Simple Perfection

ALSO BY ABBI GLINES

The *Perfection* series

Twisted Perfection

Simple Perfection

The *Too Far* series

Fallen Too Far

Never Too Far

Forever Too Far

The *Sea Breeze* series

Breathe

Because of Low

While It Lasts

Just for Now

The *Vincent Boys* series

The Vincent Boys

The Vincent Brothers

Simple Perfection

Abbi Glines

SIMON AND SCHUSTER

First published in Great Britain in 2013 by Simon & Schuster UK Ltd
A CBS COMPANY

First published in the USA in 2013 by Atria Paperbacks,
an imprint of Simon & Schuster, Inc.

Copyright © 2013 by Abbi Glines

This book is copyright under the Berne Convention.
No reproduction without permission.
All rights reserved.

The right of Abbi Glines to be identified as the author
of this work has been asserted by her in accordance with sections
77 and 78 of the Copyright, Designs and Patents Act, 1988.

1 3 5 7 9 10 8 6 4 2

Simon & Schuster UK Ltd
1st Floor
222 Gray's Inn Road
London
WC1X 8HB

Simon & Schuster Australia, Sydney
Simon & Schuster India, New Delhi

A CIP catalogue copy for this book
is available from the British Library.

ISBN: 978-1-4711-2045-9
Ebook ISBN: 978-1-4711-2044-2

This book is a work of fiction. Names, characters,
places and incidents are either a product of the author's imagination
or are used fictitiously. Any resemblance to actual people, living or dead,
events or locales, is entirely coincidental.

Printed and bound by CPI Group (UK) Ltd, Croydon, CR0 4YY

www.simonandschuster.co.uk
www.simonandschuster.com.au

Abbi loves to hear from her readers. You can connect with her on
Facebook: Abbi Glines (Official Author Page)
Twitter: @abbiglines
Website: www.abbiglines.com

To my husband, Keith.
Thanks for being my safe place.

Acknowledgments

When I decided to write about Woods I hadn't yet envisioned Della. But once I started writing her, wow. I fell in love. It takes more than just me and a MacBook to get a story written, though.

I need to start by thanking my agent, Jane Dystel, who is beyond brilliant. Signing with her was one of the smartest things I've ever done. Thank you, Jane, for helping me navigate through the waters of the publishing world. You are truly a badass.

When I signed with Atria I was lucky enough to be given Jhanteigh Kupihea as my editor. She is always positive and working to make my books the best they can be. Thank you, Jhanteigh, for making my new life with Atria one I am happy to be a part of. The rest of the Atria team: Judith Curr for giving me and my books a chance. Ariele Fredman and Valerie Vennix for always finding the best marketing ideas and being as awesome as they are brilliant.

The friends who listen to me and understand me the way no one else in my life can: Colleen Hoover, Jamie McGuire, and Tammara Webber. You three have listened to me and supported me more than anyone I know. Thanks for everything.

When I finished *Simple Perfection*, I was worried about the major twists I knew no one was expecting. I wanted to know how readers would react. These two ladies always drop what they are doing to read my manuscripts and tell me their honest opinions. I cherish that. Thank you Autumn Hull and Natasha Tomic for being my eager readers and never holding back a punch.

Last but certainly not least:

My family. Without their support I wouldn't be here. My husband, Keith, makes sure I have my coffee and the kids are all taken care of when I need to lock myself away and meet a deadline. My three kids are so understanding, although once I walk out of that writing cave they expect my full attention and they get it. My parents, who have supported me all along. Even when I decided to write steamier stuff. My friends, who don't hate me because I can't spend time with them for weeks at a time because my writing is taking over. They are my ultimate support group and I love them dearly.

My readers. I never expected to have so many of you. Thank you for reading my books. For loving them and telling others about them. Without you I wouldn't be here. It's that simple.

Woods

My mother hadn't spoken to me during my father's funeral. I had gone to comfort her but she turned from me and walked away. There were a lot of things I expected in life, but that hadn't been one of them. Ever. Nothing that I'd done had affected my mother's life. However, she'd helped my father as he had tried to destroy mine.

Seeing him lying there cold and still in the casket hadn't struck me the way I imagined. Everything was too fresh. I hadn't had time to forgive him. He had hurt Della. I could never forgive that. Even with him dead and buried in the ground I couldn't forgive what he'd done to her. She was the center of my world.

My mother had been able to see the lack of emotion in my eyes. I wasn't one for pretending. At least not anymore. A week ago I had walked away from this life I'd been born into without one ounce of remorse. It hadn't been hard to let it all go. My focus had been on finding Della. The woman who had walked into my life and changed everything. Della Sloane had become my addiction when I hadn't been available. In all her twisted perfection she had made me fall helplessly in love with her. A life without her in it seemed pointless. I often wondered how people found joy in life without knowing her.

With the sudden death of my father, the life I had just washed my hands of and been so ready to walk away from was now being placed completely on my shoulders. Della had stood beside me quietly from the moment I'd stepped foot back in Rosemary Beach, Florida. Her small hand tucked into mine, she knew when I needed her without my saying anything. A squeeze from her hand would remind me that she was there beside me and I could do this.

Except at this moment she wasn't with me. She was at my house. I hadn't wanted to bring her here, to my mother's house. My mother might have wanted to pretend that I didn't exist but I now owned everything in her life, including the house she lived in. It came with the country club, and my grandfather had made sure that when my father passed away this would all become mine.

Not once had my father thought this might be something I needed to know. He held it over my head that he controlled my life. If I wanted this world, then I had to bend to his will. Yet all along it would become mine on my twenty-fifth birthday or in the event of my father's death. Whichever came first. There was no running from this now.

I thought about knocking and changed my mind. My mother needed to stop acting like a child. I was all she had left. It was time she accepted Della in my life, because I was getting a ring on her finger as soon as I could convince her of it. I knew Della well enough to know that it wouldn't be easy to get her to marry me. With my world completely morphing into something I hadn't expected, I wanted the security of knowing that when I came home Della would be there.

I started to reach for the doorknob when the door swung

open. My eyes lifted to see Angelina Greystone standing in the doorway of my parents' house with an innocent smile on her face. The evil twinkle in her eye couldn't be masked by her attempt to appear nice. I had almost married this woman so that I could get the club that was going to become mine anyway. My father had made me believe I had to marry Angelina to get the promotion and future I deserved.

What my dad hadn't banked on was Della walking into my life and showing me there was more for me than a loveless marriage to a heartless bitch.

"We were expecting you. Your mother is in the sitting room with some chamomile tea I made for her. She needs to see you, Woods. I'm glad you took her feelings into consideration and didn't bring that girl."

The one thing I did know, despite what the witch had just said, was she knew Della's name. She might have wanted to pretend like she had never heard of her and didn't know her, but she did. She was just being spiteful. What I didn't know was why the fuck she was at my mother's house.

I pushed past her and walked into the house without responding to her. I knew where my mother was without her help. The sitting room was the place my mother always went to be alone. She would sit on the white velvet chaise lounge that had once been my grandmother's and she would stare out at the water through the large picture windows that lined the room.

I ignored the click of Angelina's heels as she followed behind me. Everything about her grated on my nerves. Her being here in the middle of a family situation on the day of my father's funeral only added to my disgust. Why was she doing this? What did she think this would win her? I owned it all now. Me. Not my father. And certainly not my mother. I was now the Kerrington in control.

"Mother," I said as I walked into the sitting room without knocking. She didn't need a chance to send me away. Not that I would go without having this conversation. As wrong as she had been, I loved her. She was my mom, even though she had always stood beside my father and never once thought of me. It had always been about what they wanted for me. But it didn't make me love her less.

She didn't turn her attention from the gulf view outside. "Woods, I was expecting you." Nothing more. It hurt. We had both lost a part of our lives with my father's death. She didn't see it that way. She never would.

I walked over to stand in her line of view. "We need to talk," I replied simply.

She shifted her eyes to look up at me. "Yes, we do."

I could have let her control this conversation but I wasn't going to. It was time I set some boundaries. Especially now that I had Della with me and we were back in Rosemary.

"At least he came alone." Angelina's voice came from the door and I jerked my head to glare at her intrusion. She wasn't a part of this.

"This doesn't concern you. You may leave," I replied in a cold tone.

She flinched.

"She is a part of this. She's going to stay with me. I need someone here so I'm not alone and Angelina understands that. She's a good girl. She would have made an excellent daughter-in-law."

I understood my mother's pain at losing my father was

fresh—and she *was* in pain. But I wouldn't let her control this. It was time I made some things very clear for both of them. "She would have been a selfish spoiled bitch of a daughter-in-law. I was lucky enough to realize it before it was too late and I ruined my life." I heard both of their sharp intakes of breath but I wasn't about to let them speak. "I control everything now, Mother. I will take care of you. I will make sure you want for nothing. However, I will not accept or acknowledge Angelina in my life. More importantly, I will not allow anyone to hurt Della. I will protect her from both of you. She is my perfection. She holds my heart in her hands. When she hurts it brings me to my knees. There is no way to explain to you the way I feel about her. Just understand that I will not allow anyone to hurt her again. I won't forgive that. I lose a piece of my soul when I see her in pain."

The tight line of my mother's mouth was the only answer I needed. She wasn't accepting this. Today wasn't the day to try to convince her about my feelings for Della. She was mourning and I was still angry with the man she was mourning. "If you need anything, call me. When you're ready to talk to me without resentment toward Della, then call me. We will talk. You're my mother and I love you. But I won't let you near Della, nor will I put you before her. Understand that if you make me choose, I will choose her without a second thought."

I walked over and placed a kiss on the top of my mother's head before walking past Angelina without a word. It was time I got back home. Della didn't do well alone. I was always anxious when I left her.

Della

He still hadn't cried. No emotion at all. I hated that. I wanted him to grieve. He needed to let it out instead of bottling his emotions because of me. The idea that he was hardened toward his pain because he was protecting me twisted my gut. His father had betrayed him by sending me away. But I had seen the look in Woods's eyes as he looked at his father, seeking approval. He had loved his father. He needed to mourn his loss.

"Della?" I turned to see Woods walk into the living room. His eyes scanned the room before they found me standing outside on the balcony. He immediately headed for the door. There was a determination in his eyes that worried me. He opened the door and stepped outside.

"Hey, did things go okay?" I asked before he pulled me into his arms and held me tightly against him. He had done this a lot over the past week.

"She's grieving. We will talk again once she's had time to process everything," he said into my hair. "I missed you."

I smiled sadly and pulled back so I could look up at him. "You were gone for about an hour. Not much time to miss me."

Woods ran his hand through my hair, brushing it out of

the way, and then cupped my face. "I missed you the second I walked out that door. I want you with me all the time."

Smiling, I turned my head and kissed his hand. "I can't always be with you."

Woods's eyes darkened with something I recognized well. "But I want you with me." He slipped one of his arms around my waist, tugging me up against him. "I can't concentrate when I'm not close enough to touch you."

I grinned as I pressed a kiss to the inside of his wrist. "When you touch me we tend to get carried away."

Woods's hand slipped under my shirt and I shivered as he moved it closer to my chest. "Right now I want to get carried away."

I wanted that too. I always wanted that, but he needed to talk. He needed to say something.

His phone rang, interrupting both of us.

His face tensed and he let his hand slide out from underneath my shirt reluctantly before reaching into his pocket to pull out his phone.

"Hello," he said in his business tone. He looked at me apologetically. "Yeah, I'll be there in five minutes. Tell him to meet me in my dad's . . . in my office."

He was having a hard time calling his dad's office "his." That was only another glimpse into the pain he was ignoring.

"That was Vince. There are several board members in town and they want to meet with me in an hour. Gary, my dad's adviser and best friend, wants to brief me first. I'm sorry," he said, reaching out to take my hand and pull me against him.

"Don't be sorry. There is nothing to be sorry about. If there's anything I can do to help you, then I will. Just tell me."

Woods chuckled. "If I could get away with keeping you in my office all day with me, then I would."

"Hmmm . . . I don't think you'd get a lot of work done."

"I know I wouldn't," he replied.

"Go, show that board that you're ready for this."

Woods pressed a kiss to my head. "What are you going to do?"

I wanted to work again. I missed seeing everyone and having something to do. Lying on the beach every day wasn't really me. "Could I have my job back?" I asked.

A frown wrinkled Woods's brow. "No. I don't want you working in the dining room."

I had been prepared for this. "Okay. Then I'm going to go find a job somewhere else. I need something to do. Especially with you being so busy."

"What if you need me? Where would you want to work? What if I can't get to you? That won't work, Della. I can't protect you if you aren't near me." I was only adding more stress for him. He needed more time to adjust. I would give him that. He needed to heal. I would have to find a way to spend my days.

"Okay. We'll wait a couple weeks and talk about it again," I said with a smile, hoping to reassure him.

He looked relieved. That was what I had wanted. "I'll call you once this meeting is over. We'll have dinner together. I won't leave you here alone long. I swear."

I just nodded.

Woods pulled me to him and kissed me. It was a possessive kiss. Right now he needed me to be there for him. For now, that is what I would do. Be there for him.

"I love you," he whispered against my lips, and then pressed one last kiss to them.

"I love you, too," I replied.

◇

Woods left and I stayed outside on the balcony looking out at the gulf. I had missed out on life for so long and now I was learning that life was about sacrifice. Especially when you loved someone.

My phone rang this time and I picked it up from the table I'd left it on earlier. It was an unknown number. That meant one thing: it was Tripp.

"Hey," I said, sitting down on the lounge chair beside me.

"How are things?"

"Okay. Woods is adjusting," I replied.

Tripp let out a weary sigh. "I should've come home for the funeral. I just . . . I couldn't."

I didn't know what it was in Rosemary that haunted Tripp. But I knew that something did. Since he'd left he had called me twice. Both times it had been from an unknown number and both times he had seemed off. Almost depressed.

"Jace said he tried to get in contact with you and couldn't. You've changed your number."

"Yeah. I did. I needed some space."

"Jace misses you. He worries about you."

Tripp didn't respond and I didn't feel like I was the person who should push him to respond.

"I'll call him. Let him know there's no reason to worry. I shouldn't have stayed in Rosemary so long. It messes with my head. I can't go back there. There're things . . . stuff I don't like to face."

I already knew this. I had no idea what those things were but I knew that they haunted him.

"Are you working again?" he asked.

"No. Woods doesn't want me working right now. He needs me to be available for him. I'm his only source of support. His mother . . . well . . . you know how she is."

Tripp paused a moment and I wondered what he was thinking about. I really didn't want him to say something negative about Woods. "Right now he needs you. I get it. But, Della, you started this journey to live life. Don't forget that. You left one prison; don't find yourself in another."

His words sliced through me painfully. Woods was nothing like my mother. He needed me right now because he had lost his father and been thrown into a position he wasn't prepared for overnight. He wasn't trying to control me. "This is different. I'm choosing to stand beside Woods. I love him and I will be here for whatever he needs. Once he's better he'll be fine with me getting a job again."

Tripp didn't respond and we sat there for a few minutes in silence. I wondered if he disagreed or if he wasn't sure what to say to that.

"The next time I call I won't block my number. I want you to have it if you need it."

I wouldn't need his number.

"Just . . . don't give it to Jace or anyone. Please."

"Good-bye, Tripp," I replied before ending the call. I didn't want to hear his doubt and concern. He was wrong. Everything was going to be fine with Woods and me. He was very wrong.

One month later

Woods

I glanced over at the phone and considered calling Della. I hadn't spoken to her in five hours. My morning had been packed with meetings and conference calls. She never complained. That bothered me. The fact was I thought she should complain. I was failing her. How was I supposed to run the Kerrington Club and take care of her? Any other woman would have been in my office throwing a fit. But never Della.

A swift knock on my door kept me from picking up the phone. I would call her in a minute. "Come in," I called out, and started looking for the papers Vince had brought me to sign earlier.

"Vince wasn't out there so I knocked." Angelina's voice wasn't what I expected to hear.

"What does Mother need now?" I asked without looking up at her. That was why she was here. At first I had been annoyed with her presence but she was helping my mother more than I could. More than I wanted to.

"She misses you. It's been over a week since you called to check on her."

Angelina was as good at guilt trips as my mother was. The

two of them were so much alike. "I'll call her later today. I've got work. If that's all, please see yourself out."

"You don't have to treat me so coldly. I'm helping you the only way I know how. Every day I stay here with your mother is for you. It's all for you. I'm in love with you, Woods. I can't compete for your heart because you won't allow me in. But what is she doing for you? I don't see her helping you—"

"Enough. Don't ever put yourself on the same level as Della. I didn't ask you to take care of my mother. I can hire someone to help me if I need it. As for Della, she's the reason I get out of bed each morning, so never underestimate her importance."

Angelina stiffened and opened her mouth to say more. I lowered my angry glare back to the contracts in front of me. I was done with this conversation. "Leave."

The clicking of her heels on the hardwood floors as she left the office was the most welcome sound I'd heard all day.

When the door closed behind her I reached for my phone to call Della.

"Hello," her sweet voice said into the phone.

"I need you," I replied.

"I just finished a late lunch with Blaire and Bethy. I'll be right there," she replied.

"Just come in when you get here," I told her.

"Okay."

◇

Exactly ten minutes and fifteen seconds later my door opened and Della stepped inside. Her dark hair was pulled up into a ponytail. The short sundress she was wearing hugged her curves more than I would have preferred. I stood up and walked around my desk.

"Hi," she said with a shy smile.

"Hi," I replied before resting both my hands on her hips and pressing my mouth on hers. Her lips were always so plump and soft. The faint taste of cherries from her lip gloss clung to my tongue.

This was what I needed. This was what got me through each day.

Della broke the kiss and placed her hands on either side of my face. "Are you okay?" she asked softly.

"I am now."

Della gazed up at me as if she were studying me closely. Then she stepped back and turned to the door. Before I could ask her what she was doing the lock clicked in place.

"Take off your clothes," she said simply, then began to slip the straps of her dress down her shoulders.

I was at a loss for words at the moment. I did as I was told. I couldn't take my eyes off of Della. As her dress pooled at her feet and she stood there in nothing but a pair of pink lace panties and a matching bra, my hands started to tremble. Seeing her like this never got old.

"We haven't made love in here yet," she said, smiling at me as she unsnapped her bra and let it drop carelessly to the floor.

"No we haven't," I managed to say. When she hooked her fingers in the sides of her panties and started pulling them down, I reached my breaking point. The moment she stepped out of the pink lace I took the two steps separating us and picked her up, and her legs wrapped firmly around me. You couldn't call what our mouths were doing kissing. It was too raw for that. We were taking each other. It was the best description I could think of.

I wanted to take her on my desk but we weren't going to make it that far. Not after that striptease. I wasn't even going to be able to enjoy tasting her and touching her. I needed to be inside her now before I exploded.

I set her down and flipped her around until she was facing the wall. "Brace yourself," I whispered into her ear.

Della leaned forward and placed both her hands against the wall. I took in the sight of her body arched out and my heart slammed against my chest. She was beautiful. Perfect. Grabbing her by the hips, I sank inside of her. The cry of pleasure was so loud I was pretty damn sure Vince had heard it outside at his desk, but I didn't care.

"So good, it always feels so good," I whispered in her ear. The shiver that went over her body made me smile.

"Harder," Della panted, pressing her sweet round ass back against me.

I slammed inside of her and stopped. Buried deep, I leaned forward and caressed her breasts. "You make me crazy, baby."

Della only moaned and wiggled her bottom. She wanted me to move.

"It's so tight. You feel like heaven. I want to stay right here for fucking ever," I swore, and I meant it. Della's pussy sucked me like the sweetest mouth I'd ever known.

The tight hole I worshipped squeezed me and I froze. Then she did it again. What the fuck? It was like she was pumping my dick. "Holy shit," I growled. She was gonna make me come way before I wanted to. I slid out of her and back in and the squeezing started again. "Baby, you're gonna make me come,"

I said in a strangled voice. I was fighting back the heat tightening in my cock. I was so close. "Della, baby, stop doing that. I'm gonna fucking explode. I can't hold back."

She stuck her bottom out farther and the walls of her silky heat squeezed me tighter. It was as if she had just taken the control of my body away from me. I felt myself erupt as I called out her name and my body jerked helplessly against her.

"Yes! Oh God, yes!" Della cried out, and her body went rigid in my arms before it began to shake underneath me. I wrapped both my arms around her and held her as we both came back down from the climax she'd sent us spiraling off into.

"What the hell did you do to me?" I asked, holding her close.

She leaned back against my chest and a smile tugged at her lips. "I fucked you and I did a real good job," she replied.

I hadn't expected that response. Laughing, I picked her up, carried her over to the nearest chair, and sank down into it with her in my arms.

"That was incredible," I told her before pressing a kiss to her neck.

"Do you feel better now?" she asked, arching her neck so I could access it better.

"That depends," I replied.

"On what?"

"If I can convince you to stay in here with me all day."

"You have to work," she said, turning her head to look up at me.

"Mmm, but if you're here with me I can concentrate. And then you can get naked for me again and be a naughty girl when I need you."

Della threw her head back and laughed. The sound of it made everything in my world right.

Della

The phone on Woods's desk beeped twice. "Mr. Kerrington, Miss Greystone is here to see you," the secretary's voice announced through the speaker.

Woods closed his eyes and laid his head back on the chair we were sitting in. "Damn. What the hell does she need now?"

Did she come here often? I fought back the jealousy that wanted to eat its way inside me. Of course she came by to see him. She was staying with his mother and helping her deal with things, which in turn was helping Woods. Unlike me. I wasn't doing anything to help him. I didn't know what to do.

I started to get out of his lap but his hands tightened on me.

"We need to get dressed."

"Don't leave me here with her."

I leaned over and kissed the tip of his nose. "I won't go anywhere. But I prefer to be wearing clothes when she walks in."

Woods let out a sigh and let go of me so I could get up and get dressed.

"You get dressed, too. I don't care what she's seen before me, I don't want her seeing it now."

Woods laughed out loud and stood up. "I'm going to put my clothes on, sexy. Calm down."

We both grinned at each other as we dressed. I liked the idea of her coming in here and seeing us together and knowing what we had been doing. It was silly for me to feel that way, but I did.

"You can send her in," Woods replied, standing at his desk while he watched me fix my hair, which our wild sex had messed up. My ponytail was barely hanging on.

The door swung open and I spun around to see Angelina strutting inside like she belonged here. "I don't know why you . . ." Her voice trailed off as her gaze landed on me. I finished adjusting my ponytail and let my hands fall back down to my sides.

"Did you really just—"

"Why are you back?" Woods cut off her question.

Angelina jerked her gaze to him as if he'd slapped her. I watched as she fought to compose herself. Woods hadn't bothered to run his fingers through his hair and it was messed up from my hands being in it. I bit back a smile as I looked at his properly rumpled appearance.

"I came back to tell you your mother wants to have you over for dinner," Angelina said tightly.

"Unless Della is invited, I'm afraid I won't be able to make it."

Angelina let out a frustrated sigh and shot me an annoyed glance before looking back at Woods. "She's your mother, Woods. She just lost her husband and she's hurting. You're all she has left. Don't you get that? Do you not care?"

She was right. Woods's mother might never like me. But she was his mother, and right now she needed him. "I want you to go, Woods," I said before he could say anything.

He looked over at me and frowned.

"Please," I said, hoping he wouldn't argue with me in front of her.

Woods ran a hand through his hair and I smiled at the way it was still messed up. He was adorable like that. "Fine. But only for an hour. This will also be a one-time thing. Next time I have dinner with her, Della will be with me."

Angelina's annoyed grimace turned into a pleased smile. She would get him tonight, too, without me around. I hated that but I couldn't let it keep Woods from his mother.

"I'm glad you're thinking with something other than your dick," Angelina replied before spinning around and heading out the door.

"She's a bitch. Ignore her," Woods said, shoving off from the desk he'd been leaning on and walking over to me.

"I know," I assured him, but deep down I worried that she was right.

◇

"They're at the door, Della. Don't let them in here. They'll hurt us. All they want to do is hurt us. We have to keep your brother safe. They tried to kill him before. They'll kill us this time. Don't let them in. Shhhh. Stop that crying, you little brat! You have to be quiet. So very quiet, then they'll go away."

I covered my mouth with both my hands to keep in the terrified cries I couldn't control. I hated when this happened. Mom would get mean afterward. She didn't like it when people knocked on our door. It upset her. And she would talk to him. He wasn't there, but she saw him. That scared me, too.

"Get up! They're gone. Go to the door and get the package they left and be careful that they don't see you."

I didn't want to open the door. I wasn't sure what was out there that wanted to get me, but I didn't want to open the door. Momma had been making me do that more and more lately. Since my sixth birthday.

Pain seared my head as she wrapped her hand around my ponytail and jerked me to my feet. I couldn't let her hear me cry or this would get worse.

"Go!" she screamed in that voice that sent chills down my body. The hard shove from her hands sent me stumbling out of the closet and into the hallway. She would stay in the closet until I came back with the package.

I glanced back at her but instead of seeing her wild, distant eyes there was blood. It was pouring out of the room and into the hallway. No . . . no, there wasn't supposed to be blood.

Then a shrill scream of terror ripped from the small room.

◇

I jolted straight up and the scream was still echoing around me as it tore from my chest. It was my own scream. It was always my scream. Not my mother's.

I was still alone. Looking around the living room, I took slow, deep breaths while my heart kept hammering against my chest. I pulled my legs up and tucked my knees under my chest. Falling asleep without Woods here wasn't something I did often. Having him near me while I slept kept me from having night terrors for the most part.

The clock on the fridge said it was after nine. He should have been home over an hour ago. Had he stayed later with his mother? I reached for my phone on the coffee table and saw that I had two missed calls and one text message. All from Woods.

I clicked the text message.

Please answer. I'm worried about you and Mom passed out during dinner. I think she hasn't been eating properly. Call me!

That had been ten minutes ago. I jumped up from the couch and started to dial his number when the front door swung open and Woods came running inside. His eyes locked on mine and he stopped and let out a deep breath. "Thank God. Shit, baby, you scared me."

I dropped my phone and walked over to him. "I'm so sorry. I just woke up. I fell asleep on the couch. How's your mother?"

Woods pulled me against him and wrapped his arms around me. "She was too weak to stand up so I called an ambulance. Angelina kept saying it could be a stroke. She rode in the ambulance with Mom so I could come back here and check on you."

I pushed at his chest. "Go! Go to the hospital. No, wait, let me get my shoes, I'm going, too."

"Are you sure? If you're tired I don't want to drag you to the hospital. We could be there all night."

I slipped my feet into a pair of tennis shoes and ran my hands through my hair. "I want to be with you."

Woods smiled and held out his hand for me. "Good. I won't be able to focus if I'm worried about you here alone. If you need to sleep, I can always hold you."

I tried not to think about the fact that Angelina was helping him take care of his mother. He had been able to leave her knowing she would be there beside his mother. What was I good for? He had to worry about me. I was weak and needy. I was one more thing for him to stress over. I wasn't any help at all.

"Stop frowning. She's gonna be okay. The paramedics said there's a good chance her potassium is low. They don't think it's a stroke but they said due to her heart rate we needed to admit her and let doctors check her out."

I nodded as he laced his fingers through mine. "Let's go," I told him.

I was going to find a way to be helpful. He needed someone to lean on right now and I was going to be that someone.

"Did you sleep okay without me here?" he asked as we stepped outside.

"Yes. I slept great," I lied, because telling him the truth would only have upset him.

Woods

Della had finally given in and curled up against me. She'd been asleep within minutes. It was after three in the morning and they had Mom in a room under observation. Angelina was in the room with her. It was better that way.

I wasn't stupid. I knew Angelina wasn't helping my mother out of the goodness of her heart. She had no goodness in her heart. She was doing it to get to me. It wasn't like my mother needed a live-in nurse. Just a friend, and Angelina was being her friend.

Della didn't seem to mind. I had been watching to make sure it didn't get to her. The moment it seemed like Della was upset about Angelina's still being in our lives in this capacity, I would end all connection with my mom until Angelina left. She would eventually leave anyway when she realized I didn't want her and nothing she did was going to change that. Della owned me. She always would.

Della started to whimper in her sleep. I pulled her into my lap, brushed her hair back off her face, and whispered in her ear. That always calmed her. She rarely had bad dreams anymore. I normally saw them coming on and stopped them before they could take over.

"I have you, I'm right here. You're in my arms and nothing can touch you, Della. Nothing, baby. I won't let it," I assured her as her breathing returned to normal and her body eased back into a peaceful sleep. Smiling, I pressed a kiss to the side of her hair. I liked knowing I could fight off her fear. It was a powerful drug to know all she needed was me.

"Doesn't that get exhausting? She's like a helpless, needy child." Angelina's icy voice annoyed me. I didn't look up at her. I'd rather have kept my focus on the woman in my arms.

"How's Mom?" I asked her.

"She's sleeping. She hasn't been eating well. I knew that but I can't force her to eat. I'm not a damn nurse. If you came to visit her more often she'd eat more. She misses you."

My mother had never missed me. She was my father's puppet. She wanted me around if he did. When she thought I was going to marry Angelina she wanted me around.

"You're choosing her over your mother and it's disappointing, Woods."

I lifted my eyes from Della's peaceful face. "No. My mother is choosing her wants over mine. I will not live my life the way she wants me to. I will love who the fuck I wanna love. She doesn't control that," I replied in a cold voice.

"You have the Kerrington Club to run, Woods. You need someone who can stand by you and help you. You have to take care of not only the club but her. She's a weight on you, not a help. You can't be a successful businessman with a burden like her," she said, pointing at Della.

I held her closer to my chest. I could do anything if I had Della. Anything.

"What you're not understanding—what my mother is not

understanding—is I can't live without Della. I can't breathe. I can't fucking concentrate. I need her. Just her. I can do anything if I have her with me. So take your snide comments and beliefs and leave me the hell alone. I know what I need and it will never be you. Did you hear that? Is it sinking in this time? It. Will. Never. Be. You."

Angelina opened her mouth and snapped it closed again. The bright red color on her face said I'd gotten through. She was furious. Good. About damn time. I didn't watch her leave. I dropped my gaze back down to Della. Just looking at her calmed me.

When the doctor came out four hours later to tell me that Mom was fine and wanted to see me, Della woke up and rubbed her eyes. I watched as the doctor looked her over appreciatively. I didn't like it when men looked at her like that but it was pointless to get mad. She was beautiful and sexy as hell. I just had to remind myself she was mine.

"Go on in and see her. I'm going to find some coffee," she said in a sleepy voice. "I'll get you some, too."

I pressed a kiss to her lips because I needed to taste her and I wanted the doctor to see exactly who she belonged to. She immediately responded by wrapping her arms around my neck and kissing me back.

"I love you," I said against her lips as I ended the kiss.

"I love you," she replied, then stood up.

She walked off in the short cut-off sweatpants she was wearing and one of my hoodies. She'd come with me in a tank top last night and gotten cold in the waiting room. I had gotten her a hoodie out of my truck.

"Is the woman in the room with your mom your sister?"

the doctor asked. I glanced over at him. He was too young to be a doctor, wasn't he?

"No," I replied, and walked past him toward my mother's room.

Angelina was sitting in the chair beside her bed looking at a magazine. She had stayed all night. Even after I'd said what I had. Either she was crazy or she really did like my mom.

"Hey, Mom," I said as I closed the door behind me.

"Hello," she replied. "Angelina said you stayed all night. You didn't have to do that."

I walked over and bent down and pressed a kiss to her forehead. "Yeah I did," I replied.

"Did you send the girl home?" The distaste in her voice wasn't missed.

"She went to get coffee," I replied. I wasn't going to fight with her over Della. "You need to eat more, Mom."

She sighed. "I know, but I just don't have an appetite anymore. I miss him."

He was an ass. He tried to control me and he lied to me. He also hurt Della and she knew about it. Forgiving those things was hard. The fact he'd hurt Della made it almost impossible. I couldn't say anything. I had nothing to say.

"I need to get to work. When they discharge you, call me and I'll come get you." Getting out of there was best. She was my mother and I loved her, but there was so much between us that needed to be forgiven. I couldn't stay there.

"I'll take her home. You go work. You're going to be exhausted since you didn't sleep all night." Angelina sounded so sincere. I didn't trust that.

"Okay, well, call if you need me," I said to my mother, and then turned and left the room.

Della stood outside the door holding two coffees. The concern in her eyes was the most sincere thing I'd seen that morning.

"Is she okay?" Della asked as she handed me a cup of bad hospital coffee.

"Yeah. She's fine. Let's go," I replied.

"Why don't I leave and you stay here? She's your mom." Della started to say more but I shook my head and stopped her.

"She's fine. She needs to eat more. I want to leave with you."

Della let out a weary sigh, then nodded her head. "Okay. If that's what you want."

Della

The bonfire lit up the dark beach. I stood watching everyone drink, dance, and laugh. Woods had left to deal with an issue with the staff. He was looking for someone to take over his old job but he hadn't found anyone yet. Right now he was doing everything himself and I could see he was growing weary.

I glanced over at the group of Woods's friends and I knew I was welcome. Bethy was laughing loudly and I was pretty sure she was drunk. But I needed time to think. I wasn't in the mood to pretend like my heart wasn't heavy. Woods had been on the phone with Angelina today when I'd walked into his office. They'd been talking about his mom and it had been friendly. She was taking a lot off him and I wanted to like her. To be thankful to her. I just couldn't.

Turning, I walked up to the parking lot. No one was up there partying and I could wait for Woods to get back. I needed to get in a better mood before he came back. The fact that I was a hindrance to him weighed heavily on me. It was getting worse every day.

If I could just get better . . . If I could just stop having bad dreams . . . If I could forget my past and move forward . . . If the fear that I might go crazy wasn't haunting me every day . . . then I might be able to help him. I might be a support for him.

"Della." Angelina's voice surprised me. I turned to see her standing behind the building where the restrooms were located. The small amount of light the moon was supplying shone down on her.

"Yes," I replied, not sure if I should be worried about being alone with her or if I was just being silly.

"Where's Woods?" she asked.

"He had an issue with some of the staff. He's dealing with it."

Angelina looked disgusted. "He has so much on his shoulders and you make it so much worse. So helpless and fucked up. How long do you think he'll want you? What happens when that crazy in your genes takes over? He won't be able to keep you then. You'll be locked up. And I know he doesn't want kids with you. He would be worried about them being crazy, too. That would kill him."

Hearing my own fears spill from her cruel lips took my breath away. She was right. Everything she said was right. Woods and I pretended like the future was possible. But it wasn't. I would never be his future. I wasn't getting better.

"What do you want?" I asked.

"I want you to leave him alone. He deserves so much more," she spat.

He did. I agreed. "But that won't be you. You're not better," I replied, shooting an angry glare her way. Even if she couldn't see me in the darkness, I hoped she could feel my hatred for her.

She walked over toward me and I fought the urge to back away from her. I wasn't scared of her. I could hold my own.

"You're a crazy bitch. You know nothing. He loved it when

I sucked his dick. He'd scream my name and hold my head as if I had the key to heaven in my mouth. He loved it."

"Stop it!" I screamed. I didn't want to think about Woods and Angelina together. It made me ill.

"He once said my thighs were magical. He loved being between them."

"Shut up!" I said, backing away.

A pleased smirk touched her evil lips. "I can still make him hard. All I have to do is rub my hand over his crotch and talk dirty and he's hard as a rock."

I turned and started walking away before I threw up. My head jerked back and I cried out in pain as Angelina pulled my hair in her fisted hand. "You're not going anywhere, you crazy bitch." She growled and pulled me by my hair while I stumbled back into the darkness behind the building. Away from the parking lot where someone might see us.

"I swallowed his come. Do you do that for him? Do you go to his office just to suck his dick and make him cry out in pleasure? Does he tell you how amazing your mouth is? Hmm?"

Tears burned my eyes. The pain in my head was nothing compared to the pain from her words. I didn't want to think of Woods with her. It hurt too much.

She slung me down onto the grass and I glanced up to see a wild look in her eyes that scared me. What was wrong with her? Why were we back there in the dark? I scrambled to get up and she kicked me in the ribs, then pushed me back down on the ground. "He stays with you. Why? Why does he stay with you? I do everything for him! Everything! I am what he needs. I was raised to be his wife. I fit into his world. I can be his helpmate but he wants you! Why?!" she screamed, and reached for my hair again, only this time she pulled out a handful.

"If you're dead, then you won't be in my way. I can make it better for him. I can ease his pain. He'll be over you and fucking me against his desk again. Not you! *Me!*" She reached for my arm and then threw me on my back. I felt her pulling my hair again. I was going to black out. The darkness was going to take me and I would be lost in myself. She'd kill me then. If I didn't stay focused I wouldn't be able to fight her.

"I can strangle you. No one will ever know," she snarled. "You took him from me. You made him cheat on me. You're the reason he broke off our engagement. He was going to marry me. You made him leave me. Now I'm going to fix that."

I knew crazy. I had seen it all my life. And right now I was positive she wasn't kidding. This was no idle threat. Something had snapped in her head and she was going to kill me. I had to do something. With my side throbbing, I wasn't sure I could fight back. I would beg, then catch her off guard and knee her in the ribs.

"No, please. Just talk to Woods. I didn't do anything. I swear. Don't, oh God."

"I'm done talking to Woods. You took what was mine. He chose you. Fine. He can have your skanky, crazy ass. But first you're gonna fucking pay for taking what was mine." She slapped me across my face so hard everything went blurry. "Hurts, don't it, bitch? You're a psycho. Why Woods thinks you can make him happy, I don't know. He'll learn. He will fucking learn not to screw with me!" she roared, then kicked my sore ribs again, taking my breath away. I had to fight back. If she kept this up I wasn't going to be able to fight back.

I started to move when she grabbed my hair again and jerked me up, only to slap me again. I couldn't keep from crying out in pain. I needed to focus on saving myself but the pain was overpowering me. My vision was blurring and I used all my willpower to push it away. I had to keep it from taking me away.

"Let her go." Blaire's voice came through the darkness like an avenging angel and I cried in relief. Then I turned to see her standing there with a gun pointed at Angelina. *Holy shit. She has a gun.*

"What the fuck?" Angelina said. Her hold on my hair only tightened. I should have done something to fight back now but I was more scared of the gun in Blaire's hands than of Angelina at the moment. Did she know how to use that thing?

"Let go of her hair and step away from her," Blaire said with command. I was impressed and terrified.

Angelina laughed. That was it. The girl was insane. She had a gun pointed at her and she was laughing. I was scared to breathe. "That's not even real. I'm not an idiot. Go mind your own fucking business and stop playing *Charlie's Angels*," Angelina said.

Blaire's gun made a sound that I knew meant she was ready to fire. I had heard that click on television before. "Listen, bitch. If I wanted to I could pierce both your ears from here and not mess your fucking hair up. Go ahead, test me." The look in Blaire's eyes might have been meant to warn Angelina but I could detect the truth in her words. I believed her and the relief washed over me. She could actually use that thing.

Angelina let go of me and I quickly moved away from her while I had a chance. I believed Blaire could use that gun but I didn't want to be anywhere near her target.

"Do you have any idea who I am? I could end you. Your ass is going to sit in jail for a very long time for this," Angelina said, but the fear in her voice wasn't lost on me, and I doubted Blaire missed it, too.

"We're in the dark and there are three of us. You don't have a scratch on you. Della's bleeding and bruised and it's our word against yours. I don't care who you are. This doesn't look good for you."

Angelina moved back as if she could run from a bullet. "My daddy will hear about this. He'll believe me," she said with a shaky voice.

"Good. My husband will hear about it, too, and he'll sure as hell believe me," Blaire replied.

Angelina laughed. "My daddy can buy this town. You have fucked with the wrong woman."

"Really? Bring it on, 'cause right now you're looking at a woman with a loaded gun who can hit a moving target. So please. Bring. It. On," Blaire replied like a complete badass. I wanted to be like her. I wanted to be tough.

I pulled my legs up and wrapped my arms around my knees and prayed this would end without her having to use that gun.

"Who are you?" Angelina asked. I hadn't realized that Angelina didn't know who Rush Finlay's wife was. He was a celebrity because of his father. I thought the whole world knew who Blaire was.

"Blaire Finlay," she replied.

"Shit. Rush Finlay married a hick with a gun. I find this hard to believe," Angelina said in her snide, uppity tone. She really did think she was above everyone else.

"I'd believe her. She's holding the fucking gun." Rush's voice came from behind Blaire. I let out the breath I was holding. *Thank God he's here.*

"Are you kidding me? This town is insane. All of you," Angelina said, on the verge of a scream.

"You were the one beating up an innocent woman over a man in the dark," Blaire replied. "You're the one who looks insane here."

"Fine. I'm over this. I'm done," Angelina yelled, and walked over to the parking lot. I sat in shock as Blaire lowered the gun and put the safety back on before handing it to Rush. She then ran over to me. I just sat there and stared up at her. She'd just pulled a gun on another woman for me. I couldn't wrap my head around everything that had happened. I felt the darkness around my eyes start to close in on me. I had to fight off the panic attack I knew was close.

"Did you really just pull a gun on her?" I asked, trying to focus on the here and now.

"She was putting a beating on you," Blaire said simply.

"Ohmigod. She's crazy. I swear, I was beginning to think she was going to beat me until I was unconscious. I kept thinking I was going to zone out and then she'd really hurt me." I looked up at her. "Thank you." Those two words weren't enough but it was all I could say right now. I was about to lose myself. The darkness was coming.

Blaire held out her hand. "Can you stand up? Or do you want to sit here while I call Woods?" I needed to stand up. I had to fight this. I slipped my hand into hers.

"I want to stand. I need to stand up," I told her. I didn't want to tell her I was about to black out. It was a weakness that I was ashamed of. Having her see me like that would be humiliating. Rush would know Woods was in love with a crazy woman. I couldn't do that to him.

Blaire pulled me up, then asked, "You got a phone?"

I couldn't talk. I needed to stay focused. I handed it to her. She was calling Woods. I knew that. I wanted her to call him. If he held me I could fight this. Blaire handed me the phone. I would have to talk to him.

"Baby?" His voice came over the line and my fear eased off.

"Hey," I replied.

"You okay?" he asked. I could tell he was walking. Hopefully he was headed back this way.

"Actually, no, not really. I had an incident with Angelina," I explained.

"Did she say something to upset you? Is she still there? Put the bitch on the phone." I heard his truck crank up. He was already heading back.

"No . . . no . . . she's gone. Uh, Blaire showed up and . . . uh, scared her off," I tried to explain, though I wasn't sure how to.

"Scared her off? What the hell did she do to you? Are you alone?" The panic in his voice was nothing compared to what he was going to feel when he found out what really happened.

"Blaire is still here and so is her husband," I reassured him.

"Rush is there? Good. Stay with them. Where are you?"

"Behind the parking attendant building."

"I'm almost there. I love you, stay with me. Don't black out. I'm coming."

"Okay. I love you, too," I replied. He knew I was close to getting lost in the monsters in my mind.

I hung up and looked over at Blaire. "He's on his way."

"Good. We'll wait with you," she replied, then opened her purse and pulled out a wet wipe. "You want to clean the blood off your lip before he gets here and goes after Angelina?" she asked, holding it out to me.

I hadn't realized I was bleeding. I took it from her. "Thanks."

The sound of Woods's truck broke through the silence and I wanted to weep in relief. He was here. His door swung open and he jumped down and came running over to me. I felt like sagging in relief. He was here and I was okay.

"Dammit!" he roared, furious, as he took in my face. He pulled me into his arms and held me tightly. His breathing was fast and hard. He was upset. "God, baby, I am so sorry. She's gonna pay for this," he said as his hands starting roaming my body to make sure I was okay. I wasn't okay. But I would be.

"It's fine. I think Blaire scared her," I assured him.

"What did Blaire do?" he asked.

"She pointed a gun at her and threatened to pierce her ears," I explained.

Woods cocked an eyebrow. "So, Alabama pulled her gun out again? Thanks, Blaire," he said before kissing my head. "I love you. I'm here and you're going to be okay. Stay with me. I got you," he whispered in my ear. He knew I didn't want them to know how close I was to getting lost in my head.

"I'm glad I found them. You need to do something about that woman; she's a crazy bitch," Blaire said, then turned to walk back to Rush.

"Thank you," I called out after her. She'd literally saved my life.

"You're welcome," she replied with a sweet smile. She didn't look like someone who had just pointed a gun and threatened to pierce someone's ears with it. I now knew that under that beautiful, innocent-looking exterior, Blaire Finlay was a tough badass. I wanted to be her one day.

Woods

I turned on the shower, then reached for Della. Streaks of blood were still visible on her face. She'd tried to clean it but she'd left some of the proof behind. A bruise was forming on her face and blades of grass in her hair clung to the tangled mess.

She wouldn't let me call the police. She'd cried and begged me not to. I was going to kill Angelina myself. She'd hurt the most precious thing in my life and she would pay for it. I'd make sure she paid over and over again. But right now I had to keep Della lucid and out of her head.

I reached for her shirt and had started to lift it over her head when she cried out in pain. I froze. "What's wrong, baby?"

"My ribs," she said in a tight whisper.

Fuck. I forced myself to calm down. The anger rolling over me was getting worse. I was going to snap. The tank top she was wearing was ruined. Blood and grass stains had made it unsalvageable. I reached up and grabbed the neckline, then ripped it in one swift move. It fell to the ground behind her and my eyes found the bruised skin. It was too much. Seeing the dark bruise covering her side broke me. I had let this happen to her. I had left her alone and let this woman into our lives. This was my fault.

My knees gave out and I fell before her. Knowing that she

was hurting was too much. The sob that filled the bathroom was mine.

"Woods, please don't," her sweet voice begged. Della's hands caressed my head in her attempt to comfort me. Me. I wasn't the one who had been attacked. She was the one with bruises and covered in blood but I was the one on his knees, crying. "It's okay, I'm okay," she tried to reassure me. She was in pain and she was worrying over me. I was a man, dammit. I couldn't break apart on her. It was my place to take care of her, not the other way around.

I forced myself to stand up and focus on undressing her. I needed to clean her. I had to fix her. Make the pain go away.

"Woods?" Her voice was soft and unsure. I knew the tears were still rolling down my face silently. I couldn't seem to make them stop. I was trying. They weren't going away.

"I need to clean you. Let me clean you," I said, finally lifting my eyes to look into hers. She wasn't about to leave me anymore. The glazed look that I'd seen in her eyes earlier was gone. I had her back with me.

"Okay," she said simply, and stepped into the shower.

I undressed and followed her inside. She wasn't standing under the warm water.

"I need to wash your hair," I told her, moving close to her body and running my hands down her arms.

"Be gentle with my head," she said.

Her head? What the fuck did Angelina do to her head? "What's wrong with your head, baby?"

She dropped her eyes from mine as she stared down at the marble floor. "She pulled a lot of my hair out. It burns," she said so softly I almost missed it.

My body trembled. *Holy hell.*

"I will be gentle. But we need to clean it. Do you trust me?" I asked as she stared warily back at the water. Then she nodded.

I moved her under the water and pressed kisses to her lips while whispering comforting words to her as she winced.

Gently, I washed her hair, then moved to clean her body. She flinched as I touched the tender spots. Each flinch from her body caused my chest to constrict. Once she was clean I wrapped a towel around her and carried her to bed. I needed to hold her but first I wanted her checked out.

"I'm going to call a friend of mine. He'll come here and check you out. I need to know you're okay. Your ribs could be broken."

She started to shake her head but I couldn't give her this. I had to know she was okay. "Della, I have to. I can't not make sure you're okay. Please, baby. He's a sports doctor. We use him at the club during tennis tournaments. He's a friend. It's okay."

She finally nodded. "Okay," she agreed.

I didn't want to leave her in there alone but I wanted to talk to Martin without her hearing me. I didn't want to scare her.

"Hello," Martin said after one ring. I had his private line for emergencies. The club had been using him for over twenty years.

"Martin, it's Woods. I need you to make a house call. My girlfriend was beaten up tonight by my crazy ex-fiancée. I'm worried her ribs could be broken or she could be internally bleeding. I don't think Angelina is strong enough to actually cause internal bleeding but I still need Della checked out. She won't go to the hospital."

Martin let out a low whistle. "Damn, Woods. That is some fucked-up shit," he replied.

"Yeah, it is. Can you come check her tonight?"

"I'm on my way. I'll be there in twenty minutes. Are y'all at your house?"

"Yeah, thanks, man. See you in a few."

◇

Della hadn't been thrilled about Martin checking her out, but I'd held her hand while he felt her ribs. She was bruised but that was it. He'd left her some pain pills. They had successfully knocked Della out within thirty minutes. I wasn't going to be able to sleep, though. I had something I needed to do.

Jace arrived ten minutes after I called him. He didn't ask questions. He just agreed to watch Della and call me if she woke up. He seemed to understand that I wasn't ready to talk about this. I started for the door.

"Don't do anything that could take you away from her. Be careful how you handle this. Don't kill a bitch; I don't want your ass in jail. I would want revenge too. Just . . . just be careful. Use your head."

Rush must have told him. I didn't look back at him. I only nodded, then opened the door and headed outside. I was going to make sure Angelina understood that this was her only warning. She had one hour to get her shit and get on a plane and not come back. I couldn't beat the hell out of a woman but I could make her wish she'd never been born. She'd crossed a line.

When I drove up to my mother's house, Angelina's car was missing. She was hiding or she wasn't home yet. I took the stairs to my mother's house two at a time and knocked once before pulling out my key and opening the door.

My mother was walking down the staircase in her robe. "Woods? What are you doing here so late? You scared me."

"Where is she?" I asked, trying to control the anger in my voice.

"She left. What did you do?"

I let out a hard laugh. "What did I do? I just stood over Della as a doctor checked her for internal bleeding and broken ribs because Angelina beat the shit out of her. If Blaire Finlay hadn't shown up and pulled a gun on her crazy ass she would have killed Della. So tell me now, where is she!"

Mother covered her mouth with both her hands as her eyes went round in surprise. "What? That's . . . that's ridiculous. Angelina is a sweet girl. She'd never do something so awful. Della has lied to you."

"No, Mother. Rush and Blaire Finlay found them and stopped Angelina. I have witnesses. She isn't sweet, she was using you to stay near me. She's a fucking psycho."

"Watch your mouth in my house. I won't listen to this. The poor girl left here in tears saying you'd hurt her too many times. She wanted to stay with me but she was going home to her parents and starting over."

She was going to refuse to believe me. I shouldn't have been surprised. She had always chosen my father over me. Now she was choosing Angelina because she was my father's choice for me. What mattered was that Angelina was gone. The bitch was gone. She had better never come back.

"If you speak to her, let her know that if she steps foot in Rosemary again I will have her arrested. I have witnesses and I will press charges. I don't give a fuck who her daddy is."

I didn't wait for my mother to respond. I turned and left the house, slamming the door behind me.

Della

I stared down at my phone after I hung up with Woods. He had called me four times today already to check on me. It had been this way all week. Since Angelina had attacked me he had been afraid to leave me. He had a country club to run but he kept calling me. I mentioned getting a job again and he panicked and begged me not to. He said he couldn't focus on work if he was worrying about me.

We were at a standstill. This wasn't healthy. He needed to be able to live without worrying over me. I needed to be able to live. His protective nature was starting to smother me and I loved him too much to hurt him by saying something about it. I was going to have bad moments. I was going to slip into my head sometimes and he couldn't always be there for me. I just didn't know how to get him to understand this and accept it. How could we make this work? This couldn't be forever.

I wanted this forever but Woods deserved so much more. I was holding him back. This relationship would destroy him. I would destroy him. I felt sick to my stomach. *I did this. I let this happen. I let myself fall so helplessly in love with him. I let myself believe he could fix me. That we could fix me. But it isn't happening.*

My phone rang and I looked down to see Tripp's number.

He hadn't called in two weeks. I thought about telling Woods that Tripp checked in with me a couple times a month, but I hadn't found the right words to explain that. Woods seemed jealous of Tripp. He had no reason to be, but he was. I didn't want to give him something else to worry over.

"Hello," I said as I stretched my legs in front of me on the sandy beach.

"How are things?"

"Good, I guess," I replied.

"You guess? That don't sound good."

"Angelina beat me up and Blaire Finlay pulled a gun on her and scared her off. Woods is now more overprotective than ever and he's always worried about me."

Tripp was quiet for a moment. I let him digest my words.

"Holy shit. Blaire has a gun?"

I laughed. *That* was his response to what I'd just told him?

"Sorry. I don't think that was the point. But damn, I can't picture that hot little blonde with a gun."

"Yeah, it was a shock," I replied, smiling out at the water crashing against the shore.

"Jace said she was from Alabama. Maybe I've been looking for a woman in the wrong states. I need to try out good ole Alabama next."

Tripp always managed to make me laugh, and he made me forget for a moment that my chest was about to explode from pain.

"Thanks," I said.

"For what?"

"Making me laugh," I replied.

"Anytime."

We sat there again for a few moments in silence.

"Where are you at now?" I asked, knowing he was on a road trip.

"I'm in South Carolina at a place called Myrtle Beach. I like it here."

"You like those beaches, don't you?" I replied.

"Makes me feel like I'm home, in a way."

"Will you ever come back here to stay?"

He didn't respond right away. It made me wonder what kept him away. There were secrets that he wouldn't share with me.

"Doubt it," he finally said.

"I don't think I can stay," I said aloud for the first time.

"Why?"

"Because this isn't working. I'm holding him back. I'm not getting better. This isn't going away and he deserves more. He needs more. Someone strong to stand beside him."

"He wants you, Della."

"Sometimes what we want isn't what's best for us," I replied.

"Yeah . . . I know that," he said quietly. "But if you leave him it will break him."

It would shatter me. But I loved him too much to ruin his future. "He will heal and then the woman who can be all he needs will walk into his life one day and he'll be glad he didn't make the mistake of staying with me."

"Don't say that. You aren't a mistake. You underestimate your worth. You make him happy. Woods is happy with you."

"For now he is," I replied.

Tripp sighed. I was frustrating him, but he knew deep

down that I was right. "When the time comes and you think you need to leave, just call me. Don't go by yourself."

"Okay," I replied. I would call him when I needed to. He wasn't tied to me. I didn't control his actions and thoughts. I could travel with Tripp and not destroy his future. At least until I was stable enough to live alone.

"I think you need to talk to Woods about this first. Don't blindside him."

I wasn't sure that was possible. He would never listen to me. "Okay," I replied.

◇

I stepped out of my car and waved at Bethy as she drove by in a golf cart toward the fifteenth hole. She was a cart girl at the Kerrington Club. It was how she had met Jace. He was a member here and I had heard them arguing over her quitting more than once. He hated seeing the men on the course flirt with her. That had been him once. She refused to change just because she was dating him. I think, deep down, he respected her for that.

After hanging up the phone with Tripp, I'd sat and thought a long time. Woods needed help and all I seemed to be doing was whining over not having a job and being a burden on him. I was stronger than that. Why couldn't I help him? I could. He would have me close by and I would have a purpose. So, I'd gone back to the house and dressed up.

I was going to go apply for a job as his assistant. I could do the tasks that caused him extra headaches. I could handle the staff. I might have been dealing with some mental issues, but I wasn't helpless. If I could prove to myself that I could do this, then I could prove to Woods and the rest of the world that I was healing.

Vince glanced up at me and smiled. “Go on in, Miss Sloane,” he said before going back to his work. Woods had informed him that I never needed permission to enter. I was free to come and go as I wanted.

I knocked, then opened the door.

“I realize that, but make it happen. I need the order here tomorrow, not Monday. I’ll switch suppliers if it doesn’t happen,” Woods said.

“Yes, sir, Mr. Kerrington, we will make it work,” the voice said from his speakerphone.

“Good,” he replied, then ended the call before standing up and walking toward me.

“I needed to see you,” he said, smiling as he pulled me into his arms. I put both my hands up to stop him before he could kiss me. If I let him kiss me I would end up forgetting my purpose here, and there was a good chance that we would be naked in minutes.

“I’m here to apply for a position as your assistant,” I said.

That stopped him. He gazed down at me, confused, and I used the opportunity to sell my idea. “You need someone to handle the staff and place orders. You have bigger things to deal with. I can handle the staff. I can put out the small fires and leave the big ones to you. I can place orders and I can help you. I can’t sit home alone and lost. I can be here near you and helping you every day.” I stopped and took a breath. He hadn’t moved, but I had his complete attention.

Finally, he stepped back enough so that he could see the pencil skirt and pair of heels I’d put on. I was even wearing a nice blouse and had pulled my hair up in a bun with chopsticks pushed through it. It was as professional as I could get with what I had to work with. A small smile tugged on his lips.

"Is this your interview outfit?" he asked.

I nodded and continued to watch him.

"You want to be my assistant. To help me. Looking like that," he said.

Again, I just nodded. Then he chuckled and shook his head. "Baby, I don't doubt that you would be able to help me, but if you intend to strut around here dressed like that, I'm going to end up fucking you every damn hour, or thinking about fucking you every damn minute."

My stomach fluttered hearing him say he was going to fuck me. I had to stay focused. "I can wear something else," I replied.

Woods studied me a moment. "You sure you want to do this?"

He wasn't going to tell me no. I tamped down my excitement. "Yes. Please. I want to do something. You know I want a job, but more than that I want to help you."

"Are you going to file a sexual harassment suit against me when I decide what I need is to touch you?"

I shook my head and grinned this time. "No. But that's not what I'm here for. I want to take some stress off you," I told him.

"Oh, that would take stress off me," he said, putting his hand on my hip and pulling me against him. "You're hired. But the minute you feel like it's too much, you tell me."

I squealed and reached up to grab his head and kiss him hard on the mouth. "Thank you, boss. I swear I'll do a good job. You just have to swear to give me stuff to do. I want to take stuff off your plate."

"You can take off my clothes," he said against my mouth before tracing kisses down my neck. I arched into him. His tongue flicked over my skin, causing me to shiver. "You can start working for me after I've had you in this sexy little outfit. Then you need to change. Because I won't be able to concentrate with you dressed like this. All I can think about is the way I want to be buried deep inside my new assistant."

His hand slid up my skirt and slipped inside the crotch of my panties. "All wet," he replied before sliding his finger inside me.

"Oh," I cried out, and his mouth got hungrier.

"Unbutton this shirt," he growled.

I did as he asked and his mouth worshipped the tops of my breasts as his finger continued to fuck me. "On my desk," he said, picking me up and putting me on his desk, then shoving my skirt up.

I watched him pull my panties down. Then he fell to his knees and spread my legs, putting my feet up on the edge of his desk. "Fuck, you smell good," he swore before his tongue began tracing circles around my clit, then dipping inside of me. All I could do was squirm and beg. He kept up the torture until I was chanting, "Please, Woods, please."

Finally, his tongue flicked over my clit, sending me rocketing toward my release. Before I could see clearly again, Woods was over me and stretching me as he entered me. I loved it when he filled me up.

"Heaven. This is my heaven. All I fucking need to breathe," he said as he shifted his hips, moving in and out of me.

I pushed papers out of the way and leaned back on my arms to brace myself. Woods's shirt was still on and I wished it wasn't. I loved seeing the muscles in his arms flex when he hovered over me. "You didn't unbutton your shirt," I said as a moan of pleasure escaped me.

He smirked. "You wanted my shirt off?"

I nodded and lifted my legs to wrap them around his waist.

"Next time, baby. I can't stop now," he growled.

I slid my legs up his back higher and he groaned, then threw his head back. I felt him grow inside me and I came apart underneath him as his hot seed poured into me.

I fell back on my elbows and gasped for air.

Woods's head dropped onto my chest and he took several deep breaths.

"Best interview ever," he panted out.

I let out a giggle that only caused him to laugh against my skin. I was going to make myself worthy of this man.

Woods

I stood just out of sight as Della calmed the feuding cooks. I wanted to handle this. I hated having to watch her stand between two men yelling at each other. But I couldn't interfere. She was so happy with her new job. At first I hadn't wanted to give her much work, but she'd put her hands on her hips and pitched a fit one day when she saw me outside dealing with a staff issue. Once I realized this was going to make her happy, I let her have more of my work.

She was good at it, too. Not once all week had she had an episode. I had been watching her closely, and I had others watching her to make sure she didn't need me. I was getting more done knowing I could just check on her at any minute. And she was in my office a lot. We were having a hell of a lot of office sex, too, which was making me very happy. Vince wasn't thrilled about it but he didn't complain too much.

"How're things working out with your new assistant?" Jace asked in an amused tone. I turned to see him dressed to play golf.

"She's very good at what she does," I replied.

Jace chuckled and looked over my shoulder as she calmed down the cooks. They were both looking at her now. She was hard not to look at when she was all fired up and red in the face. If the new waiter didn't stop looking at her like he wanted a bite, I was gonna have to fire his ass.

"Want to grab some lunch? I was gonna eat before my tee time."

I was going to ask Della to eat lunch with me but she had several things to do and I knew she'd turn me down so she could work instead. I nodded. "Yeah, sounds good."

We walked around to the entrance and the hostess smiled up at us as we went toward my table. Della came into the dining room and spoke with the hostess, then headed over to Jimmy. She had been a server when she'd first come here and Jimmy had become one of her friends. I was good with that since I knew Jimmy had more interest in me than her.

"She looks so professional," Jace drawled.

I knew he was looking at her skirt and heels and that damn bun in her hair. It was driving me nuts. She said she needed to dress this way to appear professional, but I'll be damned if she didn't look like a fantasy.

"Don't look at her," I snarled.

Jace chuckled. "Relax, man. Not interested in your woman. I have my own."

I knew this but I was feeling territorial watching her move around dressed like that and drawing attention to herself. She was writing something down on a small notepad. Jimmy was probably telling her the things the servers needed ordered. He was the head server. She put the tip of the pen she was writing with in her mouth and chewed on it as she listened to Jimmy, then went back to writing.

"Heard anything from the crazy bitch?" Jace asked.

Angelina had disappeared and I liked it that way. I had to check on my mother more and that was a pain in the ass because she was mad at me. She still believed that Angelina was innocent and I was the asshole who had run her off.

"No, and if she knows what's good for her she won't ever come near me or Della again."

The new server who had been looking at Della in ways he shouldn't have walked over to her and said something that made her smile. She nodded her head and then glanced over his shoulder to see me watching her. The smile on her lips grew before she shifted her eyes back to the guy. I saw her say something to him before turning back to Jimmy, who had an annoyed expression on his face. That told me enough.

Jimmy nodded his head my way and said something to the guy, who glanced back at my table, then walked over to us. Jimmy had sent him to wait on us. Good man.

"Hello, Mr. Kerrington, what can I get you to drink?" the server asked as he filled our water glasses.

"Della is mine. Keep your distance. If you need something, ask Jimmy. He tells Della what is needed. Not you," I told him without caring that my tone was more angry boyfriend than boss.

His eyes went wide and he nodded. "Yes, sir," he replied.

"Get me a sweet tea," Jace said.

"Coffee," I told him, and then turned my attention back to Della, who was standing back, waiting to approach me. She looked wary.

"Hey, baby," I replied, standing up and walking over to her. She smiled at me, then glanced back at the server, who had just walked away.

"What did you say to Ken?" she asked.

"He doesn't need to be looking at you and talking to you. He needs to be working," I told her.

She pressed her lips together, then nodded. "Okay. But he's new. You just hired him last week."

I slipped my arm around her. "Yes he is, and I understand that. He should have been worried about the fact that his boss had just been seated and needed to be waited on. Not the incredibly hot female talking to Jimmy."

Della shook her head, then laughed. "Okay, fine. But be nice. Jimmy needs help."

"Eat with us," I told her.

"Can't. I have to place an order for new aprons and there's an issue with the hot-tea button on the machine. I have to get the service guy here to fix it."

"You have to eat," I told her.

"I'm eating a late lunch with Blaire," she informed me, then grinned. "Now, let me work, boss."

I lowered my head to her ear. "Call me *boss* again and we're gonna end up in a cleaning closet real damn fast."

Della shoved away from me, laughing as she walked off.

I loved that girl.

Della

Blaire had called and asked me to have lunch with her that day. I hadn't spoken to her since the incident with Angelina except for the few times I'd seen her with Rush around the club. It was odd because I felt like we had a bond now that we'd faced down Angelina together. She'd been my hero that night. She made me want to be tough. I wasn't tough and I wanted to be so bad.

I walked out of Woods's old office, which he'd moved me into and told me to decorate any way I wanted. Blaire was headed toward me.

"You even have an office now," Blaire said, smiling brightly. I had to admit I loved having an office. Specifically this office. I had many good memories there. I didn't intend to change anything about it.

"Yes, I feel very official," I replied.

"Good. I'm glad Woods has you. You're perfect for him."

I didn't agree with her. He could have done better—so much better—but I was working toward being good enough. Strong enough. Tough enough.

"Ready for lunch?" I asked, wanting to change the subject.

"I'm starving. Nate isn't sleeping as much as he used to. He keeps me busy but it's wonderful. Downside is, I don't have a lot of time to eat. When Rush is home he helps out a ton and makes sure I have time to eat. Anyway, I'm ready for a baby-free meal."

Nate was Rush and Blaire's baby boy. He was an adorable mixture of the two of them. I didn't normally think guys with piercings and that rough rock star look were attractive, but Rush Finlay holding a baby in his arms was very nice to look at.

"Is Rush with Nate now?" I asked as we walked to the dining room.

"Yes. They're going fishing, which means Nate is going to sit on a blanket and eat sand, if he can get to the edge of the blanket, and Rush is going to fish for about five minutes before realizing he can't fish and watch Nate at the same time. Then he'll stop fishing and they'll sit at the edge of the water and let their feet get wet."

The happiness in Blaire's voice was unmistakable. Rush Finlay made her happy. She made him happy. That was what I had with Woods but it was different. Rush could leave her alone with their baby and not worry about her zoning out and getting lost in her head. He could love her and not worry that his baby would inherit her mental illness. Their love was easy. It was the kind that would go the distance. What Woods and I had wasn't.

Every time I saw Rush holding his baby, I wanted that for Woods. The proud look in his eyes and joy on his face. I couldn't give him that.

"You okay?" Blaire's voice broke into my thoughts and I forced a smile.

"I'm sorry. Work on the brain. I promise to shut it off and be a good lunch date," I assured her.

"As long as it's work that's causing that distressed look on your face," Blaire replied, sounding like she didn't believe me.

I hadn't been brave enough to talk to my best friend, Braden, about this. She loved me fiercely and thought I could do no wrong. She also thought I could be a mother and stable wife. She lived in a fairy tale that I didn't allow myself to step into. Would Blaire be the same way, or would she see my side and understand my fears?

The hostess snapped to attention when she saw me and led us to Woods's table. He had told the staff in the dining room that his table should be available at my convenience.

"Oh, we get the good table," Blaire said, grinning, as we sat down. "I guess you're the boss now, too."

"Woods made a big deal out of them always seating me here." I felt myself blush and Blaire laughed.

"That's sweet," she said.

I wasn't sure how to respond to that. It was sweet. Woods was always sweet. He was impossible to get mad at. Even when he deserved it. Like when he made the new server, Ken, almost pee his pants for talking to me.

Jimmy came strutting out of the kitchen, grinning at us.

"Looks like we're going to get special service, too," I said, nodding my head toward Jimmy.

"Well, hello, my beauties. I didn't know I was gonna get this lucky today," he said with a southern drawl that made most women drool over him.

"Hello, Jimmy," Blaire said.

"You broke loose from baby duty, I see," he teased.

"It's never a duty," she replied.

"Sweet tea for both of you?" he asked.

"Sparkling mineral water for me," Blaire told him.

His eyebrows shot up and then he laughed. "Well look at Alabama getting all sophisticated with her water choices. Damn, baby girl, I remember when you drank water out of the tap."

Blaire laughed. "It's better for the baby than soda or tea. That's all."

"Mmm-hmm, next you're gonna be ordering sushi with that raw shit in it," he said, shaking his finger at her. Then he shot us both a wink and turned to head back to the kitchen.

"He's a mess," Blaire said with fondness in her tone.

"Yes he is, but he runs the kitchen so well. I don't know what we'd do without him."

Blaire leaned back in her seat and crossed her legs. "You'd beg and plead with him to come back. That's what you'd do."

She knew exactly how important he was. She had once been a server there, too. Jimmy had been her first friend in Rosemary. The story went that she came into town looking for her daddy and found her daddy's new wife's son instead. Rush Finlay wasn't a fan of her father and disliked her on the spot. But he let her live in the maid's room while she worked for Woods and made some money until her dad got back from France with Rush's mom.

Rush treated her poorly but ended up falling for her against his will. They had more pain to work through in the end and a lie that tore them apart. I wouldn't have believed any of it seeing them now, but Bethy had told me all about it. She'd been Blaire's friend through it all.

"Did my gun effectively run off the wicked witch, or did Woods do that?" Blaire asked.

"I think it was your gun and the fact that she was scared of what Woods would do once he found out. She left that night and we haven't seen or heard from her since. Mrs. Kerrington isn't very happy with Woods about the whole thing. She blames him for her leaving."

"You're welcome to tell her that it was all me," Blaire said with a smile.

"Thank you, but I don't think it will matter. She doesn't approve of me. She wants Angelina for Woods."

Blaire sighed. "I understand that. I have a mother-in-law who hates me so badly she hasn't even seen her only grandchild."

Blaire was poised and beautiful. She wasn't dealing with something like a mental illness, so you would think her mother-in-law would have loved her. But she represented something to Rush's mother that couldn't ever go away. It was part of the dark past she shared with Blaire's dad.

"I heard Rush's dad was in town last week visiting Nate," I said, remembering how the entire club had talked nonstop about the drummer from Slacker Demon being in town. He was a legend, just like the rock band he was a part of.

"Yes. Dean is a wonderful grandfather. It is a bit surreal to see him cuddling with Nate and singing to him. Nate adores the man. I love to watch Rush's face while he witnesses his dad with his son. It brings me to tears every time."

"I would imagine that is special," I replied. I didn't have parents who would see any child I might have one day. If I ever felt safe enough to have a child.

Woods

My mother was driving me nuts. She was lonely. I understood that. With Angelina gone, she spent most of her time alone. Mother had never done well alone. I had seen her at the club playing tennis with a few of her friends earlier in the week. She had put on a good show for them, treating me like she was proud of me. But I knew she was still mad at me. I'd been going along with her acting all my life.

I had sent Della to my office to organize some files on my desk that didn't really need organizing. I just wanted her safely out of the way while Mother was here. I wasn't sure my mom could act as if she liked Della. And I wasn't going to have Della hurt or embarrassed.

The rest of the staff loved Della. When they saw her coming, everyone became happier and nicer. They didn't want to let her down. Whatever had been wrong the moment before they were willing to fix. It was helping me out a shit-ton. My jealousy over the fact that the males on my staff bent over backward to make her smile was difficult. But then who wouldn't want to make Della happy? I couldn't be mad at them for that. As long as they kept their hands off of her.

"Where's Della?" Marco, our golf pro, asked as he walked into the clubhouse.

"Why do you need Della?" I asked, reminding myself that this man was happily married.

"She was working on getting me a sub for next week. They're inducing Jill on Monday and I want to be with her and the baby the first week."

"I have her working on something. I'll check to make sure she has a sub for you. You should be with your wife and child," I replied.

"Thanks, Mr. Kerrington," he replied, and nodded before heading over to grab a water from the cooler.

The back door swung open and Vince stood there, looking wide-eyed. "Mr. Kerrington, sir, you need to come quick."

It was Della. I knew that look. She was having one of her episodes. *Shit!*

I ran for the door. "Where is she?" I asked him.

"In your office, sir. She came up to see you and then your mom stopped by. I tried to call you but it went to voice mail. Your mom went into the office to talk to Della. After she came out I heard Della whimpering. I knocked, sir, but she didn't respond so I went in."

"That's enough. I know the rest. Don't tell anyone about this, do you understand?" I waited until he nodded before I sprinted across the parking lot into the main offices. *My mother is off her damn leash. Fuck! I shouldn't have left Della alone for so long.*

Several people called my name as I ran for the stairs, not wanting to wait on the damn elevator. Taking the stairs two at a time, I reached the third floor in less than a minute. My office door was closed and I was thankful Vince hadn't left her exposed to whoever walked up there.

I swung the door open and scanned the room until I found her sitting against the wall with her knees pulled up to her chin. Her arms were wrapped around her legs and she was rocking back and forth, whimpering. I hated seeing her like this. She'd been doing so well. Her night terrors had eased off; she hadn't experienced any in a month, at least.

"Della." I called her name as I walked over to her, hoping she could hear me and my voice would draw her out. I bent down beside her and pulled her into my arms. She was stiff and cold.

"No, no, no, no, no," she chanted over and over.

"I have you, sweetheart. You're in my arms. I have you, Della. Shh, it's okay. Come back to me, baby. Please come back to me. I'm right here and I have you." I whispered in her ear how much I loved her; I wasn't going to let her go until her body started to ease.

Slowly, her arms loosened their grip around her legs and wrapped around me, and then she buried her face in my neck. She was back. I continued to tell her she was wonderful and she was mine and I would take care of her. Reassuring her reassured me that I had her. That she was here and I could take care of her. I had let her take on too much responsibility because she was good at it. I had started letting her work longer and I was checking on her less. This was my fault. My mother would never have gotten to her if I had been watching her closer.

"I'm sorry," Della said in a teary voice against my chest.

"Don't say that," I replied as I ran my hand over her hair

and down her back. "Please, baby, don't say that. I hate for you to think you have to say that."

She sniffled. "I need to be stronger. I want to be stronger. I want to be tough."

Did she not realize how fucking tough she was? She had lived a horror story for sixteen years of her life that had ended even more horrifically. And she still laughed and found reasons to smile. She was brave enough to live life, even after enduring the monsters that had terrorized her in her room as a child. And they weren't pretend. She'd faced real monsters and she had survived. There was no one as fucking tough as this woman.

"Della, you are tougher than anyone I know. Just because you have to protect yourself sometimes and fade away from me doesn't make you weak. You're a survivor. You are my inspiration and I love you. No matter what, I love you."

Della clung tighter to me. My mother had upset her. I would deal with her. She wouldn't get close to Della again, even if I had to ban her from the club. This would stop. I was done with my family hurting what was mine.

We sat there in silence. Della let me hold her as close as I needed to. She let me kiss her head and hands and run my hands over her arms and back to reassure myself she was okay.

The knock on the door ended our peace and quiet. Della started to move out of my lap but I held her to me. I was going to ignore whoever it was. Vince should have been out there by now.

"Is everything okay, sir?" Vince asked from the other side of the door.

"Yes, we're fine," I replied.

Della tilted her head back to look up at me. "Did he see me?"

I nodded. I didn't want to lie to her, even though I knew she hated for people to see her when she was like that.

"He's going to think I'm insane," she said with a defeated sigh.

I grabbed her chin and made her look up at me. "No, he won't. You aren't insane. You are intelligent, lovable, and beautiful. But you are *not* insane. You lived through hell and you beat it, Della. Most people can't overcome something like what you've overcome. Don't ever think you're less than amazing."

A small smile tugged at the corners of her lips. "You just love me," she said.

"More than life," I replied before pressing my lips to hers.

Della

Woods hadn't left me alone since my blackout yesterday. I knew he had work to do. I also had work to do, but he was keeping me by his side at home. Every time I mentioned going into the office, he did something to distract me. Oral sex on the kitchen counter had been his first tactic, and it worked. I had forgotten about anything but the way he made me feel.

Then he'd caught me sneaking off to take a shower when he was on a work-related phone call. I mentioned that we needed to get ready, and then he'd taken me against the shower wall. After he cut the water off and carried me to bed, we'd made love again.

Now he was outside on the phone again. I knew he was dealing with work from home and it only proved my point that I was hindering him. My weakness was a weight on him, but I wanted to help him. When he opened the door and stepped inside, I started to tell him that we should really go to work. I was going to fight off any sexual advances he tried to use to keep me there.

"That was Vince. I have two board members in my office that my mother contacted about some things she knows nothing about. I need to go into work to deal with them. I should be back in two hours max," he said before the door closed behind him.

He wasn't going to let me go. "I could go to work, too. There are things I didn't get done yesterday."

"No. I've got to concentrate on this meeting, and knowing you're there will distract me. I'll be worried about you. Just stay here and I promise I'll come right back."

He pressed a kiss to my lips before walking to the bedroom to get dressed. I stood there and let his words sink in. He was taking my job away. He was going to keep me here again. He was afraid of my being at work and having one of my episodes.

I had been working so hard to be tough. To ease his worries. One bad day and he had me in a glass box again. This wasn't fair. I wanted to live. I loved being close to him and having a purpose, knowing I was helping him. Staying here all the time was lonely. I couldn't do this again.

He walked out of the bedroom dressed in a suit and smiled at me. "We'll eat at that Italian place you love in Seaside tonight," he told me, as if that made this all okay.

Instead of telling him how I felt, I just nodded and kissed him back, then watched him leave. I didn't fight back. I just let him decide what I was going to do. This wasn't tough. Blaire wouldn't have let Rush do this. She would have fought back. She would have turned Alabama badass on him and gotten her way.

I had to show Woods that I could do this. I'd had one slipup but I was bigger than that. I could keep working. He needed me there. I was helping him. I was good at it.

I went to the bedroom and got ready for work.

Facing Woods while he was in a meeting wasn't a wise decision. Instead, I finished the work I hadn't completed yesterday. I managed to schedule a stand-in golf pro, ordered new golf carts to replace two of our older ones, and met with the manager of the golf course, Darla, about using new vendors for snacks and adding some new beers.

It was three hours before I had a chance to meet with Woods. He hadn't called me yet so he wasn't even aware that he had gone over his two hours. Either he was still in a meeting or he was so swamped with work he had lost track of time.

Vince smiled at me with relief in his face when I walked off the elevator. "Miss Della, I'm so glad you're back today. You've been missed."

I needed to go ahead and deal with this thing with Vince. "Thank you," I said, stopping at his desk. "About yesterday, Vince, I'm sorry you saw me like that. I'm very thankful you went and got Woods for me. I have those episodes sometimes and I work hard to control them, but I didn't do a good job yesterday."

He held up his hand to stop me. "I don't need an explanation. If you need me I'm here. Don't you concern yourself with what I saw. That's between us and only us."

Tears stung my eyes and I only managed to nod. I glanced at the closed door to Woods's office. "Is he in there?"

Vince shook his head. "No, he left about fifteen minutes ago. He said he'd be back in thirty minutes for a conference call he's expecting."

Crap. Was I going to miss him? "Okay, thanks, Vince."

I went back to the elevator and changed my mind. I'd take the stairs. Woods normally took the stairs. I might miss him if I took the elevator.

The moment the door to the stairs closed behind me, I heard Woods's voice from below. Stopping, I considered going back into the office. I didn't want to eavesdrop.

"I don't know how you've dealt with the crazy as long as you have." Jace's voice stopped me from leaving, as did his words. I froze with my hand on the door.

"It was what I had to do. I couldn't just let her be alone. But it's affecting my work. At least when Angelina was here she helped." Woods's words were like cold water being poured over my head.

"You need to keep your ass away from her insane shit. You have a corporation to run. Dropping what you need to do to deal with one of her batshit crazy episodes isn't fair. You need to fix this problem." Jace's words made the numbness in my heart start to spread.

"I can't. How the hell do I do that?" Woods said in a frustrated growl.

I'd heard enough. I had to get away. I had to leave. I couldn't breathe. The darkness was closing in again, and this time I wasn't going to be here for everyone to witness it.

I forced a smile at Vince when I walked back out of the stairwell and headed for the elevator. He didn't ask and I didn't explain. I just kept my focus on the elevator doors. They opened and I stepped inside. Taking deep breaths, I fought off the darkness. I would not do this here. My craziness was affecting his work. *No, no!* I would stay focused.

When the doors opened, I stepped out and walked straight

to the parking lot. When I reached my car I got inside and reached for my phone.

"Tripp," I said when he answered.

"Yeah?"

"I need you to come get me. It's time I left," I replied.

He was silent.

"Trust me. I will tell you after you get here. Don't tell Woods. Just come get me. It's past time I left."

"What did he do?"

I let out a heavy sigh and grasped at the strength I hoped was inside me. "He wants out. My issues are too much for him. He just doesn't know how to tell me. Please, it's time I left. I want to live my life now."

"I'll be there by lunch tomorrow. I just have my bike."

"I'll pack light," I replied.

"You can ship everything else. I'll text you an address."

"Okay."

"You're sure about this?"

"Yes," I replied.

Woods

My mother had called two of the board members my dad was closest to and told them that I was letting Della work at the club. Then she'd proceeded to tell them Della was mentally unstable and dangerous. She'd gone as far as to make up shit about Della trying to hurt her. My mother had lost her mind.

Jace walked into my office after I'd had a long meeting with the two men and lost my argument about Della. They wanted background checks on her. I knew what they would find and I refused to do it. She wouldn't want that.

"You look ready to murder an entire village with your bare hands, bro. What's up?" I stormed past him and to the stairwell. I needed to yell and hit a wall. That was the safest place to do it.

I ran up two flights of stairs before I stopped and slammed my fist into the wall, cursing everyone responsible. Della didn't need this right now. She was doing so much better. How was I supposed to tell her about this?

"What happened?" Jace asked from behind me. I hadn't realized he had followed me.

"My fucking mother happened. Her and Angelina. They're evil and twisted. How is it that my mother is so damn screwed up? What happened to her and my father to make them such fucked-up individuals? To make them think they can control lives? They can't! This club is mine and if I want to fire every motherfucker on the board that my father set in place, I will! It's time for a new board anyway," I snarled, taking deep breaths to calm myself down.

"I don't know how you've dealt with the crazy as long as you have," Jace said, sitting down on the steps and watching me pace.

"It was what I had to do. I couldn't just let her be alone. But it's affecting my work. At least when Angelina was here she helped," I said.

"You need to keep your ass away from her insane shit. You have a corporation to run. Dropping what you need to do to deal with one of her batshit crazy episodes isn't fair. You need to fix this problem," Jace said, as if it were easy. How was I supposed to just turn away from my mother? I was all she had.

"I can't. How the hell do I do that?" I asked, stopping my pacing and leaning against the wall. If it was a choice between Della and my mother, I would choose Della. If she forced my hand, I was going to have to turn away from her. First, I needed to decide about the board. I needed a lawyer. My own lawyer, not my father's. I was done using the people he had set in place. Things were different now and I didn't need a crazy-ass phone call from my mother sending board members to my office questioning my decisions.

It was time I made sure this place was run by me. My board would be made up of people I trusted and confided in. It was time for a new generation.

"Jace," I said, turning to look at him.

"Yeah?"

"You ready to be a board member?"

Jace frowned. "What?"

"I'm getting a lawyer. I'm firing the old board and starting my own."

A grin spread across Jace's face. "Hell yeah," he replied.

For the first time since I'd gotten the call earlier that day, I felt lighter. I wasn't going to let my mother control me. I was in control. My grandfather had left it all to me. Even her home was now mine. If she wanted to fuck with my life I'd fuck with hers enough to make her stop. She was my mom, but Della was my life.

◇

Four hours had passed since I'd left Della. Dammit. I'd lost track of time. Grabbing my phone, I headed out the door to my truck. My call went straight to her voice mail. Shit!

Della's car was in the driveway. She was there. Maybe she'd been outside when I'd called her. I had promised her dinner tonight in Seaside. I was two hours late. This wasn't fair to her. I couldn't keep her here all the time. She was coming back to work with me. I needed her help. She was good at her job.

Opening the door, the smell of roasted garlic and tomatoes met my nose. I closed it and followed the smell to the kitchen. Della was standing at the stove with a black apron on from the club, stirring a pot.

"Hey," I said quietly so I didn't startle her.

She spun around and smiled at me. There was a sadness in her eyes she couldn't hide. I'd made her sad. My leaving her here had upset her. She had wanted to go to work today. I would have to explain all that tonight.

"I decided to cook instead of us going out," she said.

I walked over to stand behind her and wrapped my hands around her waist. "It smells incredible."

"Good. I haven't made lasagna in a long time. This sauce is hard to get right."

Something was off in her voice. I hated that she was upset.

"I'm sorry about today."

"Don't apologize. Please, don't. You had work to do. I know that and I'm okay with it."

She didn't want my apology. What was upsetting her then?

"You can come back to work tomorrow," I told her.

"I don't think I'm ready for that yet," she replied.

She wasn't ready for it? Today she'd tried several times to go back to work. What had changed?

"Why do you think you're not ready? Did you have another episode today?"

She shook her head. "No, I think it's just too much on me right now. I need to get a better grip on myself first." She turned and looked up at me. "Let's not talk about it tonight. I want to cook you dinner and enjoy being with you."

I tucked my head in the curve of her neck. "Okay," I replied. We would talk about it tomorrow then. "How can I help you with dinner?"

She turned and kissed my head. "You can slice the French bread, butter it, then sprinkle it with garlic powder. I need to toast it."

"I can do that," I said, stepping back from Della and reaching for the bread.

Della

I had known deep down that this wouldn't be forever. I'd thought once Woods realized how impossible life would be with me that he would end it. But that wasn't true. He was already tired of dealing with my being "crazy," but he'd never let me know. He made me feel cherished. If I hadn't heard him talking to Jace I would still have been holding on to the belief that we could work through it all.

Years of not living among other people had hindered my ability to read them. Jace had known that Woods was tired of dealing with me but I hadn't gotten the hint. I knew now. Tonight would be it for us. I had cooked for him and enjoyed looking at him and listening to him talk. I wanted to etch every moment of tonight in my memory.

When I left tomorrow, that would be it. I wasn't coming back and Woods would be relieved. At first he would be upset. I thought he loved me. I was just more than he'd bargained for. When he realized I'd taken myself out of the picture for him, his life would get easier. He could be free of worrying about me.

Tonight, though, he was still mine. I could hold him and believe in what we had. Just once more.

We stood side by side and cleaned up the dishes. Normally

we talked and laughed but I couldn't find anything fun to talk about. My heart was too heavy.

"Are you okay?" Woods asked when he put the last dish in the dishwasher and closed it.

I nodded and smiled.

He reached over and laced his fingers through mine. "Are you sure? I'll fix whatever is wrong if you just tell me," he said, gently tugging me to him. He was a fixer. He wanted to fix my life, and that wasn't possible.

Instead of answering, I stood up on my tiptoes and pressed my lips to his neck. "I want you," I whispered against his warm skin. "Right now, all I want is you."

Woods let me kiss down his neck, and when I tugged at his T-shirt he lifted his arms and let me take it off. His chiseled chest was always tanned and perfect. I ran my fingers over the beautiful skin and each hard ab muscle that fascinated me. This had been mine for a time. It would be a chapter in my life that was hard to look back on, yet it would be my favorite.

I pressed my lips to the taut skin of his lower stomach and started undoing his jeans. He stood there and let me. I was glad there was no resistance or questions. If we were ending this chapter tonight, I wanted it to be perfect.

I pulled his jeans down with his boxer briefs.

"Fuck, Della," he whispered as I licked the tip of his cock. Both of his hands were now buried in my hair as I lowered myself to my knees in front of him. I wanted him to know I loved him. When I was gone I wanted him to know that he was a part of me. That this hadn't been empty for me.

"Oh, hell," he groaned, leaning back against the counter for support as I sank his length into my mouth until it slid into my throat. I loved the way this made him feel. Knowing the trembling in his legs was because of me was a wonderful feeling. He made me tremble all the time. I liked making him tremble in return.

"That's so damn good, baby. Your hot little mouth is fucking perfect." His voice was husky and deep. I reached up and cupped his balls in my hand. He let out a low growl and suddenly I was being jerked up. "Not gonna come in your mouth. Not tonight. I want inside you," he said, kicking off his jeans and leaving them on the floor before picking me up and walking to the bedroom.

His hands were on my shorts, jerking them off. I raised my arms and let him pull my top off. My bra and panties went just as quickly.

"You're beautiful," he said as he knelt above me and stared down at my body.

When I was with him I felt beautiful. "Make love to me," I told him as I opened my thighs and reached up to pull him down to me.

"I want to taste you," he said, stopping me from pulling him down farther.

"I want you inside me," I replied.

"Don't care. I want a taste first." His crooked grin warmed my heart. I'd let him have whatever he wanted.

"Okay," I replied as he lowered himself until his head was between my thighs.

His lips brushed the sensitive skin on the insides of my legs as he trailed kisses, switching from one leg to the other until the heat of his breath touched my tender flesh. I shuddered and grabbed handfuls of the sheets underneath me just before his tongue slipped inside of me and then moved up to my clit.

I cried out his name until I came against his mouth. Every single flick of his tongue had taken me farther under the wave of pleasure that overtook me.

As I gasped to get air into my lungs, he filled me in one swift move. I lifted my knees and pressed them to his ribs. "I love you, Della. I love you so much, baby. So damn much," he said with a hoarse voice full of emotion. It was as if he knew this was it for us. That tomorrow wouldn't come. This was the end. I fought back the tears clogging my throat and grabbed his face so that I could kiss him. I couldn't talk. I didn't trust myself to talk. I showed him how much I loved him with my mouth.

With each thrust I lifted my knees and cried out. He never stopped telling me how much he loved me. It was a chant as we both climbed to our release.

"*Woods!*" I screamed his name in ecstasy as the world blurred.

He held me to his chest as he jerked inside of me. My name was a strangled cry from his chest as he shuddered against me.

Our chapter was over. It was the most beautiful chapter in my life. I knew I'd had the happy ending way before it was time and now I had to live the rest of the story without him. It wasn't the way life was supposed to be, but it was my life. And I'd had Woods in it. That made it all okay.

◇

Woods had kissed my head, telling me to sleep late. He had an early meeting and I could come to work when I was ready. I had pretended to be sleepy and nodded, keeping my head buried in the pillow to hide my tears. When the door clicked behind him I turned over and stared at the ceiling.

My heart had just walked out that door.

I moved without thought as I showered and dressed. I boxed up the things I would be shipping that morning to the address Tripp had texted me. I then packed a small bag I could carry with me. I wasn't sure where we were going and when we would make it back to the South Carolina address I was shipping my things to.

Woods called me around ten and asked if I wanted to eat lunch with him. I didn't want to lie to him but I couldn't tell him the truth either. So I told him I was behind on work and if he wanted me to come back, then I needed to catch up. He didn't argue with me. When I told him that I loved him one tear rolled down my face. I was glad he couldn't see me.

On a piece of paper I wrote:

I will never forget you. Thank you for everything but it's time I move on. I want to see the world. This life isn't for me. It doesn't fit. It isn't what I dreamed of. Don't come after me, just let me go. I hope you find the happiness you deserve.

I'm sorry,
Della

Woods

I ended the strange phone call from Tripp and stared down at my phone for a few minutes. Nothing about that conversation had made sense. He'd asked me how life was. I'd told him it was good. He had said I should strive for great. I told him it was perfect and he had gone silent. Then he'd said, *Sometimes what we think is perfect is royally fucked up.* I had asked him what he meant and he said he was just checking in and hoped I'd figure life out soon.

What the hell had all that meant? Was he drinking before lunch? Glancing at my clock, I realized it was my tee time with Jace. When Della had turned me down for lunch I'd let her because she wanted to work. I couldn't keep making her feel like she wasn't important. So to keep myself from begging her to have lunch with me, I'd called Jace and set up a tee time for us.

I had a meeting with my new lawyer at three, then after that I would hunt her down. I thought she'd be ready to take a break then. Smiling, I let Tripp's weird phone call go and I headed down to the golf course.

Jace was standing at Bethy's golf cart with his hands on the roof as he leaned in, flirting with her. I never would have guessed those two would have made it so long. Bethy had been the wild local girl who lived in the next town over. She slept with the rich boys and they acted like they didn't know her in public. Until Jace. He'd decided that she was worth it. He had seen something more.

"You gonna stop making out with my employee long enough to play a round?" I asked as I approached them.

Jace grinned over at me, then flipped his middle finger. "Suck it, Kerrington."

"You two need me to get y'all a caddy?" Bethy asked.

"We're real men, baby. We don't need a caddy," Jace said, winking at her.

"Let's do this. I have a three o'clock appointment," I informed Jace.

The cart I'd ordered was brought around with my clubs. Jace said his good-byes to Bethy and put his clubs in the back of the cart. "It's been a while since we played a round," Jace said. "Boss man never has any time."

"Della has taken a lot off me. I need to give her a raise."

Jace chuckled and propped his feet up on the dash of the cart. "You told your momma about the new-board idea?"

"I won't be telling her. It isn't her business. I'm meeting with the lawyer today to make sure this is handled the correct way. The lawyer will make sure the board knows they've been terminated."

"You know, I always thought the board, like, owned a portion of the club," Jace said.

"My grandfather forbade it in his will. He wanted the club to always be under the Kerrington name. He didn't allow investors unless they were family. That was one of the reasons my father wanted me to marry Angelina. She would become family and he would merge her father's clubs with the Kerrington Club. My grandfather wouldn't have wanted that. I've looked over his business plan. I know his dream for this place. My father had other ideas and he was going to use me to accomplish them."

Jace let out a low whistle as we pulled up to the first tee. "Damn, no wonder your dad was ready to marry you off to a psycho. So, you really own it all now. You make the decisions. That board was just so your father had people to help him build and make decisions."

"I think he had promised them a piece of the pie once the Kerrington Club was part of the Greystone empire. Everything would have changed then. He also paid them well. I looked over the payroll."

Jace jumped out and pulled his driver from the bag before heading over to the tee. "So you're saying I'm gonna get a nice fat paycheck for being on this new board," Jace drawled.

"Yeah, that's what I'm saying," I replied, pulling the driver from my bag.

"Good. Because I'm gonna propose to Bethy and my family is gonna shit a brick. I can kiss my monthly income good-bye. I need to start using this education my father paid so handsomely for."

I stopped walking. Had I just heard him right? "Did you just say *propose*?"

Jace looked up from his stance over the ball and nodded.

"Wow," was all I could think of to say. I hadn't expected that.

"I love her. She's it for me."

I stood there silently as Jace hit the ball. He stepped back and glanced over at me. "She doesn't know yet. I'm trying to think of a romantic way to do it."

This golf game had just gotten a lot more interesting.

◇

I texted Della before my three o'clock meeting but she didn't respond before the lawyer arrived. Once my meeting was over and there was still no response, I dialed her number. I hadn't seen her all day. Neither had anyone I asked. Something felt wrong.

"I'm sorry, but the number you have dialed has been disconnected . . ." I jerked my phone back and looked down to make sure I'd dialed Della's number. I had.

I grabbed my keys and walked past Vince without a word. My mind was running wild. Why would Della's phone be disconnected? Had she forgotten to pay the bill? Was she okay?

As I got to the house, every bad scenario ran through my head. The car I'd given Della when she'd come back to Rosemary with me was sitting in the drive. She hadn't left the house today. My heart raced as I ran up the steps and swung the door open.

It was quiet. Too quiet.

"Della? Baby? You okay?" I called out as I walked down the hall toward the living room. I glanced into the kitchen as I passed and almost continued on when I saw a single piece of paper and a pen lying on the counter. They hadn't been there that morning.

"Della?" I called out again, walking on toward the living room and out onto the balcony. The bedroom was empty. It was also bare. There were no heels lying by the door or jewelry on the dresser. I stood in the doorway, afraid to walk inside and look in the closet.

I turned and headed back to the kitchen. The note would explain this. She could have cleaned up before she went shopping with Blaire. That made sense.

Reaching for the paper, I picked it up and began to read. With each word, my world began to slowly fall away. The small, ripped piece of notebook paper held the only words that could completely destroy me.

I let it fall to the floor as I stood frozen. I didn't want to touch it. I didn't want to see it. The words were imprinted in my head. I'd never be able to make them go away. I couldn't move. I couldn't breathe.

Della

Tripp hadn't said much when he came to get me. He had just asked if I was sure, and when I'd said yes he had taken my bag and put it in the compartment of his bike before handing me a helmet and a leather jacket. I put both on.

We had been riding for about two hours when he pulled into a gas station. My legs were slightly numb. I wasn't sure I could walk when I got off that thing. Tripp got off and then took my helmet and hung it on the bike. I didn't ask him why he wasn't wearing a helmet but I was glad he had one for me to wear. He then held his hand out to help me off. I managed to sling my leg over the bike and held on to both his hands as I stood up.

"Ouch," I said with a weak smile.

He grinned. "Yeah, you'll get used to it," he told me, then nodded his head toward the store. "Go in, use the restroom, and get yourself something to eat and drink. We'll take a little break before we go any farther."

I had focused on the road and the cars we passed. I'd managed to fight off any thoughts of Woods. But they were there in my head, teasing me. They wanted to haunt me. They wanted to break me. He would know soon that I was gone. "Where are we going?" I asked, trying to think of anything other than Woods.

"Not sure. We're just riding. I thought you might need that right now. I'm heading north. I figure we'll find somewhere interesting by bedtime to stop at."

This was what I needed. I nodded. "Okay."

"I gotta fill up," he told me, and I headed inside the store. I would need to call Braden now. I hadn't told her I was leaving Woods. She wouldn't have seen it my way. But once Woods knew I was gone he would call her first. She would be worried. I should prepare her. I slipped my phone out of my pocket and remembered I'd had it switched off. I didn't want to be traceable. I would reactivate it in the next big city. A new number. One no one knew.

After using the restroom I grabbed a bottle of water and some Cheetos, paid, and headed outside to sit at a picnic table that sat in a grassy area.

Tripp glanced over at me before he went inside and did the same. By the time he came outside I was finished with my bag of Cheetos. He dropped a candy bar, a bag of peanuts, some beef jerky, and a bag of gummy worms on the table. "Eat some more," he said before picking up the beef jerky and taking a bite of it.

I reached for the candy bar and broke it in half before eating it. We ate in silence. I was afraid to try to talk to him. He wanted to know why I was doing this. He didn't think I should. I could tell by the way he was acting.

"He didn't know you were leaving. Didn't even have a clue. That sucks, Della. It really does. The dude's gonna take this real hard."

I stopped eating and stood up. "I can't think about that right now, okay? I need to think about other things. Not that. It's what was best for him. That's all I can tell you. Please, let's not talk about it."

Tripp let out a weary sigh, then nodded. "Fine. We won't

talk about it. Not right now, anyway. Eat some worms, they're good for you," he said with a smirk as he pushed the bag of gummy worms toward me.

"I'm not hungry." I wasn't. I felt sick now.

"Fine. I'll take this with us. You'll get hungry again soon. You barely ate anything."

"Can I use your phone to call my friend Braden?"

Tripp nodded and pulled his phone out of his pocket to hand it to me.

"Thanks," I replied as I took it from him.

I walked far enough away that he wouldn't hear me. I was going to lie to Braden some, if only to keep her from telling Woods the truth.

Dialing her number, I held my breath, hoping that I could find a way to tell her and make it believable. She would go straight to Woods with my location and reason for leaving if she knew the truth.

"Hello?" Braden's voice sounded curious. She didn't recognize the number.

"It's me," I said into the phone.

"Della? Where are you?"

"I'm traveling the world. Living life. Woods's life isn't what I want for myself. I need adventure."

Braden didn't respond. She was thinking. I knew the look on her face even though I couldn't see it.

"What happened? Stop bullshitting me and tell me where you are and what's wrong." I was a horrible liar and Braden knew me better than anyone.

"I'm traveling. I'm not alone and I'm okay. I just need some time. I'll check in when I can but I need time to move on from things. This is why I got in your car and took off to begin with, anyway. Woods changed that but it was only temporary. I need to do this for me."

"I'm still calling bullshit. I don't believe you but I won't push. Call me when you can, and be safe. Can I trust who you're with to keep you safe?"

"Yes," I replied.

"You won't tell me who it is?"

"No. I need you to not tell Woods that you talked to me. Tell him nothing. He will come after me and I don't want him to."

Braden let out a small growl of frustration. "He loves you, Della," she said.

"And I love him. But it's time I lived. I can't be locked up in that small town."

"I hope you're not making the biggest mistake of your life," she said in a defeated tone.

"It was the best chapter. I'll have more chapters though."

"I love you," Braden said.

"I love you, too," I replied.

"Call me soon."

"I will."

I hung up and walked back over to Tripp, who was watching me.

"Thanks," I said, handing back his phone.

"Did you have yours turned off so he couldn't track you?" he asked, standing up.

I nodded.

"Damn, girl. You didn't leave the boy a bone, did you?"

"Can we go? I just want to ride."

"Yeah, let's go," he said, and headed for the Harley parked near the table.

Woods

She hadn't left me anything but a note. She'd taken all her things. I held the pillow she'd slept on last night and pressed my face to it. It smelled like her. The sexy sweet scent that was Della.

How was I supposed to let her go? She didn't want me to find her . . . she wanted to live. This wasn't living for her. She had started out on a journey to see the world and she'd met me. Now she wanted more.

I'd hovered over her. I had tried to keep her safe and not let her do things she wanted. I'd controlled her job and what she did. She wanted to spread her wings and I'd clipped them. So she'd found another way to fly.

My chest was so tight that each breath I took was painful. I hadn't called anyone. I hadn't left my house for hours. I held the pillow closer and glanced over at the clock. It was after nine. I'd been home for five hours. How long had she been gone? Had she known last night that she was leaving me?

The look in her eyes as she'd made love to me had been different. There had been something in them that bothered me. But she had been so passionate and needy that I'd forgotten about everything other than the pleasure. If I had just looked deeper and talked to her . . . Instead, it had been about sex. When she had fallen to her knees in the kitchen, I was lost to whatever she wanted.

If I'd only looked deeper.

How had she left me?

Slowly, a realization came to me and I stood up, still holding her pillow. The phone call from Tripp. He hadn't made sense but he'd been trying to tell me. *Motherfucker!* She'd left with Tripp. She had called him and he had come for her.

The pain slowly started heating up as anger—no, fury—consumed me. She had left with Tripp. He had taken her from me. His call wouldn't have made sense to anyone. It had been his way of being able to say he had warned me when he knew I wouldn't understand him.

I reached for the lamp on the bedside table and threw it against the wall. Then I threw the sheets and shoved over the nightstand. I grabbed the mirror off the wall and smashed it, but the anger was still there. I punched the wall until my fist went through the Sheetrock and my voice seemed so far away, even though I was yelling. I had stepped outside of myself as my body went mad. Then I threw the pillow in my hand and everything stopped. That was all I had. Her pillow. I walked over to the pile of broken glass and furniture and picked the pillow back up. I held it reverently to my chest.

Her scent filled my senses and for a moment the fury eased. For a moment I wasn't a hysterical madman bent on demolishing everything in my house. I had her. I could hold this. I had her.

"Holy shit." Jace's voice came from the doorway. I snapped my head up to see him looking into my room. The horrified look on his face as he lifted his eyes to me only made me angry again.

"Dude," he said, holding up both his hands. "You gotta calm down."

He didn't understand. He hadn't just lost his reason for fucking living. She hadn't just walked away from him. Left him nothing but a note and a pillow. The note . . . shit.

I stalked to the door and shoved past Jace. I had to get the note. I had the note, too. It was something of hers. I had that. I wanted it. Even if the words in it tore me wide open, I wanted it.

The torn paper lay on the floor and I scrambled to pick it up. I couldn't read the words again. Not right now. I folded it carefully and tucked it into my pocket. I'd keep it on me. This was her handwriting. Her words.

"You're scaring me, man." Jace had followed me to the kitchen.

"I need to be alone," I said without turning to look at him.

"I don't think you need to be alone."

"Leave my motherfucking house," I snarled.

"I've called Rush and Thad. They're on their way. I'm not leaving you alone."

I didn't want them here. I wanted to yell and break things. I wanted to find a way to ease the pain. "No! Why are you even here?"

"Tripp called me," he said slowly. Just hearing his name and knowing that he was the one who had Della made the monster inside of me snap. I reached for the glass in the sink and threw it across the room, shattering a picture.

"He took her!" I roared as I grabbed a plate and hurled it across the room. "He fucking took her from me!"

"She called him. She wanted to go with him, Woods. You

gotta calm down. She left of her own free will." I could hear the fear in Jace's voice but I didn't care. I grabbed a bar stool and began smashing it against the counter until the wood shattered into pieces in a heap on the floor.

"Holy hell." Rush's voice registered in my brain but I couldn't think. I didn't want them there.

"Dude! Stop him. He's gone fucking mad," Thad said.

Arms wrapped around me from behind and I fought against them, but they held me tighter. "Chill the fuck out. Breathe, man. Fucking take a breath. She isn't dead. She left. She's out there and it ain't over. So calm the fuck down," Rush said in a stern, loud voice as he held my arms back.

I took several deep breaths. He was right. She was alive. She had just left. She had left. "She left me," I said, and my voice broke.

"Yeah, she did. But you can't beat the hell out of your house. It won't bring her back and you're getting out of control. Get it together. I know what this feels like. I've been there. Losing your shit doesn't make her come back to you."

Rush had been here. He knew. Blaire had left him once. But she'd been betrayed. She'd had a reason to. I hadn't hurt Della. I had only loved her.

"I didn't let her live," I said, lifting my eyes to look straight ahead at Jace and Thad, who were keeping their distance from me.

"She needs some space. Let her have it," Rush said.

"How do I keep going? With her gone? What do I do?"

Rush let out a sigh and slowly let his hold on me go. "You wake up each morning and you go to work. You smile when you think you're supposed to. You spend your free time thinking about her. Thinking about what you'll say when you see her again. Then you go to bed and hope you get some sleep. Then you wake up and do that same shit over again."

I leaned against the wall and hung my head. "What if she never comes back?" He didn't say anything at first. We stood there in silence among the destruction.

"Then you find a way to keep living," Rush finally said, and I realized that was my biggest fear. That I'd be left needing to find a way, because Della might never come back.

"She was my go-all-in," I said as I stared down at the smashed-up bar stool.

"Your what?" Jace asked.

"Della was my go-all-in. She was my winning hand. You can't play when you go all in and lose. I'm out."

"No, you're not. This hand ain't over yet," Rush said.

I hoped he was right.

Two weeks later

Della

"Where are we now?" I asked Tripp as I got off the back of his bike—without his help this time.

"What have you been doing back there? Sleeping? We've passed several signs announcing our arrival at the home of the King," Tripp said as he grabbed our bags and headed for the hotel to get us a room.

"The King?" I asked, following him.

"Yeah, you know . . . hunka hunka burnin' love," Tripp said.

"Elvis? You mean we're in Memphis?"

"Yep," Tripp said as he pushed open the door to the hotel and held it for me so I could go inside. Our first night I had tried to stay in my own room, but the night terrors had come fast and hard. Since then, we got rooms with two beds and Tripp helped me when the dreams came, which was every night so far. We were both so tired this week that most nights we ended up falling asleep in the same bed once the terror was over, sleeping that way through the rest of the night.

"One room, two beds," Tripp told the lady, and she glanced

over at me, then back at Tripp and flashed him a flirty smile. He got that a lot. When females realized we weren't together they started throwing themselves at him. He ignored it for the most part. Sometimes there would be a girl he couldn't ignore. He would flirt back and take her number, which I thought was pointless since we weren't coming back. But he said he might just come back one day.

Tripp got the key to our room and we headed to the elevator. I didn't feel like talking much. I had called Braden earlier and she'd told me that Woods still hadn't called her. That bothered me. I should have been relieved. But I wasn't. The longer I was away from him without his calling Tripp or Braden, the more I realized this was what he wanted. Deep down, I'd given him his out. I didn't want to think about his being in pain. It made it easier to function each day knowing that the never-ending ache in my heart was something I suffered alone.

"You're quiet today," Tripp said as the elevator door opened and we stepped out onto the second floor. That was as high as Tripp would go. He had a thing about being too high up in a hotel. He said that if the place caught on fire he wanted to know he didn't have too many flights of stairs to take to get the hell out. I hadn't really thought about it but he had, apparently.

"Just not in the mood to talk," I told him.

"Your talk with Braden go okay?" he asked.

Sure. It had gone fine. She hadn't brought up Woods. She had only asked me where we had gone and what we were doing. Nothing more. "Yeah, it was fine."

Tripp opened the door to our room and glanced back at me. "You okay if I go out and get a drink tonight?"

This was code for "You okay if I go out and get laid tonight?" He didn't know that I had this figured out and I preferred that we keep it that way.

Every night he went out for a drink he came back around two in the morning smelling like perfume. He would have made a horrible cheating husband.

"I want to order a pizza and watch cable. Go, do what you want," I told him as I walked into the room.

"Thanks," he said, stepping in behind me.

"No problem. I need a shower. You leaving now?" I asked, taking my bag from his hands and heading for the bathroom.

"Yeah, I think so."

"See you in the morning," I told him. I stepped into the bathroom and closed the door behind me. I waited until I heard the hotel room door close and he had sufficient time to get away before I let the tears come. I'd been holding them back for hours. Crying didn't make the pain easier, but for that one moment I could lose myself in my sorrow. I didn't have to hide it. I could let it out freely.

Deep down, I knew what I had done was right. I'd let Woods go. My fear that I would hurt him no longer haunted me. He was okay. He was living his life and he would find that someone who could be his perfect fit. What we'd had was never going to be perfect. Love should be simple. I wasn't simple.

Woods deserved someone like Blaire Finlay. He needed a woman by his side who could pull out a gun and take care of herself. A wife who could give him babies that he could love and know they would be mentally healthy. The fear that their mother could snap would never be there.

I would never be a Blaire. I wanted to be more than I wanted my next breath, but it would never happen. I wasn't Woods's simple perfection. He would find it one day with someone else. Maybe one day I would find a way to be happy again. Maybe living life would help me find my place.

I refused to believe I would end up damaged like my mother. I might not have been wife-and-mother material, but I was a person. I could be something. I could make a difference in this world. I just had to find out what that something was. Thinking about Woods and his disinterest in finding me wasn't doing me any good. Crying wasn't healing me.

It was time I healed myself. I didn't need a man to hold my hand and cuddle me. I needed to do this on my own. Woods had wanted to help me and I'd wanted someone to cling to.

Tripp and I had pooled our money together and it had been enough for a while, but it wouldn't last forever. It was time Tripp went back to his place in South Carolina and I found a life. One that I lived alone. One in which I depended on myself.

I stood up and turned on the shower and undressed. I would wash away my tears and I wouldn't allow myself to do this again. There was a bravery inside of me that I was going to find and nurture.

Woods

I sat outside on my balcony with a beer in one hand and my phone in the other. Tripp called at nine every night. It was the only way I kept myself sane. Listening to him tell me about what she was doing, what she was saying, and even what she was wearing was the only way I held on to my last shreds of sanity.

The moment Tripp's name lit up the screen I answered.

"Hey, how is she?" I didn't care about small talk. I had decided not to find Tripp and break all the limbs from his body when he'd called me the first time and promised to keep me updated on Della. He said she needed time to deal with things and I needed to give her that. I was trying like hell but I wanted to go to her. Every time he told me which city they were in, I fought the need to jump on a plane.

"She was quiet today. Didn't talk much and couldn't wait to get rid of me. She's depressed but this is just another stage for her."

"Where are you now?"

"Memphis."

"Are you checked into a hotel?"

"Yeah. She's in the room. I'm out, giving her some space tonight."

Giving her space? Alone, in a strange city? "What the fuck are you thinking? You can't leave her alone! If she's been quiet she may be closing in on herself. You can't leave her alone. She'll need someone to bring her back. She can't—"

"Woods! Calm down, man. Calm down." Tripp's voice was commanding.

"She can't be alone," I said again as emotion lodged in my throat. I hated to think of her alone.

"She needs to be alone. She needs to cry. She needs to decide if giving you this freedom she thinks you need is going to be possible. Her leaving is all about you, Woods. She didn't want to leave you. I've told you that already. She loves you so much that she left to give you the life she thinks you want. One where you don't have to deal with her shit. So, now that she's done that, she has to live with it. Give her time. She'll come back."

I had set my beer down and stood up. Gripping the railing, I closed my eyes and fought back the pain. I just wanted her. Just Della. Any way I could have her, I wanted her. I wasn't ever going to be all right. I didn't want her to be alone. I wanted someone to hold her.

"Hold her for me. Hold her tight. Don't let her be lonely. Don't let her hurt. Please."

"I will do what she allows me to do. But my arms aren't the ones she wants."

"Fuck," I growled as sharp pains wrapped around my throat.

"Just give her more time," Tripp said.

I took several long, steadying breaths. He had to get back to her. He couldn't leave her alone like this. "When we hang up, go back to her."

Tripp sighed. "Fine. But I had plans tonight. There's a hot little bartender giving me the eye."

"Do you need more money?" I asked him. I had been depositing money into his account since he had called the first night. I wanted her in nice hotels and I wanted her to eat well.

"She's going to notice soon that we aren't running out of money. I keep waiting for her to bring up the fact that we stay in the nicest part of each town and eat in high-end restaurants instead of fast-food chains. She's not an idiot."

"I'm holding on by a damn thread. Your phone calls and the fact I know she's in nice hotels and eating good food is the only fucking thing keeping me sane."

"I'm going to see if I can convince her to go back to my place in South Carolina with me. I have a nice place there. It's safe and I have a job I can go back to. I can get her a job, too."

I just wanted her to come home. "Whatever you need to do. But she stays safe."

"I'm keeping her safe. I promise."

"You took her from me," I reminded him. I couldn't thank him.

"She asked me to. I'm her friend, too."

"She needs me."

"No, dude. Right now, she needs to find the strength inside herself. The strength she doesn't think is there. Once she realizes that she isn't a burden, she'll be back."

"She has to," I said, then ended the call before Tripp heard the pain in my voice.

Della

The pizza hadn't even arrived yet when Tripp walked back in the door. I had been sure he was going to screw a stranger. "You're back?"

He shrugged. "I decided I'd rather have pizza instead of a beer."

Something was up. He wouldn't rather have had pizza than get laid. Tripp was a bit of a man-whore. I had figured this out pretty fast. Women liked him and he liked them right back—for about two or three hours, then he was gone.

"Why are you really back? You never choose pizza over . . . beer."

A crooked grin tugged at his lips and he shifted his gaze over to me. "By the way you just said *beer*, I'm going to assume you know what I'm normally up to when I step out for a drink."

I rolled my eyes. "Uh, yeah."

Tripp sank down on the edge of the other bed. "Well, tonight I was thinking about something and I thought we might need to talk more than I needed a beer."

I wasn't sure how to respond to that so I just waited.

The knock on the door stopped him from going any farther.

"Pizza," he said, standing up and going to pay for the pizza. I had also ordered a two-liter soda. It wasn't beer but it came with the special.

I watched as he set the pizza down on my bed and grabbed the two plastic glasses by the ice bucket and fixed us a drink. I had been thinking we needed to talk, too, I just wasn't sure when we would get the chance. Before we got any farther away from South Carolina, I planned on telling him we should go there.

"Meat lover's. It's like you knew I was coming back," he said.

"No. The special tonight was a large meat lover's and a two-liter soda for fifteen dollars. I went with the special."

"Lucky me," he replied.

"Talk, Tripp. I want to know what's more important than beer."

Tripp let out a small chuckle and took a drink of his soda. Then he settled his green eyes on me. "Impatient, aren't you."

I didn't reply. I just raised my eyebrows to let him know I was still waiting.

"We need to go back to South Carolina. I need to get back to my job and I can get you hooked up with a job, too. I have a place there and it will be good for you to stay in one place longer than a day and think about stuff."

Not what I had been expecting him to say.

"Okay," I replied.

He stopped chewing. "'Okay'? Just like that?"

I nodded. "Yeah, just like that."

He finished chewing his bite of pizza and swallowed. "Why do you always surprise me? All the damn time? You'd think I would be used to it by now."

I took another bite of my pizza and shrugged. I hadn't realized I was going to be so easygoing about it either. I wasn't going to stay there permanently, of course, but I could work there awhile and save up some money. Then I would hit the road again.

"There is one thing I want to do first," I told him.

"What?"

"Go through Georgia and see my best friend, Braden, and her husband, Kent. I haven't seen them in a while and I'd like to stay at their house for a couple of days."

Tripp nodded. "Sounds good. I can get a place at a hotel in town and you can stay with them."

"They would be happy for you to stay with them, too," I assured him.

Tripp smirked. "Yeah, well, that sounds nice but honestly, I could really use a couple of nights to have some . . . beer."

The small bubble of laughter was fast and unexpected. Tripp's smirk turned into a pleased grin, and I laughed for the first time since I'd left Rosemary.

◇

Later that night, I had just started to fall asleep when I heard Tripp get up and walk to the bathroom. I thought he was going to take a shower but I heard him talking to someone. Who would he be calling after midnight? Then I heard my name.

I eased out of bed quietly and tiptoed close enough so I could hear what he was saying.

"She wants to stop by her friend's house in Georgia first. . . . Yeah. . . . I said yes. Damn. . . . Near Myrtle Beach. It's safe. I swear. . . . Probably need some more, yeah. . . . I'll call you. . . . I said I would call you. Go to sleep."

I hurried back over to the bed and crawled back in. Whom had he been talking to? Was there a girl back where he lived? Had he left someone behind to come help me? No. That couldn't be it. He slept with too many women. Maybe it was just a friend.

"Della?" Tripp's voice surprised me and I almost responded. Then I realized he was checking to make sure I was asleep. I didn't say anything.

It must have been a friend of his wondering when he'd be home. But the "safe" comment—that was weird. I closed my eyes and decided to let the exhaustion take me. I would think about this tomorrow.

Woods

I stared down at the list of appointments that Vince had put on my desk that morning. I had been putting off so much shit because I couldn't focus in the last two weeks, and now I was behind. Tomorrow my lawyer would be sending out the letters to the former board members letting them know that they were no longer needed. I expected the shit to hit the fan but I was letting my lawyer deal with the blows. I wasn't in the mood for it.

"Mr. Finlay here to see you, sir," Vince's voice said over the intercom.

"Send him in," I replied. I had called Rush's father, Dean Finlay, before Della had left. I figured if I put someone on the board who was a celebrity, then it would help with the members and the town when they heard of the new board. Besides, Dean had put a lot of money into the Kerrington Club and my father had never approved of him. He'd acknowledged him because he wasn't a complete fool but he hadn't liked him.

"I gotta say, Woods, you look pretty goddamn good sitting in that seat," Dean drawled as he sauntered into the room. He reeked of rock star, from his long hair to his tattoo-covered body and many piercings. He even had on eyeliner. The man was a legend and I had grown up with him as the father of one of my friends.

"Thanks, Dean," I said, standing up and reaching across the desk to shake his hand.

"You got me for about thirty minutes. Then I'm gonna have to get back to that grandson of mine. I had to leave him all giggly and playful and that's pretty fucking hard to do. The kid's adorable."

"Yes, sir. I will make this quick," I assured him, and motioned for him to sit down.

Dean sat down in the leather wingback chair and propped his feet up on the edge of my desk. "What's up?"

"I'm letting my father's board members go. They were close confidants of my father; however, I don't feel the same way about them. I have no need for a board that I can't share my ideas with and whose opinions I can't trust. I'm replacing the board with people I want to have input into the future of the Kerrington Club."

Dean held up a hand to stop me, then he cocked one dark eyebrow. "Are you saying you fired all their uppity asses?"

I nodded.

Dean threw his head back and cackled with laughter. "Damn, that's the funniest shit I've heard in a while."

If I could have managed a smile these days I would have smiled then. "I want you on my board, sir. Rush will also be asked, of course."

Dean dropped his feet to the floor and leaned forward, resting his elbows on his knees, and studied me a moment. "You want me on your board?"

"Yes, I do. My group of friends are all young. We need wisdom on the board and you're the only man I know that I would want advising me."

A slow smile spread across Dean's face. "I'll be damned."

Probably, but I wasn't going to agree with him. I just waited.

"Hell yeah, I'll be on your board. My grandson is going to grow up in this town and the Kerrington Club and the members here will be a big part of his life. I want to make sure he has the best."

I had hoped he would feel that way. "Thank you, sir. I appreciate it. I'm honored that you will be a part of the future of the club."

"Me too," he said, leaning back in his chair. "But, Woods, if we're gonna do this, then should you stop calling me *sir*. Makes me sound old. I bang chicks younger than you, son."

I might not have been able to smile but I was amused. "I'm sure you do," I replied.

"That was pretty damn funny. What's wrong with you, boy? I can't seem to get you to crack a smile."

I didn't want to talk about Della with Dean. He wouldn't understand. Like he said, he was with a different girl every night. "Personal stuff. I'm working through it."

Dean rubbed his chin, then tilted his head as he looked at me too closely. "It's a woman. That look is always caused by a fucking woman. Don't bother denying it. I can see it all over your face."

I didn't admit it but I didn't deny it. Instead, I dropped my eyes to the table and shifted through some paperwork. I had a contract Dean needed to sign and we needed to discuss his monthly salary, not that he needed it.

"Who is she? What did she do? She getting under your

skin and you're ready to run, or has she already got you on her hook and she's trying to let you go?"

I pulled out the contract and took my pen and pushed them across the table. "Neither. I need you to sign the contract saying everything we discuss about the club is confidential. Your salary is listed as well."

Dean didn't lean forward and take the paper. He was still focused on me. He started to shake his head and let out a low whistle. "Woods motherfucking Kerrington is in love. Damn, it's in the water down here. I need to get my ass back to LA. You young boys going manic over one pretty little girl. There's lots of fish. Lots of fucking beautiful fish. Why worry about one when you can have 'em all? Brunette on Monday and a redhead on Tuesday, twins on Wednesday, a blonde with big ole titties on Thursday, an Asian beauty on Friday, and her sister on Saturday, then on Sunday is when you get you one of each and have one big-ass party all damn day. No need to get wrapped up in just one."

This was very similar to a speech he'd given us one summer when Rush had taken us on a road trip to see Slacker Demon in Atlanta. We had, of course, been granted backstage access and hung out with the band. It was Dean's life. I had thought it was a lonely life back then. Now that I'd had Della, I knew it was a lonely life. I wasn't interested.

"Just want the one," I told him.

"She must be special," he said, and leaned forward to pick up the pen. "I'm not signing my life away or adding you to my will, am I?" he asked.

"No, just agreeing to keep the club's business confidential."

"I don't need the money. Put it in a trust fund for Nate. Have Rush set it up."

I'd expected as much. "Yes, sir"—his head snapped up—"I mean, Dean," I said, correcting myself.

He nodded. "Better." Then he stood up and slapped his hand down on the desk. "Looks good on you, boy. Looks real good on you," he said, then turned and walked out of the office.

I had Dean. Now I needed to make my next call.

Della

Braden threw open the door and wrapped her arms around me in one swift movement. I dropped the bag I was carrying and hugged her back just as fiercely.

"You're here! I missed you," Braden said as she squeezed me one more time, then pulled back and glanced over at Tripp. I didn't miss the appreciative gleam in Tripp's eyes as he took in my best friend. Braden had big, round, cornflower-blue eyes and long, dark curly lashes. Her brown curls were completely natural. I had been coveting them for years.

"Braden, this is my friend Tripp. Tripp, this is my best friend, Braden Fredrick."

"And I'm her husband, Kent," Kent said as he walked up behind Braden. I smiled over at him. I felt like I should apologize for Tripp and I was suddenly glad he was going to stay in a hotel. Braden loved her husband but when Tripp wanted to be a charmer he had it down to a science.

"It's nice to meet both of you," Tripp said with a knowing smile. I should probably have pinched him.

"Y'all come on in," Braden said, stepping back.

"I have plans this evening so I need to head on out. I'll be back when you're ready to leave, Della," he said, and winked at me. He was being cute on purpose.

"Okay. Go drink beer. I think you need it," I told him, and he laughed before turning and going back to his bike.

"He drives a Harley?" Braden asked, peering at him as he walked away.

"Stop it before Kent goes out there and tries to beat him up," I whispered, and stepped inside, letting the door close behind me.

"What? Kent knows I love him. I was just looking. I'm curious about who you've been riding all over the place with these past two weeks."

"Sure you are," Kent drawled, grabbing her ass before pressing a kiss to her mouth. "I'll go make some coffee," he said, then walked toward the kitchen.

When Kent was out of hearing distance, Braden grabbed my arm and pulled me into the living room. "Okay, how are you? How are your night terrors? Are you and Tripp getting along okay?"

"As good as can be expected, the same, and yes."

Braden frowned. "I need more info than that."

I sighed and sat down on her sofa. "I miss him. I miss him so much. But he's better without me. Even he knows he's better without me."

"How does he know he's better without you? Have you talked to him?"

"No. But he hasn't tried to find me. You said yourself he hasn't called you. He hasn't called Tripp. Nothing. I did what he wanted. Deep down he wanted this and he got it. So, I have to figure out how to live. That was my ultimate goal, anyway."

Braden pulled her legs underneath her as she sat down beside me. "You have a really hot biker dude helping you out," she said.

"I heard that," Kent called from the hallway.

Braden giggled and rolled her eyes. "Seriously. He seems nice. You aren't bonding with him? I mean, you're with him every day and night."

"I gave my soul to Woods. He'll always have it."

Braden sighed and nodded her head. "Yeah, I understand that."

"Glad I got *your* soul, Braden, because I'm not sure I can beat that biker dude's ass. He's thin but tall, and that type's always hiding muscles under his clothes that you don't see coming," Kent said as he walked into the room holding two mugs of coffee.

Braden laughed and I managed a smile. I could attest to Tripp's muscles. I spent my days with my chest pressed to his back and my arms wrapped around him. He had muscles all right. Lots of them. He also had tattoos, which had surprised me. I could see the wealthy, elite Rosemary in him at times, but he tried too hard to cover it with tats and swagger.

"Stop being jealous. Nothing is sexier than you in a suit and tie. That short blond hair and tanned skin. I know what I got and I'm not looking for another," Braden said as Kent bent down to kiss her and give her one of the mugs.

I didn't want to witness this kind of affection right now. At least with Tripp I knew it was cheap sex he was getting. The romance was a little too much.

Braden read my mind. She was good at that. "Go on and let us girls talk. We need time," she told him, giving him a look that I knew he'd understand. I didn't say anything. I needed him to go. No more touchy-feely.

"Sorry about that. I wasn't thinking," she said as he left the room.

"It's okay. I will have to learn to deal with that the rest of my life. Might as well get used to it now. Couples are everywhere."

Braden reached over and grabbed my hand. "You will find your happiness. I think you're wrong about Woods but I've told you that. He loves you. I know he does. I remember the madman who came chasing after you just a few months ago. He adores you. I hate to see you let that go."

How could I keep it? "I couldn't stay. He was tired of my craziness. I heard him say it. He doesn't know I heard him, but I did. He was talking to Jace about how hard it was to deal with me. He was tired of it."

"What! I don't believe that. You must've misunderstood him. I can't see Woods ever saying that. And let me tell you, if he did I will cut him. Cut. Him. You hear me?" She was already getting worked up. I should have kept that to myself. I knew that would send her into a blind rage.

"What did he say exactly?" she asked, setting her cup down and studying me for any sign of a lie.

"It was a conversation, really. I can't remember exactly."

"Bullshit. It is etched into that brain of yours and you know exactly what was said, word for word. Spill it."

She wouldn't give in until I told her.

"I was at the club and I was looking for Woods. I decided to take the stairs instead of the elevator, so I stepped into the stairwell and I heard him talking. I didn't want to eavesdrop but I heard Jace saying that he didn't know how Woods had dealt with the crazy as long as he had."

"And what did Woods do? Please tell me he shoved his fist up his nose."

I shook my head and let the numbness ease me. I couldn't

think about what I was saying. "He said it was what he had to do. That he couldn't let me be alone but it was affecting his work." I stopped and swallowed, then looked down at my hands. Anywhere but at Braden. "He said that at least when Angelina was there, she helped." That part hurt the worst. Hearing him say that someone like her was easier. That she was what he needed. Not someone like me. The crazy one.

"Maybe he wasn't talking about you. Isn't his momma a loony bitch?"

"No. She's just mean," I explained. There was more. Jace had said more. "Jace said that Woods needed to get his ass away from the insane shit. He had a corporation to run. He then said . . . that Woods dropping what he was doing to deal with my batshit crazy episodes wasn't fair. That he needed to fix the problem."

"Woods better have beat his ass then," Braden said, her face turning red.

I should've changed the subject so I could calm her down. But I needed her to understand that I had left Woods for him. This was what he wanted. He just didn't know how to ask for it. "Woods said he couldn't. Then he asked how he would do that."

Braden shook her head, her eyes wide with disbelief. "That just doesn't sound right. That isn't the same man I talked to . . . that I talked to back when he came to get you a few months ago."

"No. It's the man who had the responsibility of a country club and his mother laid on his shoulders overnight. He has real problems and concerns. I'm more than he can handle now."

Braden kept shaking her head. It would take her a while to process all of this. I hadn't told Tripp about that conversation.

I hadn't wanted to talk about it. He hadn't pressed me the way Braden had, either.

"You're not crazy. You're not insane."

"I know you believe that. But it's in my blood, Braden."

She gave me a sad smile. "No. It's not. There's something I need to show you and a lot I need to tell you. While you've been riding on the back of a hot stud's bike for two weeks, I've been doing some research."

"What? What do you mean 'research'? On what?"

"Della Sloane, you were adopted."

Woods

Darla Lowry, my golf course manager, was now a board member. She was the one thing my dad had gotten right. I trusted Darla with my life. With Jace planning on marrying Bethy, Darla's niece, we were just tying the family knot tighter. Darla was also wise. She was older than me and she had seen this club grow and flourish for over twenty-five years. She deserved a seat on the board. She also deserved the paycheck that came with that seat.

My phone rang and I glanced down to see Braden's number. I hadn't talked to her in a few days but she always called when she had any information on Della.

"Hey," I said, praying this wasn't going to be something bad.

"I know why she left. There was more to it, just like I said there was. But before I tell you anything I need you to make me a few promises and listen to all I have to say, because I'm not scared of you or your money, Woods Kerrington. I will hunt you down like a dog and bury you. Do you understand me?" Braden was fired up and ready to attack.

"If you can help me get Della back I will walk on fucking water," I replied.

"Good. I thought so. However, she thinks very differently.

She's of the belief that she has done you a favor. That you wanted to get rid of her and didn't know how. That she walked away and now you're relieved and living the good life."

"What? Why the hell? What the fuck gave her that idea? Did Tripp tell her that? Because I swear to God I'll kill him."

"Sit down and take a breath. You did this. Don't go pointing fingers at other people. First, I have to tell you about a conversation Della overheard the day before she ran off. You had better tell me what she really heard, because what she thinks she heard will get your ass killed, and sexy biker dude will get off scot-free. *Capisce?*"

"Please tell me what she heard, because I honestly have no idea."

"Did you have a conversation in the stairwell with your friend Jace that day?"

The stairwell? I sat down in my chair and thought back to before Della ripped my world away. I had talked to Jace that day. About my mom. "Yeah, I did."

"And . . ."

I wasn't sure what she wanted me to say. "And what?"

Braden let out a loud sigh. "What did you and Jace talk about?"

Hell, I couldn't remember. My mother was stressing me out. I was planning on installing the new board. I was going to let Della come back to work and stop smothering her. Nothing that should've upset her. "I can't think of one thing I said that would have made her leave me."

"So Jace never told you that you had to stop dealing with her crazy ass? And you didn't say that it was affecting your work and it was easier to work with Angelina? And Jace didn't say that you had to get rid of the batshit crazy because you had a corporation to run?"

I shot up out of my chair. "What?" I roared.

"I didn't think so. Didn't sound like you at all. If someone had called Della batshit crazy you would have beat their ass. Della, however, felt sorry for you for having to put up with her and thought it was in your best interest if she left."

"Holy hell! I swear to God I never said that. Jace never said that. I would've killed him. We were talking about . . . we were talking . . . oh, motherfucker." I knew what she'd heard. She hadn't heard everything. She'd just heard enough.

"Please tell me you didn't just have an epiphany and this conversation did actually happen," Braden said, warning me.

"No. Of course not. I mean, it did but we weren't talking about Della. God! Never Della. We were talking about my mother. She had just caused problems for me at the club and I was talking to Jace about how to deal with her. I . . . fuck! I can't believe she thought we were talking about her. I'm coming to get her. I can't do this anymore. I have to explain this to her. She has to know."

"*No!* Shut it, Kerrington. I told you at the beginning of this conversation that you would do just as I said. I'm not done talking to you and telling you everything you need to hear. So calm down and put your damn keys away. When it's time for you to come get her, I'll let you know, but this time I think it's real important that she come back to Rosemary on her own. She ran. She needs to find her way back. The cavalry can stay put and be patient."

"I have to see her, Braden!"

"Would you shut up and listen to me? I have information

for Della that she needs to deal with first. She thinks she's going to be mentally ill because her mother and grandmother were. She thinks that staying with you means you can't have kids because their mother could snap at any time and go insane. She loves you more than she loves herself. So she's making sure you don't suffer that ridiculous fate she's convinced you'll have with her."

"We won't have kids. I just want her. If she's scared of that, fine. We won't have kids. I have to tell her I just want her."

"Yeah, yeah, yeah, I know you do. Shut up, I'm not done," Braden snapped into the phone. I fisted my hand around my truck keys and moved to stare down at my truck parked outside. I could get to her in five hours.

"Della was adopted."

So many emotions ran through me at once, I wasn't sure if I was going to weep or cheer or fall to my knees and take deep, even breaths. Holy fuck. This was a game changer.

"She was adopted?" I managed to choke out.

"Yep. She was adopted. Her adoptive parents were scared to have kids because they were afraid that Della's grandmother's mental illness was genetic. So they adopted a boy from the foster system. He was two when they adopted him. Then a couple years later they adopted a baby girl from a teenager who wasn't ready to be a mother yet. You know the rest."

She was adopted. Her fear of being mentally ill like her mother was unfounded. "Does she know?"

"I told her today. She knows. I've set up a meeting with her birth mother. She's a kindergarten teacher. She's married and has a ten-year-old son and an eight-year-old daughter. They live in Bowling Green, Kentucky. Her name is Glenda Morgan and she wants to meet Della. She said she tried looking for her after her son was born. She realized what she had given up and she wanted to make sure she was okay. But the file was closed and it cost money she didn't have to get an investigator. Her husband had agreed that with their income tax refund this year they would find her daughter instead of taking a family vacation. So when the investigator I hired found her she was as thrilled as I was."

I wanted to like this woman, but knowing that her decision to give Della up had been the reason for the hell Della had lived through made it hard for me to forgive her. Where was the guy who knocked her up? Did he not care he'd given up a child?

"What about her birth father?" I asked.

"Glenda has contacted him. His name is Nile Andrews. He lives in Phoenix, Arizona. He's a dentist. Also married, with triplets. All girls. He wants to meet Della, too. His wife is being supportive of his decision."

A kindergarten teacher and a dentist.

"I've seen a photo of her birth mother. She looks like her."

"Please let me come. I want to be with her through this. She needs me."

"No, Woods. What she needs is to feel like she's strong. Like she can handle all of this on her own. She knows she's not going insane now. That's big. Real big. She's lived with that fear for so long. It's crippled her. She has to find her own strength now. And she needs to come back to you on her own. With the belief that she is strong and worthy of you."

"Worthy of me? What the fuck does that mean? I belong to her. How can she not be worthy of me?"

"I know this and you know this but she has to figure this out on her own. She had shit for a life. I held her hand for years. Then she left me and within months she had you holding her hand. No one can hold her hand this time."

"I don't want her to be alone."

"This isn't about what you want, Woods. It's about what Della needs."

I pressed my forehead against the window and closed my eyes. I didn't want her to be right. I didn't want to wait for Della. But this wasn't about my wants. Della loved me more than herself. She loved me enough to walk away because she thought it was best for me. It was time I proved I loved her more than I loved myself.

"Okay. But please, keep me updated."

Braden let out a relieved sigh. "I knew you'd do the right thing. Just so you know, I think you're worthy of her, and that's a high bar to reach. You promised to walk on water and I happen to believe Della already does."

Della

Her name was Glenda. When she'd given birth to me it had been Glenda James. She married when she was twenty-two. I would have been six years old that year. She married a man she met her freshman year of college. They had fallen instantly in love. They had kids. Two of them. Today I would be meeting her. And if all went well I would be meeting her family.

I was in a surreal moment. One I couldn't seem to snap out of. The mentally ill woman who raised me wasn't my biological mother. I wasn't going to become her. The woman who gave birth to me was a teacher. She was a mom and wife.

And my brother. He had been adopted, too. I didn't remember him but he'd been such a big part of my life. My mother had snapped after losing him and my father . . . or her husband. He wasn't my birth father and he had barely been my adoptive father before he was killed. There was so much my mother had told me that couldn't be true. She had said she was nursing me and led me to believe she had gotten depressed after my birth. But she hadn't been pregnant. She hadn't given birth to me. None of that was true. I didn't know what was true anymore.

"What are you thinking?" Braden asked as she drove down the busy streets of Atlanta. Glenda was driving down with her family to Atlanta. We were meeting at a coffee shop that Braden knew about. I wasn't sure I could eat a meal with this woman yet. I also wasn't sure what to ask or say to her. There was so much I wanted to know but then so much I didn't.

"She doesn't know about anything. I didn't tell her. I found her but I didn't feel like it was my story to share."

I wasn't sure I would be telling her about my life either. "What if I don't know what to say once I see her?"

"Then don't say anything. Do what you feel comfortable with. If today all you're ready for is 'hello,' then that's what we will do. When you want more we'll make arrangements to meet with her again."

Braden always made everything sound so easy. This woman had put her family in a car and had driven down to Atlanta to meet me. I had to say more than *hello*. "You won't go in with me?" I asked again. Braden had informed me that I had to do this on my own. It was my chance to prove to myself I was strong. That I was brave and that I didn't need someone to hold my hand. Though right now I was thinking I needed someone to hold my hand. I was terrified.

"Don't do this to me. I want to go with you. I hate the idea of you going by yourself, but this is for you, Della. This is for you."

She was right. Braden was always right. I nodded. "I know. Thank you."

I watched as she pulled the car into a parking spot in front of a quaint little coffee shop. There were tables outside and inside. The crowd wasn't big and I recognized the woman who had given birth to me from the photo Braden had shown me, sitting at the table in the courtyard to the left of the building. She had a cup of coffee in her hand and she was twirling it around nervously. This was scary for her, too, I guess. But she was brave. She was here alone.

"There she is," Braden said, pointing toward Glenda.

"I see her," I replied, and reached for the door handle.

"You can do this."

I glanced back at Braden and smiled for the first time in weeks. "I know."

◇

Her eyes locked with mine the moment I stepped out of the car. I watched as she stood and looked at me. I made my way over to her table, still unsure as to what I would say to this woman. She had given me life but she was a stranger.

"Della," she said as if needing to check and make sure it was me. We had the same hair, nose, and mouth. But her eyes were brown.

"Yes," I replied.

She fidgeted with her hands a moment, then covered her mouth with one hand. "I'm sorry. I just . . . I don't know . . ." She dropped her hand and gave me a wobbly smile. "I've thought about this day. I've thought about it so many times and now I'm actually standing here, looking at you." She studied my face, taking in the features I already knew were hers. "You have Nile's eyes. He'll like that. He always loved his eyes," she said with a smile. "They're his best feature. I'm glad you got them."

I knew I should say something but I didn't know what. I decided that it didn't matter if she liked me or approved of me. I wasn't here to gain her admiration. I wasn't perfect. I was damaged but I was a survivor. I had that to be proud of.

"I like my eyes," I finally said.

She let out a soft laugh. "They're beautiful eyes. I was

always jealous of Nile's eyes. I used to tell him they were too pretty to be wasted on a boy."

It sounded as if she still kept in touch with my birth father. I wanted to know about that, too. "Should we sit down?" I asked, pulling out a chair.

Glenda nodded and sat back down. Her coffee cup sat forgotten. "Your friend, Braden, she didn't tell me much about you. She said that you should be the one to decide what I got to hear. I want to know it all, at least everything you feel comfortable telling me. What do you do? Are you in college?" She stopped and smiled at me. "Sorry, I'll let you talk."

There was one thing I was sure of: Glenda wasn't going to push for my life story. It wasn't easy to tell, and I wasn't sure I wouldn't fade out while telling it to her. That was a part of me that I would keep to myself. If this woman remained in my life then maybe one day, but not today.

"I've been traveling around. I wanted to see and experience new things for a while. Then I plan on going back to college."

"That sounds like fun. Are you traveling alone?"

I thought of Tripp and realized I was going to have to send him on to South Carolina without me. I wasn't going there now. I had to decide what my next move would be. "I was traveling with a friend of mine. He's going back to his home in South Carolina this week. I'm not sure yet what I'll do next."

"That sounds exciting," she said, watching me carefully. I knew she wanted me to delve deeper into my life but she didn't deserve that.

I didn't say anything else. I had nothing else to say really. Now that I had seen her and I knew this was my mother, I felt like I was finished here.

"I almost kept you. I wanted to. I loved Nile back then. He was the captain of the basketball team and everyone fell under his charm. But he'd picked me. I was his girl and I worshipped the ground he walked on. When I found out I was pregnant I wanted to keep my baby. I wanted to marry Nile and I wanted a family. But I was sixteen. I knew nothing of love and heartache. I didn't know what paying the bills was like or how much babies cost. My mother worked as a nurse back then and my father was a construction worker. They made a modest living and we lived from paycheck to paycheck. I, of course, didn't understand any of that. I was wrapped up in the romance of it all." She stopped and took a drink of her coffee. She was nervous telling me this but I realized I wanted to know why. Why had she given me up?

"Nile came from money. Lots of money. His mother's father was a congressman and his father was a surgeon. They had big plans for Nile. Being a teenage father wasn't on their list. I think he loved me back then. I really do. I've always thought he did. He told me he'd get some money and we would run away and raise our baby. We would get married when we turned eighteen. I was giddy with excitement. Until everything changed." There was a sadness in her eyes. As if remembering this was hard for her. It had been twenty years ago. I couldn't imagine she still regretted it. Especially with the life she had now.

"Nile was offered a full-ride basketball scholarship to the University of Arizona. He decided to take it. He told me he wasn't ready to be a dad and he didn't think I was ready to be a mom. We were too young. We had no idea what we were doing. I knew he was repeating his parents' words back to me. I was angry and hurt. He tried for a long time to talk to me and get me to forgive him but I was done with Nile. He had betrayed me. He had chosen a scholarship over me and our unborn child. As the months went by and my stomach grew bigger, he would go out of his way to help me at school and do things for me, like bringing me my lunch tray. I continued to ignore him. He wasn't standing by my decision to keep the baby. He wanted me to give it up." Tears filled her eyes and she gave me a sad smile before wiping them away.

"As the days drew closer to your delivery date, my dad lost his job. My mom had been forced to sign us up for food stamps just so we could eat. They were fighting all the time and I knew it was because they were scared. Soon there would be another mouth to feed. A baby who would need diapers and formula and child care if I was going to finish school. I didn't want that for you. I didn't want you to live the life I had been living. I wasn't ready to be a mom and I wanted you to have more. I loved your father. You were a product of that love. It took me until I held you for the first time to realize I couldn't do this to you. I couldn't take you home to the life I could give you. It wasn't enough." She paused and took a deep breath. "I kissed your fat little cheeks, then handed you to the nurse and told her I couldn't keep you. To find you a good home."

I sat there and stared at Glenda. Her story made sense. Sixteen-year-olds weren't ready to be parents. I felt sorry for her, and she had been young enough to believe that handing me over was a better option. Maybe if my adopted father and brother hadn't been killed, then it would have been. My mother may not have snapped mentally if they had lived.

"I'd like to meet your family," I finally said.

A grin broke across her face. "I would love that. Thank you, Della."

Woods

I walked over to the bar and took the glass of bourbon that Mitch, the club's bartender, pushed my way. It was after-hours and I was expecting someone. He'd texted me an hour ago.

Just as I lifted the glass to my lips, Grant walked in the door and scanned the room until he found me at the bar. He had been out of town more than usual this year. It was summertime. He should have been in his condo, living it up in Rosemary.

"Give me one of those, Mitch," Grant said as he approached the bar, and leaned against it before looking at me. "I'm back. What's up?"

"Where have you been?" I asked.

His mouth was in a firm, set line before he gave in and let out a sigh. "You don't want to know," he said, then took a long swig of the bourbon.

That meant he'd been with Nan. There was a story there I wasn't sure I wanted to know. Grant was Rush's best friend. They were like brothers. Rush's mom had been married to Grant's dad when they were kids. The marriage only lasted a few years but they bonded. What no one expected was for Grant and Nan, Rush's half sister, to do anything more than fight. They fought when they were kids and they fought now. Grant was a good guy. Nan was the world's second-biggest bitch. Angelina was the first.

"Nan," I said simply.

Grant took another swig and handed the glass back to Mitch. "Another," he replied.

"That's twenty-three-year-old Kentucky bourbon. It's meant to be sipped and enjoyed, not thrown back like a shot of cheap tequila," I pointed out.

"You're an elitist, Woods. Kiss my ass. I need more alcohol."

"Anyone who spends five minutes with Nan needs alcohol. The question is, why the hell do you do it?"

Grant threw back his second glass of bourbon and then looked over at me. "Not talking about her tonight. Why did you call me? What is going on?"

Good. I didn't really want to know about Nan anyway. If she came back to town, Rush was gonna be pissed. He loved his sister, but she hated his wife. So Nan had drawn a line and Rush had stayed on Blaire's side. Nan's coming back to Rosemary wouldn't be cool. I'd hoped she was staying in LA with her daddy. She'd recently found out the man she had grown up thinking was her father was not. Her real father was the lead singer of Slacker Demon. Apparently, Rush's momma liked sleeping with the band back in the day.

"I fired the board. I'm choosing my own. My father's board isn't for me. I want you on my new one."

Grant set down his glass and stared at me a minute. "What did you just say?"

"The club has a board of directors. The old one has been let go. Will you be on my new board?"

Grant motioned for Mitch to refill his glass. "Damn, I'm glad I'm back. Crazy shit happens here all the time. No place is as drama-ridden as Rosemary. Not even fucking LA."

"Does this mean yes, you will be on my board?" I asked, taking a sip of my bourbon.

Grant grinned over at me. "Hell yeah, I will."

I knew he would. That made four. I still needed to talk to a few more. "I have paperwork in my office for you to fill out. But tonight, let's drink. I need a distraction."

Grant pulled out a stool and sat down. "Where's Della?"

I had been expecting this question but hearing her name jolted me. She had met with her birth mother today. Braden was supposed to call me tonight and let me know how it went. I was anxious and needed to think about something else until I got that call.

"She left." I couldn't bring myself to explain anything else.

"She left? What the fuck did you do?"

"Screwed up. Missed some signs I should have noticed. Got too busy to see what she needed. Smothered her." There was a long list of things I had realized I was guilty of.

"Damn. Last I saw you two, you were worshipping at her altar. How the hell did it go south so fast?"

"It's not over. I'm waiting. She'll come back. I'm letting her decide if she can do this. In the meantime, I'm drinking a lot and living for phone calls from Tripp."

Grant put his glass down and let out a low whistle. "Ah, hell no. She left with Tripp?"

I just managed a nod.

"Shit, dude. I'm sorry. If you want my help kicking his playboy ass I got your back."

At one point that would have been exactly what I wanted,

but not now. Tripp was taking care of her. He was making sure she was safe. It was all I had. I shook my head. "No. It's okay. He's keeping me updated. He's making sure she has what she needs to be free."

Grant frowned and leaned toward me. "Am I understanding you right? Your woman is off with Tripp and you're okay with this?"

"She loves me."

Grant nodded. "Yeah, she does."

"She'll be back. This hand isn't over. It can't be. I went all in."

I didn't have to explain that to Grant. He got it. He smiled and leaned back with his drink in his hand. "You got this one, Ace."

My phone rang and I pulled it out to see my mother's name on the screen. I stuck it back in my pocket. I wasn't talking to her. I was sure she was aware that the old board members had been released. She wouldn't be happy about that.

"Is Nan coming back?" I asked.

Grant held the glass to his lips a moment longer than necessary. He was stalling. I knew that move. When he finally set it down he turned his head toward me. "Yeah. She's coming back. I'm heading over to Rush's when I leave here to tell him. He needs to be prepared."

"You ask her to come back?" I asked. Grant's attraction to Nan made no sense to me. He had seen how evil she could be. He had seen her at her worst. How could he want that?

"Hell no. But she's coming. Kiro bought her a nice, big, fancy house. The light blue one that sits over the hill on the south end of the beach."

Kiro was the lead singer of Slacker Demon and Nan's father. "Damn. I like that house. How'd she get that out of him?"

"He's trying to get rid of her. She hasn't been easy to deal with. She gives him hell every chance she gets and he's pretty desperate."

"Can't say I blame him." I would have done whatever I could to get away from her, too, if I was him. Nan was dangerous when she wanted to be.

"I feel bad for her, man. She knows he bought it for her to move her as far away from him as possible. She just wants his attention."

"He's the lead singer in the biggest, most legendary rock band of our time. He ignored her for most of her life. He isn't daddy material."

Grant frowned and I could see he was dealing with something. "He has another daughter. He treats her differently. He's affectionate with her. He loves her. It's obvious. But she's not like Nan. She doesn't demand things and she's quiet. I think that's what he wants. A meek, sweet daughter. Nan will never be that."

"Another daughter? Really?" I'd never heard of Kiro having a daughter.

"Yeah. She lives with him, too. She has what Nan wants and will never get. Because Nan can't be her. She can't be what Kiro wants. It sucks for her. She's always just wanted attention. Both her parents denied her that. Rush is all she ever had and now he has Blaire and Nate. She lost him, too. I can't help but feel bad for her." He took a drink and set it down, then stood up. "I get that no one understands why I have anything to do with her, and I'll be honest: at times, I don't know either. She's all kinds of fucked up and mean."

I nodded, because he was right about that.

Della

"I shouldn't have got you. If it hadn't been for you crying and keeping me up all night I wouldn't have been needing a nap. I wouldn't have let my little boy go to that store. It's all your fault, Della. All your fault. He knows it, too. He wanted to stay with me but I was so sleepy. So very sleepy. You wouldn't let me sleep." Mother roared and reared back and slapped me across the face. I stumbled backward and grabbed the edge of the bed before I fell down.

"If you had slept at night and let me be a good mommy to my little boy he would be alive. But you ruined everything. I didn't want another baby. Your father wanted a little girl. He said it would complete our family. You didn't complete us! You destroyed us!" I braced myself as Mother hit me again. I tried not to cry. I tried not to whimper. If I whimpered she would get angrier. I had to stay calm. I had to let her scream. She would cry soon and go to her room.

"Get on that bed and don't move. The monsters under it will get you. They will come get you for being such a bad girl. They know it's all your fault. They know what you did to me."

I never understood her when she blamed me for my brother's death—I was a baby when it happened—but I let her yell and hit me. If I fought back she only got angrier. Once she had hit me at breakfast and I didn't wake up until the middle of the night. I had been on the kitchen floor with a pillow under my head and a blanket over me. She had put two plates of food beside me.

I didn't fight back anymore. I was scared to.

"Get on that bed!" she screamed as I scrambled to do as she commanded. "Don't come out. I don't want to look at you," she said before walking away and slamming the door behind her. I heard the familiar click and I knew she'd locked me in. My door had always locked from the outside. She controlled it.

"Good night, Momma," I whispered as I pulled my knees up to my chin and rocked myself back and forth while I pretended that I had a better life. One where I could go outside and ride a bike.

◇

I opened my eyes and stared at the ceiling fan. I was in the guest bedroom at Braden's house. I hadn't woken up screaming. I had never dreamed of my mother and not woken up screaming with imaginary blood on my hands. Something had changed. The memory was one I'd forgotten but her words that day made sense now. I sat up and swung my legs over and stood up. I had dreamed and not screamed. I was afraid to hope, but I had never been able to do this. I opened my door and stepped out into the dark hallway. Braden would be asleep and I didn't want to wake her. But I needed to process this.

I walked to the kitchen to get a drink of water.

Braden was standing at the counter with a glass of milk, staring straight ahead in deep thought, when I walked into the room. Her eyes shifted to me. "Della? Are you okay? I didn't hear you."

I stood there as it really sank in. I had dreamed of her. Yet I hadn't had a night terror. "I dreamed about her. About my life then. And . . . and . . . I just woke up. No blood. I never saw the blood. I just woke up."

Braden stared at me as she processed what I had told her. Then she set her milk down on the bar and ran over to me. Her arms wrapped around me. "You're getting better. Already, you're getting better," she said in a teary voice.

I wanted to cry, too. I wanted to cry because I realized I might just have a chance at happiness. What if I was strong after all? What if, underneath all that fear, I had buried someone deep inside who was brave and could take on life without someone to lean on?

"I think I'm going to be okay," I said out loud, because I needed to hear myself say it.

Braden squeezed me tighter. "I know you're going to be okay. I know it."

We stood there holding each other in the kitchen for several moments before I pulled back. "I'm not going to go crazy. I won't snap one day and become her."

Braden wiped at the tears streaming down her face. "I know. I've always known that."

"But I didn't. I had seen her. I knew what she could be. I didn't want to be that, too."

"She was the woman who raised you but she wasn't your mother."

I nodded. I knew that now. I was going to be okay. "I want to meet my . . . I want to meet my birth father. I need to see him. I need to see his family, too."

Braden nodded. "Good. I think you should."

I stepped back and turned to go back to the bedroom.

"Della," Braden said.

I glanced back at her. "Yes?"

"Call him. He needs to hear from you."

She wasn't talking about my birth father. She was talking about Woods. I would have given anything to hear his voice. But I couldn't. He had moved on. He hadn't looked for me or tried to contact me. I had let him go and he'd walked away. I couldn't bother him now. "I can't."

"He misses you," she said.

"You don't know that. You assume it because you think what we had was a forever thing. But Woods has plans and I'm not in them. I gave him what he wanted. I'm not going to bother him again."

Braden let out a frustrated growl. "Della, a call from you wouldn't be a bother to him."

She loved me and didn't understand what I was trying to tell her. I knew better. "No, Braden. I'm letting him live. I'll find my way soon. First, I have to figure out my past."

She didn't say more as I walked back to the bedroom. I closed the door and waited a minute to make sure she wasn't following me before I let the tears fall. I didn't want her to see me cry. She would call him. She would try to fix this. There was nothing there to fix, but she didn't see it that way.

But now I knew I was going to heal. I was going to be okay. I had a future. I had to face what I'd lost. Losing Woods was my biggest mistake. I shouldn't have left him. I should have been stronger then and fought harder. But I hadn't. I would deal with that the rest of my life.

Woods

The ringing was in the distance. I heard it but I couldn't find it. Everything was dark. My eyes snapped open and the ringing started again. *Shit!* It was my phone. I sat up and grabbed it. It was after three in the morning and Braden was calling me. *Della. God, please let her be okay.*

"Is she okay?" I asked the moment I answered the phone.

"Yes and no."

"What does that mean?" I asked, standing up and looking for my jeans. If I needed to go to her that night I would.

"She had a dream about her mother. She didn't wake up screaming. She just woke up."

I stopped searching for my jeans. "What?"

"She had one of her dreams but she didn't have a night terror. She didn't get lost in her fears. She just woke up. She's already getting better."

"I'm coming there. I've had enough with waiting. I'm on my way. Tonight."

"No! You're not. You have to give her time. She's meeting with her birth father next. She met with her birth mother and then had dinner with her family all on her own. She needs to do all this alone. She's realizing she can do this. She's also finding out that she was crippled by her fears. She's overcoming that. Don't come here and confuse her. She has to come to you this time, Woods. She thinks you don't want her. She needs to face that fear on her own, too."

Fuck no! "You can't expect me to stay here and let her think I don't want her. That's not okay, Braden. It's not fucking okay. She shouldn't have to overcome a fear that's pointless. How can she think I don't love her? That she isn't my heart, my soul, my future? That's the one thing she should never doubt. That, she needs to know."

"Listen. I know this is hard and you've been great so far but give her just a couple more days. Please. She needs this. Remember this is about what she needs, not what you want."

I started to hit the wall again and stopped myself at the last minute. That wasn't going to help anything. I had to calm down. "When she left here she took my soul with her. I will always belong to her. I don't want her to ever think differently."

"Trust me, I know this. But she doesn't. She thinks you haven't tried to contact me or Tripp and you don't care that she's gone. That you're relieved she left. Before you run out to your truck, take a deep breath and remind yourself that you'll get to correct her belief in a few days. Just give her a few more days. She doesn't need you here messing with her emotions while she's facing her demons and figuring out that she's going to be okay. When she sees you again she needs to feel like she can be what you need."

"Two days. That's it. She comes to me in two days or I'm coming there. I can't do this anymore. It isn't for me that I want to come. It's because I can't let the woman I love believe I don't want her. I've done this for as long as I can stand it. Two days is all I'm promising," I told her.

"Fine, two days."

I dropped the phone to the bed and sat down beside it. Della had overcome her night terrors. She was getting better. She was going to be whole. If I could make it just two more days.

◇

My mother had called and woken me up that morning. I told her I'd be at her house in an hour to talk. She was furious and I had been avoiding her calls. It was time I talked to her. She would know soon who the new board members were when I held a party at the club to celebrate their new positions. Everyone would know and she wasn't going to be happy about it. Dean Finlay might send her into a rage. She should be prepared.

When I arrived at her house, Harry, the chauffeur I'd hired for Mother after I fired Leo when I returned to Rosemary, was loading my mother's bags into her Benz. She was going somewhere, obviously. Good. That was probably best.

I nodded as I passed Harry. He was my employee. Leo had been my father's. Leo had also left Della in handcuffs for five hours in the back of a car and hadn't let her use the restroom. I'd fired him before I could get my hands on him.

"She's leaving, I see."

Harry nodded. "Yes, sir. I'm taking her to the airport at nine," he replied.

"Thanks, Harry."

I headed to the door and didn't knock. It was standing open. The house cleaner, Martha, was standing there, wringing her hands nervously. I was sure she'd seen and heard my mother's anger. I smiled at her reassuringly. Stopping at the bottom of the stairs, I called out, "Mother. I'm here."

Then I turned to look back at Martha. "It's okay. You can finish doing what you were doing. She won't kill me. Even if she's threatened to."

Martha didn't look too sure but she nodded and scurried off.

Mother came to the top of the stairs with her purse over her arm. "I'm leaving," she stated, as if I hadn't figured that out already.

"I see that," I replied.

She walked down the staircase and I waited for more of an explanation.

"You have chosen to defy your father's memory. You have taken everything he set into place and thrown it away. Those men you let go were a part of the Kerrington Club for over thirty years. They are trusted confidantes. You thumb your nose at that. You're a foolish child. I don't want to stay here and watch you destroy this legacy. Your grandfather was a silly man. He shouldn't have left anything to you. A twenty-five-year-old boy isn't old enough to run a business like this one. You know nothing."

I let her angry words seethe from her mouth. She needed to get this out and it was time I let her. When her furious gaze leveled on me and stayed there I decided it was my turn to speak.

"Those men were my *father's* confidantes. Not mine. I put in place those who are close to me. It's time for a change. The club will be run differently now. I'm not Father. But I strive every day to be like the man who built this club. I admire my grandfather and hope to be worthy of his legacy one day.

I hope you travel safely and will check in with me so that I know you're doing well. I love you, Mother. You may not believe me or even care, but I do. You're my mom. That will never change."

She opened her mouth, then snapped it closed again. I believed, deep down, that she loved me, too. But right now her pride was too big to accept that emotion where I was concerned. She pulled her purse up to her shoulder and looked at the door. "I'm going to our apartment in Manhattan. I have friends there, and I prefer to live there now. Rosemary has changed."

Yes, it had. And I hoped it would keep changing. "I wish you happiness," I replied.

She didn't look back at me. I watched as she walked out the front door with the click of her heels echoing through the house. She would come back one day. She would love me one day. But for now, she had to go. She had to be mad. And letting her go was something I could do.

Della

Nile Andrews had my eyes. Or I had his. When his eyes met mine as I stepped into the restaurant, I could see that he noticed it, too.

I was more nervous about this than meeting Glenda. I'd never had a father. I didn't know what that felt like. What a meeting with the man whose sperm gave me life would even be like. My first question had been, did he really want to have this meeting? The answer was clearly yes. He'd boarded a plane to Atlanta hours after I'd called him that morning. He said he could meet me at seven at this restaurant. I had been surprised by his desire to come here so soon. I had even expected him to make excuses.

"Hello, Della," he said as he stood up and held out his hand for me to shake.

"Hello, Nile," I replied, slipping my hand into his. He was tall. Glenda had said he played basketball and I could see why. His hair was a dark color that contrasted greatly with his blue eyes. He was a handsome man. I could see what Glenda's teenage heart had seen.

"I'm so glad you wanted to meet me. I've been waiting for that call since Glenda let me know she found you."

He hadn't wanted me. But he'd been a seventeen-year-old boy. I couldn't hold that against him. It wasn't like he had been an adult who had made the decision to give me away. He hadn't been old enough to be a parent yet. Not really.

"I like Glenda," I said simply.

Nile grinned and he sat down after I did. "Yeah, she's something else."

There was a tenderness in his eyes that surprised me. He had loved her once. It had been young love but he had loved her. It had been real. And somewhere deep down it had never really gone away for him. Glenda didn't get that soft look in her eyes when she talked about Nile. She admired the man he had become and said his wife was gorgeous and perfect for him. Nile reacted differently.

"I guess she told you about what happened," he said.

I nodded. "She did. I understand. You were both young."

He studied me a moment, then shook his head. "You look so much like her. It's amazing. But you got my eyes. My other girls don't have my eyes. They got their mother's. But you got them."

His other girls. He hadn't called them *his* girls. He hadn't made them sound exclusive. He had said *other*. Something in me warmed. In his mind I was one of his girls. I didn't know him. I hadn't even known about him until a few days ago. But he had always known I existed.

"Did you know that I was a girl . . . before you heard from Glenda?"

A frown creased his forehead, then a small smile touched his lips. "Yeah. She told me. After you were born she told me she held you. That you were perfect and that she'd given you away. I got drunk that night. Real drunk. Wrecked my dad's car and almost lost my scholarship. I went a little self-destructive for a while. I was a kid myself but I kept seeing this small baby whose face I had never seen, and I knew she was mine. But I'd never held her. I'd never been able to kiss her." He shook his head. "It was the hardest thing I'd ever experienced. Then Glenda moved. Without a word of explanation she was gone. I didn't see or hear from her for over thirteen years. Then one day she called me. She wanted to find you. I didn't want to. It wasn't because I didn't want to see you, because I did. I was just afraid to see her. She, uh . . ." He cleared his throat and tugged at his collar. "She's my one that got away. You never quite get over that one."

I felt like pointing out that she hadn't gotten away, that he'd sent her running, but I didn't. That ship had sailed. They were both married with kids. "What are your daughters like?" I asked. I had never had siblings. Not ones that I remembered. To know I had half siblings in this world was hard to comprehend. I was curious about them. I wanted to know if they were anything like me.

Glenda's daughter was young but she had a free spirit. She'd told me I looked like a princess. She asked me if I could fly a plane and told me that one day she was going to fly planes. I had been fascinated with her. All her long blond hair, like her father's. Her name was Samantha but they called her Sammy. I liked knowing she was my sister. That what she was could have been me. I could have been like that as a child. I could have been so free. Knowing she would get a chance to live her dreams and have a family around her that loved her made me happy. It made the heaviness on my shoulders ease.

"Three of them are difficult but they're fun too. Jasmine is the oldest by one minute and fifty-six seconds, and she doesn't let the other two forget it. Jocelyn is the middle child and she's the most like me. She plans to be a basketball star. Then there is my baby, July. That's the month I met their mother. She's what warms me when I need it most. July is the perfect name for her. She's also the sweetest and most forgiving."

"They all have J names," I said, smiling at the idea.

"Their mother's name is Jillian."

I liked that. "I would like to meet them," I said.

Nile's smile grew. "I would love that. So would they. I told them about you after I got the call from Glenda. Jillian already knew about the baby . . . about you. So, she stood behind the idea of me meeting you. She would like to meet you, too."

"Okay," I replied.

The server appeared and we ordered our drinks and Nile asked if I wanted an appetizer. I wasn't really hungry at the moment so I told him no. Once the server left he turned his attention back to me. "What was your life like growing up, Della?"

This was a question that Glenda hadn't asked me. I had been prepared for her to ask me but she never did. Because of that, I had let my guard down with Nile. He was different. He wanted to know. He wasn't afraid to hear the answer. I could tell that Glenda was afraid of the truth.

"It wasn't easy. I wanted to meet you because I needed to know what the people who created me were like. I needed to know I was going to be okay. But I'm not ready to share my past with you. Honestly, I don't think you want details. If I were you, I wouldn't want to know."

Nile's face paled at my words and his jaw worked back and forth. I picked up my water and took a drink. I was more honest with him than I had planned on being. But the words had come out without a filter.

"You're wrong. I want to know," he said in a quiet tone.

I shook my head. "No, you think you do but you don't. And I don't like talking about it. I'm still working through some things. Meeting you and Glenda and seeing with my own eyes that you have healthy, happy children is what I need right now. It eases fears that I've lived with a long time."

Nile leaned his elbows on the table and studied me. "You're scaring the shit out of me," he said.

He had no idea.

"Nile, I want to get to know you. But I plan on taking that slow and doing it when I can deal with it. One day I'm sure I'll be ready to tell you about my life. Until that moment, I don't want to discuss it again."

He took a long, deep breath through his nose, then nodded. "Okay. Fine. But the father in me wants to fix things."

He wasn't my father. He was someone else's but he wasn't mine. He just provided the sperm that helped create me. "The male in you wants to fix things. Not the father in you."

He started to say something and stopped. A smile broke across his face and he leaned back. "Who is he? The man who wants to fix things for you?"

I fidgeted with the napkin in my lap. "I'm not talking about that, either."

"Why not? Did he hurt you?"

I shook my head. "No, he never hurt me."

Woods

I stood looking out the window of the conference room while I waited on my new board members to arrive. I had now talked to all of them. Everyone I had asked had agreed. Well, everyone except one of them. He would come around though. In time.

My thoughts went back to Della. I had twenty-four more hours before I was going after her. She would arrive here by then or I was going to Georgia and Braden could get over it. I had agreed with her at first but I didn't agree now. It was taking too long. Every day Della was away from me, she convinced herself even more that I didn't want her.

"I feel like a badass," Jace drawled.

I turned to look at him. He was standing in the doorway with a cup of coffee and a grin on his face. "When did we get so damn old?" he asked, then chuckled and walked inside.

"We're not old," I replied.

"Who's old? I'm not fucking old," Thad said as he followed Jace into the room.

I had debated asking Thad to be a part of the board. He was rarely serious and he still thought he was seventeen most of the time. But he was one of us. His father had been a board member. He should be one too.

"I'm old. That's who's old," Darla announced as she walked into the room with her iPad in her hands, typing away at it. She was always working. That was why she was the best.

"No, you're not. You're wise," I assured her.

She snorted and barely glanced up from what she was working on before she took her seat.

"This kind of feels like the knights of the fucking round table," Grant said as he sauntered into the room with a grin and a glass of what I assumed was bourbon. He really was drinking a lot more these days. I wondered if Rush knew about this.

"This needs to be quick. Nate's checkup is in two hours. I have to be there. They weigh him and shit. I don't want to miss that," Rush said as he walked into the room, followed by Dean.

"I'm not missing it either," Dean said, reaching into his pocket and pulling out a pack of cigarettes.

"No smoking in here, Dean," I told him.

He grumbled. "You bunch of prejudiced asses. No one lets me smoke anywhere around here. It's fucking insane. I need to go back home where I can smoke a joint on that street if I get the urge."

I ignored his rock star hissy fit. We were all here. At least the ones who were in Rosemary. We were missing two. One would take her place soon. The other still had his shit to figure out.

"Are you drinking bourbon this early?" Rush asked, looking at Grant with a frown.

Grant rolled his eyes and leaned back, propping his feet on the table. "Yeah," was his response.

"Really? You've started drinking whiskey before lunch?" Rush wasn't giving in and I really didn't want them having this fight in here.

"He's fucking your sister. Hell, anyone that stupid has to drink to stay sane," Dean said in a bored tone.

Shit. This was gonna go downhill fast.

"Don't respond to that, either of you," I said, standing at the head of the table.

"It's okay. It's true," Grant said, and held up his drink with a grin that didn't reach his eyes.

Rush swore under his breath.

"Harlow's too damn sweet for you. You know that, don't you, boy? She don't need Nan's seconds. She's too good for that. She's the kind of girl you can look at but can't touch. They're too unattainable for guys like us. Only those who can reach the pedestal she's on can touch her," Dean said.

"Harlow?" Rush asked, looking at his dad in confusion. "What's Harlow got to do with this?"

Dean just grinned. "What happens in LA stays in LA." He winked at Grant. "Don't it, boy?"

Yeah . . . there was a lot I didn't know. I was pretty damn sure I didn't want to know either. "Okay, let's get off Grant's private life and let's focus on the point of this meeting. As you all know, you are now my board of directors. I don't make decisions without meeting with this group and discussing it. You are my advisers. It's time to take the Kerrington Club into the next generation. We're going to do that together."

Darla's pleased smile as she sat back and listened to me talk meant more than she could have known. She was proud of me. Right now, I needed someone to be proud of me.

"Does this mean we can get rid of those damn coming-out balls? That shit is ancient," Jace said.

"Hey. Don't knock the coming-out ball. The girls get all sentimental, which leads to horniness," Thad argued.

"Could you please watch what you say in here, Thad? We have a lady on the board and another will be joining us soon."

Thad looked properly guilty. "Sorry, Miss Darla," he said sheepishly.

"No worries, Thad. I've been watching your horny ass screw through my cart girls for years."

The entire room went silent, then burst into laughter. This was a good group. We would make my grandfather proud.

Della

I opened the door as Tripp came walking up to it. I'd been expecting him. I had called him over an hour ago. Told him we needed to talk.

"You look good, Della. Much better than the girl I left here," he said before stepping into the house.

"Thank you. A lot has changed," I said, then motioned for him to go to the living room.

"Apparently it is a good change. You look almost happy."

Almost was a stretch. I wasn't happy. I missed Woods. I missed him so much it hurt. "Not sure if I'll be able to achieve happy, but I hope to," I said simply.

Tripp sat down in the closest chair, stretched his legs out in front of him, and looked up at me. "Talk, Della girl. I'm listening."

"I'm not going to South Carolina. I'm not sure what I'm going to do next but I won't be going with you. Thank you for everything. Thank you for putting up with me for the past two weeks and helping me when I needed it. What you did means more than words could ever express. I promise to pay you back every penny you spent. As soon as I get a job I'll start sending you money. I have your address."

Tripp frowned. "Don't send me any money. Keep it. I had fun. I had a traveling buddy for a while."

I wasn't going to let him get away with that. I had taken two weeks of his life on the road and now he was staying in Atlanta this week while he waited on me. "No. I'm paying you back."

Tripp smirked and shook his head. "I won't argue with you right now," he said.

"I found out some things this week," I told him. "I'm not having night terrors anymore. I still have dreams and there're still bad memories but I don't get scared. The fear is gone. I just wake up."

Tripp's eyes went wide and he beamed at me. "That's awesome, Della."

I nodded because I agreed. It was amazing. I had conquered something. "Yeah, it is."

"Are you going back to Rosemary?"

I wasn't sure. Every minute that passed in which I didn't have a panic attack and have to fight off the fear that used to overwhelm me, I wanted to go back. I wanted to show Woods that I was complete. I wasn't broken anymore. I was whole. He could love me. I was safe to love. But had I burned that bridge?

"I don't know," I replied.

Tripp bit his bottom lip. He did that when he was thinking. Finally, he let it pop free. "Listen. I can't say much because it isn't my place, but go back. If you want to go back. Be brave and go back."

I wish it was that easy. "What if he doesn't want me back?"

Tripp shook his head. "Not possible. Trust me."

"I left him. All I left was a note. He hasn't looked for me. He must hate me."

Tripp stood up and paced back and forth in front of the fireplace while biting his bottom lip again. What was he so worked up about?

I watched him, waiting for him to say something.

Finally, he stopped and ran his hand through his hair, pulling on the ends a little, like he was having a hard time with something. "Tripp, what's wrong?" I asked.

He stared at me hard a minute. He knew something. *Is Woods dating someone else already? Surely not. Oh, God. I'm going to be sick. Could he move on like that?*

"The money, it was all—"

"All because he was a good friend and wanted to help you, Della. Wasn't it, Tripp?" Braden's voice startled me as she interrupted Tripp.

He swallowed hard, then nodded. "Yeah," he finally said.

That wasn't what he was going to say. Braden knew what he was going to say and she had stopped him. She was keeping something from me. What was it?

I stood up and spun around to look at her. "Is he with someone else?" I asked. Just saying it ripped me into pieces. If she said yes I would crumple to the floor. I wouldn't be able to deal with that.

Her eyes were determined. I could see she wanted to tell me but she wasn't going to. "I think you need to go back to Rosemary and take back your man, if that's what you want. I think that if you love Woods Kerrington, then you need to be brave enough to put your heart on the line and go after him. You need to stop fearing things, Della. This is your last obstacle. Face it." Her voice cracked. "Please, Della. Go get him. If you want him. Go get him."

He had moved on. I sank back down on the couch. "Oh, God," I gasped as the pain started filling every inch of my body.

"No, Della—"

"Shut up, Tripp," Braden snapped. She wanted me to know the truth. Tripp was trying to ease my pain because he was a good guy but Braden loved me enough to be honest.

"How do I go after him? He doesn't want me," I said, my voice no more than a whisper.

Braden knelt down in front of me. "You are beautiful, smart, kind, and selfless, and you're the best friend I've ever had. I love you like a sister. You are my family. I've watched you hurt and I've watched you hide from your fears as if they really were those monsters under your bed that your mother threatened you with. In two days I've seen you face life with a strength I knew was in there but I'd never seen you use. If you want Woods Kerrington—if he is your forever—then go get him. Don't doubt yourself. Don't doubt your importance. People don't love you and forget you, Della. You're unforgettable."

I covered my mouth to smother a sob. Braden didn't reach for me and hug me. She didn't offer words of comfort. She just knelt there and watched me. She was waiting on me to decide. She was betting on me. When the rest of the world thought I was hopeless, she bet on me. She believed in me.

So had Woods.

"Can I have one last ride?" I asked Tripp as I raised my gaze to meet his.

"You know it," he replied.

Braden let out a loud sob as she stood up and wrapped her

arms around me. "I'm so proud of you. You did it, Della. You did it," she said into my hair as she cried in my arms.

I smiled over her shoulder at Tripp, who was getting a little teary-eyed himself.

He gave me a thumbs-up and winked, then he turned and walked out of the room.

Woods

I walked into my house and went for my suitcase. Della had four hours left to come back to me. I was packing. I was going after her. She wasn't going to come back. She was scared, and I'd be damned if I was going to continue to let her think I didn't want her. Whatever reasons Braden had could go to hell. I was going to get my woman. I was going to make sure she damn well knew I loved her with all my heart.

My phone rang and I froze. *It could be her. She could be coming back.* I was almost scared to hope. I reached into my pocket and pulled out my phone. It was Tripp.

"Yeah," I said, then held my breath.

"Get your ass ready. She's coming back."

I sucked air into my lungs and threw my head back as my heart started beating again for the first time since she'd walked away from me. Della was coming back.

"Are you sure?" I asked.

"She's packing her bag and telling Braden good-bye. I ain't gonna lie, dude. That was a tough scene in there. I was real damn close to telling her the truth and sending her back to you, but Braden is hard-core. She was determined that Della make this decision. When she broke and agreed to come back, even though she thinks you've moved on, it was emotional."

"What are you talking about? Why does she think I've moved on? What the hell does that mean?" Had Braden lied to her?

"She's convinced you're with someone else now. That the secret she can sense between me and Braden is that you've moved on to someone else. So, she's coming to Rosemary to win you back. She isn't just coming back to you—she's coming back thinking she has to fight for her man."

As much as I didn't want Della ever thinking I could even touch another woman, the idea of her coming to fight for me made me smile. "Are you bringing her?"

"Yep," he replied.

"Bring her to my house. Drop her off and leave. I'll be here," I told him.

Tripp chuckled. "Ah, damn, you mean I don't get to watch the make-up sex?"

"Careful," I warned him as my mind started making plans. I had a lot to do before she got here. "Go rent a car. Use the money I just put in your account. Don't put her on the back of your bike again."

"I'm a good driver," Tripp argued.

"Don't give a shit. If I have to think about her arms wrapped around you one more time I'll lose it. I don't want her on the back of your bike. Ever. Again."

Tripp let out a sigh. "Fine. I'll rent a damn car."

"Bring her back to me safe. And hurry."

"Yes, sir. Gotta go, here she comes," he said.

I hung up and looked around my living room. It was time

to start getting ready. She was coming back to me. I was going to make sure she never regretted it.

I dialed Jace's number. I needed Bethy's help.

"Hey."

"Bethy with you?" I asked as I began cleaning up the kitchen.

"Yeah, why?"

"I need her help. Give her the phone."

"Okaaay," he said. I heard him telling her it was me and that I needed her help.

"Hey, what's up?"

"Della is on her way back to me. I need rose petals. Where do I get a bunch of rose petals this late?"

Bethy squealed. "She's coming back! That's wonderful. I'm so happy for you!"

"Focus. I need rose petals," I told her as I put the last dish in the dishwasher and turned it on.

"I will get you rose petals. Don't worry about it. I'll be by in about an hour."

"Thanks," I told her before hanging up. I glanced over at the wall where the picture I'd smashed once hung.

I quickly dialed the next number on my list.

"Hey, Rob. I know it's late but the picture I brought you to frame—I need it. Now."

"It's not ready and I close in the next hour."

"A thousand dollars if you can get it to my place in two hours."

"Shit. Okay, yeah. I'll make it happen."

"Thanks."

Hanging up, I walked to the bedroom and started stripping the sheets. I hadn't changed them because they smelled like Della. My girl needed clean sheets. Once I had my room cleaned I dialed one more number.

"Boss?"

"Jimmy, I need your help. Close the dining room early. Tell everyone that there's a private member meeting or some shit. Just close it. I need the kitchen staff's help."

Della

"You didn't have to rent a car. I was fine with the bike," I told Tripp again when we pulled out of the car rental parking lot.

"Yeah, I did. Trust me," he replied with a smirk.

I was tired of arguing with him about it. He had been determined to rent the car and now it was too late to change his mind. I leaned back in the seat and stared out the window. I would be in Rosemary in five hours. I wasn't sure if I would go to Woods's house or if I would go to a hotel. Maybe I could call Bethy. There was always Tripp's condo. I could ask him for one last favor. I'd asked him for so many already.

"Are we going straight to Woods's place?" Tripp asked.

"Um . . . I don't know. Maybe I shouldn't blindside him. I could just go see him tomorrow while he's in his office. That way I won't have to just show up at his house in case . . ." I couldn't bring myself to say *in case he's with someone else*.

"What? You getting cold feet now? Can't do that. You want to get your man, then go get him."

"I'm not sure if that's the way I should do it."

Tripp shifted in his seat and cleared his throat. "Okay. Picture this: Woods is at his house with another woman. One he can't love like he loves you. You haven't been gone long enough for that. She's gonna get to sleep in his bed, where you belong, tonight. Unless you march up to his door and take back your man."

The idea of this faceless woman sleeping in Woods's bed and touching him made me physically ill. *No.* He was mine. She couldn't touch him. He was mine first.

"You're getting fired up, aren't you? Ready to take back what belongs to you? I think it's about damn time. Shame to let him sleep with her another night when he would rather be with you. She's just filler."

He was right. Woods wasn't in love with her. He had been in love with me. I could make him love me again. I could show him I wasn't weak. I was worthy of his love. I was going to fight for it. I would get him back—no one was sleeping over there tonight except for me. She was leaving. I'd make her leave.

"Take me to Woods," I told him.

Tripp let out a whoop and patted my leg. "Attagirl. You got this," he said.

I sure hoped I did. If not, I might've been on my way to making a complete fool out of myself.

◇

When we were ten minutes away, I started having second thoughts.

"Maybe I should just go to your place tonight."

Tripp let out a short laugh. "Uh, yeah, no. Woods is already going to want to hurt me when he gets ahold of me. I'm not about to bring you back to Rosemary and take you to my place."

"But if he's with another girl . . ."

"Della, do I have to give you another pep talk? Because I will. You can do this. You came back here. You wanted Woods enough to come back and face this. It's time to face it, baby."

He was right. I knew he was, but I was scared of what seeing Woods with someone else would do to me. I'd come so far this week. I didn't want to turn into a whimpering lunatic in front of him. I wanted him to see the new and improved Della. Not the girl he had gotten rid of.

"He's gonna want to see you. I know you don't believe that but he will. I'm a guy. I know these things."

"He may want to see me, just not when he has another . . ." I couldn't say it.

"Remember, you aren't gonna let her have him tonight. You're back."

I nodded. Right. I was going to take back what was mine. Even if it wasn't mine anymore, I was gonna fight like hell.

"Okay. Hurry before I change my mind again."

"Two more minutes," Tripp said with a smile.

Those two minutes felt like hours. When Tripp finally pulled into Woods's driveway I almost wept with relief to see that his truck and my car were the only two vehicles there. That didn't mean he was alone, though. He could have brought someone there. The "she" in my mind still existed.

Tripp squeezed my hand. "Go get him," he said.

I couldn't talk. I was too nervous. I just nodded and opened the car door and stepped out. I hadn't even asked Tripp if he was staying and waiting on me or if he was going back to Macon to get his motorcycle. I couldn't think about that now.

I closed the door behind me and moved toward the stairs.

Then he drove away. I turned back to see Tripp pulling back onto the street. He stuck his hand out of the window and waved good-bye before speeding off. He'd just left me there.

I looked back to the front door and took a deep breath. Woods was in there. I was going to plead with him for a second chance if I had to. I was going to make sure I was the woman in his bed tonight.

The lights in the house were off. All I could see was a dim light in the bedroom. It almost looked like candlelight. *Please, God, don't let it be candlelight.* I gripped the railing as I walked up the stairs to the front door. He was never in bed this early. *Maybe he isn't here. Maybe he's with Jace.*

I reached the top step and stood there staring at his bedroom window. I was pretty sure that it was candlelight I was seeing there. It was flickering light. This was a bad idea.

No.

It wasn't.

He was mine, and I'd be damned if I was going to let some other woman have him. I would shove the candle up her ass.

I closed the distance between me and the door and knocked several times, then stood back and waited. If it took a while, that meant he had to get his clothes on.

The door swung open and there he stood. He had on a pair of khaki shorts and a white button-down shirt. The sleeves were rolled up to his elbows. I loved it when he wore white. His dark skin was startling in white. I sucked in a deep, fast breath at the sight of him.

He didn't move. We just stood there, staring at each other.

It had been almost three weeks since I'd left. It felt like forever since I'd seen his face.

"Hi," I managed to croak out.

"Hi," he replied, still standing in the doorway, looking like a beautiful fallen angel. Whom had he gotten dressed up for? My nose caught a scent from inside and I stiffened. Someone was cooking. In the dark?

"Can I come in?" I asked.

He stepped back so I could enter the house. I didn't see her yet. But I smelled the food. *Maybe she isn't here yet.*

"Are you expecting someone?" I asked without looking back at him.

"Yes," he replied. His voice was low. He didn't want to tell me that. At least he was honest.

"Oh, I'll—" I stopped myself. I almost told him I'd be quick. I almost apologized. I wasn't going to do that. I was here to fight for him. Not lie down and let her have him.

"You should probably call her and tell her that your plans have changed," I said, turning around and facing him.

Something flashed in his eyes but the stupid lights were off and I couldn't see him well enough.

"Why's that, Della?" he asked as he took a step toward me.

I stood my ground. He was hurt. I had hurt him but I was back. Dammit. I was back. "Because if she steps foot in this house I will have to kick her ass." I snapped my mouth shut. I couldn't believe I'd said that.

A grin tugged at the corner of Woods's mouth as he took another step toward me. I didn't move away. I wanted him close. I wasn't going to run. "Hmm, someone's jealous," he said as he reached out and ran a finger along my jawline. I shivered.

"Very," I admitted. I wasn't ashamed of it. I was livid with jealousy.

"Why are you jealous, Della?" He took another step toward me, causing me to back up against the wall. His hands rested against the wall on either side of my head. "Who would you ever have to be jealous of?"

I was having a difficult time breathing normally. He smelled so good. The tanned skin of his throat was right there. I wanted to lick it. Taste him. "Anyone you touch," I said breathlessly.

"Then you only have one person to be jealous of," he replied, and lowered his head to nuzzle my neck. I trembled and reached up to touch his shoulders. I needed some support. There was someone else. He was admitting it. I wanted to hit him and scream and I wanted to grab his shirt and kiss him. Claim him.

"You left me, Della. You left me. You broke me," he whispered against my skin, and then ran the tip of his tongue up my neck and took a small nip at my ear.

"Who is she?" I asked, needing to remind myself that he'd been with someone else.

"Who is who?" he asked, pressing against me as he continued his assault on my neck as if it were a delicacy he craved.

"Who have you . . . who are you cooking for? Who's coming here? Who have you touched?" I asked, holding on tighter to his shoulders as my body went warm and weak.

"You. Always, you. Just you," he said, lowering his mouth to my collarbone.

What did he mean "me"? "I don't understand," I panted breathlessly as he ran his lips over my cleavage slowly and murmured about how good I smelled.

"What don't you understand, baby?" he asked as he moved his hand from the wall to cup my right breast.

I let out a strangled cry of pleasure. I wasn't going to be able to think clearly if he kept this up.

"You said there was someone else," I said as my body betrayed me and moved closer to him like a magnet.

"No, I didn't. You asked if I was expecting someone. I said yes. I was expecting you. You asked who I touched. I said only one person. You. Always you," he said, finally lifting his head to look at me. The heat I expected to see in his eyes wasn't what I saw. His heart was in his eyes. He loved me. It was right there for me to see. He was showing me with a look that he hadn't given up on us.

"You knew I was coming back," I said, wondering if it had been Braden or Tripp who had clued him in.

Woods cupped my chin gently in his hand and ran his thumb over my bottom lip. "I've known exactly what you were doing every day since the day you left me. I've made sure you had money to stay in hotels that were safe and food to eat. How do you think I kept from going crazy? I had daily calls to tell me how you were. Where you were. I stayed away because I wanted you to come back to me. I wanted you to want me. To want us."

He had been keeping tabs on me. He had cared. He hadn't just let me leave. Tears filled my eyes and I didn't care. I wanted to cry. I was happy. I was loved.

"Don't cry," he said as he began to kiss each tear from my face. "I can't stand it when you cry. Please, don't cry."

"You love me," I said, smiling.

Woods pulled back enough to look down at me. "Della.

That should have never been a question in your mind. You should have known that. If you didn't know that you had my soul, then I'm doing something wrong."

I reached up and grabbed his face and kissed him. With everything I had, I kissed him. I didn't have the words to make any of this right. So I showed him how I felt. How much he meant to me. His arms wrapped around me and he met each stroke of my tongue with his own. We stood there tasting and indulging in each other. It was perfect. I was home.

When I broke the kiss so I could catch my breath I reached for his shirt. I wanted that shirt off him. I wanted his clothes off. I wanted him inside me. "Now, I need you, now," I told him as I began unbuttoning his shirt.

"I have food. I was going to romance you first. Convince you to stay with me," he said as I pushed his shirt off his shoulders.

I caressed his chest. His broad shoulders always made me feel so small but safe. "I'm hungry and we'll eat but right now I need you inside me," I told him as my hands got busy with the buttons on his shorts.

"Then come to the bedroom," he said, his breathing as out of control as I felt.

"No. I can't wait." I reached for my sundress and jerked it over my head. I started to push down my panties and Woods let out a growl and took over. His hands covered mine and he pulled them down, and then he ran his hands over my bottom and pressed kisses to the insides of my thighs. "Get inside me," I begged. I wanted all the sweet kisses and I wanted to taste him, too, but right now I needed to be full of Woods.

"Fuck," he groaned, and stood up, turning me around to

face the wall. "You make me crazy, Della. I was gonna be romantic. You deserve romantic."

"I want you to fuck me hard. Fill me up and remind me that I'm yours," I begged.

Woods's body shuddered behind me just before he grabbed my hips and entered me with a yell.

"God, yes! So tight. So hot. This is mine," he said as he stopped and caressed my butt, then slapped it hard one time. "Mine. All this is mine."

"Yes, it's yours," I told him, and pressed back against him.

He let out another animalistic grunt and began moving in and out of me. With each thrust I climbed closer to the release I knew would fill me with completion.

"No one touches my pussy. This is my pussy, Della," he said in a growl before slipping his hand around me and running his fingers over my clit.

I went off like a rocket from his touch. "Yes! That's it, baby, come on my dick. That's my girl." His words made me wilder. I bucked against him and begged him to keep fucking me.

My words caused his body to pause, then jerk again as he began chanting my name over and over. Each tremor through his body made me tingle.

"My Della," he whispered as he rested his head on my back. I moved so that he came out of me, then I turned around and pulled him into my arms.

"Always your Della," I told him.

He held me tighter and we stood there as our bodies hummed our pleasure and our hearts healed.

Woods

My welcome-home for Della hadn't gone off in the way I had planned. I hadn't meant to take her in the foyer against the damn wall like a madman. But she'd been saying things that made me lose it. She wanted to be fucked and my body wanted to give her what she was asking for.

That hadn't been the plan. But I'd needed it. I had needed to hear her say she was mine. The thought of Tripp riding that damn bike while sitting between her legs ate me alive. I hated it. I wanted to remind her who belonged between her legs. Only me.

The idea that she believed I could be with anyone else still blew my mind. If she didn't know how completely I loved her, then that was my fault. I had failed her. I would fix that.

After I dressed her I brought her into the dining room. Jimmy had brought the staff over and set up a table complete with a linen tablecloth, candlelight, and roses. He had also brought the meal. It was Della's favorite special that we offered at the club. I watched as she took in the room. I had an Erick Baker playlist playing low over the sound system. She shifted her gaze over to mine and smiled at me shyly.

"This is beautiful."

"You were coming home. I wanted it to be special." *I didn't mean to fuck you against the wall before you could even completely get in the house.* Although I didn't say it aloud, her blush made me think she knew what I was thinking.

She turned and then stopped. She had seen the picture. The one Bethy had taken of us at the beach one afternoon. We had been lost in each other and hadn't noticed that Bethy was taking our picture. I had been sitting on the sand and Della had been straddling me, facing me. Our gazes were locked, and even in the photograph you could see the way we felt. There was no question as to how much I adored her in that moment.

"You had it framed," Della said, staring at it. I walked over and turned the dimmer on the lights up so she could see it better.

"Yeah, I did."

"I love that picture," she said, glancing back at me.

"Me too."

She turned around and looked at me. "That girl in the photo was scared. Of her past and her future. She was scared to love you. That's not me. I'm not scared anymore. My past is what made me who I am. My future . . . as long as I get to spend it with you, then I can't wait to live it. I'm going to be okay, Woods. I'm not going to . . . snap. I have a lot to tell you."

I already knew but I wanted to hear her tell me. I wanted to know her thoughts. I knew she'd met with both her birth parents, and I wanted to hear all about that.

I walked over to her and reached out and took her hand. "I always knew you would be okay. I was with you. I would never leave you. I was here to be strong when you were weak."

"And I love you for that. But I want to be the strong one sometimes. I don't always want to be the weak one."

"I just want you. In whatever way I can have you. But I'm glad you're happy. I'm glad you feel strong. I want you to be happy with yourself. Because you make my life amazing."

She sniffled and then smiled. "We need to eat. I'm fighting the urge to force you to make love to me again or cry because that was so sweet."

I tugged her hand and brought her to my side. "Baby, if you want me inside you again you just crook your finger. This food can wait," I told her before pressing a kiss to her lips.

"I want you inside me again," she said.

I was at least getting her to my bedroom this time. I had plans in there.

I pulled her behind me to the bedroom and opened the door, then stood back and let her walk inside.

The room was filled with candles and the bed was covered in pink and red rose petals. Della gasped, then looked back at me and gave me a naughty grin. "I thought I was going to have to come in here and beat someone up because they were in your room. That's what I thought when I saw the candlelight in your bedroom window."

I chuckled and reached for her. "Mmm, as sexy as it sounds to see you go badass over me, I would never touch another woman. Much less bring one in here. This is our room."

Della leaned into me and sighed. "I think Braden and Tripp wanted me to think that you had another woman."

I smiled into her hair. "Yeah. I think they did, too."

"I'm going to kick their asses. I was all ready to kick someone's ass because of them. It's only fitting I kick theirs."

I laughed, then picked her up and carried her over to the bed and laid her down on the bed of roses.

She was beautiful. "Take off your dress," I told her. She sat up and pulled it off. We hadn't bothered to put her panties and bra back on in the hallway. She was naked and back where she belonged.

"Good girl. Now lie back and open your legs," I told her, and watched as she did exactly as I said.

My release from earlier was on her inner thighs. Her pussy was wet and swollen from the rough loving we'd just had. I pulled my shirt off and took off my shorts before kneeling on the bed between her legs. I ran a finger down her silky heat and watched her body tremble.

"My come is still leaking out of you," I said as I rubbed it over her clit.

Her breath stuttered and she bucked beneath my touch.

"It's so fucking hot to see my release on you like this."

I dipped my finger inside her, then ran it down her thighs. The possessive monster inside of me roared to life. "I want to mark you," I said as I slipped my finger back inside her to coat it with more of our mixed come, then rubbed it on the top of her mound.

"Oh God, Woods. Please," she begged, and moved against my hand.

"My come looks so good on you." I was fascinated with it. Seeing it soak into her soft skin. Knowing it was a part of me.

"Then please put some more in me," she pleaded this time.

I rose up over her and teased her entrance with the head of my cock. She cried out and tried to get closer. I slowly sank into her until I was completely inside.

"You're my all-in, Della. I'll throw it all away for you. I just want you. I'm all in, baby. This life with you, I'm planning on us."

She ran her legs up mine and smiled up at me. "This is it. This is our start. Take me home, Woods."

I dropped my head to her shoulder and began moving inside of her while our breathing hitched and we gradually climbed to the pleasure we knew awaited us. The place we could only reach with each other.

"Now, Della. Come with me," I ordered when I felt myself ready to explode.

Her immediate strangled cry as she began clawing at my back sent me flying off into nirvana.

Della

I opened my eyes and stared into Woods's eyes. He was already awake. The way he looked at me made me feel treasured. Like I was some precious jewel he wanted to protect. "Good morning," he said as his fingers continued to trace the length of my arm with a featherlike touch.

"Good morning," I said, smiling at him. "How long have you been awake?"

"You mean how long have I been staring at you?" he asked teasingly.

"Yes, that too," I replied.

"About an hour. I woke up and you were so damn gorgeous curled up against me I couldn't go back to sleep. I didn't want to sleep and waste time that I could spend looking at you."

My heart squeezed. "You have a way with words, Mr. Kerrington," I told him.

"You think?"

I nodded. "I know."

"Good, because I want to ask you about the past two weeks and I want you to tell me everything," he said.

"I thought you knew everything already," I replied, realizing it had to be Tripp he'd been talking to. Braden hadn't been with me for most of those weeks.

"I know what Tripp and Braden told me. I want to know everything that Della knows."

So they'd both been in on this. I couldn't be mad at them. Not now. I was in Woods's arms. They had brought me back here. They had made me face my fears.

"I almost didn't come back. I was scared to face you. I was afraid you didn't want me. Braden and Tripp talked me into coming back."

Woods smiled at me and reached over to tuck a strand of my hair behind my ear. "Sweetheart, I was coming after you. Your time was almost up. I had told Braden you had forty-eight hours. I had started packing my bag when I got the call from Tripp saying you'd be back in four hours. Don't get me wrong. I'm glad you came home to me. But I wasn't going to stand back any longer. I'd given you two weeks. I wanted you back."

He had been coming to get me. That was why Braden was so insistent that I come back to him. She wanted me to be the one to come back. "I'm not sure what I did to score a best friend like Braden, but I'm so thankful I have her."

Woods kissed the tip of my nose. "There were a few times I considered locking her up long enough to get you and run."

Giggling, I moved closer to him. "But I came home."

"Yes, you did. And it was so damn sweet."

He wanted to know about all that had happened. I wanted to tell him about everything. "Do you know I was adopted?" He nodded. "Well, I met both of them. I even met Glenda's—that's my birth mother—family. She has a daughter and a son.

Her husband was quiet but he seemed nice. I mostly watched her daughter. I wondered if I would have been so free and outspoken if I had lived her life. And I have my birth father's eyes. His name is Nile. He was the high school heartthrob. I can look at him twenty years later and tell that. He's handsome and I think he may still be a little in love with Glenda, which is weird. But I try not to think about it."

I continued to tell Woods all about meeting the people who gave me life. I hadn't told Braden much about each meeting and she hadn't pressed, but with Woods I wanted to tell him everything. I wanted him to know that Nile smoked cigars and Glenda used to sing. She wanted to be a country singer once.

By the time I had finished telling him about everything, he had sat up and leaned against the headboard and pulled me into his lap. He made small circles on the palm of my hand and stayed silent. So I talked more.

I told him about my fears and why I had left him. I told him that my night terrors were gone. I wasn't waking up screaming anymore. I was whole. I wanted to be a mother one day. I wanted so many things I'd been scared to want before.

He slipped his hand down over my stomach and I felt fluttery in my chest. "One day I want my baby tucked safely in here."

I covered his hands with mine. "Me too."

We sat there like that for a while and didn't talk. I had told him everything. Every feeling, every fear. He knew it all now. And he loved me. Through it all, he had loved me.

"Della," he said in a gruff voice.

"Yeah?"

"The idea of you on the back of Tripp's bike, with your

arms wrapped around him, and him sleeping in bed with you and holding you through your fears—it's gonna be hard for me to get over. I'm thankful he took care of you, but you're mine to take care of. I don't want to have to see his face for a while. I need time to get over it."

I moved so that I was facing him. "I never thought anything of those things. I don't have any feelings for Tripp at all. You were the only thing on my mind."

"I know. That's why he gets to live. But it doesn't take away the fact I'm a man and I'm possessive of one thing. You."

He could be so sweet and romantic at times and then so tough and male at others. I shifted to my knees and gave him a wicked grin. "Let me see if I can get that image out of your mind and give you a new one," I said as I kissed down his chest and moved his legs apart so I could get between them.

He was more than ready when I got down to the bottom of his flat, hard stomach. I grabbed his thick length in my hand and held it while I flicked my tongue across the head.

"Baby," Woods groaned, and bucked underneath me.

"Mmm," was my reply as I looked up at him while I slid him into my mouth until he touched the back of my throat, causing me to gag. He always liked it when I gagged.

Both his hands grabbed my head. "Ah, that's good, baby. So damn good. Take it deep. Oh, hell yeah, gag on it." His words came out thick and raspy.

I continued to work my mouth over his cock while he praised me. I wanted to give him a memory that I could send him back to every time he thought about me and Tripp. I wanted to remind him who I belonged to. He never needed to worry. My body was wired for him only.

"Come up here," he said as he caressed my head. "I'm gonna come in your mouth if you don't stop."

I wanted him in my mouth. I grabbed his legs and continued to take him as deep as my throat would allow me to while sucking hard on the tip.

Woods's hands got more frantic and he now had handfuls of my hair. Each gentle tug made my pussy clench. "Gonna come. Your hot little mouth wants it, doesn't it? My naughty baby wants it down her throat. Fuck, yeah. That's my mouth to fuck," he said before yelling my name and holding my head as he shot his release exactly where we both wanted it.

When he eased his hold on my head, I slowly slipped my mouth up his cock, then back down again, cleaning him. I licked the sides and then pulled his head back into my mouth.

"Motherfuckinghell, baby, you're gonna kill me. Stop," he groaned, pulling me up and away from his sensitive flesh. He held me against his chest as he caught his breath.

I traced small hearts around his nipples with my finger. "Woods," I said.

"Yes, sweetheart?"

"Next time you think about me with Tripp, remember that instead. Okay?"

His hold on me tightened, then he chuckled. "I'll do that."

"Good."

Woods

I'd had Jimmy bring breakfast, too, so all I had to do was get up and get it out of the fridge. While Della finished getting dressed after I'd feasted on her in the shower, I went and got everything ready.

I cleared the table from last night and toasted her Belgian waffle, then added the orange cream and shaved almonds to the top of it. I also put out a bowl of honey yogurt with figs and goat cheese. These were all items that Jimmy said Della ordered off the breakfast menu.

When she came walking out of the bedroom, her hair was pulled up in that sexy bun again and she was dressed for work. Good. I had to talk to her about the new board.

"I hope it's okay if I go to work today," she said as she walked into the room.

"Whatever you want to do," I told her, then pulled back her chair.

She took in the food on the table, then cut her eyes back at me and smirked. "You got Jimmy to help you with this."

I shrugged. No use in denying it. "I wanted to get it right."

She stopped and pressed a kiss to my lips. "You get everything right." Then she sat down at the table and let out a pleased sigh. "I'm starving."

"Wild, hot sex all night and morning will do that to you," I replied, and sat down across from her.

She blushed and reached over to take a fig. "Yes, I guess it will."

I was sticking with a Belgian waffle and butter. The fancy shit wasn't my thing. I took a bite and watched her eat some before taking a drink of my coffee and preparing myself to ask her to be on my board.

"I fired the board of directors. I hired a new one. People whose opinions I care about," I said, getting straight to the point.

Della put her fork down and stared at me. "Good for you. You're in charge; you need those close to you helping you with this."

I was glad she agreed. Not that I expected her not to. "I want you on the board, Della."

She had started to pick up her juice but she set it back down and looked at me like I'd just spoken a foreign language. "What?" she asked.

"I want you on my board. I already have your paperwork ready. You just need to sign it."

Della shook her head. "I don't think that's a good idea. I mean, maybe later when you're sure, but right now . . . that's a hasty move. I mean, just three weeks ago you and Jace were worried about my, uh, problems being an issue. I can't be on your board. I'm better, but what if I relapse? You don't want that there and I know your friends agree. I heard Jace. He's gonna want to see that I'm better."

I had forgotten about that damn conversation she'd overheard. I stood up and moved around the table, then knelt down in front of her. "Della, I need you to listen to me. What you heard wasn't what you think it was. We weren't talking about you. Never you. We were talking about my mother. She had called board members and caused problems for me. We were discussing her because, unlike you, she really is crazy. Baby, I would never call you those things or allow anyone else to call you that."

I could see the relief in her eyes. She believed me. She hadn't brought it up all night and I'd been so damn happy to see her that I hadn't thought about it. But damn, she was here in my arms thinking I'd said those things. It was humbling.

"Oh," she said simply.

I smiled and stood up and kissed her. "Yeah. Oh."

"I should have asked you about it. I was . . . I didn't want to hear the truth. I was scared of it."

"Never be scared to hear the truth from me," I told her.

She nodded. "I'm sorry I didn't ask you about it."

"I'm sorry you thought we were talking about you."

She sat there and studied her hands a moment, then looked up at me. "I want to be on your board."

"Good. I can't do this without you."

She went back to eating and I had to force myself to eat, too, and not watch her. I just wanted to watch her do everything. Letting her out of my sight today was going to be hard.

◇

I stepped off the elevator and Vince looked up to greet me. He started to speak and stopped. I watched him as he observed me.

"Miss Della is home, then," Vince said.

"Yes she is. How did you know?"

Vince let out a low laugh. "I'm old, Woods, not blind. It's all over your face, boy."

The grin that broke out across my face stayed while I went through my morning notes and made scheduled phone calls.

Right before lunch, Della stepped into my office with a sexy little smile on her face that was going to get her fucked up against my desk if she wasn't careful.

"I missed you," she said.

"I missed you more. Come here," I told her, holding out my hand for her to come to me. She walked over to my side of the desk and I pulled her down to my lap. "Have you had a good morning?"

"Yes. Have you?"

"It could have been better," I replied, slipping my hand up her skirt. She wiggled in my lap and slapped my hand away.

"Stop that. We have work to talk about," she said playfully, and then tried to stand up. I held her to my lap.

"Go ahead and wiggle, baby. It feels real good."

"You are so bad," she said, stopping me from slipping my hand between her thighs.

"I'm playing catch-up. I have three weeks' worth," I told her.

"Mr. Kerrington, Mr. Rush Finlay is here to see you," Vince announced over the intercom.

"Damn, Rush. Forgot he was coming by."

Della jumped up out of my lap and straightened her skirt.

"Send him in," I said as I watched her fix herself. I was going to mess it up as soon as Rush brought me the info on Nate's trust fund that he'd set up for Dean.

Rush walked into the room with Nate in his arms and a baby bag over his shoulder. That was funny shit. Rush Finlay, badass rock star's son, had a baby bag and a baby in his arms.

"Oh, you brought Nate!" Della's excitement interested me.

I watched her walk over to Rush and take Nate from him. She walked over to the sofa with him, cooing and making him laugh.

Rush's chuckle reminded me he was there. I shifted my attention back to him.

"She likes babies," Rush said with a smirk.

I hadn't known she liked babies. I liked watching her with Nate. Rush was going to be hard to concentrate on. "Yeah, she does."

"When did she come back? Or did you chase her down?"

"Last night. She came back to me," I told him.

"Told you that hand wasn't over," Rush said, then took a seat across from my desk. "Stop mentally fucking her while she's holding my kid."

I shot him an annoyed glare that just amused him. "Here's the paperwork for Nate's trust. Do the same with my paycheck from here."

"Done. I'll get the direct deposits set up today."

Rush let out a sigh. "I might just sit here a minute and take a break. Della looks like she's having fun and I'm beat. Grant was at my house late last night and we had to deal with some shit."

"Is Nan back?"

Rush let out a weary sigh and rubbed his forehead. "Yeah. She's back."

"Damn," I said, more for Rush's sake than anything.

"Yeah," Rush agreed.

Della

Nile was coming to Rosemary today with his family. They were staying in one of the condos on the club property. He had insisted on paying but Woods had gotten him to accept the free condo. I wasn't sure what he'd said but he had talked him into it.

I was excited about introducing Woods to him. I wanted to know what Woods thought about him. Deep down, I also wanted to show Woods that the blood in my veins came from normal people. I often forgot that myself.

"You look beautiful. Stop fidgeting. Nothing you do can make you any more beautiful than you are," Woods said as he reached over and took both my hands in his to keep me from pulling down the mirror and checking my face one more time.

"I know I'm being silly. I'm sorry. I just . . . I've not met Nile's family yet. His daughters . . . they're my sisters."

"And they're about to find out that they have the most beautiful, talented, sweet, brilliant older sister in the world. So stop it. Take a deep breath and know that you're amazing and they're lucky to get to sit in the same room with you."

Woods could say some of the sweetest things in the world.

"I really want to kiss you right now but it will mess us up."

He laughed and pulled the car into the valet parking line at the club. We were meeting Nile and his family there for dinner. "I'll get messed up any time you want to put those plump lips of yours on me."

"Save it for later, sexy," I said just as my door was opened by Bradley. I was glad to see he was still working out. I had hired him a month ago.

"Good evening, Miss Sloane. You're looking lovely," he said with a twinkle in his eyes.

"She's always lovely; hands off," Woods told him, taking my hand and tucking it in his arm.

"You scared that poor valet to death," I said, scolding him.

"Good."

I didn't argue. I followed him inside the club, trying not to smile like an idiot.

"Mr. Kerrington, right this way, sir. Your party has already arrived," Jimmy announced when we stepped into the dining room.

Jimmy shot me a wink before leading us over to the formal dining area reserved for special guests and parties. Woods had requested it so that we'd have privacy.

Nile stood up when we walked in. Woods squeezed my hand to reassure me.

"Hello, Nile," I said in greeting, then turned to Woods. "Woods, this is Nile Andrews. Nile, this is Woods Kerrington."

Woods and Nile shook hands and I heard Nile thanking him for the accommodations, which I had no doubt were extremely impressive, knowing Woods. I looked over at the three girls sitting at the table, studying me. Each one had a different expression. They ranged from nervous to curious.

"Della, I'd like you to meet, Jillian, my wife."

Jillian was tall and slender with long, dark red hair. Her skin was a creamy ivory color and her eyes were hazel. "It's so nice to meet you, Della. Nile has told me all about your visit. I'm anxious to talk to you myself, as are the girls." She had kind eyes. The high cheekbones and excellent bone structure made me think of an uppity elitist woman but Jillian was very nice and down-to-earth. She was what I would have expected Nile to be married to. I couldn't picture him with Glenda. They were nothing alike.

"I'm glad y'all could come visit," I said, glancing down at the girls again. All three of them had their mother's hair color and eyes.

"Della, this is Jasmine, Jocelyn, and July. Girls, this is your sister Della," Nile said, standing to my left. I hadn't expected him to call me their sister. That was surprising. I also wasn't sure how I felt about that yet.

"It's nice to meet the three of you," I said.

"I love your dress. Is it a Marc Jacobs? I swear, I saw one in the new Marc Jacobs line just like it."

"You have Daddy's eyes. I've always wanted Daddy's eyes."

"Do you live on this beach?"

All three of them began talking at once. I was a little overwhelmed but I liked that they wanted to talk to me. I started with Jasmine. "I have no idea who Marc Jacobs is. I bought this dress on a shopping spree with my best friend at a thrift store in Atlanta." I could see the fascination in her face at the idea that I'd shopped in a thrift store.

"I do have your dad's eyes. It was a pleasant surprise but yours are equally beautiful. You have your mother's fantastic hair." Jocelyn blushed prettily and I wondered if she was the shy one.

"And yes, I do live on this beach. It's a wonderful place to live," I told July.

"Do you always shop in thrift stores? I've always wondered what they were like inside."

"I can play the piano. Do you play the piano?"

"Do you know how to surf? I've always wanted to surf."

Again all three of them asked me a question at once.

"Girls, let Della sit down and breathe. You will have plenty of time to drill her with questions, but don't scare her away just yet," Jillian said before I could start answering their questions again.

Woods pulled out my chair and I took a seat. He then took the one next to me. I was seated across from Jillian and he had taken the seat across from Nile. July sat to my right. Jimmy came up and put my napkin in my lap.

"Sweet tea, Miss Sloane," he said as he set the glass down in front of me. I could see the impressed gleam in Nile's eyes as he watched Jimmy deliver our drinks and appetizers without our having ordered.

"Thank you, Jimmy," I said, smiling up at him.

He shot me a quick grin before leaving the room.

"He is swoony. I saw him when we came in and he winked at me," Jasmine said from across the table.

I bit back a smile. Jimmy was beautiful and he knew how to make women of all ages drool over him. And while they were checking him out, he was checking out their men. I'd caught him appreciating Woods's backside on more than one occasion.

"Jasmine, please," Nile said, frowning down at her.

"Sorry," she mumbled.

"July just kicked me. I was just asking her to pass the bread and she kicked me," Jocelyn said as she crossed her arms over her chest.

"All right, girls. That's enough," Jillian said, then looked over at me apologetically. "They were in the car all day and now they're overly excited about being here and meeting you."

"I'm fascinated. I've never been around little girls like this. Or sisters. It's very entertaining."

Jillian's laugh reminded me of tinkling bells. "You may not feel that way anymore before the meal is over."

Woods's hand slid over my leg and rested on my upper thigh. I had faced Nile the first time alone but it was nice to have Woods beside me now.

"I invited Nile to play a round tomorrow morning with me, if that's okay with you," Woods said, leaning closer to me as he spoke.

I liked the idea of his getting to know Nile. "Of course. That's fine," I assured him, and smiled over at Nile.

"Are you married?" one of the girls asked. I glanced back at them and saw Jocelyn elbow July.

"She's not wearing a ring. Don't ask that," Jocelyn hissed.

"No, we're not. But it's okay for her to ask," I replied, unable to keep from smiling at them. Their constant fighting made me wish I'd had a sister.

"Why not? You live with him, don't you?" July asked.

"July." Jillian was the one to scold her this time.

"It's okay, really. I want them to ask me questions," I assured her. Then I looked back at July. "I do live with him. He's my boyfriend."

"Mommy and Daddy lived together for two years before they got married," Jasmine announced from across the table.

I saw red splotches appear on Jillian's face but she just laughed and shook her head. "You need to stop listening to adult conversations. I swear, you know more than you're supposed to," Jillian said as she tried to cover her amusement.

"Does that mean you will be getting married, too?" July asked.

They really weren't going to let the marriage thing go.

"Maybe I will get married one day. I don't know that right now."

"Let's ask Della questions that don't pertain to her personal relationships. Okay, girls?" Nile said with a stern voice. I watched as all three nodded with a look of defeat.

"I have a boyfriend. Can we talk about him?" July asked.

"I would love to hear about him," I assured her. She beamed.

I heard Jasmine sigh from across the table. "Great, here we go," she muttered.

Woods

Della had opened up more than I expected to Nile and his family. Mostly it had just been to Nile's daughters. They had been drawn to her, too. Watching it had been heartbreaking and amazing all at the same time. Della could have had a normal life. Her father was a good man.

I had also watched Nile most of the night. He had watched Della and his girls, too. The pleased look on his face was hard to miss. He might never be someone that Della considered a father but I had hopes that she would form a relationship of some kind with him and his family. I thought she needed it.

"Tell me what you thought of Nile and his family," Della said as we walked into the house. She had been quiet on the ride back and I had left her alone with her thoughts. It was a lot to process without my trying to pull things out of her.

"I think he's a good man and he's a good father. The girls are well-adjusted and they are fascinated with you."

Della grinned as she slipped off her heels. "I liked the girls. Each one was so different. It was like they made this one complete person. I wonder what it must be like to know you have someone on your side all the time, knowing you can make snide comments and even push and shove but they'll love you when the rest of the world is against you."

I walked over and wrapped my arms around her from behind. "I'm always on your side. You can push and shove—hell, you can even slap me—but I will still be right here, ready to face the world with you."

Della leaned back against me and wrapped her arms around mine. "I know that. I meant growing up. Having a sibling to stand in your corner."

I understood what she meant and it broke my heart to think about the little girl who was so alone in dealing with a mother who wasn't there mentally. "You did find Braden."

"Braden found me. And you're right. She was always in my corner."

"I like knowing you have her. She loves you almost as much as I do."

Della laughed. "Don't let her hear you say that. She'll fight you for that title."

I wondered what Braden would do when I asked Della to marry me. Would she grill me? Make sure my intention was to treat her like a princess? I had no doubt I'd hear from her when the time came. I just wasn't sure about the right time.

I loved Della and I knew no one would ever take her place in my heart. She was the one. But marriage also meant a commitment that scared me. I'd been ready to ask her before she left me. Now I knew how quickly she could rip my world out from under me. Could I handle that kind of pain if she were my wife? It was making me even more vulnerable. I needed time to adjust to having her back. Having a Della who didn't wake up screaming and one I didn't worry about all the time.

"I love you," she said as we stood there together.

"I love you more," I replied. And I meant it. That was what kept me from asking her to marry me. That was my roadblock. I loved her more.

A knock on the door broke into my thoughts and Della stepped out of my arms to look back at me. "Who could that be?"

"Not sure. I'll get it."

◇

Jace was pacing back and forth on my front porch when I opened the door. His head snapped up when he saw me. He shook his head and went back to pacing. This was woman trouble. I looked back at Della, who stood watching me from the other end of the hallway.

"Looks like Jace needs to talk. We'll be out here if you need me," I told her.

A worried frown pinched her forehead but she nodded. "Okay."

I closed the door behind me and watched as Jace continued to pace.

"What's wrong with Bethy?" I asked. I knew that was the only thing that could get him to pace like a madman.

He stopped his constant moving and shoved his hands in his pockets. "She's . . . She wanted to get married. I mentioned it to her and she wanted to. But she's started to act different lately. So I dropped the marriage thing. I thought that was what made her go crazy. But she's just getting worse. Hell, what was I supposed to do? I can't get married if she's not ready. I sure as hell can't ask her. I don't know what I was thinking. Just because Rush and Blaire are playing house doesn't mean the rest of us are ready."

I was going to be here a while. I could tell by the frantic tone in Jace's voice. I sat down in the swing. "So you've changed your mind on the marriage thing? Sounds like it scared Bethy anyway. Maybe you two need more time just being a couple."

Jace let out a hard laugh. "Yeah, I thought that, too. But she's just . . . reverted."

"Reverted?" I asked, trying to figure out what in the hell he was talking about.

"You know, reverted to the way she was before. She's drinking and wanting to go out partying all the time. She rarely sees Blaire anymore because she said it makes her sad. She wants what Blaire has but she says it's rare. We can't measure ourselves against that. But that makes no damn sense. I've been in two bar fights in the past week. Two fucking bar fights. Me. I don't fight, dammit. But she's forcing me to go save her drunk ass from men who want to touch her."

I thought about Della playing with Nate the other day and how sweet she was. But not once had she asked for the same thing. She never pressured me for more. I wasn't sure what I'd do if she did. I would probably give it to her.

"Do you want Bethy? Forever? Is she who you see yourself spending your life with?"

"I did. Before all this. I did. I thought we were ready. But now she's changed. She's acting like . . . she's acting like she did before. When all I wanted to do was fuck her because she was so damn good at it. I was addicted to sex with her. Then she stood up to me and drew a line in the sand and I came barreling through it because I realized, through all that sex, that I had started to care for her. I wanted more than just the sex."

Everyone knew this story already. No one had expected it. Jace was a trust fund baby and Bethy was a trailer park baby. The two didn't seem to fit . . . until they did. "She could be drawing the line in the sand again. Forcing you to pick her."

Jace walked over and sat down on a padded bench and dropped his head into his hands. "If I thought that was it I would just propose. I would just ask her to marry me. Because, yeah, I love her. But I think she's hiding something. I don't know what. I try to overlook it but there are times—and they're rare—when she withdraws from me. I can't pinpoint when it happens. I can't figure out a reason—she just does. Then suddenly she's back the next day or a few days later, however long it takes, and she's my Bethy again. I just . . . she has to tell me everything. She has to explain to me what haunts her and why the hell she thinks going to a honky-tonk dressed like a cowboy's wet dream is okay. I'm tired of getting into fights with dudes bigger than me."

Della never did any of these things. I couldn't sympathize and now I was pretty damn sure he shouldn't propose because they had shit to figure out.

"You two need to talk," I said. I had no other words of wisdom.

Jace ran his hand through his hair and sighed. "I know we do. Every time I try and ask her about it, she starts drinking. The next thing I know, she's dancing on a bar somewhere. When she starts to sober up she tells me she wishes she was enough for me and that she wishes she was someone I could love forever. I tell her she is but she needs to tell me why she's doing this. Why she pulls away from me sometimes. She either starts crying or sucking my damn dick. Both get me completely distracted."

I had thought Jace and Bethy were fine. They were good. They were always together. I hadn't imagined any problems with the two of them. Bethy was always so happy and bubbly. The Bethy he was describing wasn't someone I'd ever seen.

"I love her. I'm gonna do whatever the hell I need to to stop this. Because I can't lose her. I love her. She's the best thing that ever happened to me. All relationships before her pale in comparison. If she wants to get married, I'll propose. I wanted to wait but I don't think she'll ever tell me why she pulls away sometimes. Maybe if we're married she won't do that. If I put a ring on her finger then it will stop this drunken partying shit she's doing."

The only thing he'd said there that even came close to a reason as to why he should marry Bethy was the part where he said he loved her and she was the best thing that had ever happened to him. The other stuff wasn't good logic. "I think you need to get her to talk to you sober first. Lock her in a room and make her talk. Don't just propose because she's forcing your hand with this drinking shit. That isn't what marriage is supposed to be about. You gotta want this, man."

Jace glanced back at the door to my house. "What about Della? Do you want it with Della?"

Yeah, I wanted forever with her. "One day, but she isn't pressuring me. When the time is right."

Jace nodded. "Yeah, that's what I thought, too. But Bethy seems threatened by that idea." He stood up. "Thanks for listening. I needed to unload on someone. I couldn't go back to the condo and deal with Bethy after tonight. I just needed to talk."

"You're my best friend. I'm always here to talk when you need to. Besides, you kept me from losing it when Della left me."

Jace chuckled. "More like Rush did. I was scared to touch you. You were going apeshit."

"Rush was the only one strong enough to hold me back. But you listened to me and kept me sane while she was gone."

Jace nodded. "You're my family."

And he was mine.

Della

"Hush, little baby, don't say a word, Momma's gonna buy you a mockingbird." Momma's voice rang out shrill and off-key as I stood outside her bedroom door and peeked inside. She was in a rocking chair in her room with the baby doll I wasn't allowed to touch wrapped tightly in a blanket. She sang to the baby doll when she was sad.

"Yes, he's a good boy to sleep for Momma. He sleeps like he's supposed to." She cooed at the doll and touched its plastic face tenderly, as if it were real. For a long time I thought the baby doll was real. But it never made any noise and she left it forgotten in its crib in her room for days at a time. Eventually I realized it was just a baby doll.

Then I'd made the mistake of picking it up and rocking it, too. Momma had been very upset with me. I had gone three days without food, locked in my room.

"Sweet little baby, Momma's joy. I'm gonna go buy you some new toys." She sang the made-up words. She always made up words to this song. I wasn't sure if she didn't know the real words or if she just liked singing about what she was doing.

Then she threw the baby doll across the room and screamed, "Demon child!" over and over again as she stomped her feet. I ran back to my room as fast as I could and prayed she wouldn't come after me.

"Della?" Woods's voice broke into my dream and my eyes snapped open. I looked up into his concerned face.

"You okay? You were breathing hard."

That was all? I smiled. I was okay. I could live with the memories. If the terror didn't come with them. "I'm fine," I assured him, and cuddled against his side. "It was just a memory."

Woods ran his fingers up and down my arm. "Do you want to talk about them? Maybe if you told me, you would stop dreaming them altogether."

I started to say no and stopped. I had been telling people no for years because it sent me into the darkness when I let myself think about it. But I was better now. What if I did tell him my dreams . . . what if it could actually help?

"Okay," I said, not looking up at him. I kept my eyes on his chest. I wasn't scared of the memories now. I just wasn't sure how I was going to open myself up to him that completely. It would make me feel more vulnerable than I had ever felt. He would know my horrors. No one really knew them.

It was time.

Woods tightened his hold on me and I focused on the warmth of his arms. I was safe. Telling him was safe.

"She was rocking the baby doll. She always rocked the baby doll when she was in one of her dark times. She sang to it and made up words to lullabies. I knew, even at five years old, that her singing to a plastic doll was wrong. Something was wrong. So, I would watch her. She never rocked me. Seeing her rock the doll confused me. Why would she rock a plastic baby doll? The baby was a he. She called it a him. She never called it by a name. Just 'sweet baby' and 'baby boy.' That was weird, too, because the boy they'd adopted before me was never a baby when they had him." I stopped a moment and thought about looking up at Woods to see what he was thinking. But I had more to tell and I didn't want to watch his eyes and see his reaction.

"If she ever saw me watching her rock the baby she would yell at me and often hit me. She would tell me to be quiet, that the baby was sleeping. Or to go fix my brother some food and make sure he ate it. I hated making my brother food. I knew he'd never eat it and that it would get old and stinky before she'd finally give in and throw it away. The smell of rotten food permeated our house. I hated the stench." I lay still in Woods's arms. I knew that what I was telling him was disturbing. I knew it would bother him, but it was helping. He had been right. Talking about what I'd lived through with someone who loved me, not just a psychiatrist, helped.

"When she was rocking the baby doll she would eventually realize it was plastic. I never knew what it was she saw but she would start screaming *demon child* and she would throw it across the room like it was on fire. Then she would claw at herself and pull her hair. She would tell the doll she was sorry that she had let him go to the store. She was sorry that she hadn't kept him safe. But then she would point and scream *demon* at it again. I didn't usually watch that part except for once. It terrified me. When she started screaming I would hurry back to my room and close my door. That's what I was dreaming about tonight. One of those moments."

Woods let out a long, shaky breath. "Shit," he whispered, then pressed his face to the top of my head. He didn't say anything else. He just held me. That was what I needed the most.

It didn't feel like I thought it would, opening myself up like that to him. I had always thought that showing someone what was inside, what had been my life, would expose me in a way that would make me unlovable. But I didn't feel that way in Woods's arms. He held me tightly to him and kissed my head. No other words were needed.

My eyes closed and I relaxed in his arms. I had always felt safe with Woods. That wasn't new. But now . . . now I felt like I'd found my anchor. My entire life I'd held on to anything I thought could hold me still and keep me from going under. I had clung to Braden for years, hoping that having her would remind me I was normal. That I wasn't in that house anymore. But even though she loved me, she had never made me feel completely secure. She couldn't give me the grounding I needed. I thought no one would ever be able to give that to me. Not after all I'd seen and lived through. I knew now that it wasn't true. With Woods's arms wrapped around me and the beat of his heart pressed against my chest, I knew he would hold me steady. If I ever fell, I'd have him to catch me.

Woods

I had drunk three cups of coffee that morning to prepare myself for the early tee time I had with Nile. After Della had told me about her dream last night and shared her memories, I hadn't been able to sleep. I'd wanted to hold her and watch her sleep. The idea of her having another dream like that and my not being awake to stop it scared the shit out of me.

That was fucked up. What she'd lived through was more fucked up than I could even imagine. She worried that she wasn't strong enough, but, damn, anyone who had lived through what she had and still functioned normally day to day was strong. Della did more than function. She laughed, she made friends, she enjoyed life, she made me smile, and she completed my world. She was the strongest person I had ever met.

"Sorry I'm late. The girls woke up early and I was trying to get them something to eat so they could watch television and let their mother sleep late," Nile said, interrupting my thoughts.

With his dark hair and blue eyes, he looked so much like Della that it was hard for me not to stare at him. There was no arguing that this man was her father. "No worries. I haven't been here long," I assured him.

"You want a caddy?" I asked. I never used one but most members did.

Nile glanced over at the golf cart I had already pulled around with my clubs and a set from the clubhouse. He had mentioned last night that he hadn't brought his clubs with him.

"No, I think I'd like it to be just us," he said with a smile.

He wanted to talk about Della. I figured as much. Which was why I hadn't already had a caddy on standby.

"All right, then we're ready to go. I have water in the cooler but if you want something more, a cart will be around by the time we get to the third hole. We can order something from it if you prefer."

"Water's great. Too early for anything else," he replied.

I drove us to the first hole. "Della is looking forward to meeting the girls and your wife down at the beach today." They had planned a beach day. Nile was going to join them after our game. I was going to go work and give Della time alone with them.

"The girls can't wait to see Della again. They really took to her. Jillian adores her, too."

I parked the cart. "Della's hard not to adore," I said before getting out.

"Yeah, she is. She's much like her mother . . . uh, Glenda, that way."

I hadn't met Glenda but I wanted to. Della looked like her birth father but she didn't have his personality.

Nile pulled his driver from the bag. "Della seems happy here," he said.

"She is," I replied.

He didn't move to set up his shot. He studied me instead. "You haven't proposed to her. And I couldn't help but notice she didn't make it sound like marriage was in her near future last night when the girls were questioning her."

Not a conversation I had expected to have with him today. I pulled my driver from the bag and tried not to get pissed by this line of questioning. "We haven't talked about marriage yet."

Nile nodded. "I see," he said.

What the hell did "I see" mean? I was going to marry Della.

"I'm going to shoot straight with you, Woods. You're a good man. You have a bright future. When the woman you want to marry walks into your life, you will know it and you will want to be married to her. So, seeing as how you aren't thinking of marriage to Della just yet, I know, as a man, that you aren't sure she's the one for you. I was going to wait but I have decided to ask Della to move to Phoenix and live with us. Jillian is on board with this idea. We stayed up most of last night talking about it. We have an extra bedroom and Della can finish school. She's only twenty. She needs a family around her."

I could hear what he was saying but I felt like I had just stepped outside of myself and was watching this conversation happening. This wasn't real. It couldn't be real. This man was not suggesting taking Della away from me. I shook my head before he finished talking and he stopped midsentence.

"No," was all I managed to say. He had blindsided me. I hadn't expected this.

"No?" he repeated as if he didn't understand that word.

"No," I repeated. "You're not taking Della away from me. I'll follow her. Anywhere she goes I will follow her. She's it for me. She isn't going to Phoenix. She's staying here with me. I'm going to marry her. No, I haven't proposed yet, but I intend to. She just came back to me. She's finally facing the horrors of her past and letting me help her heal. She's mine, Nile. She is mine. She's not going anywhere."

Nile studied me a moment, then he nodded. A smile touched his lips. "That's what I wanted to hear," he said, then turned and walked to the tee as if the conversation were over. It wasn't fucking over until he told me he wasn't asking Della to move to Phoenix.

"What does that mean?" I demanded.

Nile glanced back at me over his shoulder. "You showed passion and determination to keep her. You want her forever. I wanted to make sure. Now I just need to make sure she wants the same thing."

"You mean you lied to me to get me to admit I was going to marry her?" I asked. I wasn't sure I liked this man anymore.

"No. I'm very serious. If Della wants to move to Phoenix with us, then I'm taking her. I will spend every damn dime I have making up for the fact that I was a kid when she was born and didn't know any better. I will give her a family and I'll make sure she feels loved and a part of my family. But I needed to know that if I leave her here, then she'll have someone who loves her with the passion that forever requires."

Wait . . . he was still asking her to move to Phoenix? "Della isn't just mine. I belong to her."

Nile nodded. "Good. If she feels the same way she will tell me no when I ask her to move to Phoenix. If she does, I will know that she has a happy future ahead of her. I will also expect an invitation to the wedding."

"She won't leave me," I said with more force than necessary.

"I guess we will see. Won't we?" he said before giving his complete attention to his swing.

Della

Jasmine may have only been a couple minutes older than Jocelyn but she seemed years older. She laid out on a towel as if she were a teenager and talked to me about name-brand clothing, which I knew nothing about, but I tried hard to follow along.

Jocelyn and July asked me to build a sand castle with them, then we played in the waves until seaweed wrapped around July's leg and sent her screaming to the shore.

Jillian and I talked when the girls gave us a chance, but I preferred playing with them. They were so full of life. Nile had been a good father. They loved him. They all called him Daddy, which I thought was endearing.

"Are you going to come live with us? I heard Daddy talking to Mommy about it late last night. They thought I was sleeping." Jasmine watched me carefully.

I wasn't prepared for that question. She had waited until her mother had gotten up to take July to the restroom. I couldn't figure out why Nile would even think to ask me to come live with them. I was happy here. I had a home.

"I have a home here," I told her.

She nodded. "Yeah, but Daddy said you aren't engaged

and it didn't look like you were going to get engaged. He was thinking you could live with us and go to college. We could be your family."

I was pretty sure Nile had never meant for me to know about this conversation. "I don't think we should be talking about this. If your dad wants me to know about it, then he will talk to me about it."

Jasmine rolled over and looked up at me. "He's going to. Just so you know."

Was this kid really nine? She acted like she was fifteen.

"Here comes Daddy now," she said with a smirk.

I glanced back over my shoulder to see Nile walking toward us in a pair of blue and yellow plaid shorts and a white polo shirt. He looked like he'd just walked off the golf course.

"Daddy," Jocelyn squealed from next to her attempts at another sand castle, and went running to him. He reached down and picked her up and hugged her. Then he pretended to care that she'd gotten sand on him. It was cute.

"Hey, Daddy, what did you shoot?"

"Seventy-nine. I'm rusty. Woods shot a seventy. It was impressive."

I was glad that they'd gotten to spend time together. Nile and his family were going home tomorrow. I wasn't sure if, or when, I would see them again.

"How have you girls fared out here on the beach?" he asked, sitting down beside me.

"Other than the time July got seaweed on her leg, I think we've done brilliantly," I told him.

Jasmine laughed. "It was epic."

Nile looked over at her and grinned. "I can only imagine." He looked around. "Where are Jillian and July?"

"Restroom," I explained.

We sat there a few minutes and didn't say much. Jocelyn kept calling out to us to look at her sand castle, but other than that we all remained quiet.

Finally, Jasmine and July returned and July plopped down in Nile's lap and told him every second of everything he'd missed. He listened to her like he was hearing the most intriguing story ever told. She expected it, too. She was secure in the fact that her dad wanted to listen to her. He wanted to know what she had to say.

"Girls, let's go down and get our feet wet and leave Daddy to talk to Della for a few minutes," Jillian said, standing up and holding her hand out for July to take.

I glanced at Jasmine, who was giving me an *I told you so* look before she stood up and followed her mother and sisters down to the water.

"Why don't you and I go for a walk?" Nile suggested, standing up and holding out his hand for me to take so he could help me up. I didn't need his help but he was wired to be a gentleman, so I let him.

We began walking and I waited for him to say something.

"I want you to move back to Phoenix with us, Della. We have an extra bedroom over the bonus room. It would give you privacy and you would have a separate entrance into the house. You could go to school out there and we could all get to know each other better. The girls love you. Jillian thinks you're great. We all want you to come live with us, though I know you have a life here."

"Della!" Woods's voice broke into Nile's surprising offer and I stopped and turned around to see Woods running toward me. What was he doing here?

"Well, I'll be damned," Nile said beside me with an amused tone. I didn't have time to focus on him and his offer. Woods looked upset.

"Woods?" I searched his face to see if there was something wrong. Was someone hurt?

"Don't leave me," he said, grabbing my arms and taking a deep breath like he had been running for a few miles.

"What are you talking about? I'm not leaving you."

He looked over at Nile, then back at me with determination in his eyes. "I love you. You're my one. My all-in. Don't leave me."

Had Nile told him he was going to ask me to leave with him? If he had, then why would Woods even think I would go? Had I made him feel that insecure about us? Of course I had. I had run off and left him with nothing but a letter. I reached up and grabbed Woods's face and looked into his eyes. I needed him to hear me.

"I'm not leaving you. Ever. You'll have to send me packing to get me to leave, and then I plan on fighting back. I will handcuff myself to you and refuse to budge. Nothing will make me leave. Nothing." I brushed my thumbs over his cheekbones; it was really unfair how they were so perfect.

"He's going to ask you to go to Phoenix," he said, watching my face.

"I know. He just did. Doesn't mean I'm going," I told him, and smiled up at his beautiful, troubled face.

"So, you're not leaving me?" he asked.

I shook my head and dropped my hands from his face and turned to look at Nile. "The fact that you and Jillian and the girls would be willing to accept me into your family so easily is humbling. I am touched. I want to get to know you and them. But I won't be leaving Rosemary. I won't be leaving Woods. He's my family. The people here are my family. I don't need another one. I have what I need here."

Nile didn't look hurt or ready to argue. Instead, I could see a pleased expression light up his face. "As much as I wanted you to come live with me and give us a chance to become a family, I'm thankful that you have someone who loves you like that," he said, nodding his head at Woods. "I can trust him to take care of you and know you're okay. I didn't take care of you when you needed it. Now that I've found you, I want you to be happy and safe. I believe this man can give you that."

Woods pulled me against him.

"He can. He does that and so much more," I replied.

Woods

It was time for the end-of-summer beach bonfire. The past two months had been perfect. Della was sharing more and more of her past with me and her dreams were starting to completely go away. She'd woken me up in the middle of the night the week before last to tell me she'd had a dream about us. That we'd been having sex on the kitchen table. She'd been so excited to have a dream that didn't contain the horrors of her past that she'd been ready to play it out in real life.

It was a pretty damn good way to wake up.

I watched as she held Nate and danced around with him as the music pumped through the speakers. Blaire was in Rush's lap and they were watching Della with their son. She was beautiful. I wanted to see her dance around and laugh with our baby. I wanted her to have a child to love the way she was never loved. I wanted to know we had created something from the love that bound us so tightly together.

"She's happy," Jace said.

"She's perfect," I replied.

Jace laughed and slapped me on the back. "Just go ahead and do it. You know you want to. Put that little ring on her finger."

"I'm planning it. Has to be special."

Jace sighed. "Yeah, I'm planning it, too. Bethy and I've had a hard summer but things are looking better. She's stopped running off to bars. I think she just had a dark time there for a while. She's been spending time with Blaire and Della again. That helps."

Jace hadn't shown up on my doorstep upset about Bethy in two months. I was hoping things were better. "Good. Glad you two are working it out."

"Oh, shit. Is that Nan?" Jace said, pointing her out to me. "I thought she left and went to Paris for the summer. Seeing Nan is gonna send Grant into a tailspin again." Grant wasn't at the party; he was out of town. That was happening a lot lately. He would show up for a couple of days then leave again. I was just glad he wasn't wasting time with Nan.

"Grant has moved on. If Nan's back, then he'll be fine. She was a bad mistake. He knows that now."

Jace let out a low whistle. "She's with August Schweep. What, did she bring him back from Paris with her?"

"No. August is our new golf pro. We needed more than just Marco. When August hurt his rotator cuff his pro career was over. He wants to retire here, so he bought the Spencer house. He's working for me now."

"Looks like Nan is all over that."

"Good. At least it's not Grant."

Jace snorted. "Ain't that the truth."

I was going to get Della and take her for a walk. The dark beach was a great place to get her alone. Turning, I glanced out over the water and saw Bethy staggering out to the waves. She knew better than that. There was a red flag up. Had been all week. The riptides were intense and it was dark. You don't swim in the gulf in the dark.

"Jace, man, what's Bethy doing?" I asked, afraid to take my eyes off her.

"What is she doing now? She was drinking tequila shots earlier and I cut her off. She'd had enough . . . shit!"

"She's getting too deep," I said, taking a step toward the water. Jace took off running toward the water. I followed behind him. I heard someone scream from the crowd as Bethy's head went under the water. *No.* This couldn't be happening.

Jace dove into the waves and took off toward her. I pulled my shirt off, afraid it would slow me down, before I dove in after him. I wasn't letting my best friend go into this alone.

Bethy's gurgling scream filled the air.

"Relax, baby! Relax. Don't fight it. Please don't fight it. You'll go under and won't have the strength to rise back up," Jace was yelling as he swam toward her.

I saw him grab her just as the deathly pull of a rip current grabbed him. This wasn't happening. No.

"I need you to take her, Woods!" Jace yelled over the water's roar.

"Give me both your hands!" I shouted.

"*No!* Take her. I got this. Take her, dammit! It's strong!" Jace yelled.

How was I supposed to take her and leave him out there? "Come with me, Jace!" I demanded.

"Woods, listen to me—" His head went under and he came back up as he held a panicking Bethy in his arms. "You have to take her or we'll all die. I'm not gonna let her drown. Help me!"

I nodded. I had to do this. He could get out of the current.

He was strong and he was smart. We had grown up knowing how to fight rip currents. I reached for Bethy as she screamed Jace's name.

"I love you," he told her as he let her go. She cried as she clung to my arms.

"Don't say that!" I yelled at him. "You're getting out of this. Don't fucking say that."

"Just get her out of here!" he yelled, pushing her away from him and toward me as he held on to her arm.

I could feel the pull getting closer. If I stayed here much longer I was going to get pulled into it, too. I wrapped my hand around Bethy's arm and pulled her out of the current, then tucked her under my arm and I started swimming back to shore.

Rush came swimming up to us and relief surged through me. I was going to be able to help Jace.

"Give her to me," Rush said as he reached for Bethy.

"Go get him," she cried as Rush pulled her from my arms.

I didn't wait for them to leave before I turned back around to get Jace.

But Jace wasn't there.

I glanced back at the shore to see if he'd made his way back up there and I'd missed it, but all I saw was Rush carrying Bethy out of the water.

I turned back to the dark waves. I was met with silence. Nothing.

He was just here. I just saw him. He isn't gone. It didn't happen that fast.

I went under and forced my eyes open in the salty water, but all I could see was the darkness. I needed light. I reached around me, feeling for anything. My lungs started to burn. Kicking up, I broke the surface and took a deep breath. I heard my name from the shore. They were yelling for me. I also heard Jace's name. I couldn't go back without him.

I went back under. I had to find Jace. I couldn't lose Jace. Not like this. Not now. We were supposed to be grumpy old men together. I fought back the panic starting to set in with each second that I couldn't find him. I swam underwater and fought the pull of the current as I reached out for some sign of him. Anything I could get my hands on.

When my lungs couldn't take it anymore, I swam back to the top, only to be taken back under by a wave before I could breathe. I wasn't going down like this. I had to find Jace.

Two arms grabbed ahold of me and jerked me to the surface as I started gasping for air and coughing.

"Dammit, Woods. Come on. You're gonna drown in this. He's gone, man. He's gone. I'm not letting you drown, too." Rush's words sent a shock through my system. *He's gone? No. No! He isn't gone.* I fought against Rush's hold on me.

"Stop it! Della is up there in a crumpled mess, crying. Do you want to leave her? Is that what you want? To leave her like this?"

Della. Oh God. Della. I couldn't leave her. But I'd lost Jace. I had lost Jace.

Rush pulled us out of the waves and when my feet hit the sand he let me go. We stood there staring at each other and breathing hard. We knew what had happened and what we were going to face. I would have been gone, too, if Rush hadn't come after me. I would have left Della behind.

I turned to see her getting up from the sand where she had

been on her knees. Her face was red and soaked with tears. All she said was, "Woods," before she threw herself into my arms.

I watched in a daze as Blaire stood holding a hysterical Bethy. Sirens wailed in the distance. Sobs and cries filled the beach. And I stood there. Della clung to me. Her sobs eased but her hold never did.

Rush walked over to take his crying son from Nan's arms. He held him to his chest, and although he wasn't crying the loss and pain were in his eyes.

Me . . . I just felt empty.

Della

I had thought that I knew terror. That I knew fear. I had seen my mother lying in a pool of her own blood. That was fear. But seeing Woods out in that water going under and not coming up—that had been all-consuming terror. Nothing compared to that. Nothing.

Jace hadn't come back up, though. My chest hurt so bad I couldn't take deep breaths. Jace was gone. I had seen it happen, and the broken sobs coming from Bethy as Blaire held her on the sand only ripped through me harder. I couldn't imagine that. That had almost been me. That could have been me on that sand, knowing the man I loved wasn't coming back to me.

Woods's body shuddered and reality started to hit me. The idea of losing him had been all I could think about. But he'd been out there for a reason. He had gone to save his best friend. He'd watched his best friend be pulled under, unable to save him.

I tightened my hold on him. How was he going to survive this?

Bethy continued to wail and Woods's body went stiff. He was strung so tight he was trembling.

“Get her the fuck out of my sight!” he roared. I jumped back, startled by the angry hate that laced his words. His eyes were glaring and focused on someone behind me. I turned to see that he was looking at Bethy.

Blaire’s face went pale and Bethy cried harder.

“I said to get her selfish, trashy ass off my beach! *Now!*”

I swallowed hard and watched as Bethy looked up at him with big, pain-filled eyes.

Rush was behind Blaire, helping Bethy stand up. I heard him telling her they needed to take Bethy somewhere else. Woods was yelling at Bethy. He was blaming her.

“Woods?” I was almost afraid of the man in front of me. He swung his gaze to mine and there was an emptiness in them I couldn’t reach.

“She killed him,” he said simply.

Maybe she had. She had gone into the water and almost drowned. Jace had died saving her. But she had been drinking.

“She loved him,” I said.

Woods shook his head. “No. She didn’t love him. You don’t do what she did and call that love.”

I glanced back and saw Blaire lead Bethy up to the boardwalk. The cops would want to question her. She wouldn’t be able to go far.

“Woods, she lost him, too. We all did,” Thad said as he stood watching Woods, afraid to get too close.

“I lost him because he wanted me to save her worthless, drunk ass. I did what he wanted and I lost him.” Woods’s voice was cold and emotionless.

Headlights lit up the beach as ambulances and police cars arrived. Paramedics swarmed the stretch of sand and I watched as they were told by several of the people at the party what they had seen. A paramedic approached Woods.

"You were one of the people who were in the water?" he asked.

"Yes," Woods replied.

"We need to check you out," he said.

"No."

I watched as the paramedic started to argue and stepped between him and Woods. "He's fine. If I think he needs medical attention I will make sure he gets it. Please, he needs to be left alone."

The man looked up at Woods and then back at me. "Okay," he said, then turned away.

"I'm not leaving until they've found him," Woods said.

I turned around and reached for his hand. He laced his fingers through mine. "Okay," I said. "We'll stay right here."

"You'll stay with me?" he asked.

"I'm not leaving your side."

"Thank you."

◇

We sat there for the next four hours. Rush had brought Woods a blanket from one of the ambulances to keep him from getting cold since he was soaking wet. He didn't say anything, he just dropped it on his shoulders. Rush had been out there, too. He had been the reason Woods hadn't drowned. They had both lived this nightmare.

After the police questioned Bethy, Darla came and took her home. Blaire took Nate and went home at Rush's insistence. The crowd had thinned. Helicopters spotlighted the dark water and boats searched in vain. It was impossible to see in the dark.

Woods sat there beside me, not letting go of my hand and staring at the water. Watching them look for Jace. He wanted Jace's body found. I understood that. He didn't want to leave the beach until he knew Jace wasn't out there alone.

Finally, the helicopters left. The boats went away. The paramedics packed up and drove off. A police officer tried to get us to leave but they weren't going to argue with the owner of the Kerrington Club. They finally left us.

We weren't alone, though. Rush stood off in the distance, his hands in the pockets of his jeans. At some point he'd changed clothes. He was staring off at the dark water, too. I kept thinking this was a dream I would wake up from, but it never ended. I glanced over to our left and Thad sat there on the sand with his arms wrapped around his legs and his knees bent, like a little boy who was lost.

They all hurt.

And there was nothing I could do. Nothing anyone could do.

The sound of the ocean crashing against the shore wasn't soothing like it had once been. It now felt like a taunt. Reminding us that it was stronger. It was in control.

Someone else moved in the darkness and I watched as Grant came running down the boardwalk. He hadn't been at the party. I never knew if he was in town or somewhere else. The guy never stayed in one place.

He stopped at Rush and Rush turned his eyes to look at him. They stood there for a moment, then Grant hung his head and dropped to his knees.

It was morning when the searchers found Jace's body washed up one mile down the shore.

Woods

I stood under the shower spray and let Della wash me. She washed my hair and body so methodically and thoroughly. She never said a word. She didn't ask me questions. She was just there beside me. I needed her to stay there. If she left me I was afraid the reality would set in and I couldn't let it. It hurt too fucking much.

"You're clean," Della said softly, opening the shower door and stepping out. She picked up a towel and began to dry me. And I let her.

When she was finished she wrapped the towel around herself and pressed a kiss to my chest. "Go, get in bed. You need to sleep," she told me.

She turned to walk away and I reached out and grabbed her hand. "Don't leave me." The words sounded more like pleading. They didn't sound like me at all.

She shook her head. "I'm not. I just need to get dry. I'll be in bed in a minute," she assured me.

"I'll wait," I told her as I stood there. I was scared of my own nightmares now. I couldn't lie down and face them without her with me.

"Okay. I'll hurry," she said. I saw the sadness and pain in her eyes.

She dried off her body and wrapped the towel around her hair, then went to the dresser. When she opened it and pulled out a pair of panties, I moved toward her.

"No. Don't wear clothes." I wanted her in my arms just like this. I wanted her warmth to reach my empty coldness inside. She was the only reason I was still alive. If it hadn't been for her I wouldn't have stopped until I'd drowned, too.

"Okay."

She reached for my hand and took me over to the bed. I lay down and she climbed in beside me, then pulled the covers up over us. *If Rush hadn't come back I wouldn't be here now.* I held on to her tighter.

She would've been here without me. I didn't want to think about that. Not being there to protect her. To hold her. Not being there to spend forever with her.

"I came back for you." My voice sounded hoarse.

She tilted back her head and looked up at me. "Thank you."

I didn't say anything else. I wasn't sure what to say. Within minutes, my eyes were too heavy to hold open and the smooth heat of Della's skin gave me the comfort I needed to fall asleep.

◇

When I opened my eyes, I stared at the ceiling. It was late afternoon. I could tell by the sunlight through the windows. Della's slow, even breathing told me she was still asleep. I hadn't dreamed. Thank God.

I hadn't wanted to dream. It all replayed over and over again in my head. Jace was going to propose to Bethy. He'd been ready to spend his life with her. We had been right there together and everything had been fine.

Then Bethy had changed all that. She'd turned a summer night we were all supposed to enjoy together into a nightmare. One that would never leave us. One that we would all relive over and over the rest of our lives. Remembering the helpless feeling of knowing he was gone and there was nothing we could do to bring him back.

I had lived on this beach my entire life. We had seen more than one death from the water but it had never been a death that impacted me. It had never been someone I loved. It had never been real.

It was real now.

Della moved in my arms and I held her tighter. She was my glue right now. Being able to touch her was keeping me together. Last night she'd sat right there on that beach, refusing to let go of my hand.

When they had found his body she had wrapped her arms around me and used every ounce of strength to hold me as they covered him and took him. I couldn't have made it without her. Holding her reminded me that I was alive. I hadn't drowned. When she walked away from me or left me for even a moment, I was under that wave again, being sucked away and unable to fight it.

"Woods?" Della's concerned voice brought me out of my head and I blinked, then focused on her face. "I'm here," she said simply, and brushed the hair from my forehead.

I reached up and touched her face. I didn't have words just yet. I couldn't talk about it. I just needed her near me.

She moved her body over mine until she was on top of me.

She straddled my waist and pressed small kisses to my neck and shoulders. This was her way of easing my pain. I could feel it in each gentle brush of her lips. Her hips moved down until I could feel her wet heat slide over me. The contact was all I needed to be ready.

Della lifted her hips and I slid into her with ease. When I was completely inside she leaned forward and rested her head on my heart. We stayed there a few moments. Joined in a way that only she could achieve.

When her hips began to rock against me she didn't seek my mouth or get frantic with her need for release. She just loved me. She used her body to love me and hold me in the most intimate way.

I wrapped my arms around her and held her against me. We moved with each other in a perfect rhythm that was selfless. Its purpose was to heal and comfort. When Della's warmth began to tighten around me and her body started to tremble, I cried out her name and she followed me.

After I filled her with my release she didn't move from me. She held me inside her as we stared into each other's eyes. All the pain and devastation of last night was there. We didn't need words.

"He would have wanted you to come back," she finally said.

"I know," I told her.

She pressed a kiss to my cheek. "He loved you."

"I know."

Della

The beach was empty. It was the middle of the day in August and the beach was empty. Almost forty-eight hours had passed since Jace drowned. Tourists had already gone back to their lives. It was the locals who were left to mourn. Woods hadn't wanted to leave the house yet. I was going to have to make him eventually but I didn't want to push him.

I thought I should call Tripp but I didn't know what to say. He was probably with family. I would see him tomorrow at the funeral. I knew that. I just felt like I should call. Say something. He would mourn this just as hard as Woods. Jace was his cousin. He was like his little brother.

Then there was Bethy. I hadn't called Bethy. I wasn't sure how Woods would react to that. He obviously blamed her for Jace's death. I was afraid he always would. I wasn't sure if forgiveness could be granted to her for this. Not from Woods.

Rush had dropped by that morning to check on Woods. He had still been sleeping. I'd told him I'd let Woods know he came by. Grant had stopped by an hour later. His red-rimmed eyes reminded me of Woods's hollow look.

Woods hadn't been awake then, either. He had slept until eleven. When he realized I wasn't in bed with him he had jumped up and come after me. He hadn't said anything but pulled me into his lap. We had sat there for an hour in silence.

Finally, I had told him about Rush and Grant stopping by. Then I'd convinced him to get dressed and eat something. I turned from my view of the gulf and walked back into the kitchen to check on the chicken Parmesan I had put in the oven.

Woods walked out of the bedroom freshly showered and dressed in jeans and a T-shirt. "I need to go to the office today," he said.

"Lunch is almost ready. Can you eat first?" I really wanted him to eat.

"After we eat I want us both to go. I want you with me."

I didn't ask why, I just nodded. Right now he seemed to need me. I would be whatever he needed me to be. It was my turn to be the strong one. This time I would be his shoulder to lean on.

"It smells good," he said as he walked around the counter to kiss me. He was doing that a lot lately too. More than normal. Sometimes they were desperate, hungry kisses that led to more, but most of the time they were kisses that held words he couldn't say.

"I need to go to the store. I worked with what we had," I explained as I pulled the chicken out of the oven. I kept myself busy fixing us each a plate and toasting some bread and buttering it.

"Soda?" I asked him.

"Do we have sweet tea?" he asked.

We did. I had made it that morning. I fixed him a glass while he carried our food to the table.

"Thank you," he said as I set the drink down in front of him.

"You're welcome."

He reached up and grabbed my hand. "No. Thank you for being exactly what I needed and knowing when I wanted to speak and when I didn't." That was one of the longest sentences he'd said since we'd come home from the beach.

"I will always be whatever you need me to be," I said simply before taking my seat.

We ate for a few minutes in silence.

"I need to see his parents . . . and Tripp. He's called my phone twice. I should see him, too."

"Okay."

"I want you to go with me."

"Okay," I agreed.

Woods looked out at the water. "Do you know when the funeral is?"

"Yes. Rush said it was tomorrow at two."

His jaw worked as he stared out the window. "Will Bethy be there?"

"Yes. I'm sure she will be," I replied.

His jaw continued to shift like he was clenching his teeth.

I reached over and took his hand. "Woods. She loved him, too. She made a mistake that she'll have to live with for the rest of her life, but she did love him. You know that."

"I can't forgive her," he said.

"I understand that. But remember, he loved her. He loved her enough to die for her. She's suffering. Don't doubt that. She's suffering because she knows why this happened. You can hate her but try to remind yourself of the pain she has to be going through. And that Jace loved her more than he loved himself."

Woods didn't say anything; he just sat there, letting me hold his hand while he stared out the window.

◇

Everyone in Rosemary was at the funeral. There were more people there than I'd ever seen at any event in town. Bethy was lifeless. Her face was pale and her cheeks were hollowed. She stood beside her aunt Darla and a man I assumed was her father. Jace's parents I had seen a few times at the club. His mother's eyes were red and swollen as she clung to his father's arm. Tripp stood to the side of them. He was dressed in a dark suit. You couldn't see his tattoos and he looked nothing like a biker bartender but more like the Ivy League graduate that he would have been if he hadn't run from his parents' plans for him.

Woods held on to my hand like it was his lifeline. He hadn't let it go since we arrived. Rush also held Blaire's hand just as tightly. Nate wasn't with them today.

Grant stood on the other side of Rush, his hands tucked in his front pockets and his face pinched in a permanent frown. It looked like he was trying not to cry.

The others were there, too, but I couldn't see them from where we were standing.

Each one of them had had an impact on the others' lives.

They all had stories.

They had all loved, and many had lost.

They had expected to grow up and become adults together. Get married and let their kids play together.

They'd planned on being the next generation in Rosemary.

What they hadn't planned on was losing one of their own. Losing a member of their tight group. They hadn't seen their future minus one. Death hadn't touched them before. Not like this. Not one of them.

Everything was about to change.

Bethy

My entire life I had loved the sound of the waves. The natural beauty of the gulf. I was proud to live in such a special place.

But that had all changed.

The crashing waves were cruel. It had been two weeks since the water had taken Jace from me. Two weeks since I cheated death and it had taken the man I loved instead.

"It should have been me," I screamed at the water. I wanted it to know it had messed up and taken the wrong life.

"He wouldn't have agreed with you."

I didn't want to hear that voice. Not now. Not now that Jace was gone. I wanted him to go away.

"No one should have died, Bethy. And Jace made sure it wasn't you. It wasn't the water who took the wrong person. Jace made that decision." I wanted to cover my ears like a child and scream at him to go away. I didn't want him here. Why was he still here? He knew it was my fault. He knew this was all my fault, yet he didn't look at me with hate in his eyes the way Woods did.

"Go away," I said without looking back at him.

"I'm not leaving again."

Those were not words I wanted to hear right now. Maybe

five years ago I would have loved to have heard Tripp Newark tell me he was staying in Rosemary, but not now. Any and all feelings I had for Tripp had died the day I walked out of the abortion clinic Aunt Darla had taken me to, with an ache in my chest where my heart used to be.

"You can do what you want. Just stay away from me," I snapped, finally turning my angry glare on him. He was still just as beautiful as he had been when I was sixteen and stupid. He had said pretty words and I had believed him.

"I will for now. But I've been running for five years, Bethy."

It wasn't my fault he had been running. He had left me without an explanation or apology. He hadn't answered my phone calls. Nothing. Not even the message I'd left him after I had killed our baby. I had been devastated. He hadn't even called me back then.

"*I loved him!*" I yelled, and pointed my finger at Tripp. "*I loved Jace!* It was *real*! Damn you! It was real. Don't come to me and tell me you're coming back. Don't tell me you're tired of running. I don't give a motherfucking shit! I loved him." My angry screams had turned to sobs, but I didn't care. He'd asked for this. He should have stayed away from me.

"I loved him," I said one more time before turning to walk away.

"I loved him, too. He was like my brother. He was everything I wasn't. He was good. He was honest. He was strong. He deserved you."

I stopped and let the pain slice through me. *He's gone. How could he be gone?*

"I'm sorry, Bethy. I'm sorry that I just left you that summer. I was young and stupid. My parents wanted things for me I didn't want and I was scared of becoming my dad. So I ran like hell. I wanted to tell you. Dammit, I wanted to take you with me, but you were sixteen years old. You were an even bigger kid than I was. What was an eighteen-year-old trust fund brat going to do taking care of a sixteen-year-old?"

It was the past. Nothing he said made up for what he'd done. It was over. I had let it go and buried it and moved on.

"I was in love with you, Bethy. You were the first girl I ever loved. You've been the only girl I've ever loved. I never wanted to hurt you. When Jace was smart enough to fall in love with you I knew you'd be okay. He would give you everything you deserved."

"Shut up!" I snapped, spinning around and glaring at him "Just shut up! He didn't know! He loved me and he trusted me and he didn't know. I never told him. I wasn't worthy of him. I was never worthy of him. I was a liar. I'm tainted. I'm dirty."

Tripp took a step toward me. "No, you're not. Just because you trusted me with your love and then gave me your virginity . . . Bethy, that doesn't make you tainted or dirty. What we had wasn't wrong. It was real. I was too young to deal with it but it was very fucking real. It never left me."

Giving him my virginity was stupid. I had been a good girl then. Sex had equaled love to me. But Tripp had changed all that. He had turned me into something that Jace saved me from. The girl Tripp had destroyed, Jace had salvaged and cherished.

"No. Loving you was stupid, not wrong. Trusting you with my virginity was a mistake, not dirty. But killing the baby that we created because you didn't care enough to return my calls . . . that's what made me unworthy of someone like Jace."

I turned and walked away. This time he didn't try to stop me.

Della

I sat in the window of Woods's office and watched him read over some new contracts he needed to sign with a distributor that I had found for the clothing line in the clubhouse. What we had was for an older crowd. The members of the Kerrington Club weren't all fifty and above.

He hadn't wanted me out of his sight for longer than a few minutes. It had been two weeks since the funeral and he was still clingy. It was easing up each day, but he still needed me close by. We were also having sex more often than normal, and that was a whole lot of sex.

Blaire had called and invited me over for lunch today at one. That was Nate's nap time, so she was hoping we could meet at her house. Bethy was also invited. She wasn't working or showing up anywhere anymore. Blaire was worried about her and I was, too. Woods still wouldn't talk about her.

"Blaire has invited me to lunch today at her house at one. Are you okay with me going?" Normally I wouldn't have felt like I had to ask Woods's permission to eat lunch, but with his need for me to be close to him at all times, I wanted to check and make sure.

He looked up from his contract and frowned. I could see the sadness in his eyes and I almost wished I hadn't asked him and had just told Blaire no.

"I'm sorry, Della."

I stood up. "For what?"

"For making you think you have to ask me to go somewhere. These past couple of weeks I've been needy, and I'm sorry I've done that to you."

I pulled his chair back and straddled his lap, then grabbed both of his shoulders. "Do not apologize to me. Not for that. You needed me and I was able to be what you needed. I was the strong one this time. Not you. Me. I got to be the one to hold your hand. It was my turn to show you how much I love you. So, don't apologize for that."

Woods grinned. He hadn't grinned since before the accident. He lifted his hand and traced my jaw. "You're straddling my lap in a skirt. I want you to go but I'm also thinking about your panties and wondering if they're wet, or if I can get them wet. Hurry and stand up and get away from me before I do something that changes your plans."

Laughing, I jumped out of his lap. "Not that I wouldn't enjoy you checking to see if you could get my panties wet, because I assure you that you could, but Blaire seemed to really want to do lunch."

Woods nodded. "Go eat lunch with her. I'll be fine."

I blew him a kiss that he caught and pressed to his lips. Then I stepped through the door and closed it behind me.

"I heard laughter. It was nice," Vince said from his desk.

I nodded. "He's better," I told him.

"Because of you," he replied.

I just smiled because I knew he was right. I had helped Woods. It had been me.

◇

Blaire opened the door with Nate on her hip. His small hand was fisted in her long platinum hair and he was tugging pretty hard on it.

"Come in," she said with her head tilted in his direction. "Let me detangle myself and get this one in bed and I'll be right back. There's glasses and tea on the table in the kitchen. *Oh!* Nate, that hurts Mommy."

I tried not to laugh but a giggle leaked out.

She grinned and rolled her eyes. "He likes my hair. I'm going to end up bald because he's pulled it all out."

"Go save yourself. I'll get a drink," I told her, and she flashed me an appreciative smile and headed for the staircase. It was a grand, elaborate set of stairs. The whole house was pretty fabulous. It had been Rush's before Blaire. His dad had bought it for him when he was a kid. His mother used to live there when she was in town, but he wasn't on speaking terms with her at the moment.

I walked through the house and stopped to look at the life-sized portrait of Nate above the fireplace in the drawing room. His hair was going to be as pale as his mother's, or at least it looked like it now. The longer it got, the blonder it was.

The kitchen was at the other end of a long hallway with really high ceilings. There were framed photos of the three of them covering the walls. They weren't professional pictures but casual family photos of them playing at the beach or opening gifts at Christmas. There was even one with Rush on a slide with Nate in his lap. He so didn't look like the kind of guy to go down a slide.

Once I got to the kitchen, I fixed myself a glass of tea. The pantry door stood open and I walked over and peeked inside. I had heard about the hidden room under the stairs that you got to through the pantry. It had been where Rush had stuck Blaire when she first came to Rosemary looking for her dad.

Smiling, I wondered if they ever went in that room . . . to remember.

The doorbell rang again and Blaire's footsteps echoed as she came down the stairs. I had wondered if Bethy would come. I hadn't seen her anywhere else so I wasn't sure she would show up, even though Blaire was her best friend.

Both women walked into the room and Bethy's sad, empty eyes met mine. I set my glass down and went over to hug her. She looked like she needed a hug.

"I've missed you," I told her.

She wrapped her arms weakly around me. "Thanks," she sniffled.

"No crying. We're going to eat the cookies I made and not think about calories, and we're going to talk," Blaire announced as she picked up a covered tray, walked over to the table, and set it down.

I wasn't sure if this was going to work, but Blaire looked pretty determined. I watched Bethy as she tried to gather herself and took a seat across from me.

"Okay, so maybe we need to cry first," Blaire said as she saw Bethy's face crumple. "Talk to us. We're here to listen."

Bethy lifted her eyes and shook her head. "No, I'm tired of

crying. I'm tired of being sad. I just want to be able to smile again."

"We haven't lost the man we love but we both have lost people we love. I've lost my mother and my sister. Della lost her mother. We know it hurts and we want you to scream and yell, whatever you have to do to get it out. Then you need to eat cookies and think of funny stories that make you laugh. Think about things that Jace did to make you laugh. Remember him in the good ways. They will overcome the bad memory of that night. I promise you, they will."

Woods

Jimmy had called to tell me I needed to get Grant from the bar. He had drunk too much and was now calling my new golf pro a douchebag. Not a good thing. He'd regret that tomorrow.

I walked past Jimmy, who was shaking his head with an amused grin on his face. Grant was leaning on the bar, trying to convince the new bartender that he was a congressman and demanding another drink.

"I got this," I told the new guy, who looked very relieved.

Grant spun around and almost fell over a stool. "Hey, Woods! It's you. Get me another shot, buddy," he slurred. Grant only called people *buddy* when he was drinking.

"Not a chance in hell," I replied. "Come on, you're going home. You're done for the night."

Grant jerked his arm out of my grasp. "I don't wanna go home. I wanna stay here. I like it here. It's better here. If I go back to my place"—he lowered his voice, although he was still talking really loudly—"she will come."

"Who is she?" I asked, grabbing his arm and jerking him up. I started pushing him toward the door before he could protest this time.

"She is *she*," he said, whispering loudly again.

"She is she? Really? Man, how much have you had to drink?"

Once we were outside, Grant looked around and realized we had been walking. "Aww, damn. You tricked me. We left."

"Why don't you want to go to your place? You need to sleep this off."

Grant looked around us like he was looking for someone who might be hiding and waiting for him to tell a highly important secret.

"She's Nan. Always Nan. And she's pissed. When she gets pissed she gets possessive, then naughty, then she does things and I end up letting her, but now I don't want to let her 'cause I don't even like her. So I can't go home."

Nothing he had said made sense except that he didn't like Nan. Neither did the rest of the world. I was pretty damn sure there was a Twitter hashtag that said #NanHater.

"You want to crash in one of the rooms here?" I asked him as he stumbled and sat down on a bench.

"Can I? She can't find me here. Can she?"

I was pretty sure I hadn't seen him this drunk since boarding school. Nan had done a number on him. "You would think by now you would have learned your lesson about messing around with Nan. She's poison. Why even go near her?"

Grant let out a loud sigh and leaned forward.

"Do not puke on the damn brick. It's a country club, dickhead, not a bar."

He lifted his head and his eyes were glassy. "It ain't Nan that's making me drink. It's her. She's so damn . . . so damn . . . hell, I don't know what she is. She messed up my head. She fucked me over, literally. She won't see me. Won't talk to me.

Nothing. She's guarded like the damn queen. Bunch of damn rock stars act like I'm a problem. I'm not a problem. I just want to see her. I need to explain."

What the hell was he talking about? "I'm lost, dude. You're not making sense anymore. Come on, let's get you a room."

"She's got these legs that go on forever. Lots of legs . . . lots of 'em. They're soft. So fucking soft," he muttered as I jerked him up and walked him over to my truck.

"Nan?"

Grant spit. "Fuck no. I told you this ain't about Nan. She's the evil bitch that fucked it up. She fucks up everything."

I put him in and closed the door, then got in on my side and rolled down the windows. "If you need to hurl do it outside of my truck," I told him before cranking the engine.

"She's got these legs," he said again.

"Yeah, you told me."

"You don't understand, they're like legs from fucking heaven."

Someone had done a number on him. I was thankful it wasn't Nan. That was the only thing I was thankful for at the moment. If I could get him out of my truck without his puking, I'd be thankful for that, too.

"She was a virgin," he whispered.

Wait . . . what? "Now I know we aren't talking about Nan."

Grant leaned his head back on the leather seat. "A virgin. She didn't tell me, either. Now she won't talk to me. I need her to talk to me."

So Grant took a virgin and some rock stars are holding her captive. That doesn't make any . . . oh shit.

"Grant, are you talking about Harlow?"

"Yeah, who the fuck did you think I was talking about?"

That might just be worse than Nan.

Yeah . . . it's definitely worse than Nan.

He was in deep shit. Nan would never let that happen. Ever.

Two months later . . .

Della

Braden was pregnant. I had hung up with her over ten minutes ago but I hadn't moved from the swing on the porch. I continued to swing. I needed to let this process. *Braden . . . a mommy. My Braden. Wow . . .*

The door to the house opened and Woods stepped outside. "You off the phone?" he asked as he walked over to the swing.

"Yeah," I replied, scooting over so he could sit down with me.

"What is Braden up to?" he asked as he put his arm around me and pulled me over to his side.

"She's . . . she's pregnant." It was hard to even say it. I had always imagined Braden as a mom. She would make an excellent one, but just knowing that she was about to start another new step in life was a surprise.

"That's good, right?" Woods asked.

I smiled and nodded. I guess in the moment I took to process, I looked upset. "Yes, it's wonderful. They've been trying for a while now, apparently. I didn't know. She hadn't said anything. But she's now three months along and they heard the heartbeat yesterday. She feels it's safe to tell people now."

Woods pushed the swing with his feet so I curled mine back behind me and let him do the work. "She'll be a wonderful mother," I told him.

"I agree with you. She's pretty damn fierce when she loves someone."

I laughed and looked up at him. "Yes, she is."

Woods bent down and kissed the tip of my nose. "I love you."

"I love you more," I said in reply. That was always his line. I figured I would take it away from him.

He chuckled. "Thief."

I pinched the skin covering his abs and he squirmed.

We sat there for a while and enjoyed the evening breeze. Fall was here and Rosemary was peaceful again. The crowds were gone. Jace's absence still clung to us. We all felt it. We knew we always would. But lately we had all been able to talk about him again. Someone would tell a funny story about him and we would all laugh instead of cry.

Bethy was at work again but Woods still wasn't ready to speak to her. He knew he was wrong. He admitted it to me one night. But he said he couldn't forgive her. I let it go. I knew he just needed more time.

Tripp was also back in town. He had been gone for about a week and packed up his place in South Carolina. Then he'd moved back here into his condo. Woods had given him a place on the board of directors at the club.

"Della?"

"Yes?"

"Do you believe in fate?"

I thought about it a minute. I wasn't sure. I hadn't given much thought to the idea of fate before.

"What exactly do you mean by that?" I asked.

"I mean . . . do you think things happen for a reason, and no matter what we do or what we choose they'll happen anyway?"

He was thinking about Jace's death. He didn't want to hate Bethy. But his heart wasn't letting him forgive her because of his love for Jace.

"I think that everyone's life is controlled by a series of events. They choose what they want and if it is in their control they can reach it. Sometimes luck shines on them and sometimes it doesn't. I also think accidents happen and we are placed in situations where we have to do things for those we love that we don't want to do."

Woods didn't say anything.

I let him think about it. I wasn't going to push him to forgive Bethy.

That would be something he'd have to find within himself when he was ready.

Woods

I slipped my phone in my pocket and waited by my truck for Della's car to pull into the gas station. I had made sure her tank was low before I left the house an hour ago. She was going to need gas before she met me at the Mexican restaurant where we'd gone before our one-night stand. I had convinced her earlier that she wanted the quesadillas for dinner. Talking about melted cheese had been all I needed to get her to agree to drive the short distance out of town.

Her car turned the corner, and just like I'd planned she pulled up to the tank. She had already spotted my truck parked on the other side of the pump when she pulled up.

Her car door swung open and she was grinning at me like I was crazy.

"What are you doing here? I thought you were waiting on me at the restaurant."

I stepped around the pump and leaned against her car. "I believe we've been here before," I said, watching as she realized what I was talking about.

Her smile grew and her eyes twinkled with laughter. "Yes, I believe we have. But good news: this time I can pump my own gas," she said.

I had met her for the first time in this very spot. She'd been wearing tiny little shorts, looking sexy as hell, and had no idea how to pump gas. I had needed a distraction from my life and there she was.

"Damn, I was hoping I could pump it for you," I said.

She pressed her lips together in a smile and shrugged. "If you really want to, then you can."

"I need you to pop the door," I told her, pointing to the little door where the fuel went.

"Oh! I saw you and forgot to do that." I watched as she turned around and bent inside the car to push the button.

I reached into my pocket and pulled out the small box that I had kept hidden in my sock drawer for a week. Della turned around and started to say something but stopped when I went down on one knee.

"A year ago I was lost. My life was a fucked-up mess. I stopped to get gas right here and found this gorgeous brunette who couldn't pump her gas. I then somehow convinced her to eat with me. She made me laugh and made me horny as hell. When the night was over and I had to leave her sleeping on that bed in the hotel, it was hard. I didn't want to. But my life was fucked and she was traveling the world, finding herself."

I stopped as Della reached up and wiped a tear that was running down her face. Her big blue eyes were swimming with tears.

"Then she came back into my life and saved me from hell. She changed my world. She taught me to love and she owns my soul."

Della's small hand went up to cover her mouth and a sob came out.

"Della Sloane, will you marry me?"

She was nodding before I could get the words out of my mouth. I stood up and slipped the diamond that I'd spent weeks trying to find onto her finger. When I found it I had known it was the one. It was worthy enough to grace Della's hand.

"Yes," she finally said before throwing her arms around my neck. "Yes, yes, yes," she chanted, clinging to me.

I held her against me and realized that if there was no such thing as fate, then someone had to be up there dealing out winning hands.

"Can we skip the Mexican and go back to that hotel room instead?" I asked her.

She tilted her head back and flashed me a saucy smile. "What about your truck? I don't want to skip that part."

Neither did I.

Read on for a sneak peek at the next novel
by Abbi Glines set in the world
of Rosemary Beach

Take a Chance

The first book about Grant and Harlow

Grant

Why was I here? What was the fucking purpose? Had I gotten this bad? Really? In the past, I'd been able to shake her loose and walk away. Nanette had been my go-to fuck for years, but then she'd gotten needy. And I'd liked it. Somehow, she had managed to get under my skin. I had wanted to be wanted—I was that pathetic. My dad rarely called me; my mom had decided she preferred French models over me years ago.

I was screwed the hell up.

It was time I let this go. Nan had needed me for a time when she felt like she was losing Rush, her brother and safe place, to his new life with his wife and child. Not that Rush wouldn't welcome her with open arms—it was just that she was such a bitch. All she had to do was accept Rush's wife, Blaire. That was it. But the stubborn woman wouldn't do it.

Mine had been the arms she'd run into, and like a fool I had opened them up for her. Now, all I had was a lot of damn drama and a slightly damaged heart. She hadn't claimed it. Not completely. But she had touched a place no one else had. She had needed me. No one had ever needed me. It had made me weak.

To prove my point, here I sat in Nan's father's home, looking for her, waiting on her. She was running wild again, and Rush wasn't coming to the rescue. He had hung up his Superman cape and decided his days of coming to Nan's side were over. I had wanted that. As sick as it was, I had wanted to be her hero. Damn, I was a pussy.

"Drink, kid. Fuck knows you need it," Kiro, Nan's father, said as he shoved a half-empty bottle of tequila into my hands. Kiro was the lead singer of the most legendary rock band in the world. Slacker Demon had been around for twenty years, and their songs still skyrocketed to number one whenever they released a new album.

I started to argue but changed my mind. He was right. I needed a drink. I didn't think about where the dude's mouth had been when I touched the rim of the bottle to my lips and tipped it back.

"You're a smart boy, Grant. What I can't figure is why the hell you're putting up with Nan's shit," Kiro said as he sank down onto the white leather sofa across from me. He was in a pair of black skinny jeans and a silver shirt, unbuttoned and hanging open. Tattoos covered his chest and arms. Women still went crazy over him. It wasn't his looks. He was too damn skinny. A diet of alcohol and drugs would do that to you. But he was Kiro. That was all that mattered to them.

"You gonna ignore me? Hell, she's my daughter and I can't put up with her. Damn crazy bitch, just like her momma," he drawled before taking a pull off a joint.

"That's enough, Daddy." The musical voice that was finding its way into my fantasies lately floated from the doorway.

"There's my baby girl. She's come out of her room to visit,"

Kiro said, grinning at the daughter he actually loved. The one he hadn't abandoned. Harlow Manning was breathtaking. She didn't look like a rock star's kid. She looked like an innocent, sweet country girl, with long, dark hair and eyes that made you forget your fucking name.

"I was going to see if you planned on eating dinner at home tonight or if you were going out," she said. I watched as she stepped into the room and purposely ignored me. That only made me smile.

She didn't like me. I had met her at Rush and Blaire's engagement party and then spoken to her at their wedding reception. Both times hadn't ended well.

"I was thinkin' of going out. I need to party a little. I've stayed inside this house too damn long."

"Oh, okay," she said in that soft voice that I swear was intoxicating.

Kiro frowned. "You lonely? Locking yourself away in that room with your books getting to you, baby girl?"

I couldn't take my eyes off Harlow. She rarely came around when I was here. Nan wasn't exactly kind to her. I got why she didn't like Harlow. She was eaten up with jealousy where Harlow was concerned. Even if it wasn't Harlow's fault that Kiro loved her and didn't seem to give a shit about Nan.

"No, I'm fine. I was just going to wait and eat with you if you planned to eat here. If not, I'll just eat a sandwich in my room."

Kiro started shaking his head. "I don't like that. You're in there too much. I want you to stop reading for tonight. Grant is here and he needs some company. He's a good guy. Talk to him. You can have dinner together while he waits for Nan to return."

Harlow stiffened and finally glanced my way, but only for a moment. "I don't think so."

"Come on, don't be a snob. Grant's a family friend. He's Rush's brother. Have dinner with him."

Harlow's spine stiffened even straighter. She went back to not making eye contact with me. "He's not Rush's brother. If he were, it would be even more disgusting that he's sleeping with Nan."

Kiro grinned as if Harlow was the funniest person in the world and he was proud of her spunk. "My kitten has claws, and apparently only you bring them out. Sleeping with the evil sister has put you on my baby girl's shit list. Now, that's funny as hell." He looked extremely amused as he took another long draw from his joint.

I wasn't amused. I didn't like the fact that Harlow hated me. I wasn't sure how the hell to fix it, though. Turning my back on Nan wasn't possible. She wouldn't be able to handle someone else dropping her. Even if her slutty ass deserved it. I wouldn't let myself think about the boy band she was currently sleeping with. Guess I was wrong about those guys. I thought for sure they were sleeping with each other. Instead, they were all sleeping with Nan.

"Have a good night, Daddy," Harlow said, then turned and walked out of the room before Kiro could demand she stay with me.

Kiro laid his head back and closed his eyes. "Shame she hates you. She's special. Only known one other like her, and it was her mom. Woman stole my heart. I adored her. Worshipped the fucking ground she walked on. I would have thrown all this shit away for her. I had planned on it. I just wanted to wake up each morning and see her there beside me. I wanted to watch her with our baby girl and know that they were mine. But God wanted her more. Took her the fuck away from me. I won't ever get over it. Never."

This wasn't the first time I had heard him ramble on about Harlow's mother. He did it whenever he got high. She was the first thing that came to his mind. I hadn't known that kind of love. Scared the shit out of me, though. I wasn't sure I ever wanted to know it. Kiro had never recovered. I had met the man when I was a kid and my dad had married Rush's mom. Rush had begged his dad, Dean Finlay, the drummer for Slacker Demon, to take me with them on one of his weekend visits.

I had been in awe. It had been the first of many weekends. And Kiro would always talk about "her" and curse God for taking her. It had fascinated me, even as a child. I had never witnessed that kind of devotion.

Even after my dad's short marriage to Rush's mother, Georgianna, I had remained close to Rush. His dad still came to pick me up sometimes when he got Rush. I had grown up personally knowing the most legendary rock band in the world.

"Nan hates her. Who the hell can hate Harlow? She's too damn sweet to hate. Girl hasn't done anything to Nan, yet Nan's mean as a goddamn snake. Poor Harlow stays away from her. I hate to see my baby girl so defenseless. She needs to toughen up. She needs a friend." Kiro set his joint down in an ashtray and turned his head to look at me. "Be her friend, kid. She needs one."

I wanted to be a lot more than Harlow Manning's friend. But she wouldn't even look at me. "Not sure I can be her friend and Nan's at the same time."

Kiro frowned, then sat up and leaned forward. "Three kinds of women in this world. The kind that suck you dry and leave you with nothing. The kind that only want a good time. And the kind that make life worth a damn. That last kind . . . the right woman's the one who gives as much as she takes, and you can't get enough. She's the kind . . . if you lose her, you lose yourself."

His bloodshot eyes told me he hadn't just smoked a joint today. But even high, he made sense. If anyone knew about women, it was Kiro Manning.

"I've had all three. Wish like hell I'd stayed away from the first. The second is all I touch anymore. But that third one . . . I won't ever be the same. And I wouldn't take back one minute I had with Harlow's mom."

He ran his hand through his stringy hair. "Nannette, she's the first kind. Be careful of the first kind. They will fuck you over and walk away laughing."

About the Author

ABBI GLINES is the author of *Fallen Too Far* and *Never Too Far,* in addition to the young adult Sea Breeze and Vincent Boys series. A devoted book lover, Abbi lives with her family in Alabama. She maintains a Twitter addiction at @AbbiGlines and can also be found on Facebook and at AbbiGlines.com.

For the latest news on Abbi's books check out www.abbiglines.com
or follow her on Twitter @abbiglines

Want to find out what happens next?

Here's a SNEAK PEEK!

A tempting *Too Far* novel

Fallen Too Far

Abbi Glines

"Each as sizzling as the one before. We love."
COSMOPOLITAN

Chapter One

Trucks with mud on the tires were what I was used to seeing parked outside a house party. Expensive foreign cars weren't. This place had at least twenty of them covering up the long driveway. I pulled my mom's fifteen-year-old Ford truck over onto the sandy grass so that I wouldn't be blocking anyone in. Dad hadn't told me that he was having a party tonight. He hadn't told me much of anything.

He also hadn't shown up for my mother's funeral. If I didn't need somewhere to live, I wouldn't be here. I'd had to sell the small house that my grandmother had left us to pay off the last of Mom's medical bills. All I had left were my clothes and the truck. Calling my father, after he had failed to come even once during the three years my mother had fought cancer, had been hard. It had been necessary though; he was the only family I had left.

I stared at the massive three-story house that sat directly on the white sand in Rosemary Beach, Florida. This was my dad's new home. His new family. I wasn't going to fit in here.

My truck door was suddenly jerked open. On instinct, I reached under the seat and grabbed my 9 millimeter. I swung it up and directly at the intruder, holding it with both hands, ready to pull back on the trigger.

"Whoa . . . I was gonna tell you that you were lost but I'll tell you whatever the hell you want me to as long as you put that thing away." A guy with brown shaggy hair tucked behind his ears stood on the other side of my gun with both his hands in the air and eyes wide.

I cocked an eyebrow and held my gun steady. I still didn't know who this guy was. Jerking someone's truck door open wasn't a normal greeting for a stranger. "No, I don't think I'm lost. Is this Abraham Wynn's house?"

The guy swallowed nervously. "Uh, I can't think with that pointed in my face. You're making me very nervous, sweetheart. Could you put it down before you have an accident?"

Accident? Really? This guy was beginning to piss me off. "I don't know you. It's dark outside and I'm in a strange place, alone. So forgive me if I don't feel very safe at the moment. You can trust me when I tell you that there won't be an accident. I can handle a gun. Very well."

The guy didn't appear to believe me, and now that I was looking at him he didn't appear to be real threatening. Nevertheless, I wasn't ready to lower my gun just yet.

"Abraham?" he repeated slowly, and started to shake his head, then stopped. "Wait, Abe is Rush's new stepdad. I met him before he and Georgiana left for Paris."

Paris? Rush? What? I waited for more of an explanation, but the guy continued to stare at the gun and hold his breath. Keeping my eyes on him, I lowered my protection and made sure to put the safety back on before tucking it under my seat. Maybe with the gun put away the guy could focus and explain.

"Do you even have a license for that thing?" he asked incredulously.

I wasn't in the mood to talk about my right to bear arms. I needed answers.

"Abraham is in Paris?" I asked, needing confirmation. He knew I was coming today. We'd just talked last week after I'd sold the house.

The guy nodded slowly and his stance relaxed. "You know him?"

Not really. I had seen him all of two times since he'd walked out on my mom and me five years ago. I remembered the dad who'd come to my soccer games and grilled burgers outside for the neighborhood block parties. The dad I'd had until the day my twin sister, Valerie, was killed in a car accident. My father had been driving. He'd changed that day. The man who didn't call me and make sure I was okay while I took care of my sick mother, I didn't know him. Not at all.

"I'm his daughter Blaire."

The guy's eyes went wide, and he threw back his head and laughed. Why was this funny? I waited for him to explain, when he held out his hand. "Come on, Blaire, I have someone you need to meet. He's gonna love this."

I stared down at his hand and reached for my purse.

"Are you packing in your purse, too? Should I warn everyone not to piss you off?" The teasing lilt to his voice kept me from saying something rude.

"You opened my door without knocking. I was scared."

"Your instant reaction to being scared is to pull out a gun on someone? Damn, girl, where are you from? Most girls I know squeal or some shit like that."

Most girls he knew hadn't been forced to protect themselves for the past three years. I'd had my mother to take care of but no one to take care of me. "I'm from Alabama," I replied, ignoring his hand and stepping out of the truck myself.

The sea breeze hit my face, and the salty smell of the beach was unmistakable. I'd never seen the beach before. At least not in person. I'd seen pictures and movies. But the smell, it was exactly like I expected it to be.

"So it's true what they say about girls from Bama," he replied, and I turned my attention to him.

"What do you mean?"

His eyes scanned down my body and back up to my face. A grin stretched slowly across his face. "Tight jeans, tank tops, and a gun. Damn, I've been living in the wrong fucking state."

Rolling my eyes, I reached into the back of the truck. I had a suitcase and then several boxes that I needed to drop off at Goodwill.

"Here, let me get it." He stepped around me, then reached into the truck bed for the large piece of luggage my mom had kept tucked away in her closet for that road trip we never got to take. She always talked about how we'd drive across the country and then up the West Coast one day. Then she'd gotten sick.

Shaking off the memories, I focused on the present. "Thank you, uh . . . I don't think I got your name."

The guy pulled the suitcase out, then turned back to me.

"What? You forgot to ask when you had the nine millimeter pointed at my face?" he replied.

I sighed. Okay, maybe I'd gone a little overboard with the gun, but he'd scared me.

"I'm Grant, a, uh, friend of Rush's."

"Rush?" There was that name again. Who was Rush?

Grant's grin grew big once again. "You don't know who

Rush is?" He was extremely amused. "I'm so fucking glad I came tonight."

He nodded his head toward the house. "Come on. I'll introduce you."

I walked beside him as he led me to the house. The music inside got louder as we got closer. If my dad wasn't here, then who was? I knew Georgiana was his new wife, but that was all I knew. Was this a party her kids were having? How old were they? She did have kids, didn't she? I couldn't remember. Dad had been vague. He'd said I'd like my new family but he hadn't said who that family was exactly.

"So, does Rush live here?" I asked.

"Yeah, he does, at least in the summer. He moves to his other houses according to the season."

"His other houses?"

Grant chuckled. "You don't know anything about this family your dad has married into, do you, Blaire?"

He had no idea. I shook my head.

"Quick mini-lesson then, before we walk inside the madness," he replied, stopping at the top of the stairs leading to the front door and looking at me. "Rush Finlay is your stepbrother. He's the only child of the famous drummer for Slacker Demon, Dean Finlay. His parents never married. His mother, Georgiana, was a groupie back in the day. This is his house. His mother gets to live here because he allows it." He stopped and looked back at the door as it swung open. "These are all his friends."

A tall, willowy strawberry blonde wearing a short royal-blue dress and a pair of heels that I'd break my neck in if I tried to wear them stood there staring at me. I didn't miss the distaste in her scowl. I didn't know much about people like this, but I did know that my department store clothing wasn't something she approved of. Either that or I had a bug crawling on me.

"Well, hello, Nannette," Grant said in an annoyed tone.

"Who is she?" the girl asked, shifting her gaze to Grant.

"A friend. Wipe the snarl off your face, Nan, it isn't an attractive look for you," he replied, reaching over to grab my hand and pulling me into the house behind him.

The room wasn't as full as I'd assumed. As we walked past the large, open foyer, an arched doorway led into what I assumed was a living room. Even so, it was bigger than my entire house, or what had been my house. Two glass doors were standing open with a breathtaking view of the ocean. I wanted to see that up close.

"This way," Grant instructed as he made his way over to a . . . bar? Really? There was a bar in the house?

I glanced over the people we passed by. They all paused for a moment and gave me a quick once-over. I stood out bigtime.

"Rush, meet Blaire. I believe she might belong to you. I found her outside looking a little lost," Grant said, and I swung my gaze from the curious people to see who this Rush was.

Oh.

Oh. My.

Where Hope Lives

Wendy Robertson

headline

Copyright © 2001 Wendy Robertson

The right of Wendy Robertson to be identified as the Author of
the Work has been asserted by her in accordance with
the Copyright, Designs and Patents Act 1988.

Many thanks to Tom McGuinness who has kindly given his
permission to reproduce his pictures 'Miner and Child' and
'Underground Stable' in this book.

First published in 2001 by
HEADLINE BOOK PUBLISHING

First published in paperback in 2002 by
HEADLINE BOOK PUBLISHING

10 9 8 7 6 5 4 3 2 1

All rights reserved. No part of this publication may be reproduced,
stored in a retrieval system, or transmitted, in any form or by any
means without the prior written permission of the publisher, nor be
otherwise circulated in any form of binding or cover other than that
in which it is published and without a similar condition being
imposed on the subsequent purchaser.

All characters in this publication are fictitious and any resemblance
to real persons, living or dead, is purely coincidental.

ISBN 0 7472 6605 0

Typeset by Avon Dataset Ltd, Bidford-on-Avon, Warks

Printed and bound in Great Britain by
Clays Ltd, St Ives plc

HEADLINE BOOK PUBLISHING
A division of Hodder Headline
338 Euston Road
London NW1 3BH

www.headline.co.uk
www.hodderheadline.com

To Bryan with love

ROTHERHAM LIBRARY &
INFORMATION SERVICES

B48 862953 8

Askews

GENERAL £5.99

RO000062923

Acknowledgements

The characters and events in this novel are entirely and absolutely fictional. However, in writing it I was inspired by the work of the Settlement Movement, a charity funded in the 1930s by the Pilgrim Trust, which established a series of Settlements in the most deprived parts of England. The Trust's objective was the provision of a meeting place where people could experience the intellectual stimulation of wide discussion, participate in the practice of arts and crafts, and have access to artists of national reputation.

For a time, this objective was most fully realised in Spennymoor, the town where I grew up. Fortunately, the Depression has become part of history and Settlement-type activities have been taken over by schools and arts centres nationwide. However, the little theatre built by the remarkable warden Mr Farrell is still there, and a small group of dedicated actors still put on several plays a year. For them the Settlement spirit lives on and I would acknowledge them as part of my inspiration.

It is worth noting also that the Settlement was funded in part for some years by CEMA (Council for the Encouragement of Music and the Arts), which was the forerunner of the Arts Council. In recent years I have been working for the Arts Council in prisons. In that work I have noted that for certain individuals in confinement, creative experience can both enhance self-esteem and change lives. I think my insight into the lives of Gabriel, Greta, Marguerite and Tegger, confined as they were in the prison of the Depression, has sprung directly from my Arts Council experience.

I would like to thank Gillian Wales for her inspiring friendship and for access to her extensive research into the Settlement, with Robert McManners, in preparation for their forthcoming *Mining Art in the Great Northern Coalfield*.

Finally, I would like to acknowledge the inspiration of the writing of Sid Chaplin and the work of painters Tom McGuinness, Norman Cornish, the late Ted Holloway and the late Tisa Hess. Looking and looking *and looking* at their work has been, for me, the most pleasurable part of the research for this novel.

Wendy Robertson, 2001

'Miner and Child'
Tom McGuinness

'Underground Stable'
Tom McGuinness

Prologue

22 November 1963
Notes for a Eulogy
Mention synchronicity, The assassination today of President John Kennedy.

We're here to celebrate the life of another great man who had his finest hour some years ago, many, many miles from this sunny place with its wide bright skies and long golden sands. (*Steady on! Sounds more like Miami than Bournemouth.*)

In order for you to grasp what this man took on, you'd need to know about the small town in the North called Brack's Hill. (*Say how strange it is that he chose to come to the South Coast to retire. No jokes. There'll be local people here!*)

Brack's Hill sprang up in the nineteenth century in the burgeoning Northern Coalfield, that cradle of the railways which supplied the coal that fired the Industrial Revolution in Great Britain.

Like many others, this town had its steel necklace of colliery wheels and nearby ironworks, threaded together by rows and rows of crude houses thrown up close by, so that a miner or ironworker could roll out of bed and into work in a matter of minutes. (*Once underground, of course, he might have to walk a full mile or more to reach the face where he would do his actual shift. We called it 'walking inbye'. Should I say this too?*)

Picture Brack's Hill. In the best days of full employment and good pay, this network of streets was well serviced by a Saturday market, by shops and travellers, pubs and chapels, a chip van and a football field, by racing tracks for horses, dogs and men who ran for money. The spirit of the people was served by a Salvation Army Citadel and chapels of every persuasion, as well as a couple of substantial churches with spires, whose vicars were compensated for their trouble with handsome vicarages and a clutch of servants.

Brack's Hill always remained a very working-class town. Even so, people felt the need to mark themselves out. Subtle levels of snobbery still flourished: skilled against unskilled; in-work as opposed to out-of-work: physically strong as opposed to the physically weak: pigeon men against the rest; football men against the rest; garden men against the rest; respectable women as opposed to those not so respectable; people with bay windows at the end of pit rows as opposed to those with common straight windows: people with clout – (such as councillors, and shopkeepers, doctors and clerics), as opposed to those without clout – which was more or less the rest of the population.

The man we honour today belonged to none of these groups.

Brack's Hill had its Grammar School, of course, but many of those who went there often fled the town to find work elsewhere in what they saw as more congenial places. A few individuals – legendary 'good scholars' – turned from pupil to apprentice teachers in their old schools, and then to full-blown teachers courtesy of the Durham colleges. Roots and old loyalties kept such individuals at home with their own families, despite the interior distance engendered by their book-learning. (*No such trap for Greta Pallister, when you think of it . . .*)

Others, who fled the North East, joined the more fluid social systems of the Midlands and the South of England. They had to lose some of their accent, of course, to avoid being called *Geordie* all their lives; they could join orchestras or drama and choral groups and complain of the philistinism of the poor little town whence they came. (*Is this becoming autobiographical? Then again, any eulogy for Archie would have to be so, as he changed lives. In order to talk about him, you have to speak of yourself.*)

The single tier of superiority in Brack's Hill consisted of the doctors and clergy who met monthly with the dogged social compulsion of castaways on a desert island. At their regular monthly dinner, they reassured each other with urbane conversation and the power of shared values. They consoled each other about the difficulty and thanklessness of the task before them in this dour town with these sometime strangely unforgiving people. Our man – the man we speak of today – made a difference even to this superior group.

When the world demand for coal and iron faded, this small town just about died. By the 1930s, many Brack's Hill people had no work, little food, less dignity. Families went from comparative affluence to poverty at a stroke. Those with savings had to raid them to survive. When the savings were drained and the humiliation of the Means Test raised its ugly head, pure poverty, isolation and boredom stared every man and woman in the face.

Many shops in the High Street closed for want of custom. Others stayed open a little longer, giving extended credit to customers in dire need until the shopkeepers themselves went bankrupt. In some cases, formerly proud and self-sufficient individuals became the walking wounded. In less fortunate cases they were the living dead. (*One of the first to lose his job after the General Strike, my own father, was one of these living dead. In doing what he did to himself in the end, he was merely confirming that for years he had lived, day by day, as a dead man. Why have I written that? I want to say it. I* do *want to say it.*)

Into this dour and difficult place came a magician called Archie Todhunter. A strange, ambiguous man, his creative energy redeemed the pride and self-esteem not just of the lucky group of individuals with whom he was in daily contact, but of the town itself. He changed these people (*he changed me*) for ever. Archie Todhunter showed us that no matter how hungry you were, life was not just about parcels of clothes and food. No matter how powerless you felt, it wasn't just about the right political party being voted in or out. Archie was not one for party politics. (*What about today? Don't digress into the present-day politics!*)

He saw the significance of you, me, anybody, as *an individual*: who you were, how you viewed the world. His was a kind of secular religion; his temple, you might say, was the Settlement. This place was about the individual, about what made you tick, what you made of your life and how in turn you could transform the lives of others.

I, Gabriel Marchant, speak to you here because it was my privilege to know all this at first-hand. Archie Todhunter's magic worked for me so well that the dark places, in the end, were transformed into my raw material, my avenue to the light.

Some might say it was the Prince, the Prince Charming of his age, who made the difference, coming to see us like he did that year, bringing Brack's Hill into the spotlight. But I say it was Archie Todhunter. And Rosel. And Marguerite. The exceptional Tegger MacNamara. And, of course, thc redoubtable Greta Pallister.

(I wonder who'll make it here to the funeral today? Some of them might want to say something as well. Or perhaps, like everyone else, they'll be running round in circles about the Assassination. How can something that happens so far away, that comes to us through the flat television screen set off so much panic? The cheese girl in my local Sainsbury's was crying her eyes out as she cut the Cheddar with her fine wire.)

Think of it. Think of Archie Todhunter. Of Brack's Hill in 1936 . . .

Chapter One

The Petrified Forest

On my seventh birthday, my father brought home these stones in the pocket of the suit in which, seven years before, he'd married my mother. He wore this suit of working-class legend on alternate Sundays. Like thousands – even millions – of others, my mother folded it into a brown paper parcel to go in pawn on Monday and took it out of pawn two weeks later on pay Saturday.

That suit did have capacious pockets. My father tipped the stones out of them on to the table, throwing up a cloud of coal dust which shimmered in the light of the fire. I put them in lines and peered at them. One by one my fingers touched their gritty surfaces. I brought them up to my eye to see more clearly the ferns, the fish and the lizards so perfectly impressed there. One of them was so very small I had to put my eye really close. It was a fragment of blue-grey slate revealing the shape of a sea urchin. A magic creature.

'Why?' I asked him. 'How?'

He was still answering me in those days. 'The petrified forest,' he said, unlacing his big boots and shaking them over the hearth.

They spat out grains of coal and the air again was ignited with fireflies. 'The coal we win, like – those deep seams – once were forests. Millions of years ago, Gabriel. Millions. I've seen whole trees down there. Believe me, son. Once those fish swam in rivers on the surface. Once those leaves fluttered in the bright sun.'

I've a vague image now of my mother, long ago, picking up his boots and cradling them in her arms like a baby.

I tip-fingered the hard stone. That ancient world was alive in my head. The pit in my mind grew into a magical place, a place of wonder. I already knew it was a place of pain; I'd seen the sealed up blue scars, like blue buttons (medals earned when my father's back scraped the roof in the low seams). I'd felt the scabs on his knuckles from mis-timed blows from his pick.

But now my father, with his careful words, had shown me a different world: a place of endless time and natural splendour.

I took the notebook bought for me by my grandmother at the corner shop and began to copy on to its lined pages the plants, the seahorses and the antique lizards. My father, one Sunday morning when his hands were clean, showed me how to veil the stones with paper and rub my stubby pencil over it. This made a shadow image of the leaf or fish, perfect in every detail.

Such times of unemphatic joy came to an end, of course, in 1926. By November in that year the miners had just been forced back to work, the last to stay out after the National Strike. My pregnant mother, exhausted by her own fight for survival, gave birth too early and died, taking my baby brother with her into the night.

My father, active in the Union, never worked in a pit again. He was not alone.

* * *

From time to time I've wondered if I got my love of drawing and painting from my Aunt Susanah, wife to the teacher Jonty Clelland.

She was first married to an uncle of mine who died in prison at the time of the Great War. They don't talk of him much as he was a 'conchie'. So too was this schoolteacher called Jonty she married after my uncle. Jonty still dabbles in politics. He got into bother a while back over some Blackshirts, and he, too, ended up in prison. It was in the papers.

Aunt Susanah drew and painted pictures. She was known for it. In the house I share these days with my father there is this picture of hers – *Kingfishers by Glittering Water*. She gave it to me for my fifth birthday. But Aunt Susanah lives in Priorton, five miles away, so I don't see much of her.

There's a chance, then, that I get my delight in drawing from Aunt Susanah. But I think it's much more likely my grandmother who set me away. She'd never, though, have called herself an artist. And she'd no more sense of politics than that sublimated into chill anger at having to feed her family on strike wages, or on no money at all; or into the fury at seeing her daughter-in-law die of hunger and having her grown son home again trailing his motherless child.

Me and my dad came to live with her in 1927; for three years she fed us and took care of us, then she fell ill herself five years ago and died. She was still wearing her crossover pinny when she breathed her last. In her coffin she looked like a silver-haired doll.

This narrow house of hers, where we eventually came to live, seemed to me to be flooded with colour and distinctive shapes. My grandmother showed me that you could recreate the sun and the moon; how you make balance in a square; how you create order in a rectangle; how you could make explosive red stand out against dense black: how yellow lives when set against green.

Her choice of colour was bold and uncompromising: not for her the safe blacks and greys of a mining life. Such a freight of colour burned in her head that neither wall nor picture frame could contain it. Her canvases were the circles, squares and rectangles of home-made rag rugs, designed to cover the floors in this meagre house. Those mats are still here, faded now but still doing service as a barrier to the damp cold coming from stone laid straight on to soil.

When I was very small I would sit under the framed canvas which she stretched across two chair-backs, peering up at the shadow of her prodding hands, and watch the stubby back of the mat grow and grow. Here were the sun and the moon in negative: the underside of outrageous sunflowers and plump sprawling geraniums. Later, when my hands were bigger, she would let me wield her big scissors and cut useable strips from old clothes and discarded furnishing cloth.

For the dyes, I helped her to strip berries off bushes and floral lichen from stone walls, and pound them to coloured juice which drenched the dull cloth with startling brilliance.

Together we stirred the dye, me dipping my fingers and holding them up to see how the light made my flesh glow through the reds and greens. One day I swirled my dripping fingers across my father's newspaper, making the image of a coiled red snake. He hadn't read it, and I got a beating with a fire iron for my troubles.

My grandmother charred larchwood and made charcoal for me. The first pictures I drew were messy but it was good making that hard black mark. She also bought stubby pencils for me, using her eternal 'tick' – her credit – from the corner shop.

One birthday she managed to persuade my father to buy me my first tin of paints. He'd got a rare month's work with a company which moved furniture for families who were going to the Midlands and the South of England to find employment. Two or three households to a wagon. 'In my wagon,' he'd say, 'are packed the lives of twenty people. You don't have to live inside a stone tent, son, if you can pack your life in a van.'

He liked this work. 'Your own boss out on the road. See a bit of the world away from the pit,' he said. 'I wish I'd known that before. I'd not have spent all those years underground.'

Then the company went bankrupt and he lost that job as well. That was the last time he worked and the last time I saw him merry. As for me, at least I had my paints and I could make my mark. I painted on old newspapers and broken-down cardboard boxes. The woman at the Co-op kept back big sugar bags and flattened them for me. They were poor things, those paintings: scrappy copies of my grandmother's mats, pictures of things around the house – pots and pans, my father's old bent boots, my grandmother's Singer sewing machine.

I won a prize for a painting in my first week in school. Always the good scholar. My teachers said I could use this to get work, this talent to draw. More than one of them took me aside and told me that I was too good for the pit. My talent would be my salvation.

All this made not one jot of difference, of course, when I turned fourteen and my father got wind of a job at White Leas Pit. It was just on the screens of course, but it was a start. I had to go. I'd no great confidence in my teachers' judgement, nor had my father. 'They're just flattering themselves and flattering you. There's nothing in it!' he said. 'People looking after their own jobs.'

My grandmother was dead by then and I had no one to fight my corner. I had to fight for myself now. More so if I was to paint as well as win coal for a living.

Chapter Two

Susanah

The first pay Saturday after I start the pit I turn up at home to see my Aunt Susanah standing four square on my grandmother's sunflower rug. My father stands, arms folded, in front of her. The crackle of a recent quarrel zings in the air.

She smiles when she sees me. In her arms is a large flat parcel. 'I brought this for you, Gabriel,' she says, placing the parcel carefully on the table.

My father lifts a stoneware milk jug and a cup and brushes past me as he takes them through to the scullery. I hover uneasily on the hearthrug. Aunt Susanah looks at me. 'You have the pit all about you, Gabriel,' she says. 'And so young.'

I catch sight of this stranger in the mirror above the mantelpiece. The black pit dirt is on my cheeks, on the inside of my eyes. I curse the blush that shows itself underneath the grime.

'So how was the pit?' she says.

I shake my head, wary. 'It's only the pit,' I mumble.

I can hear my father clashing about in the scullery. He's avoiding coming out to where my aunt is.

'Sad, I was, to learn that you'd had to go down there. My own brother Davey changed for ever, the day he went down the pit.' The Welsh sings in her voice.

'Davey?' I say. I've heard of no Davey.

'Killed in the Great War. He liked the army better than the pit.' There's this dark look on her face. 'Much better.'

I rub my chin. One or two bristles are appearing on it these days. 'I can see what he meant,' I say.

She puts a gloved hand on the parcel. 'Yes, sad I was, hearing you'd left the grammar school, you being such a good scholar.'

'I needed to work.'

'So your father tells me.' She sighs. 'They are crying in the street for work.' Out of the brown paper she pulls a great flat book, the name *Rembrandt* scrawled diagonally across its slate-coloured cover. 'It's a book of picture plates. I bought it at an auction of the property of a schoolmaster in Priorton. I thought it might do for you.' She opens a page and tips the book towards the window. 'Look,' she says.

Many of the plates are black and white but some are coloured. Such colour. Such harmony of flesh and light. I'm drenched in sweetness, as though I've drunk a cup of Golden Syrup all at once. The colours lambast me from the page: the glow of the flesh, the subtleties of the folds in the garments, the mysterious life in the eyes of the subjects. 'Crikey,' I say.

'As you say. *Crikey*.' There's a small smile on her face.

I don't know what to say further. 'Thank you,' I say loudly. 'Is this really for me? I've never had nothing like this before, like.'

She looks round. 'Is there anybody else in this house who's an artist? Of course it's for you.'

'I'm not an artist.'

'Oh, yes you are. You're an artist and a good scholar, and if that . . . if your father wants to forget it then you must not.' She pulls on her gloves. 'Well, Jonty's waiting for me at the station. We're off to Durham. We have a meeting there – branch of the Peace Pledge Union.'

'What's that?'

'Trying to stop another war. You know, two or three gathered together . . .'

'Don't go, Aunt Susanah. How about something to drink? Some tea?'

She laughs a contented, confident laugh. 'Indeed, I think your father'll only settle when I get out of this house, Gabriel.' Her voice sings in the air in the narrow cluttered room. She puts her clean glove on my dirty pit jacket. 'Promise me you'll draw still, and paint still, in spite of the pit? In spite of those men there who'll think it's, well, a cissy kind of thing?'

'Well, I don't really know.'

'Promise!'

'To be honest, Aunt Susanah, I don't think I can stop myself.'

Her laughter rings out now and she reaches up and kisses me on my black cheek. For minutes after she has gone I can feel the soft imprint of her lips on my cheek and my heart aches for a mother who I don't know if I loved, who I am not sure that I remember properly.

If my father sees the tears in my eyes when he comes in with the clean pots, he doesn't say. He puts the pots in the press, and with his back still to me he says gruffly, 'What was that about then?'

'She brought me this book of paintings.'

'She wants to mind her own business.' It is more a growl than a voice. 'She's nowt to us.'

I wrap the book carefully in its brown paper and, holding it gingerly in my coal-black fingers, I take it upstairs and put it on the windowsill of my bedroom where it may catch the light.

It might be an obvious thing to say that the pit, when you first enter it, as I did at fourteen, is dark. But this is no ordinary kind of blackness. It's not the darkness of night which you know for sure will be followed by dawn, nor the dark of the Northern Hemisphere when you know the South is in light. Down there there is no light at all, nor promise of a light. In a thickly curtained room you know there will be light out there behind the curtains the next day. In the pit there is dark behind the dark. There is no next-day dawn down there. No outside-the-curtain.

The darkness underground is unrelieved. The flickers of our pathetic firefly lamps barely pierce the gloom. You know that beyond this blackness stand rooted walls and lines of rock which were born in darkness and which will remain in darkness until the death of the world.

This can make it very hard to feel, to think about. But I was lucky, could make my feelings change when I brought into my mind the petrified forest, whose leaves once fluttered in the light of day, where fish once swam on a sunlit seashore, and seahorses bobbed in the ebb and flow of primeval tides. That was my father's gift to me.

And having been in such dark, when you come up in the cage and step out into the dusty world of the pit yard, you've never known such light! You've never seen such blues, such distinctive ochres, such sultry and vibrant greens. The very faces of the boys coming from the screens are baby pink, their eyes are blue sapphires, the inside of their lips, their slipping tongues, are carmine.

In time my own eyes became attuned to the peculiarly dense existence of light and colour in the pit. I began to relish the dark rainbow of the mining seam: the intense blues and purples, the odd prickle-pinpoint of red which, when you get to it, turns out to be the stray beam of a miner's lamp as he returns from the face. In time the pit, that great warren, began to disclose for me the colours of the old forest which has buried inside it the sunlight of ancient times. Down there the rainbow has darkened, has imploded. Yet it is nonetheless present.

I've spent a lot of time pondering on the impossibility of reproducing this colour, of sharing with the unknowing world the density, the vibrancy which invade my eyes down here in the depths.

Of course I kept my pondering to myself among the pitmen, who value more direct and masculine talents. You can't deny they appreciate the facility which I do have to draw cartoons and likenesses, as they relish others who can spout facile poetry or sing songs. The overman even got me to draw these cartoons about safety measures which are hung up in the lamp cabin.

But if anyone ventured into the wilder aspects of colour and more outrageous flights of verbal fancy they would usually dismiss them as womanish.

I quickly learned to keep my own counsel down the pit, and am known to be close and silent even among those reserved men. I am like this with all except my workmate, my marra Tegger who's given to flights of verbal fancy himself from time to time.

Tegger and me went to school together from when we were five. He was the bright noisy one; I was always quiet. Tegger has broad cheeks and a smile that flickers across his face at the slightest excuse. He is sunny, easygoing. Even so, don't be deceived by his manner: Tegger's no simpleton. I never knew a wiser man. He has heavy, almost fat shoulders. His hands, chunky as a span of butcher's sausages, beat the air as he tries to make a point. He'll pat you on the shoulder, almost hug you when he is really excited about something. This hugging is not so common round here, but men shrug it off genially enough. 'Only Tegger's way,' they say. 'Daft as a brush, that one.'

Like I say, Tegger and me've been together right since our first day at school. I grew tall while he stayed small. We went on to the grammar school together and left on the same day, to start the pit. Within three months he began to grow again and broadened out, putting the meat on even in the leanest times. His mother says he shows every ounce of his keep. His father says he grew in the dark, like a bloody great mushroom.

We always worked the same shifts. Tegger would knock me up at three-thirty and we'd trudge side by side along the pit road. Our feet would crunch companionably over the cinder and dirt which, ground together, makes the black path. Our feet knew the way themselves. The yellow lights strung on drooping wires every thousand yards made sure we weren't tempted to stray southwards or northwards to escape this place of deep fissures and dark caverns.

Tegger would hunch his shoulders against the morning cold and keep his head down all the way. But me, after a while, I'd look up, my eyes skinning for the shades of black, grey and purple which define the very early morning. The sky at this time was the densest black. Soon, though, the morning star would rise, poking like a chalked billiard cue through the blanket of night. At those times I'd dwell on the thought that beyond this well of darkness there existed a world of light, a rainbow universe where the whiteness shatters into ribbons of colour.

When I'm feeling low this blackness is the worst of the pit. In my lowest times then it seems to me that this black was the blackest of blackness, the essence of absence. The pit men have a word for it down there. They call it the *goaf*.

But in the end you get to see wonderful colours down the pit, believe me. Just a flicker, a touch of light from your lamp, liberates colour from the *goaf*. Underground, I learned to feast my eyes on the purple sheen on coal and the glitter of fool's gold; the red of a man's inner mouth, the gleam of his eye the flutter of the silver-grey moth surviving down there and the skittering roll of blind mice rolling like feathers along the rails.

In the hierarchy of the pit, strength and judgement are considered of the greatest value. Strength – well, me and Tegger had that in abundance. We were young and fit. In the matter of judgement we were probably suspect. Tegger had his own kind of manic wisdom but they often called him a fool. My judgement, I'd claim, was mostly sound, but I had this habit of daydreaming – of light dreaming – which sometimes got in the way of concentrating on serious work. I did once have such a dream of light down there, a dream which set away something which is still resounding through my life.

Chapter Three

Dream of Light

One particular shift, Tegger and me stand shoulder to shoulder in the cage crowded in by other men. Their faces are already filming with a first layer of dust; mouths tight with grim anticipation, weary acceptance. The talk fades as the space fills. Tegger turns his bulk sideways to make room for two more men at the other end of the creaking cage.

By the time we get inbye – nearly a mile's walk – the putter has a tubful ready for us to push on its way. When you start a shift it yawns before you like an unleapable chasm. But in truth it's broken up in pieces; full tubs to move, empty ones to return. There is the dicey pull of the turns on the road, the low ceilings which leave only a breadth of space between your fingers and the roof. There are the occasional calls and communications of the hewers; there is the roar of song from Tegger who loves music from the theatre and the pictures. The men call him a daft bugger but still encourage him. Such things break up the time, rescue you from the yawning cavern of the shift.

Sometimes when Tegger's voice echoes in the galleries a

distant voice will join in. Then someone else will bawl that he should shut his noise and let a man get on with his work.

Me, I wonder how Tegger finds the spit to sing. My tongue and throat are silted up like a river mouth and I have to pace myself with my water bottle or it won't last a shift.

We always stop for bait time. My father says that in his early days they used to work straight through, eating as they worked. At bait time you can hear and see different things in the mine. The beat and the grind of excavation, the clashing of tubs, the grate of shovelled coal cease on the air. The wandering firefly lights of helmet and lamps are dimmed to rest the miners' straining eyes. A moment of peace pervades the galleries: a quietness undercut by the drum and thrum of the pumps as the men, in their holes and corners, enjoy a bit of crack with their marras.

Tegger and me go to a niche in an old bit of face, well out of the way of the stinking place where men squeeze through to relieve themselves. We crouch on an old prop placed across two pieces of stone and get out our bait tins. We flick off our lights and feel our way to our food. We eat simple enough fare – jam sandwiches cut thick as Bibles fill my bait tin. In the dark I can't see my black fingers staining the white bread. If the taste is a bit gritty I put that down to the pips in Mrs McVay's blackberry jam.

There in the dark we talk on a bit. Then Tegger sings a new song for me about four pit lads and a dog that lost a crucial race. His rendition gets applause from further along the gallery. 'Give us another one, son!' 'Yer should be on the stage, you, lad!'

He gives them one more: this one is about a pigeon man who had a winning pigeon which survived an epic storm on its way back from Whitehaven. After that there are no new requests and the murmur of voices tells us that more important discussions are afoot – like those rumours of the pit closing, and the pros and cons of the Jarrow March, the mingling of pride and despair.

I close my eyes against the dark and listen to the murmuring in the gallery. Tegger's shoulder lies heavy against mine and I realise he's having his five-minute nap to keep him going for the rest of his shift. I close my own eyes. Around me the gallery stills. Tegger's breathing drifts to a sustained snuffle that a puppy dog might make.

I open my eyes, blinking. The pit face before me is ablaze with light, the dark behind it glowing through threads of silver. I lean across to feel my lamp but it is still in the off position. I look back at the old coal face and the gleam is still there. Phosphorous! I've read about it. Heard about it in old pitmen's tales. But the gleam's too great for phosphorous. The hair on the back of my head prickles and I scramble with my lamp to light it. The gob of light throws itself into the black chasm, chasing away the luminescent glow.

The chasm is no longer gleaming, no longer a place of magic. Beyond the beam of the lamp the darkness sulks away in its space. But now there's a figure! I screw up my eyes, then lift up my lamp to make it out more clearly. Is it another man, moved into the dark to relieve himself? A pony on the wander? Worse has been known.

But it's not a man. It's a woman with a shadowy face, her dark clothes only relieved with a glittering red patch on her shoulder: a brooch maybe, or a flower. I have to squeeze my eyes together to see her properly. A strand of light from my lamp touches her hands, which reach out to me: long slender fingers. I pull back hard against the wall. The stone cuts into my shoulder-blade.

Women are not allowed in the pit. They bring bad luck. It's a common superstition. Like a ship at sea, the pit is a place of men. Here, men are free to be themselves: to work and fart and talk and swear among their own absolute kind. I've heard the most saintly of men swear down here, using the old words which echo back from the lacerated wall of the chasm and resound down through years.

The woman is moving towards me. I push my face sideways against the crumbling coal. I don't want to see the face. It's in my head somewhere that this is my mother or my grandmother, both dead. Or it's the face of all the mothers of all the lads killed in these galleries. Perhaps the intensity of their pit-gate mourning vigils have created a disembodied presence down here who searches for their lost ones. My head runs with questions.

Answers flow into my head, through my veins. This is more than any of that. It's the earth herself enfolding us all in work and sleep. She forgives us our gouging, our cutting and harvesting and reclaims us for her own. In our blind wander, our sparkle of imagined colour, our helpless charging and working of the depths, we're her unborn children. We're born into the bright world at the end of each shift. Then at the beginning of the next shift we're sucked back into her overwhelming void as the cage drops yet again and spews us out into the galleries which are the wounds we cut in her side.

My lamp calls forth an answering glint in her hidden eye and I grab Tegger's meaty arm. 'Tegger! Tegger! D'you see her? D'you see the woman?'

'Gabriel! Gabe, what is it, man?' Now it's Tegger who's shaking me. My head's groggy and full of shadows.

'What is it, man? Yer dreaming.' He grabs my shoulder hard.

I am shaking and sweating. 'Tegger. Do you see the woman?'

'Mistake to go to sleep, marra.' He turns up his lamp and our end of the gallery blossoms into dark normality. 'Come on, lad. Tony Arkwright'll have a tub near ready for us.'

'I didn't sleep, Tegger. You went to sleep, not me.'

'Me? I've never gone to sleep down here in my life. Dangerous, that. *She* takes hold of you when you've gone to sleep. Ask the old lads. Never gan to sleep down below.'

I shake the woman, and the drowsiness, out of my head. I know better than to discuss the vision with the other men, but I wonder how many of them have already had it, this dream of the earth as a woman in a place where no woman must enter.

After this experience, I feel the need for, and the benefit of, heavy work. In hard, grinding work all these fantasies of engulfment and possession fade away. And I'm the better for it.

I had two years down below to participate in this visual feast, this primal battle into the earth, before I was cast out of the darkness into the light of unemployment. Until now, my 'lad's wages' had kept my father and me afloat in bare poverty. My father lived his days in dark dreams and conjured up rough food for when I came back from the pit. But then even that comes to an end and, like the rest, I was thrown out of work.

Bereft of the black inspiration of the pit and with too much time on my hands, I start to use remembered images in my drawing. I make my own charcoal in the way my grandmother showed me and beg paper from Mr McVay at the corner shop. I iron it with my mother's flat-iron and I draw my pictures. My father makes no comment on this activity: merely sucks on his empty pipe and stares at the guttering fire.

I spend a lot of time over at the pit heaps. This town is

pockmarked with these manmade hills, which rise like pyramids from the green valley floor. My favourite is the one by the dog track. This is the highest of them all. The rail that used to pull the trucks full of spoil up this particular heap is rusted now. No engine has puffed its steam up here since 26 May, when the big strike started. The spoil heap hasn't grown, but with every winter's frost and every spring rain, the waste settles and moves, throws up its treasure. I never come here but I find a fish or an elaborate flower, a seahorse or a scaly animal. The collection of fossils in our frontroom cupboard grows apace, but we are tidy. The woman who ventures here with a charity pot of stew for 'the poor men', even while she mutters about a house of men having no comfort, has to admit that those Marchants, father and son, do keep their place clean.

I confine myself these days to three fine specimens a trip. First I collect a whole lot of them in my canvas sack. Then I sit on a high rock and lay them out, examining them minutely before I make my selection.

I sometimes think my father misses the pit more than he misses his wife. Pits of one kind or another have mothered him, swallowed him whole since he was ten. But now he has been spat out and prevented by the mean machinations of men from returning to the depths. His spirited activity in the strike led to his banishment. Now at last he's learned to be quiet, his spark is quite extinguished.

He always loved the pit but he loved the surface too. When I was small, before my mother died, he'd take me on long, leg-aching walks out of the town, beyond the clanking iron wheel. We'd tramp to the woods and ancient coppices that thickened in the crevices of this hilly land like hair on the human body. We'd gather bluebells and yellow aconites and, on two or three days a year, we'd fill the raised hem of my jersey with mushrooms which glowed grey-white against the late spring grass.

In the woods we'd watch the water voles and the hatching drone flies. We'd turn over Roman building stones. We'd climb the old trees, scrape off lichen and roll it in our fingers till it stained our skin green, red and purple. One time, high in a tree, I disturbed a ball-like bundle of sticks and sent it flying. My father told me the squirrel now would have to make a new home and he would chatter about me to his friends, telling them how I had destroyed his dray.

The one consolation for my father these days is that, away from the narrow rows of houses but still within the shadow of the great wheel, he has his own strip of land which he farms like any small farmer did in feudal times.

At the time I sensed the perverse satisfaction in my father when the main seam at Brack's Hill closes and I lose my job. I sensed his prickly disapproval when I came in the next day to say me and Tegger's got jobs in a drift mine out by Killock Quarry. But in these last winter months it has proved to be a cold and weary trudge, which makes me wish I could stay at home with my father even in his present misery. But I have to do this for the money. Turning down work is like blasphemy in a church: a sin against God and, worse, it demonstrates contempt of your fellow man.

My father's allotment is a long strip set alongside five other strips behind the last row of houses built by Lord Chase for the first opening of Brack's Hill Pit. The houses are small and narrow and overshadowed by the long pit wall. The allotments, however, look out over open land towards Priorton. It's not an unpleasant place to spend a fine Sunday afternoon.

Years ago, my father built himself a little shed made out of the packing cases which brought the new winding here up to the pit in 1920, before the first strike. The shed is orderly; his tools and implements (most of them handmade by his own father) each have their own special hook. In the worst days these spades and forks have travelled back and forth to the pawnbroker's. I am sure my father resented this more than the pawning of his best Sunday suit.

The vegetables he grows in the neat rows, the rabbits he breeds, the eggs from the clucking chickens: these are all we had to keep us going from 1926 to 1930 when I left school to go down the pit. After that, my father and I paid no rent to Lord Chase's agent for the house and my wage, small as it was, made a difference.

As I say, my father doesn't like this, me earning a wage. On pay days he'll be missing down the garden, way past the coming of darkness. He doesn't like to see me come in with bought goods from the shop. He rarely speaks to me in the house – ignores the scribbles and drawings on scraps of paper which I leave on the table for him to see. After a day or so I pile them up and put them in the drawer of the press in the parlour.

Saturdays and Sundays I walk the lanes and climb the slag heaps for new specimens. Then this one Saturday I see a woman moving between the whinbushes which are starting to root at the foot of the heap. She's tall and slender. She wears a long wool coat and a close hat around her face. Even from a distance I can see that she's not from round here. The coat is sweeping and well cut. The face is too soft: no sharp angles from hunger kept barely at bay.

She is there again on the Sunday.

That Monday, me and Tegger are laid off at the drift mine.

We tramp round other places looking for work, with no result. There are a hundred men in front of us in the queue for work. My father grunts when I tell him but I know there's some perverse satisfaction in him.

When I go up to the heap on the following Saturday, that woman is there again. The next day I wait for her by a sprouting lime tree which hooks improbably over the path leading to the heap. I spring forward and take her arm. She smells of fresh lemons. 'So what is it?' I say. 'Here again, are we?'

She twists away from my grasp. She's older than I thought, perhaps as much as thirty-five. 'What are you doing? Stop that!' she says. 'Will you stop it?' Her talk is strange.

'You've been watching me,' I say. 'I've felt your eyes on me.'

Her face is a long oval and her eyes a clear grey. Her hair, the colour of clean putty, is swept across her brow and away under her hat. No one, though, would call her pretty. More one of your plain Janes if you ask me. There's many a bonnier girl here in Brack's Hill turns up at the chapel dance or clusters at the entrance to the Priorton Odeon.

'I simply walk here. This is what I do. I walk.' Foreign. She must be foreign.

'You were spying on me.' I'm beginning to feel like a fool.

She smiles. Her teeth are small and even and very white. 'Why would I spy on you, whoever you are?'

'Why do you come to this place? It's not for the likes of you.'

Her head goes up. 'So! What is the likes of me? I walk where I will. Now let me pass.' She moves past me and I watch her narrow back as it recedes down the lane towards Brack's Hill. Her feet, clad in boots fine stitched in green leather, crunch on the cinder gravel of the pathway. Behind her, in the air, is the faint smell of lemons.

By the time I get back to the house I'm in a fine stew. I clash the pans about while I put together some kind of dinner. I survey the low dark scullery with loathing. I sit on a stool to clean my best boots but no matter how much I spit and polish they look what they are: worn-down patched boots which have seen much better days.

And still the woman in the green leather boots is on my mind.

Chapter Four

The Magician

Rosel Smidt knocked twice on the glass panes of the front door. From inside the stone house came the intermittent sound of a sweet contralto voice. Rosel knocked again. The singing stopped and there was silence.

She waited at the door for five minutes then made her way down the side alley that separated the house from the next one. The long back yard was enclosed by a low wall. A woman was pegging clothes on a line which drooped the full length of the yard. Her frothy hennaed hair was barely confined in an artfully tied turban; a few long rusty curls bounced on to her cheeks. Her pouting, lipsticked mouth gagged on three wooden gypsy pegs.

'Mr Todhunter?' said Rosel. 'Does he live in this house?' She reached her hand over the gate to open it from the inside.

The woman spat the pegs into her hand and tucked them into the pocket of her apron. 'So he does.' The voice was low, modulated, unlike the gruff, almost swallowed tones Rosel had been hearing on the train and in the bus on her way to this place.

'Come on inside. You'll be this German artist Archie's been on about? Von something, I think he said.'

'Yes. Yes. Rosel Von Steinigen!' She saw the frown on the other woman's face. 'Perhaps just Vonn will do. The other, *vielleicht*, is too hard for the English tongue.' Perhaps it was just here. Her London friends had had no problem with the name, but they were mostly very well educated, even for artists.

'Yes, Vonn, that's better,' said the woman. 'Rosel Vonn.'

She led the visitor through a neat scullery into a place which was half-kitchen, half-office, with books and ledgers heaped on a dresser and loaves of bread stacked on a bookshelf.

Rosel put down her heavy bags and rubbed her upper arm.

'Through here.' The woman led on. They went into a room that was bare but for chairs: chairs of all sizes and shapes pushed together in a rough circle. Behind them were stacks of folding chairs. 'Not in here,' said the woman, moving on into a cluttered hallway then out into a corridor, where the walls were cluttered with a jumble of paintings, drawings and prints. The only straight line was a set of lithographs of actors in roles: Othello, Henry V, and Touchstone. Sir Henry Irving predominated.

'Come, come.' Rosel was bustled on. She could smell the other woman's inky, intense perfume. Something from a very dark bottle. 'Come on in.' The woman opened a door off the corridor. 'If you'll just go in here.'

The room was overstuffed and over-furnished. Books and battered sheaves of paper languished on every surface. In the corner was a desk which, in contrast to the room, was surprisingly neat. On it sat an inkwell and a small rack with what looked like cigarette-holders and a fancy Eastern stand for a matchbox. The fire was laid but not lit. Still the room was not cold; it was stuffy with the residual heat and scent of other days and many other bodies.

The woman leaned on the doorjamb, eyeing Rosel up and down. 'I'd sit down if I were you. He could be a time.'

Rosel chose a seat by the window. 'Thank you,' she said. 'Thank you very much.'

The woman vanished. Rosel could hear her call, the modulation now roughened to a raucous shout. 'Archie! Get down here. Your German artist's here.'

There was a muffled shout and scramble above Rosel's head.

'Yes,' the woman called. 'Wrong day, I know. But never mind, she's here.'

Rosel could hear the pad of the woman's steps as she went up to the next floor. Then there was silence. If they were speaking, they were doing so in the lightest of whispers.

Rosel leaned across and lifted the lace curtain to peer out into the street. The January afternoon was overcast to the point where it might be evening. In the row opposite, lit faintly from the inside, were a greengrocer's shop, a butcher's shop and a tobacconist. Each window displayed a pitiful pile of goods. A hollow-eyed woman with a child on her back and one clinging to each hand emerged from the greengrocer's. The taller child held a paper bag as though it contained great treasure. Rosel wondered what was in it. A few apples? A turnip? Outside the tobacconist's, two gaunt men were crouched almost on their knees, sharing a cigarette.

'Viewing the sights of Brack's Hill, Fraulein Von Steinigen?'

Rosel turned in her chair and rose to shake hands with Archie Todhunter. Although barely taller than she was, his voice resonated from somewhere deep inside his chest. His face was pale and finely boned, masked by glasses with no rims. He carried with him the aroma of old tobacco and used-up alcohol. His reddish-grey hair was glossy and swept back in the manner of a screen idol. Ronald Colman, perhaps. So this was the one, the magician who they said could spin gold out of coal dust. He looked much more ordinary than that.

'Hello, Mr Todhunter.'

'Call me Archie – that's my name. No room for fakery and titles at the Settlement.'

She blushed at the anger in his tone. 'And my name is Rosel,' she said. 'I have decided to keep to Rosel Vonn. The whole name is, how you would say, too much of a mouthful. And *Fraulein* is far too solemn. Far too . . .' She sat back down in her seat. 'German, perhaps.'

He dragged a wooden chair close to the window and sat beside her. 'Your English is very good, Rosel. I thought I'd have to try a bit of my schoolboy German on you.' He was staring at her too closely, as if his eye would eventually penetrate her skin, and know all about her. '*Ein. Zwei. Drei*. That sort of thing.'

She laughed. 'I've been here some time. I lived in Sunderland as a girl with my uncle and in London for a time. I studied at the Slade. I come just now from London.'

'Sunderland?'

'My uncle worked for a glass company there.'

'Yes. Yes. One of your recommendations came from Sunderland. Yes, I remember this.' He stared at her. 'And what makes you want to come here and work in a place which both God and Lucifer have forsaken?' His tone was challenging.

'I was at a party . . .' She flushed. She could not say it was a funeral. It seemed somehow so indelicate.

'Oh yes?' he said. 'A feast, no doubt.'

'I was at a function and I met a member of the Trust.'

'Yes?' he said again.

'A Mr Belgique. American, I think. He told me of the wonderful work you're doing among the unemployed in the Settlement here. He called you a magician.' She paused. 'Then I went back to London. I am a member of Artists International. Duncan Grant. Vanessa . . . Ben Nicholson. You know these artists?'

'I have read of their work in the *Manchester Guardian*.' Archie Todhunter took a minute or two to fix a cigarette in a short black holder. 'So you thought you'd join me in my missionary work?' His deep voice resonated through the dense air of the room. 'A sorcerer's apprentice here in County Durham?'

'No. No. It is not this.' She searched around in her head. 'I have a need,' she acknowledged finally. 'For many years I have drawn and carved. Sometimes I have exhibitions. I live in Paris, then London. A little success, a little praise. My friends in London are very kind. But then I have a long talk with Henry Moore. Such a fine man. But after talking with him, I can carve no longer. Now some bad things are happening in Germany. My father speaks up too much, my brother is in trouble with the army. I should go home. I am afraid. I cannot paint. Then I talk with the man Belgique at the party and he suggests I join you for a year. Offer what I can. Perhaps I will start to paint again. Perhaps I will teach others. Or, perhaps I will gather the courage to go and join my father and my brother in their troubles.' She paused. 'I do not feel like a missionary. I feel myself in need of enlightenment.'

Archie Todhunter nodded. His laughter barked out. 'Bravo! What a speech, my dear! And in a foreign language. Perhaps I should draft you into my drama group. You'd have a great deal to offer there.' He went to the door. 'Cora! *Cora!*' he bellowed. 'Tea!'

Rosel blinked.

Archie turned round. 'So you know all about the Settlements?'

'Well, Mr Belgique . . .'

'Set up to keep unemployed workers occupied and perhaps even fulfilled. Perhaps even give them something which may be more useful than soul-rotting years on the dole?' His glasses were opaque in the light from the window.

'And this is what you believe?'

He shrugged. 'I might believe that it keeps the clamour down and delays the revolution. But if, on the other hand, day by day a man or a woman finds dignity in what we do here, that suits me. For me the individual is more important than the whole. In truth, I make a poor revolutionary.'

'And what do really you do? What do you do here?'

He shrugged. 'We study literature and philosophy. We have a class in French. Classes in Current Affairs. We cobble shoes, we make boxes and cabinets, we write stories, we put on plays, we have a Drawing Society which is mostly self-taught. So that's where you come in.'

She looked around the cluttered room. 'And where do you do all this?'

'You'd be surprised, my dear. We bought two nearby shops and extended, with the help of pit bricklayers and joiners. There's a good deal of skill in these parts, going spare. We also extended the sheds out the back of this house. Sometimes it's not enough of course, and we have to use our own parlour here for the discussions.'

'There is a stage? You do drama?'

'Aye. Well, in a way. We use a church hall round the corner which happens to have a kind of platform.' He inhaled deeply on his cigarette. 'One day we'll have our own theatre.'

'And you really put on plays? What plays?'

He shuffled a pile of papers, and placed some of them in her hand. 'There. The programmes – Shaw, Ibsen, Chekhov, Shakespeare. Modern stuff – T. S. Eliot, Sean O'Casey.'

Magic indeed. She peered at the paper in the half-light. 'And do people attend these plays? The Brack's Hill people?'

He chortled. 'In their hundreds. What is it, Fraulein Rosel Vonn? Do you think these miners are mere beasts of the field, that they would not have the soul or the stomach for such great works?'

She blushed. 'I did not say . . .'

She was saved by the housekeeper kicking the door open and bringing in a tray loaded with a big brown teapot and three large white cups without saucers.

'Ah, Cora,' said Archie. 'Did you introduce yourself to Rosel?'

The woman called Cora smiled, rubbed a hand down her dress and held it out. 'Cora Miles,' she said. 'Pleased to meet you, Miss . . . Rosel, was it?'

Rosel's hand was clasped in a strong grip.

'Cora runs the acting and poetry workshops at the Settlement,' said Archie, 'and occasionally takes the lead in the plays. She does a doughty Lady Macbeth, and a winsome Rosalinde. In her time our Cora has trodden the boards in West End theatres. She is no lightweight.'

'Take no notice of Archie, Rosel. He was born with a mocking tongue in his mouth.'

Rosel felt very relieved that she had not betrayed her

assumption that this hardy woman was Archie's housekeeper.

Cora passed them each a cup of tea and, taking one for herself, perched on the arm of Archie's chair. Her apron had been removed to reveal a tight-fitting dark green wool dress and she'd applied another layer of lipstick to her full lips. 'So, Rosel, will you join the happy band here?' She glanced at Archie. 'I use *happy* in its freest, most metaphoric meaning, of course.'

'Yes, I am here for this.' Rosel turned to Archie. 'Would you like me to come to this Settlement of yours? I wish to do it. I will help with your Drawing Society.'

He shrugged. 'We can but try. You might hate it. The people here might hate you. Half their brothers and cousins were killed on the Somme, so your being German will not help, I'm afraid.'

'Archie!' Cora warned.

'It's a fact.' His tone was flat. 'There's strong feeling here on the subject of Germans. Ignorant and mistaken it may be, but the sense of genuine injury is there.'

A silence prickled the room.

'My uncle and my two cousins were killed in France,' said Rosel at last. 'I was fifteen then. I can remember it well. I also am injured.'

'Ah!' Archie put a finger on his nose. 'But the English won, so their loss is greater.'

'Archie, you're disgraceful.' Cora turned to Rosel. 'Take not a bit of notice of him, dear. He is nothing but an old grump, that one.'

Then Archie asked Rosel some questions about Berlin and about the person he called 'Old Adolf'. He listened intently to her answers and told her of an affair a year or so back when there had been some trouble with some local Fascists. A schoolteacher had ended up in prison in trying to expose them.

Archie's tone was friendly, even intimate. Rosel knew she'd been accepted.

The need to defend Rosel from Archie caught Cora's sympathy. She and Archie had planned to place the German woman in lodgings but actually meeting Rosel face to face made her change her mind. Glancing at Archie for confirmation she offered the newcomer a room at the top of the Settlement house. 'We had a commercial traveller in there at odd times. A bit extra for the funds, you know? But he went missing with some goods from a grain warehouse so it's been empty for a while.'

Rosel stood up. She was grateful to have a roof over her head after her long journey from London. On their way upstairs she asked if Cora could arrange for someone to collect her big case and the boxes from the railway station, if not tonight then first thing tomorrow.

Cora went off to arrange this and Rosel threw herself on the bed. She was so exhausted that she slept half the night with all her clothes on, then stripped off and slept another six hours, only waking when a hammering on her door told her that her boxes had arrived.

By the next night Rosel had discovered that Cora was not only some unique kind of housekeeper, nor was she merely a leading lady although her name was on the playbills. It seemed that she and Archie shared a bedroom. The banter between the two of them evoked the sense of years of intimacy if not absolute domestic harmony. They were certainly married, or something close to it.

Chapter Five

The Artist

In the first few days at Brack's Hill, Rosel spent much of her time in her room contemplating just how she'd managed to end up at the age of thirty-eight in a depressed village full of hungry men and women in the far North of England.

As Herr Freud would have it, it was all about her parents. She knew that. Her mother, now ensconced in an asylum for the very mad, had been a great beauty called at birth Lilah Burgandorf. As a young woman she'd modelled for many painters in Berlin. Then she'd fallen in love with the aristocratic Max Von Steinigen at a party in the studio of his friend Heinrich, who had studied art with him in Paris and was also Lilah's lover before and after she met Max.

Max, having rejected the life of an army cadet, was abandoned by his family with a small allowance to the dissolution and comfort of art. In return he honoured his aristocratic heritage, was proud of his family, and did not betray them by word or deed. Rosel thought her father would be very alarmed at her reducing their illustrious old name to *Vonn* for the benefit of the tongue-tied of Brack's Hill.

Within a year of their marriage Lilah gave birth to Rosel's brother Boris, to be followed by Rosel herself two years later.

Until their offspring were four and six respectively, Max and Lilah left their children with a nurse in Max's home village. Parties and posing, exhibitions and affairs did not really mix with small children. When Rosel was five, she and her brother were brought to Berlin to live with their parents in their vast apartment by the Kurfürstendamm.

But Lilah didn't care for their changed lives: the crush of nurses and cooks, the wail of frustrated children. Within a month she left them to concentrate more fully on being the doyenne of the cafés and bars, the muse of the studios. She had her own life in the stews and ateliers of the city.

Max, now on his own, became reclusive. He focused his passion on Rosel and Boris. They ate at his table and slept in his bed. He taught them and played with them. He painted them in the dress of princes and the dress of street urchins. Their days and nights were filled with his obsession.

They lived like this with him in Bohemian luxury until Boris joined the army when he was sixteen and Rosel, stifled with her father's attention, ran away to find her mother.

She lurked outside cafés and talked to waiters. She carried one of her father's small sketches of Lilah and showed it to them. 'This is my mother.' They laughed when they saw it. They knew Lilah, all right! They would tell Rosel to return another night. But Lilah never turned up – she always seemed to be in another place, at another café.

Rosel slept in attic places near the cafés and the waiters fed her on scraps. She was often sick with bad food and sometimes overwhelmed by their touching and petting.

Then her father came and found her. He held her hand tight all the way back home on the rattling train and the swaying tram. When they got home he clutched her to him and wept, then slapped her about the head for betraying him. Then he comforted her, drying her tears with the sleeve of his fine linen shirt and held her until he fell asleep.

That night she sneaked out of his bed and went to the kitchen where she found a sharp knife and carved her mother's name on her wrists.

After that her father sent her to schools for girls, from which she ran away every second day, still looking for her mother. Eventually he took her over to England, putting a sea between her and Lilah. They spent one night in London then caught a series of trains, chugging their way North through darker and darker districts to Sunderland, a heaving place by the sea. Here Max left his daughter with his Cousin Berti who lived and worked in this town as an artist in glass.

Berti Von Steinigen was more of an artisan than an artist. He'd trained in the great workshop of Bohemia, and was valued at the works in Sunderland as a gifted craftsman and designer. He spun glass like an angel.

Rosel lived with Berti, whom she called 'Uncle', in a tall house by the sea. From the window of her room she relished the sight of the churning waves. Unlike her father, who made her gag with his attention, Uncle Berti allowed her to live for herself. They dined together each night. He took her to his workshop and introduced her to the young men who worked for him. He arranged for her to work at a small art institute where they took her through the rudiments of art, which were already second nature to her.

The Great War came and she and her uncle were interned.

In Germany her brother welcomed the war. He was clever and beguiling and a great favourite with his comrades. The disorder of his early youth made military discipline very attractive to him. When war came he fought for the Kaiser with pride.

In that war Max Von Steinigen was a stretcher carrier; he also drew and painted the scenes around him. His paintings (ordered recently to be destroyed by Chancellor Hitler as defeatist and decadent) were exhibited widely. His drawings were collected. His studies of the helpless human being amid the hatefulness of trench warfare were compared with the German expressionists Max Beckmann and Otto Dix, while his landscapes of war were deemed on a par with the Englishman Paul Nash.

At the end of the war Rosel returned to her studies and her uncle to his glass. Then Berti died in an accident at the glassworks and she was alone in England. By this time Rosel had no wish to go back to Germany. She often thought of her brother but he was preoccupied with the state of their homeland. These days, he was becoming very wary of the growing promise of Adolf Hitler, the man Archie Todhunter called *Old Adolf*. For three years now his letters had been threaded though with foreboding. Their mother, overwrought from excitement and appetite, had ended up in an asylum. Boris wrote with great unease about learned academics who proposed to put mad people out of their misery, as you would do with a dog.

It was at her Uncle Berti's funeral that Rosel met the M. Belgique from the Trust who told her of the work in the Settlements. It was he who mentioned the one here at Brack's Hill, and the magician Archie Todhunter, who spun something out of nothing. M. Belgique's arms had flailed around so much with enthusiasm that he nearly spilt the port with which they had just drunk Uncle Berti's health. 'This Todhunter discusses with these people the Industrial Revolution and the immoral imperatives of imperialism. It seems he even advises the poor on their rights and defends them in court.'

So, here she was. It took only a few days in Brack's Hill to become acquainted with the range of Archie's efforts.

It seemed he wanted her to teach some German, and to lead the van with the art and drawing. In writing and theatre work, he himself could clearly take the lead. He tutored writing, taught social affairs alongside a man called Jonty Clelland whom he obviously admired. Above all, Archie wrote plays, directed and performed in them.

'And, although I join in the painting, Rosel, I am a mere dauber. Not even as good as some of the miners, sad to say. We have this annual exhibition and they usually outshine me. So at the moment it's a sort of self-discovery group. There's no leading expertise, you see, so they lose out.'

Archie did so much. He had such intellectual energy. An amazing man. Rosel noted too that he had an inner watchfulness and a very odd kind of lethargy, which belied all this activity.

On the first day Archie led her through to the big room which had been the dark front shop. It was here, he explained, where they had their largest meetings, where the library books were laid out on library days and where much of the craftwork was done. 'We have to box and cox a little, to be honest.'

She looked round. Some attempt had been made to brighten the place with cream paint. 'I am to have my class in here?'

'This is what there is.' He watched her keenly.

'I could have six or seven people here only. The tables are very cramped. The light is not good.'

He nods. 'I thought of that. There is a shed out the back, with skylights. Perhaps we could fix that up?'

'And paints?'

This time he smiled, then strode across to a cabinet which, she imagined, had once held tobacco and flints. With a flourish he pulled out a stack of fine sugar paper and two cardboard boxes of pretty decent charcoal. 'I managed to get these. Don't ask me where.' He leaned down, dragged a low cupboard door open and lifted out three large boxes. 'Now these I obtained from Sunderland.'

They were boxes of watercolour and oil paint, partly used and very serviceable. Very high quality. Rosel recognised them. 'I know these paints,' she said.

'Your uncle had them sent to me a month before he died. He said he had not really painted for years and had no use for them,' Archie said. 'It seems you were meant to come here to Brack's Hill, Fraülein.'

'He knew about this place?' She was surprised.

'I had occasion to commission a window from him on behalf of a friend in London. A very fine window it was – a study of the sea and boats. We met one Sunday in his studio and I suppose inevitably I talked about my work here. He came to visit us. Shook his head at me burying myself here in what he called this land beyond hope.'

She smiled slightly. 'But you would say that this is the place where hope lives. Is that not so?'

'A wise thought, Fraulein.'

She touched the paints. She could smell Uncle Berti's studio.

'My uncle was a quiet man.' She could not think of anything else to say.

'He wouldn't know you'd end up here,' said Archie. 'I suppose.'

She thought of M. Belgique drinking her Uncle Berti's health. She clicked the box shut. 'Well,' she said, 'I'm ready to join the artists here, if you can fix up the shed with the skylights. The paints are fine.'

'The classes take place on Tuesday afternoons and evenings, and on Saturday afternoons. Some people can come in Tuesdays as there is so very little work, but we need the Saturdays for one or two people who are still working. They too need food for their souls. They only have Saturdays after a hard week.'

'And what do I do the rest of the time?' The thought of empty time in this grey place was not entrancing.

He shrugged. 'You're an artist. I imagine that you'll draw and paint. There are unique sights indeed in this place, very individual characters. They all need recording.'

'It is all so grey. The very air is dark.'

'Is it?' He raised a finely arched brow. 'Your father found images aplenty in the dingy trenches in Belgium. He rendered them very fine.'

'You know that book? His work?'

He looked around, then behind him, as though the book was actually in this room. 'I have it here, somewhere. In my room upstairs, I would think. I have it from your uncle. It came with the paints.' He smiled grimly. 'Perhaps he did know that one day you'd be here. Perhaps he thought that these were your trenches. That Brack's Hill was your Ypres. I think you should record something of the landscape and people here. There's raw material aplenty.'

So, for want of any other preference she started to wander the streets of this small town with her little notebook. Men in doorways, women at street corners. Men crouching down by a wall. A dingy house with rags instead of windows. The people were polite. They merely looked at her sideways as she scratched away, using them as raw material.

One day she wandered right out of the town, through the dense remnants of woodland, past the silent tangle of pit machinery and the blank-windowed warehouse sheds. Then she made her way down the pit road which skirted the great pit heap.

She wrote of the pit heap in her first letter to her brother Boris. *The great pit heap is like one of the circles of hell. This pyramid of grey stones and shale moves and shifts in the greyer air. It is dull even in the brightest sunlight. Here and there, wisps of smoke drift upward from some stony niche. The housekeeper here (who isn't really a housekeeper, by the way,) told me that this is where a pocket of coals, ground together by the slipping shale, begins to spit and spark, smoulder and burn. Sometimes such pockets explode and make hidden black holes for the unwary scrambler. Cora (the not-housekeeper) told me this. She also told me a tale of how, in 1927, a small child fell into one of these chambers and was dead when he was found a week later.*

It was at the pit heap where Rosel came upon the young man, poring over his stones like a miser. He drifted around the place with his face almost to the ground. He would see something that seemed to please him and hold it up directly against the wintry sun, creasing his eyes to give him some perspective. His greasy fair curls were hardly contained by the cap stuck on the back of his head. Sometimes he stood absolutely still for minutes on end. On this heap of slipping stones and shifting shale he seemed himself to be a rock.

Rosel's fingers itched to trace the high thick cheekbones, to run her palms across his muscular shoulders, to mould the hand which held up the stones to the spring sun like some kind of offering.

He burrowed on the tip as though he owned it. He had a kind of rhythm, putting some stones into a sack and throwing others away. The rejects he pitched high into the sky, his arm arcing through the air like that of a discus thrower, the muscles on his shoulders rippling under his thin coat. Then he would wait and watch as the stone found another resting place on this mountain of shale.

He was so engrossed in his task that she observed him for three days, had five sketches in her book before he saw her. On the fourth day he lay in wait and grabbed her. 'So what is it?' he said. 'Here again, Missis?'

She twisted away from him. He was much younger than she had thought at first, perhaps only eighteen or nineteen. He had the face of the boy in a Titian painting. Rosel felt very old. 'Stop that!' she said. 'Stop it.'

'You've been watching me, I felt your eyes on me here. Monday.'

'I simply walk here. This is what I do. I am walking to get to know where I am.' She was glad that her notebook was tucked down in her long pocket. 'I do not know this district.'

Red patches stained the straight planes of the boy's cheeks. 'Why do you come to this place, watching us in our misery? It's not for the likes of you.'

He was so young, so perplexed. He made her smile. 'So why would I spy on you?'

'Why do you come to this place?' he repeated. The voice was harder now, the tone ugly. 'It's not for the likes of you.'

She could feel the menace in him now. She held her head high. 'What is the likes of me? I walk where I will. Now let me pass, will you?'

He seemed about to say something, then he stood back. She brushed past him and walked steadily, steadily away. In her long pocket was her sketchbook with the first decent drawings she had done in two years.

It seemed to Rosel that now, perhaps, she had cause for rejoicing.

Chapter Six

The Mission

Gabriel's friend Tegger threw open the door and twenty-one faces turned towards him. 'Sorry, I thought . . .' He drew back, red-faced. The speaker stopped. The room faltered into silence.

'No, no. Come in.' The man with filmstar hair gestured towards him with the book which he held in his hand. 'Please – come on in, sir. We're nearly finished here.'

So this, then, was Archie Todhunter. Tegger had heard talk of him in The Lord Raglan. The conversation there was mostly dogs, horses, ways of outwitting the spies from the Means Test, or black jokes about Colledge the undertaker benefiting from everyone else's bad luck. For a good while now there had been gossip about this Todhunter. Word was he'd been a doctor. And a failed actor. They said he was Scottish, a bit of a 'Red' and a lot of a wizard. He got people to write, to paint, to act, he obtained wood and leather so lads on the dole could make and mend shoes and bags for themselves and their families. Word was, though, they weren't allowed to sell stuff.

Word was also that this Todhunter was an agitator who gave

talks on Lenin and said people should take things into their own hands. None of this bothered Tegger. 'Speak as you find' was one of his many mottoes.

At the Settlement now the men and women returned their attention to this Todhunter. He continued: 'So, friends, perhaps Chekhov *is* our man. He talks sense and he talks deep. His people wait for the future as we do. He, like ourselves, is caught in the web of the past. I've four copies of the play, so you'll have to pass them amongst you. You'll need to hand-copy your part when you get it. Anyway, perhaps you'd see what you think. If you don't care for this one then I do have a play of my own . . .' He paused. 'But see what you think about this one,' he repeated.

Some of the people were getting to their feet when Archie stopped them with a raised hand. 'Oh yes, and we have a new volunteer at the Settlement, sent by an association called International Artists. She is a very accomplished artist who'll work with the painters and drawers on Tuesdays and Saturdays. She'll also help us with our design – set and costumes – for the plays. We need more artists to work with her, so get the word out. Her presence is an honour. Good news for our work here.'

Tegger watched as the people sorted out the books between them, made arrangements to read together or pass the book on, then drifted away. A striking, rather ugly woman dressed in bright colours stayed behind and helped Archie collapse the trestles and put the folding chairs up against the wall.

'Now then, my boy.' Archie came across to shake Tegger by the hand.

'Tegger MacNamara,' said Tegger, taking off his cap. 'I've come about—'

'And here is Cora Miles, the actress.'

The woman's hand slipped into his, warm and firm. It was a

long time since Tegger had shaken hands with anyone at all. And here was a second time in minutes. It was a fussy habit, unwelcome among reserved pitmen. '*Dinna be soft, man!*' the men would say.

Cora Miles shrugged on her jacket: a graceful, tidy movement. 'I'll go up now, Archie,' she said to Todhunter. 'Brew some coffee.'

That was another thing. Rumour had it that Archie Todhunter lived tally with the ugly woman. No one did anything about it, of course. Dour comment was possible, but interference was not the style of the people of Brack's Hill. Tegger had made it his business to study these people. When the spirit moved him he even wrote stories about them in the back of an old ledger he'd taken when shifting the stock of a bankrupt shop.

The people did nothing about Todhunter and his peculiar arrangements. Tegger observed that underneath the Bible-thumping of chapelgoers and the gossip of the rest there still lay the philosophy of 'live and let live'. This, he reckoned, was because the ebb and flow of work meant people were always moving in and out of Brack's Hill.

Many of these men and women, though virtuous themselves, had seen and known enough to realise that conditions for virtue were not written on tablets of stone: that bad individuals did good things, that good people had bad edges. Every family had its grey sheep. 'There but for the grace of God go I,' was not an uncommon saying in Brack's Hill. As was 'leave well alone'.

The pragmatism of moving and settling, moving and settling meant it was wise to keep your own counsel and not interfere with others. Tegger knew this was especially so in the case of Archie Todhunter, who'd brought such bounty to the town with his American funding, his workshops, his playmaking and what was grandly termed his Poor Man's Law Centre. It was this latter which had enticed Tegger MacNamara into alien territory on this cold evening.

In his office Todhunter settled in a hard wooden chair by the open fire and pulled up another for Tegger. 'Now then, young feller. What can I do for you – Mr MacNamara, was it?'

'They say you give advice, about the Means Test and that. They say you're a poor man's lawyer.'

Todhunter fitted a cigarette into a short amber holder and held a newspaper spill to the fire to light it. He took a deep, grateful draw. 'Well,' he said, the smoke trailing from his lips with the words, 'we've a few books, some government pamphlets, and a lot of goodwill. So we can give advice. What advice would you need, Mr MacNamara?'

'It's just . . . well, me ma and da is there at home with three little 'uns. I won't get the dole when I'm with them, or they can't have the dole when I'm there. The Means Test people are hot on that. Working age and all that.'

Todhunter shook his head. 'That is the case. And as you say, Mr MacNamara, it's a mistake to cross the Means Test man. Only worth fighting a winnable cause.'

'Then I'll have to go away. Down London or Coventry like some marras of mine. Plenty doing that these days,' said Tegger. 'But me ma'd sure miss us. She needs my help with the little 'uns, see. Me da's in his chair day and night, coughing. She really does need someone to help with the bairns. I couldn't afford to move, any road.' He was too shy to add that he didn't want to move, that he was rooted in this place like any oak.

'It seems the only sensible thing, these days, is to move away.' Todhunter stared into the fire. 'Men in your position sometimes go up behind Trent Street, in the vans.'

'Vans?' Tegger was shocked. 'What? Go up there, live like a tinker?'

Behind Trent Street on a bit of wasteland was a huddle of vans, covered with canvas on an iron frame, where men gathered who had no other place to go. He'd walked past Trent Street on many a dark afternoon and seen them gathered round their flickering bonfire. The place seemed impregnable. It was a glimpse of another time, another place. 'They're shiftless, those lads. Layabouts.'

'Ha!' Todhunter barked into the air. 'Is it up to you to judge men you've never met? The pit they work in may have closed, their families moved on or even died. People are dying like flies now. Mortality here's greater than anywhere in England. D'you know this? They have no roof over their head except that stretched canvas. Some of them come here for classes. Good people.' He drew again on his cigarette. 'I know that one of them is moving out, going across to Liverpool on his way to Canada. We've just kitted him out, found him his passage money. His van will be free. If you move in there then the Means Test man must give your family their fair money.'

'Well . . .' said Tegger.

Todhunter sighed. 'Is there no one else you could move in with?' he said patiently.

Tegger shook his head. 'I've this friend who'd welcome me, I know. He lives with his da. But he's just been laid off from the drift mine and he'd be in the same boat if I moved in. They'd cut his dole.'

'Right. Shall I walk up to Trent Street with you tomorrow to talk to this fellow? The one I know?'

'I could go and see my family during the day?'

'Yes. But you should be careful not to be there in a routine daily fashion, or it will be noted.'

'Bloody spies. Excuse me. Well, I suppose I'll have to do it then,' said Tegger sorrowfully. 'Live in the van.'

Todhunter smoked on in silence and Tegger wriggled in his seat, wondering how he could escape. 'Well, Mr Todhunter . . .' he began.

'What job did you do in the pit?' said Todhunter abruptly.

'I was a putter, pushing and pulling the tubs underground.'

'It must take some strength, a job like that.'

'Yer either get strong or give up, I can tell yer.'

'Have you done anything else down there?'

'A bit of joinery. I was 'prenticed to the pit joiner first off but I gave up because the pay was poor. Strength pays, in the pit.'

'Were you any good at joinery?'

'Yeah. Close enough for pit work, like they say.'

'Ah. Good,' said Todhunter. 'Good. Well, there's no pay here at the Settlement but we do need a joiner to help with repairs on the hut that we're going to use as an art workshop. And we'll need help to build sets for our new play, whatever it turns out to be. It's not quite decided yet.'

Tegger shook his head. 'I canna do that, man. I wouldn't know where ter start, making stage stuff.'

'We've got a time-served joiner here already – out of work, of course. He could do with a hand. He'll tell you,' said Archie patiently.

'I don't know . . .'

'Well,' said Todhunter briskly. 'Just think. You'll be stuck down in the van at Trent Street. You can't spend all day at home. What else have you to do?'

'If you think . . .'

Todhunter stood up. 'That's fixed, then. Meet me here at two tomorrow and I'll take you up to Trent Street to meet this fellow with the van.'

Tegger made for the door, then looked back. 'That drawing class,' he said. 'Can anyone come?'

'Well then,' said Todhunter. 'Are you a painter as well as a joiner?'

Tegger laughed. 'No fear of that. Happier with a pen than a paintbrush! Words and songs, me. No, it's me marra. He draws, even paints sometimes. And he has time on his hands now, like the rest of us.'

'Tell him to come then. He'll be more than welcome.'

'I don't know. He's a close bird, is Gabriel. Quiet, like. Stubborn. I doubt you won't get him in here.'

'They're all quiet round here. And stubborn. But we'll see about your friend,' said Archie. 'We'll see.'

Archie Todhunter's zeal for the 'common good' was not unique to him in his family. He'd inherited it from far-off ancestors, those bog and hedge ranters who'd roared their conviction to the heather and bewildered locals since the Reformation. His great-great-grandfather had been a church minister: his great-grandfather, a missionary in Africa, and his grandfather, a missionary in China. His father, a medical missionary born and bred in China, came home once on leave and (to the genteel despair of his Edinburgh cronies) had fallen for a very simple woman who worked in a manual trade in the Glasgow shipyards. He married this common woman when she was pregnant and sailed away to China with her after she'd given birth to Archie whom she left to her Glasgow sisters to bring up.

Despite this pious inheritance, somewhere in his young life Archie lost God and transferred his vocation to medicine. Even so the cadences of the King James Bible stayed in his heart and informed his love of poetry and drama. This passion was his undoing as a medico as it led to his involvement with the student drama group: student orations, rehearsed readings, plays, the impromptu staging of a wide range of dramas. The plays, for him, had the fascination of dreams made fact.

There was no time for study so he dropped out and joined one small repertory company after another and played small roles. He took to the skill of lighting and stage production very quickly and, on taking up a hammer and saw, found he'd inherited his Glasgow grandfather's carpentry skills, rather than his Edinburgh grandfather's belief in God.

In his time he played hundreds of small towns at the end of freezing train journeys. Still, he took delight in the warm reception his troop might get in the smallest dingy place and in acting in everything from the plays of Demosthenes to those of Mr J.B. Priestley. His other delight was, in any town where they stopped, to put on classes for local young people in drama and stagecraft. He enjoyed that as a powerful antidote to playing the second policeman or the man who was murdered in the First Act.

The highlight of Archie's theatrical career was a year with the great actor-manager Tyrone Guthrie, that lanky giant in slippers, that natural Irish aristocrat, that genius of the mundane and the everyday.

It was Guthrie who was his nemesis. As they walked to the theatre one day, the Irishman wound his long scarf more tightly round his neck and pulled down the wide brim of his hat. 'Teaching, Todhunter. I can see that that's your bent. Any eye could see it. We, mere players . . .' he paused, allowing the power to rise into his voice from that elongated body '. . . mere players are weaklings by comparison. Can't think why you don't go for it hell for leather, Todhunter. Go for the full thing, old boy. Give up this precarious, silly existence. Turn aside from this bumpy road on which we walk. Give it up! Go! Do the thing you were born to. Help those poor people.'

The muscles in Archie's neck had stiffened then, with the effort not to cry. For nearly a year he'd waited, watched and learned from this great man. He'd treated him with an attention close to idolatry. He'd learned so much and offered every fibre of himself in return. Now his idol was casting him to one side like the discarded peel of an orange. 'Give it up?' he said hoarsely.

'More to the world than the theatre, dear boy . . .' Tyrone began.

Inside the long sleeves of his coat Archie's hands knuckled up into fists. He coughed. 'You might be right, Tony,' he said brightly, using the intimacy of that name for the first time. 'You might just be right. I do like working with those youngsters. Bringing light to their eyes. Giving them hope for the future.'

This speech, thrown off so very lightly, was the finest piece of acting he'd ever achieved. He'd been graceful. He'd been modest. He had to retrieve what he could.

Tony Guthrie slapped him on the back. 'Good man, Archie,' he said, returning the compliment of the friendly Christian name. 'Play to your strengths. Play to your strengths, dear boy.'

So, Archie noted, my acting is my weakness. Thank you *very* much!

The thought came to him. Here he was, at thirty, embarking on a career not unlike his father's. There would be no God or gospel of course, no wise Chinese eyes. But for him, like his father, the greatest satisfaction would be to bring light where there had been darkness; to bring The Word where there had been silence.

Yes, the Settlement was his fate, his mission, as surely as his mother's mission was in that village up the Yangtze. Was it the Yangtze? He couldn't quite remember now, and the dreams of her in her coolie hat were fading. They were not even revived when he read, in *The Times*, of her murder by anti-Christian Chinese. *The Times* made her out to be quite the heroine. So that was all right.

'So,' said Cora, pulling back the sheets and jumping in. 'Who was the big lad who came to see you? He has a nice face, like an unshorn lamb.'

Archie fastened his last pyjama button and stood before the mirror combing back his hair. 'He needed some help about the Means Test. I think he'll join us. Could make a very good contribution. He has carpentry skills and, according to him, he writes songs. I like him. He has a glint in his eye.'

'A glint in his eye!' Cora snuggled down under the quilt. 'Oh, Archie, you and your converts!'

'And he has this friend, a painter according to him. A genius. Candidate for our Fraulein Rosel, perhaps?'

'Oh Archie, come to bed, will you?'

Chapter Seven

The Tree

I've spent my life being angry with my father. Or, more properly, it seems that I've spent my life with him being angry with *me*. And now I'm spitting black-white-hot-angry with him – angrier than he ever was with me. How *dare* he? How dare he do this to me? I'll burn in hell before I forgive him for this.

I've been out of doors all day. Took a bottle of water and walked through the woods to the open-cast mine that's now closed and sealed. Poking around as I go, I find a nest of a long-tailed tit (all camouflaged with lichen) and some starling and blackbird nests with eggs. I don't bother to take one. My egg collection was complete by the time I was fourteen and I wouldn't take eggs for the sake of it.

The farmer whose field edges on the wood is cutting hay and leaving it like sleeping green snakes on the ground. In the woods the bluebells and yellow aconites line up in ragged regiments among the juniper and the ash trees. I wish now I had my paint box in my pocket. I draw outside but I've never yet dared to paint in the open where I can be seen.

Nudging around my mind is the familiar feeling of guilt that I'm out here in the light of day. Although these days me and my father have to live on garden stuff and our fire is made from pit-heap gleanings, here I am out in the daytime light, my eyes drowning in the colours of late spring.

Foreshift time. I should be in the dark.

I circle round and pause close to the pit heap where I scavenge a few more lumps of coal and a near-perfect fossil of a dragonfly. That woman is hanging around again but I ignore her and move on. She draws in a small book. I know now from Tegger just who she is, but I've not bothered with her after that first challenge. I can't be fashed with the disturbance she makes in my world. So I've avoided her by going further on from the heap, towards the open-cast.

This means I'm a long time away from the house. This hardly matters, as there's little to return to except my father's sullen looks. It's dusk when I finally make my way down the yard. The door's open but the house is empty, and the fire's dead although the ashes are warm. I stir the ashes, get a scrap of kindling and relight the fire with the coals I've brought from the tip. Like most miners I cannot bear a house without a fire, summer or winter.

By the time I've got the fire riddled and set, it's dark outside and my father's still not home. This never happens. He's home with the coming of dark every day, as there's no light down the allotments, not in his little clapboard hutch nor those of any of the men. You can't garden by candlelight, after all.

Stewing more with resentment than worry, I reach into the cupboard by the fire and rake out his old pit lamp. It takes a bit of a fiddle to light it but I manage. Once it's lit it exudes a scent that is all pit: the metallic smell of coal dust; the stink of sweat, human waste. For a second my brain fills with dark fear. I shake it off and set off back up to the allotments.

As I pass the windows of the houses I catch the silver gleam of gaslight. Here and there, light streams through an open door and I hear the lively bustle of laughter and talk, a sound which always calls up a kind of envy in me.

Soon I'm past the rows and the darkness moves in. The pit lamp lights my feet on their way just as it must have lit my father's feet on his many walks inbye, in those far-off days when he did work, like any normal man.

The allotments are deserted. The darkness distils the smell of chickweed and the air is filled with the uneasy rustle of stock not quite bedded down for the night.

I know something is wrong before I reach my father's patch. His hens are outside clucking and his cockerel is strutting around squawking and grumbling. They fly at me as I kick open the gate and I nudge them aside. The door of his hutch is slightly ajar. I put my palm flat on it and it scrapes open across the earth floor. There's a cup on the old table beside some broken-out plants. Scraps of white paper litter his potting table and sit on the clean earth floor like confetti.

I look around. The broken-backed chair on which he normally sits is missing. I know! Now I know. I lift my lamp to illuminate the hooks where he keeps the rope and his tools in a row against the rough wall. Like the chair, the rope which usually sits on its hook is missing.

Now I turn and run, my lamp swinging high then low to light my way. There's this tree at the edge of the allotment, on the far side, away from the pit wheel. It's old, older than Brack's Hill itself. Nearly as old as Durham Cathedral. My father told me this when I was young. I make for this tree. The lamplight passes first over the old chair. It has been kicked away and lies awkwardly on its side. I set my gaze on it and lift it to put it straight before I look upwards. I can barely make out the figure which hangs there still and very lumpish, suspended from a stout branch.

'You bugger! You bugger! You fucking stupid old man!' Underground words bubble from my mouth. My eyes are blind with angry tears. I drag the chair across and climb on to it. I try to hold him up, to take the tension off the rope. The rope jerks. His face swings towards me and I fall back. It's the face of a dead man staring and swollen, his tongue thick in his mouth. Relief flashes through me. This doesn't look in the least like my father. But the stuff beneath my hands is my father's jacket. The swinging boots, with their pattern of segs and studs, are his old boots. I place his feet back up on the chair and he slumps over, not swinging any more, just wedged between the chair and the tree, some inanimate thing.

Then I climb into the branches of the tree and cut him down with the knife I always keep in my pocket to scrape the clay off the fossils. I kneel beside him and loosen the cruel knot. Somehow I hold him in my arms. I whisper my hatred of him for doing this thing to me even as I hold him close as any mother and rock him as though he really is my exhausted child.

My brain stops racing and the thought occurs to me that if I'd come out straightaway to look for him, instead of fussing over the fire, I could have stopped him doing this.

I have to leave him. Forgetting the lamp, I stumble in the dark all the my way to Trent Street to find Tegger. He's in a van now, dossing with the other men. They live like tinkers just to get their families the dole. He gets dressed straight off, cocking an ear to my babble. 'Dead? You're sure? Naw, Gabriel, it canna be true. Dead?'

'As mutton. As a doornail. I'm tellin yer!' I shout the words, scream them. I don't know my own voice.

He buttons his jacket and puts a soft hand on my shoulder. 'I'm sorry, old lad. Really I am.'

I shake off the hand. 'Don't know what to do,' I mutter. 'I don't know what the hell to do.'

Tegger, ever practical, takes me literally. 'We'll gan for the doctor right off, marra. Then—'

'No,' I say, at the door already. 'We'll get him home first. Then you can fetch the doctor.' I look round the bleak caravan space. 'I'll stay with him.'

My father is not so heavy in my arms: a mere bundle of frail flesh and dense bone. He's eaten like a sparrow for years, begrudging the food that passed his mouth. Tegger walks ahead of me, swinging my father's lamp, turning round occasionally to flash the light high, to illuminate a lump of wood or stone which might be in the way. But for the weight of my dead father we might be walking inbye on night shift.

At the house Tegger stops me from taking the cut rope properly from my father's neck. 'Naw, bonny lad. Leave it there.' His voice is tender as a mother's. 'The doctor'll need to see it.' He places a blanket right up over my father's gaping face. 'Yer dinnat want to be seeing that, marra. Not at all.' Then he steers me back down the stairs and puts me in a chair. 'Now, bonny lad, you sit there an' I'll go and get this feller. This doctor. Now stay!' He might have been gentling a wild dog.

He puts coals on the fire which I relit nearly two hours ago and leaves me. The door clicks behind him. By the time I've watched the fire burn in, and flare up again he is back with the little bald doctor with the thick accent.

This fellow takes a look at my father, prods his face and his neck then makes a note in his book. 'He is dead.'

'I know that.'

'From the rope.'

'I know that too.'

'Where did this happen?'

'In the wood, just beyond the colliery.'

'You should leave him there so I can see.'

'Aye. And you'd think I'd leave my father hanging from a tree like a common felon? Naw. I cut him down and brought him home.'

'Well. Well.' He sucks his very fat lips. I notice he has pyjamas on under his long tweed coat. 'I will need to see the site tomorrow in the light. The tree.'

'Ah'll tek yer there,' says Tegger. 'Ah'll tek yer.'

'No. The son must come. He found his father. I will need him to tell everything. Now we will go to the police station to report this.' He turns to me. 'You should have gone straight to the police,' he says. 'They will not like this.'

The next day, along with the doctor and the policeman we tramp back down to the allotments. All the fellows from the allotment are there. They're about their business with the spade and the fork, sure enough, but as we pass they greet me without looking into my eyes.

'Now, Gabriel, bad business.'

'Aye, it is.'

'Now Gabriel. A bad day, this.'

'Aye, it is.'

Some greetings are no more than grunts, but there is sympathy, fellow feeling even in that sound. At my father's place his neglected marra Stevie is there, putting water and grain out for the banty hens. 'Now, Gabriel,' he grunts. 'I heard about thee father.'

'Aye, Stevie. Thanks for seeing to the stock.'

He shakes his head and vanishes, the gate creaking gently behind him.

I show the sergeant the hut: how neat it is. The scraps of white paper are like random flakes of snow in all that neatness. The sergeant gathers these bits carefully and puts them into a used envelope that he places in his pocket. We make a weary procession, threading our way through the allotment paths, past the colliery and up towards the oak tree. Then, up on the clearing the sergeant examines the cut rope very carefully and writes things in his notebook with a licked pencil. Just beyond the line of trees a band of hawk-eyed children watch us very carefully.

'We'd better have this down,' says the sergeant, 'or that lot'll be playing hangman . . .' He coughs. 'Sorry, lad. Not too delicate, that.'

Back at the house he proceeds up the narrow stairs with the doctor. Tegger and I, drinking thick sweet tea below, hear the rumble of their voices above. The fire burns merrily in the black grate.

When the doctor and the sergeant come downstairs they refuse Tegger's offer of a cup of tea and stand uncomfortably on my grandma's clip-mat whose rising golden sun is slightly dusty now. The doctor has replaced his pyjamas with a much-creased three-piece suit. I bet when he takes it off at night it stands up with the shadow of his shape inside it. He looks at me through thick glasses. 'No doubt, I fear, that he is hung.' Even his shoes are creased into the shape of his foot.

'I know that.'

The sergeant says, 'We need to be sure that your father did it to himself.' He takes the envelope from his pocket and tips out the scraps of paper on the table. 'Bit of a jigsaw, this.'

I move beside him and we spread the pieces out. It takes us thirty minutes to get them into some kind of order. Then the words jump out at me, scrawled across the paper in my father's immaculate hand. *God, I ask Thee, is this all I am to have? If so then it is not sufficient.*

'This writing,' says the sergeant, gently enough. 'It will be your father's?'

'Aye,' I say. 'Look in the Bible on the shelf. He used to copy bits when he was still bothering.' I leaf through the Bible and find the policeman a marked passage: some miserable stuff from the Book of Job.

The doctor and the policeman compare the writing and nod their heads. The policeman returns the paper scraps and the paper from the Bible to his creased brown envelope. 'There'll be an inquest,' he says. 'But I think . . .'

The doctor nods. 'There are so many of these deaths . . .' We can hear their voices still rumbling as they walk down the yard: rough against smooth; rough against smooth.

'Why, you bugger!' says Tegger.

I look up at him wearily. 'What's that?'

'That pair thowt somebody'd done that to your old feller. Done him in. Mebbe even you. That *you'd* done it!'

'Well, they was wrong, wasn't they? He did it to himself, anyone can see that. Wanted a get-out. Stupid bugger.'

Tegger comes and puts an arm round my shoulder. 'Come

on, Gabe. Sit down here. I'll sit with you.' Then he goes across and draws the curtains. I hear him moving round the house, closing curtains in all the rooms. It's our custom to close curtains when you have the dead in the house. I remember we did this when my mother and the baby died.

Tegger comes and sits beside me, shoulder to shoulder in the darkness. Only the flicker of fire tells me we're not fifty fathoms below sitting on a block of wood waiting to go outbye, back to the cage and up into the light.

Chapter Eight

The Painter

In the days after my father's funeral Tegger calls three times at the house only to have me shout at him to go away. The fourth time I open the door blinking like a pit pony coming into the light. 'Tegger.' My voice is as raw as a piece of broken crockery. I've spoken to no one for a week.

Tegger's glance moves round the room which is awash with my drawings and paintings. I've pinned them everywhere: on chairs and cabinets, on walls and curtains. Every painting and drawing I've done since I was eight or nine is here on display in this narrow house.

Tegger's a sharp lad. He knows without me saying so that I'm shouting, 'This is me!' in defiance of my father never having been comfortable about my soft habit of drawing all the things I see. *What good are such things? The workings of a marshmallow mind.* The old man's thoughts have trembled through the house all week, to be defied by the sketches and boards pinned around the room.

'Hey Gabe, these all yours? They're bloody good.' He has

two packets of chips. He offers me one.

'You would say so.' The chips are clay cold but my stomach heaves with relief. I can't remember when I last ate.

Tegger is staring, almost scowling, straight at me. 'I've told you before, marra. You need to go to this group the German woman runs at the Settlement. They like her, the lads down there. She's got some of them carving, some of them framing their pictures. They're hung up about the place. Like real pictures they are – but none of them as good as yours here. Some are not even as good as those you did when you were a kid. But this one . . . And this one! Brilliant. You should get yoursel' down the Settlement. Fool if you don't. There's paints there, the whole kit. This artist woman working there. And drama with actors to teach you. Queer feller that's running it. Talks about the playwrights like they were his best marras. George Bernard Shaw he calls "GBS". Can yer credit it? Bliddy Communist, shouldn't wonder. But a very canny feller. Get yerself down there, man. Better than going crazy in this hole.'

I finish the chips. 'Thanks for them, Tegger.' I rub my hands over my tired eyes. 'Will yer go now, lad? Leave it, will yer?'

The knocking on the door is very loud. Tegger again. I wish he'd go away. I shake the sleep from my eyes, push my fingers through my hair and open the door. But it's not Tegger. It's my Aunt Susanah and her husband, Jonty Clelland.

'Gabriel?' she says. 'We heard about Matthew and are come to say sorry.' The Welsh lilt of her childhood is still in her voice. 'A terrible thing it is. We were away, and when we came back . . .'

I stand there, sleepridden, unshaven and stare at her. I must smell like a stoat.

She peers past my shoulder into the dark kitchen. 'Perhaps we could come in?'

I stand back and feel a flutter of shame as they stand helplessly on the fireside mat, unable to find a place to sit. My aunt shivers. 'No fire, Gabriel? Cold spring, it is.'

I stare helplessly at the dead fire. 'It went out.'

Jonty Clelland takes off his jacket. 'Now then,' he says. 'I'll light the fire while you two . . . well, talk.'

She looks round the room at the drawings I've pinned to the walls, the front of the press, to the fireplace. 'I didn't realise you'd done so much, Gabriel. You kept it up, I see.'

'You gave me that book.' I nod at the battered, much-fingered book propped up on the press. 'I've used that.'

Despite that gift, we're not close, Aunt Susanah and I. Like I say, her first husband was my father's cousin. Died at the hands of the military in the Great War. Conchie. This second husband, now mildly raking out the ashes that have been there since my father hung himself, was a conchie himself, some say beneath contempt. But he doesn't lack courage. There was that do, a year back, where he took on the local Blackshirts. It was in the papers.

'Gabriel? Gabriel!' Her sharp voice brings me back to myself. 'I said how were you doing for work?'

'Work? Are you having me on? There is no work round here,' I say. 'I was one of the last to lose work when the drift mine closed. No work for anyone in Brack's Hill.'

She peers at a drawing pinned to the back wall; it's a picture of a pit pony at his stall. 'You're very good,' she sighed. 'I wish I'd kept up my drawing.' She glances at Jonty Clelland's back. 'But there is so much to do.'

He looks up at her. 'You can draw, Susanah. You know you

can draw as much as you like.' He stands up, balancing a bucketful of ash in his hand. He is frowning.

She smiles at him. 'I know, Jonty, love. I know that. It's all right. Get that fire done now, will you?' She turns to me. 'Jonty was saying there's a good art class at the Settlement. There's a German artist there – she's very good. Archie Todhunter sings her praises.' She looks round at the drawings and paintings hanging in the room. 'You'll get inspiration,' she said. 'You'll develop with the help of a proper artist.'

I look again at my work, which now seems dark and tawdry. Picture after picture of men underground. Some are almost mirror images of each other. I am saying the same thing time and again. 'These are rubbish,' I say. 'A lot of rubbish. Me father always said so.'

She puts her hand on my arm. 'Now, Gabriel, sorry for yourself, is it? We'll have none of that. Right – let's you and me go in the scullery and clear it up. By that time Jonty'll have the fire well away and we can have a cup of tea.'

'I . . .' I say.

She burrows in her bag. 'You've no tea? Well, lucky it is I've brought some. And scones from the Co-op.' She laughs. 'Bought cakes. Aren't I shameless?'

It's nearly an hour before we manage to sit down and eat the scones and drink the tea. By now I'm soothed by their presence. I look across at her. 'You should go and learn off this woman yourself,' I say. 'Take it up again.'

She shakes her head. 'No. That'd not do, Gabriel. Jonty and I have other fish to fry.'

I look at the man closely for the first time. He looks quite a bit older than her, his eyes are netted with fine wrinkles, his curly hair is thinning. 'I heard they put you in prison over that do with the Mosley men,' I say.

'So they did, son, but I survived.' His voice is modulated like the schoolteacher he used to be.

'D'you still teach in school, like?'

He shakes his head. 'They don't want jailbird schoolteachers,' he says cheerfully. 'Been sacked more than once.'

'Jonty puts in a bit of teaching for free at the Settlement here, where the art class is. Where the woman does the art.'

'What do you teach there?' I say it for something to say.

Jonty shrugs. 'Teach some folk to read, who never could. A bit of history, decent stuff about the Chartists and Cromwell.'

I remember now that years ago he was sacked for all that conchie stuff, even before the Great War. And here he is, sacked again from a job that was a thousand times easier than hewing coal. He doesn't look like a revolutionary. Mild-faced, slightly built in his shiny black suit, you'd have taken him for a down-at-heel preacher, or indeed a poor schoolteacher.

Later, I see them out of the house and watch them make their way down the narrow back street. Within six steps she's put her arm through his and is looking up at him, smiling, talking twenty to the dozen.

I pass slowly through my tidied scullery into the tidier kitchen with its bright fire and sit in my father's seat by that fire.

I'm floored again by that linking of arms, that intimacy. I suddenly remember my mother very well. She comes to me again out of the mists. I remember how she tucked my hand in hers on the way to chapel. How she spat on her hankie to scrub my face outside the gates on that first day of school.

But I cannot remember any affectionate moments between her and my father. I think that in none of those young years did

I see a gesture between them as tender as my Aunt Susanah putting her arm through Jonty's in our back street.

'You see?' Rosel Vonn leans forward; her pencil moves swiftly across the paper. 'Dark to light, dark to light. We represent the forms of objects on the flat surface of this paper.'

If I sit half-sideways I can peer across and see the tall water jug and the small kettle taking shape beneath her hand. The background recedes. The objects bloom into three dimensions on the page. For me this is familiar magic.

She sits across the wooden school chair as if it were a horse. I can see the fine serge of her skirt pulled taut across her knee, the indentation of her suspender button. 'There, you see?' she says. 'You lift them out of the darkness.' She unpins her own drawing from the easel to expose again the honest effort of the middle-aged miner beside her. 'You see?' she says. 'The truth is that nothing has an outline. The outline grows from the depths you dig out with your shading. You make the shape with the transition from light to dark. You may *see* the outline but it doesn't exist, not truly. Do you see? No outlines.' Her voice is quite severe.

'Aye, I see.' He moves to unpin his own sheet from the easel. She puts a slender hand on his. 'You do not need to start again.'

'Aye, I do. This is like a bairn's drawing. Look at it,' he says. I can see what he means. He turns the paper over and re-pins it on the other side. 'If what you say's right, this thing's beyond retrieval. It's all filled-in outlines. I'll start again.' Then he turns away from her and peers closely at the jug and kettle, narrowing his eyes. His heavy jaw is set like granite.

Now she drags her chair to the next man who's painting, at her suggestion, from a limited palette: Flake White, Raw Umber,

Black and Yellow Ochre. (The words roll round my head like a poem.) From the other side of the room I listen to her tentative suggestions to him. I see the section of the man's painting grow under this new instruction; I watch his frowning concentration increase a hundredfold.

She has circled the room twice and has still not approached me, not once. I don't know whether I want her to or not. My chair creaks as I sit right back and half-close my eyes to increase the perspective in my drawing.

It was really my Aunt Susanah who got me here. Tegger thinks it's him, so I haven't disabused him. When he finally pushed me through the door I took one look at the set piece – the tall jug with the kettle beside it standing before a drape of thick cloth – and almost walked straight back out again. I had lessons like this at school and just loathed them. I was pulled in, though, by the fine smell of linseed and the seductive pile of high-quality paper on the side table, by the thick pottery jar full of sharpened pencils. These things made me change my mind. I've never drawn on such fine paper; I've never handled pencils like these. So I was tempted to follow the actions of some of the other men; I pinned my sheet of paper to a board and selected three pencils, an H, an HB, and a 3B.

The drawing that grows under my hand is not a delicate in-depth study of the jug and the kettle so carefully arranged before us on the stool. It's the inside of a garden shed lit by a stream of light through the window. Every detail is there: the spade and fork stand against the wall, a pile of jam-jars, broken plants and a bucket are scattered on a bench. From a hook on the wall hangs an old coat with gaping pockets and creases at the elbow where the wearer's arm bent a hundred times digging earth and planting seed potatoes. Its pockets still bulge with stones and ancient unused seed and the hairy string which he had used to tie up last year's runner beans. From another hook beside the door a heavy rope snakes against the wall, its end fashioned into a noose.

The German woman circles the room again, watching the drawers and painters, talking to them briefly or sitting beside them, drawing swiftly as she does so. Twice she comes up behind me and twice I tense up, waiting for her comment, but each time she passes me without a single word.

Then she settles by her own board and begins to draw, allowing a wall of concentration to build up around her. And I forget her and become absorbed again, relishing the fine paper, the dense impact of pure graphite on its flawless surface. After so many years drawing on waste cardboard and flattened sugar bags, this is heaven.

I know I'm good. Better than any of these here. But you wouldn't think that for the attention I'm getting. She's taken no more notice of me than if I were a block of wood. If it weren't for the decent paper and the new pencils, I wouldn't have wasted my time. Even they aren't worth being treated like a block of wood. This is the last time I shall come here, paper or no paper.

She's off her chair now, on the other side of the room, talking to a fellow about warm tones and dark tones. I unpin my own picture, roll it up and put it inside my coat. Her head goes up. She knows what I'm doing, but still she goes on demonstrating the need for a highlight on the edge of the kettle.

The man beside Rosel looked across the room. 'What's up with young Gabe,' he said, 'marchin' off like that?'

Another man nodded. 'That young feller? Rolled up his drawing and went off.'

'Weren't drawing the right thing though, was he?' said the other. 'Some jumble down his old man's shed. I bought eggs from the feller one time. But did you see that drawing? Gabe had that shed there to the last nail, the last knothole, the last sunbeam.'

Rosel went back to put the finishing touches to her own drawing.

'Gabriel Marchant,' said the first man. 'Queer business, that, about his father.'

'What was that?' said Rosel.

They looked round at the art woman in surprise.

'Why, hinny, the old man hung himself,' said the first man. 'Out of his mind, they reckon. More'n one feller done that with the unemployment. It gets to you. No money, yer kids hungry . . .'

Rosel closed her eyes for a second. 'How terrible.' She thought of herself, and the days when she cut her wrists when things went wrong in her own life.

'Aye, terrible enough,' said the first man. Then the two men turned away from the topic. Miners don't waste time dwelling on death: it's such a certainty in their lives that to focus on it is seen as an unholy waste of time.

Archie, who was packing up his own things after a pleasant afternoon daubing at a very passable image of the still life, looked up at Rosel. 'I thought the boy's drawing was quite fine. It seems to me that he needs a bit of encouragement. Don't you think so, Rosel? You said nothing to him.'

'I have work to do,' she said stiffly. 'He is ill-mannered. I met him outside and he is very ill-mannered.'

* * *

This man who was in there painting catches up with me by Trent Street. 'In a bit of a hurry to get off, weren't you, my lad?' he says breathlessly. He's been running. 'One minute you were there, the next you weren't.'

'Nowt in it for me,' I say, looking down at him.

(With the gaslight behind him, all that Archie could see was a face in shadow inside a halo of curly hair.)

'You're very good, certainly,' the man says. 'I said so to Fraulein Vonn.'

'She didn't think so.' I wonder who he is, this busybody with the slicked-back hair and the round glasses. I watched him painting and didn't think much of his efforts.

'Others needed her more than you do, obviously. And she knows them. She's been working with them for weeks. She needs to get to know you.'

I shrug my shoulders. Wish he would go away.

'One more time,' he says. 'Just try it one more time.'

'If it bothers yer. One more time.' And I turn away, eager to escape. It's only later, when I'm talking to Tegger, that I realise that the bloke I talked to was Archie Todhunter, boss of the whole caboodle at the Settlement.

My next time in the class is all too short. Light is a serious problem there. The single bulb is not enough to compensate for the fading external light which is barely making it through the skylight. The German woman climbs up a ladder to remove the shade in an attempt to get better light.

Some of the artists still grumble and the woman takes off her glasses and glances at everyone except me. 'Well, next week we can meet at one instead of two, if you wish. That is one hour more.' Still the light in here is better than home where the gas throws off a bluish shade and drowns the colour so that it's not true.

There's a mutter of agreement and we collapse the easels and stack them in the corner cupboard. They are crude things, joiner-made, but they certainly do the job. I go to the pegs to get my coat, pull it on, roll up my picture and put it in my inside pocket. When I turn round, the woman is gone. The bile within me rises so high I can taste it.

Archie Todhunter looks across at me. 'Go and talk to her. Go after her,' he says. 'If you feel like that, go and tell her.'

By the time I get to the outside door she's half a block away. My boots spark as I crash along the pavement. I nearly trip over the sprawling legs of two men who are on their haunches outside the tobacconist's.

'Watch it, man, will yeh?' One of them looks at me angrily.

I catch up with her on the corner. 'Hey!' I grab her arm, which she wrenches away.

She looks me in the eye. 'Do you always attack people?'

This stops me. I look down, not able to meet her eyes. 'I was not attacking anybody. Trying to see what you're about, that's all. Why you think you're too good to talk to . . . to . . . people.'

'Well, Mr . . .'

'Marchant. Gabriel Marchant.'

'Well, Mr Marchant, what I am about is what you saw in there, in the room. Painting. Drawing.'

'I saw you there. You know what you're about. You're good.'

'Yes.' She doesn't deny it.

'But . . .' I don't want to whine about her not giving me any attention. I gag up.

'You're a very good draughtsman yourself, Mr Marchant.'

I'm hot with embarrassment now. 'I thought you had no time for my stuff. In there, like. You never bother to look. Never say nothing.' Now she'll think I'm fishing for compliments.

'You seemed to be getting on fine. You've had lessons, surely? You have style, a sense of perspective. Light. You know about light.'

'Yeah. I had lessons. At school, like. Not since then.'

'You've not drawn since you left school?'

'I didn't say that. I draw all the time, like.'

In the silence which follows I feel her withdrawing, going away from me. Then she speaks. 'Well, Mr Marchant, perhaps you'll come next Saturday? I look forward to that.' And she's away, clicking along the pavement in those bobbin-heeled shoes of hers.

I stand for a second, quite lost. I don't want to go home again to sit in my father's chair and feel him all around me. A hand on my shoulder spins me round. 'What cheer, Gabriel? In the land of dreams, are yeh?' Tegger slaps me on the back, makes me jump. 'Is that the German woman? I bet she thought you're some kinda genius, eh?'

'Nivver said a word to us. Not till just now.'

'Jealous, man, that's what she'd be. Ready to help the ignorant. Not so ready for the not-so-ignorant.' He sets off the way I have just come.

I feel the space he has left behind. 'So where you off to, marra?' I shout after him.

'I'm goin' just where you came from. I told you before. That play! The feller Todhunter said I could help with his play. Hey!' He comes back and punches my shoulder. 'You come along, Gabe. All hands to the plough. You can carry my nailbox. You can even carry my pencil.'

'Don't be daft, man.'

'Come on! What else have you to do? What have yer to lose? Come on!'

So now, thanks to Tegger, it seems I've got mixed up in this play as well. That Todhunter has more tentacles than an octopus.

At least I don't have to go back to that empty house.

Chapter Nine

The Players

The room where they will do the play is not the scruffy painting shed, but the long front room of the Settlement which used to be the main shop when it was a shop. When Tegger and me get there it's crowded with twenty or so bodies on hard wooden chairs.

I know some of these people. There's Nathan Smith who was a putter once at White Leas Pit; there are a couple of other pitmen whose faces I recognise but whose names I don't know. There's McVay, the man who used to work in the hardware shop where my father got his nails. It's now closed so he must be out of work.

A couple of older women, dressed neatly in their Sunday coats and hats sit head to head, talking. The three seats under the old shop window are taken up by two younger women and a girl with plaits wound round her head who's wearing a navy-blue Grammar School tunic.

They're sitting in a meandering circle. In the corner near the inner door is the slender man with the glasses, Archie Todhunter, the one who came after me, that first night at the art class. Beside him sits a heavy-featured woman, wearing make-up.

I've made sure Tegger and me sit by the outside door in case I want to leave.

'That's Archie Todhunter, who's in charge of this whole shebang.' Tegger's mouth is to my ear. 'Feller with the glasses.'

'So you said. I told you, he came back to me that first night. He was at the painting. He's nothing of an artist, mind. Paints like he's doing pokerwork.'

'Well, mebbe that's what he does for relaxation. This is his thing – this play. We can't be good at everything. I'm a proper dunce at darts, but I'm a dab hand with me hammer and saw, and me pen and a bit of paper.'

Todhunter shuffles his papers on the table and looks up over his glasses. An instant silence settles in the room. The man has the still concentration of a foot runner at the start of a paying race. The level of concentration in the whole room is powerful. The people on the chairs forget about whether there's food on their table at home; whether the bairn would have to miss school on Monday; about the baby being off his food. They know their man. They focus on Archie Todhunter's face and wait.

'Well,' he says, examining our faces in the circle one by one. When he reaches us he nods at Tegger. 'Nice to see you, Mr MacNamara.' His gaze turns to me. 'Another newcomer. Are you a joiner as well as a painter? We are twice blessed. We'll need you in this new play.'

Faces turn towards me. A murmur of interest flutters round the room.

'Nah,' says Tegger. 'Gabriel here's a putter. No joiner here. He can paint you a scene, mebbe. Dab hand with a paintbrush.'

'All the better,' says Todhunter firmly.

'I didn't . . .' I glance behind me at the door, wondering how long I should stay.

But Todhunter has moved on. 'Now then,' he says. 'Our *Richard III* last month was very well received.'

'Except for the *Priorton Chronicle*,' says a small, bird-like man at the back. 'What does *bowdlerised* mean? It said it had been bowdlerised.'

There are one or two lewd suggestions *sotto voce* but Todhunter waves his hand.

'It means we – I – plucked the heart out of the play and adapted it for the little stage in the Methodist Hall. He was criticising my writing. We don't worry about Herbert Grossmith of the *Chronicle*, ladies and gentlemen, because he's an overwhelming ass, a big fish in a small bowl, a cockroach among ants.'

There are shouts of appreciative laughter at this.

He goes on. 'No, friends, it was successful because in all, over the Friday and Saturday, from Brack's Hill, we had a total of a hundred and thirty people who saw our play. They appreciated the irony, wept at the tragedy and applauded you to the roof at the end. Beside this, the sainted Herbert Grossmith is as a feather in the wind.'

The painted woman sitting beside Archie joins in the laughter. 'Mr Grossmith was very cross that he did not have a front-row seat,' she says. 'He asked me did I know who he was?'

The inner door opens and we all watch as that German woman comes in. She's changed to a jersey and trousers and her hair is brushed now, tied with a green ribbon close at her neck. She looks younger. Todhunter waits till she settles down and turns back to his eager audience.

'Well, ladies and gentlemen, I thought we might do with a

change. We did the Shaw to some effect. Some of us tried out the Chekhov which, though a wonderful play, seemed a little to tangle on our tongue.'

There was a murmur of rueful agreement at this.

'So I thought we'd try something different.'

A buzz of interest.

'It'll give Herbert Grossmith something to blather about. He'll have a field day on this.' From a battered black folder he pulls out a wadge of papers. He puts his palms underneath it and holds it towards us, like some kind of offering. 'It is called *Coal and Blood*.'

Nathan Smith calls from the back, 'So who's this one by? Mr Shaw again? Zola? You talked of Emile Zola once. He wrote of coal – I read that. You'd think the man had spent his life underground. A writer, but—'

Archie shook his head. 'No, Mr Smith, this is . . . well, an unknown writer.'

'Archie won't tell you,' says the woman beside him. 'But—'

'I wrote it myself,' says Archie gruffly. 'No doubt you'll do me the kindness of telling me where I've gone wrong. You usually do. I'm quite sure that Herbert Grossmith will be only too eager to tell me.'

'You can be sure that we'll be pretty eager ourselves,' says Nathan. The rest of them laugh loudly at this.

'So what's it about?' says Tegger.

'It's about *Coal and Blood*.'

'Gan on,' says Tegger. 'Tell us the story.'

Archie puts down his sheaf of papers and stares at us. 'Well,' he says, 'first I want you to see our stage. Stage left, a tunnel in the trenches in the Great War. A group of four men, miners-turned-soldiers, are trapped. They huddle under a muddy tarpaulin. The roof of the trench is nearly to their heads. It's 1916, bang in the middle of the Great War. Stage right, a coroner's court here in Durham, where they're investigating an explosion in which nine men have been killed. On a half-height platform, stage centre, are a group of women. At some points in the play they mourn the deaths of their sons and brothers. At some points they read the letters from their loved ones in France. They talk about the war. They carry white feathers.'

'Flipping heck,' says Mr Conroy, the pit joiner. 'Three sets on one stage?'

'Stage right, sits a coroner on a dais. Before him, five chairs. It is, in miniature, a coroner's court.'

'What happens?' asks the young girl with plaits.

'A very good question, Greta. It is not, after all, a tableau.'

'Something's gotta happen,' says Tegger. 'Yeah.'

'Well, what happens is, in the course of the inquest we find out about the blast which killed these nine men underground and how the managers tried to blame it on the men, though it's due to their negligence. The wives act as a chorus singing the praises of their menfolk; and second by second undergo the agony of their extinction.'

'What about the lads in the trench?' says McVay.

'These men, from the same families, are trapped by a fall. They spend their time talking about the war and how things will be so much better afterwards.'

'Little did they know,' said McVay to a ripple of laughter. '*A land fit for heroes!* What?'

'Well, just as we learn bit by bit about the extinction of the lads in the pit, the soldiers are finally rescued by other miners, soldiers who are tunnelling for them. They survive, for the time being at least, but the miners at home do not.'

'Cheerful sort of feller, ain't yer, Archie?' says McVay.

'So, what's it really about?' asks Nathan. 'This play.'

Archie Todhunter glances round at us all. 'It's about sacrifice and whether it's worth it.'

'And we all know the answer to that,' says McVay. 'All that for life on the dole and your children hungry.'

'Well?' says Archie. His face is strained. He's worried whether they like it. The silence goes on too long.

'I think it's bloody brilliant.' The words burst out of me. 'I've never heard anything like it.'

They all turn round to look at me.

'Me too,' says Tegger. I can feel his excitement. 'Ah think it's bloody brilliant. Real people. Real lives. I never knew you could write about such things.'

'Folks want cheering up, not making miserable,' says McVay gloomily. 'Misery enough out there.'

'There are jokes in it. Some very funny,' says the made-up woman, called Cora.

The painter woman speaks up. 'The set will be very interesting. The darkness of the trench. The polished wood of the court. The village, the pit wheel in the background.'

'How d'yer get three stages on one?' Mr Conroy the joiner is still anxious.

'Well,' says Todhunter, 'that's where you and young MacNamara come in. I thought we could have some rollers or tracks. Something like that.'

'Turntable,' says Tegger suddenly, 'like the ones they turn the trains on, in Priorton station. Turn it round, you get the new scene.'

Todhunter's glance glitters round the circle, from one of us to the next, to the next. Satisfaction pours from him. He knows he has won. 'Well?' he says. 'Is that possible? There is scaffolding to be had. I saw a set done in London which was just scaffolding. A different scene on each platform.'

A heavy man next to McVay speaks up then. 'No reason why not,' he says. 'Use rollers. Make a special—'

'So we can do it?' asks Todhunter.

'Don't see why not,' the man says.

Todhunter lets the silence sit in the room. 'Well then, shall we do it or not?' he says, surveying us all again.

'Aye. Gan on,' says Nathan Smith. 'We'll give it a try.'

'Good,' says Todhunter.

'No point in wasting all that work you've done,' says Mr Conroy. 'Yeh must've burned the midnight oil over that.'

'You're sure there are some jokes in it?' says Tegger.

Todhunter nods towards the made-up woman, who hands out wadges of paper to each person. I look down at my sheets and try to pass them on to Tegger. 'I'm not . . .' I start to say.

The woman puts a hand on mine. Her nails have polish on them. 'Keep it,' she says. 'You never know. It's all hands on deck here.'

Todhunter glances at a scrap of paper in his hand. 'Nathan, I thought you could be the coroner. Mr McVay, I thought you could be the corporal in the trench . . .' He goes on giving out the parts with assurance. Seems like he's written the parts with many of these people in mind. He'll know their turn of phrase, the idiosyncrasies in their voices. Nathan Smith, as a lay preacher, who knows how to impose his tones on the air, is the obvious choice for the coroner.

Todhunter turns to the schoolgirl. 'Now, Greta. You did such a good job last time I've written this specially for you. You'll be Dorothy whose father was killed in the explosion and whose sweetheart Arthur is in the trench, afraid for his life but putting a brave face on it.' His eye moves round the circle and finally settles on me. My collar is suddenly too tight. 'Perhaps you could take the part of Arthur, Gabriel? You're the only one here young enough, as far as I can see – apart from Tegger and he's going to build the set.'

I shake my head so hard my cap comes off, and I have to scrabble on the floor to get it back. 'No. No. I'm just here . . . I said I'd help Tegger with the joinery, the painting.' Even that was more than I'd thought when I came in. Why on earth did I agree? What am I doing?

Todhunter rubs his head with his hand. 'Oh, what a pity. Never mind. Perhaps you would read the lines today, till we get someone else?'

Tegger nudges me. 'Gan on, Gabe,' he says. 'Nowt to lose.'

I blow out a very long sigh and keep my head down.

'Very well.' Todhunter is obviously satisfied. He turns to the painted woman. 'Now Cora will read Mrs Olliphant, who is the most . . . er . . . opinionated of the women and I will read Mr Jerry Molloy who, as the mouthpiece of the coal company, is the villain of the piece.' He turns to the painter 'Miss Vonn?' he says.

She shakes her head firmly. I wish I had her resolve. 'Absolutely not, Mr Todhunter. I will help you in every other way, but no, I will not climb on the stage and be an Englishwoman. It is impossible.'

'Well, there were Belgian refugees here during the war. I thought . . .' He stares at her for a moment. You can see his tactlessness dawning on him. 'Well, perhaps you will listen hard and tell us of anything you think might make it better.'

Then, with a few false starts, we embark on the reading. It's hard to read and concentrate, to bring to mind the movement between the coroner's court, the trench, and the cluster of women. All this when sitting round in a circle. But as the reading becomes more assured, the characters so cunningly dreamed up by Todhunter start to rise in the room between us. The sense of the arguments which lie there like bombs beneath the lines begin to infect us.

Nathan Smith becomes measured and magisterial, Todhunter combative, McVay quick, choleric and soldierly. Cora Miles is strident, bitter, euphoric and mournful as her lines demand. I even find my voice breaking with Arthur's terror, then becoming stronger again as Arthur thinks of his father's courage down the mine. This thing in the trenches is no worse than his father's plight in the pit. He sees that. I see it.

It takes us more than an hour to read it through. When it is finished, we all sit back, somehow drained. Funny that, as it's only words.

'So,' said Todhunter. 'Is it a play?'

'Aye. It is a play all right,' says Nathan heavily. 'But it'll make folk angry, about the war and the mines both. They'll go out sparking into the street.'

'But that's what it's about.' I can't resist it. 'We've cause to be angry, all of us. This is important.'

Todhunter takes off his glasses, breathes on the lenses one by one and polishes them on his shirtsleeve. 'So you'll do the role of Arthur then, Mr Marchant?'

'Well, I . . .'

'Gan on,' says Tegger.

'Well then, yes,' I say, knowing I'll regret it. 'Yes, I suppose I will.'

I leave Tegger behind, talking to Mr Conroy about the logistics of a turntable on which they may set the scenes, and walk slowly out and along the street, contemplating my own folly. A clatter of feet sound in the street behind me. 'Wasn't that wonderful?' It's a female voice. 'Isn't Mr Todhunter wonderful?'

It's the girl who read Dorothy's part, the one they called Greta.

'What?' I'm mad at her; I don't know why.

'That play. Isn't Mr Todhunter clever?' She has a plain narrow face and snapping black eyes behind round glasses. Her school gabardine is tightly belted. She's no child, even if she is a schoolgirl. 'I thought you read Arthur very well.'

I'm nonplussed. Do you say thank you when somebody says something like that to you? 'Thanks,' I try. 'You too.'

She falls into step beside me. 'Where do you live?' she demands.

'Past Sinker's Row.'

'I'll walk with you as far as Inkerman Street,' she says firmly. 'That's where I live.'

'Well,' I say. 'I . . .'

'Well what?'

'Just well.'

She talks on about the Settlement, about how wonderful the *Richard III* had been, how clever Mr Todhunter was. 'And Cora! You wouldn't believe it, looking at her, but she's such a good actress. Can be an old crone or a young girl in a blink. Makes you really believe.'

I wish this kid who isn't a kid would shut up. I want to think of some of the things Archie Todhunter has put into the mouth of young Arthur in the play. How glad Arthur was, to get out of the pit into the army! Like Aunt Susanah's brother, Davey. *At least way above the trenches*, Arthur says in the play, *is the deep blue sky*. But then he goes on about how here at the Front, the digging and the tunnelling make him think of the pit. Of course he doesn't know that their present dilemma, their caved-in trench, exactly parallels that situation back home with the men trapped, and killed, in the pit.

'And both our fathers die.' The voice chirrups beside me.

My father hanging from the allotment tree.

'What?'

'In the play. Arthur and Dorothy's fathers die together in the explosion. Their names are read out at the court.'

'Yes. Yes.' I wish this kid would go away. 'Which school did you say you went to?'

'Alderman Harrington. I'm in the fifth form. Top of my class in English, History and Maths. I do extra lessons in Latin and Greek and also extra lessons in German now with Fraulein Vonn. My French is not really so good.'

'That's a pity. Not speaking French must be a real problem in Brack's Hill.'

My sarcasm flows over her. 'I would be good at it. I can do anything, you know. Our French teacher Monsieur Mercat is asleep half the time. The other half he throws blackboard rubbers at you. Look at this.' She stops and I have to stop too. She puts her head up to the gaslight and lifts the heavy plait from the side of her face. There is a healed cut, still livid. 'See, he did that.'

I'm angry, even though it's not my business. 'What did you do about it?'

'I got two hundred lines. He gave me two hundred lines and called me *une imbécile*. That's imbecile in French.'

'Sounds nasty, him. Never met the feller. He wasn't there when I was there.'

'You were at the Alderman Harrington?'

'Aye.'

'But . . .'

'But what?'

'But you're a—'

'Pitman.'

She flushes a very bright red. 'I'm sorry, that was—'

'Stupid. Aye, it was,' I say. Then I let her off the hook. 'Mebbe you're wondering why I'm not an unemployed clerk or shop assistant, rather than an unemployed pitman?'

'Well . . .' she sighs. 'Yes, I am, if you want to know.'

'I left school when I was fourteen and went down the pit. Easy as that.'

'Oh. I'm sorry.'

'Why should you be sorry?'

'Well, the pit . . .'

'The pit's a very special place those fathoms down in the earth. You'd never know.' This finally shuts her up and we walk the rest of the way to Inkerman Street in blessed silence.

As we walk along, my mind starts running on girls and that sort of thing. To be perfectly honest, they are a mystery to me. Naturally there were no touches of affection, no talk of love between me and my father, but I was comfortable enough with him at first as we lived our men's life together. My Aunt Susanah came to the house but he didn't make her welcome and the visits stopped. He never seemed to care for the woman's touch.

The girls in the school were a different species from my mother or my Aunt Susanah. They had different classrooms and there was a great stone wall between their part of the playground and ours. At the Grammar School we sat on different sides of the classroom. Even with the other boys I was known to be silent. I never got a beating for this, which was quite surprising. They stood at a distance, or I stood at a distance. Which way round it was I do not know.

Then I went to the pit and even that slight contact with girls was all over and I lived quite comfortably in a world of men. They would tease me about being the quiet man, or make fun of the drawing but there was no harm in that.

I liked being with the miners underground. There was enough variety among them to keep you entertained. There were the silent strong men who won respect through their work; there were the religious ones who quoted from the Bible like daily doses of honey; there were the singers who sang and the poets like Tegger who spouted; there were the drinkers and the cursers, the gamblers who worked out their odds, the clever and the simple, the sly and the transparent. Here was always enough stimulus for me without the complication of women.

With Tegger it's different. Even at school he was one for the girls, lying in wait, teasing, throwing pebbles at them from high places, attacking them with snowballs in the winter. The first poem he ever wrote was about a girl who passed us on the way home from school. I know he's been with women but he doesn't brag about it. To my certain knowledge, married women are his weakness. It's unspoken between us, of course. He wouldn't talk about that to me.

It's not that I haven't had those feelings, the knowledge that my own body has intrusive powers and sometimes reacts of its own volition. I look at portraits in my Rembrandt book. Those sensuous Dutch burghers' wives and winsome boys with smooth faces – I'm drawn to their beauty with more than a painter's inclination. The very hairs on my body respond to the round arms, the artfully displayed full necks, white as winter stoats.

These were the feelings that suffused my impotent body when I saw, or dreamed I saw, that woman, that time down in the pit seam. But no real woman has aroused these feelings. Housewives with aprons on thickening bodies, giggling school-girls – such females live in a world which is not my own.

But these days, things are changing. There's the irritating German painting woman, old enough probably to be my mother. When she ignored me in the class the rage I felt prickled my skin and made everything about me erect. I read something somewhere – maybe in the Bible – that a body is an unruly servant.

Todhunter soon has us working through our parts. For me, the play comes as a series of pictures. In one of these, the women are clustered centre-stage, coats supplemented by shawls against the cold. A child grasps her mother's skirt. Two elegant white whippets – have I dreamed this? – sit, ears pricked, at the back of the crowd. Behind them, framed within a frame, is the gateway of the court. Within a frame again the coroner sits, a black cat beside his chair.

A messenger enters stage left, his white beard shining in the improvised spotlight. He's an old miner who says his lines flatly and they are the stronger for that. The natural balance of his fine old face is warped by a purple cloth binding a lump over his left ear. The lump is a roasted onion which was his grandmother's sure remedy for earache. He's been suffering from earache all afternoon but will not give up his role, even for one rehearsal.

His role is important. It's his character who, from time to time, comes out to tell the waiting women of the deliberations of the court. It's he, on his first exit, who tells them about the black cat who sits curled at the feet of the coroner.

This is his sixth announcement.

'And now they're reading out the names of the dead,' he says slowly, deliberately. 'One by one. Injury by injury.'

'Have they mentioned our John Joe?' says one of the women. This is the one who, in real life, helps to serve the soup in the soup kitchen.

'Aye. So they have.'

'Have they mentioned our Walter and young Sidney?' says another. This woman comes to the quilt class as well.

'They got a whole list,' he says. 'Such injuries.'

Maggie Olliphant, played by Cora as a large woman whose head seems laid on her shoulders with no neck, comes close enough to the messenger to smell the onion on his ear. 'And what are they saying in there, about why it happened?'

'The agent has been on the stand,' he says, giving every word its weight. 'He's saying it's the men's fault. Their negligence caused this!' Behind them the crowd of women draw closer together. The child cries. I imagine the dogs howling.

Maggie Olliphant/Cora puts a hand on the old man's arm. 'That can't be,' she says. 'That can't be, my friend.'

He shakes his head. His ear is hurting like twisting knives. 'It's not over yet, Missis. That judge, or coroner, or whatever is no fool. He has a hungry look. He'd not be swayed by prince or potentate when he knows he's in the right.'

'Not bad,' says Todhunter, clapping his hands briefly. 'It's coming along, this play of ours. Now then. Shall we all sit down so I can go through my notes?'

* * *

There's big news all round Brack's Hill. The Prince of Wales is to make a visit. Here. To Brack's Hill. He'll visit the town on one of his tours to comfort the afflicted. He'll go to the Club, to the Miners' Welfare, the poultry scheme and the allotment scheme. He'll hear the brass band. And the word is, he'll see the play put on at the Settlement.

I can see that, as clear as I just saw the rehearsal. In the front row the equerry will cough and the Prince will cross one immaculately-clad leg over the other. He'll take a snowy handkerchief from his pocket and half-pat the film of sweat from his face and manage to give his nose a rest from what he perceives as the earthy half-human scents in the room.

But what a big thing for Brack's Hill. The Prince of Wales!

Chapter Ten

Collaboration

Archie Todhunter's brief from thc Trust was to maintain relationships with the agencies which had helped with the original survey. This had pinpointed Brack's Hill as a suitable location for the project. The local council, the local doctor-clergy group, the Welfare Services, the Miners' Union, the schools, Durham University – all these supported and to some extent took responsibility for the Settlement enterprise and made appropriate contributions in cash, kind and in flesh.

As men of liberal persuasion, the members of these various agencies had endured a decade of feeling helpless in the face of the juggernaut of the Depression. To have Archie Todhunter and his progressive, enlightened project on their doorstep gave them a little faith that something might be done. It also gave them something to talk about with colleagues in other hopeless environments.

Archie did not have an easy run with the local people, however. Many had fought in the Great War for a better England. Even in these hard times such men and women tried to keep things together. They were shrewd people who were used to bargaining, often suspicious of the offerings of Art and Literature and generally more comfortable with the straight forward patronage of the food and clothes parcels from other parts of the country and as far afield as America.

These people could be quick to criticise if Archie made an 'unsuitable' choice of play or class. They always sat in the front row, solid hard critics unfazed by the greatest poets of this or any other day.

In the abstract, Archie admired them, but face to face it was, as he would say, 'a different kettle of fish'. They seemed so preoccupied with the practical issues of so many people out of work that often their heads could not be raised to the higher aims he had for his own flock.

One man whom he both admired and treated with caution was Dev Pallister, both a 'big' Union man and a Town Councillor who was on his way to becoming a County Councillor. Dev it was who, in the teeth of opposition, had got Brack's Hill citizens their Public Jubilee Park. He'd been in the van when they'd converted the Higher Elementary School to a Grammar School to put Brack's Hill schooling on a par with that of other towns in the district.

Dev Pallister was a man you needed on your side. He was also the father of Greta, the young hopeful in the drama group. One day Archie found himself sitting in his office defending to Dev Pallister the practicality of the Settlement provision. 'We offer classes here in basic literacy, Councillor Pallister, and in Literature and Higher Economics. In the French and German language. Basic Physics. You must agree with me that all these might allow some people at some time to hoist themselves out of this morass.'

'Aye, Mr Todhunter.' Dev took a half-smoked cigarette from his top pocket and lit it, flicking the match with his nail. 'But we have basic classes already, down at the Club. Wednesday, Thursday mornings. We tek care of our own.'

Archie wriggled a bit in his office chair. Although he liked to sustain an atmosphere of informality with his clients and students, he always made sure he was at his desk when he talked to Dev Pallister. 'There are seventeen thousand people in this town, Mr Pallister. How many of them do you have in your classes? Ten? Twenty individuals? Surely there's more need than this. The men who don't get into the Club for one reason or another. Young people. Women.'

'Women?' Pallister blew on the end of his cigarette and made it glow. 'Young people?'

'Your own daughter benefits from classes here.'

'If you want to bring personalities into it, Mr Todhunter, that young woman's in no need of extra classes. She has a full week of lessons at the Grammar School. Homework too. Your drama is just the icing on an overegged cake.'

'Six of the men involved in that play are unemployed miners from your own union.'

'I'll give yer that,' said Pallister.

He let a silence hang in the air that Archie had to break. 'It's not the drama we're on about just now, Mr Pallister. I've got an application in with the council for a year's support for these new classes in Literacy and Economics.'

Pallister leaned over and stubbed out his cigarette in Archie's half-full ashtray. 'The council's sympathetic with the aims of the Settlement, you know that, Mr Todhunter. They can see what you and what this place is doing in the town. All credit to you. But our first priority is food, clothes, boots for men whose boots have worn out and no wherewithal to replace them. Some of the children canna go out in bad weather, canna go to school because they have no shoes. There's some old 'uns drink tea instead of taking a meal. Think of money in relation to that. They've done their Practical Economics, Mr Todhunter.'

Archie bit back the retort about not living by bread alone and stood up. 'Well, Mr Pallister,' he said evenly, 'I just thought it might be useful to have a word with you.'

Pallister stood up and brushed the flakes of ash from his shiny jacket. Archie didn't reach over to shake his hand, as he would have if it had been Dr Gilliphray. These miners saw touching as affected and overfond; he'd learned to stick by that unspoken rule.

At the door Pallister turned. 'Far as I can, Mr Todhunter,' he said, 'I'll support your application in the committee.'

'I'm obliged,' said Archie.

Pallister paused. 'Our Greta. She's doing all right at the drama?'

Archie nodded. 'She's very keen. She has a remarkable memory.'

'Aye. Saying whole nursery rhymes when she was two, was that one. Read when she was three.' And he was gone.

Archie put his head down on his hands and closed his eyes. Five minutes later Cora came in to find him like this. 'Now what's up, you poor boy?'

'Just had Pallister in.'

'Seems too old to be father to that girl,' said Cora thoughtfully.

'Tried to warm him up about those funds for the new classes.'

'And did you?'

'Perhaps. To be honest, I've no idea. He's harder to read than an orang-utan.'

'What did he say?'

'Feller can't see beyond his nose. All wrapped up in cries for food and clothes. Like the rest of them he can't lift his eyes to the horizon.'

'Listen to yourself, Archie. It's you who don't see past your nose. Some of the men and women who come here do worry because of the state of their clothes and shoes. Down to their last jacket and where will the next one come from. Yet they still come.'

He shook his head. 'They have no culture, these people, not a shred. Nothing to build on. We're in the land of the barbarians, Cora. Our offerings are as nothing.'

She came close to him, put her arm round his shoulder and pulled him to her. 'You talk such rubbish sometimes, Archie. Two hundred people came through our doors last month. They're hungry for culture, this lot. Eagerly seeking what we have to offer.' She put him from her. 'Anyway, they do have their own culture. The football, the bowls, the pigeons, the Club. The singing. They have all the newspapers in the Club – and they're read. You said so yourself.'

'The Club's about beer! About men comforting each other into oblivion. Low culture where poetry is anathema.'

Cora sat down in the seat which Pallister had just vacated. 'You're getting to be an old grouch, Archie. And you're not seeing straight. This football, these bowls, these pigeons – maybe that's a kind of poetry to them.'

Archie smiled, suddenly cheered up. 'Really, Cora, you are a joke. You do get strange ideas. Just you concentrate on keeping this place straight and the classes organised. When I want your advice about culture I'll ask for it. Aren't I the expert, after all?'

Archie lit a cigarette from his, and leaned over to hand it to her. 'Smoke?' As they sat for a while in companionable silence Archie thought she was the easiest woman he had ever known. 'Remember the day you turned up on my doorstep? What a day that was.'

'I though you were a bit of an old grouch even then,' she said, surveying the glowing tip of her cigarette. 'But not a bad old stick, all things considered.'

She'd turned up at the Settlement the second day after Archie took possession of the building. He'd been working on his own, unloading several vans of kit he'd begged, borrowed and stolen from people of goodwill up and down the country. Inside the house two men were working, converting two small front rooms into one large one. Men out the back were converting outhouses to workshops. Painters and plasterers sloshed away upstairs.

He moved three boxes to get at the table which would be his desk and sat there surveying the bustle and the boxes, from which he would conjure his kingdom. There was no denying it. He was pleased with himself.

As he told the man from the Trust, he relished a challenge.

Someone knocked hard on the door then pushed it open immediately. A tall, elegant, faintly ugly woman came straight to him and shook him by the hand. 'Cora Miles,' she said. 'I'm staying here in Brack's Hill and the woman I'm staying with told me what you were doing here and I thought I'd come to help. I have ten years in rep, a good Socialist conscience, and lots of energy.' She paused. 'You don't recognise me, do you?'

Archie held up a protesting hand. 'Stop! Stop! Sit down, will you, and get back your breath.' He surveyed the Amazon figure: the over-defined face with its carmined lips. He shook his head. Then to his alarm she stood up, closed her eyes and opened them and at once seemed taller, narrower. Her eyes glittered.

> 'The quality of mercy is not strained,
> It droppeth as the gentle rain from heaven
> Upon the place beneath . . .'

She was a statuesque Portia to be sure and there was authority in her tone, implicit power in her stance. She had an old-fashioned theatrical delivery but she was not bad, not bad at all.

'Brighton,' she said. '1928. The Goodwill Players. Didn't you work with Tyrone Guthrie?'

He stared at her. So, there was to be no such thing as a fresh start. How could he come here to be the big impresario when this woman knew of his humiliation? Then he shrugged. 'Sit down, Miss . . .'

'Miss Cora Miles. Née Wilkinson. But I thought that wouldn't look so good on a poster.'

'So what makes you want to work in this . . .'

'Dingy old place?'

'Well, what?'

'Let's see. I broke my arm, went to hospital, and when I looked up, The Goodwill Players had got a new female lead and left me behind.'

'A bit extreme.'

'Well, I did break my arm when I threw a left hook at the manager. He bounced off the stage.'

'Have you got a very bad temper, Miss Miles?'

'Me? Gentle as a lamb. But that heel was trying to get into my . . . er . . . favours and wouldn't take no for an answer. So I socked him.' She surveyed her red enamelled fingers. 'Good riddance to bad rubbish, I say.'

'So they left you behind. A bit short of goodwill, eh?'

She laughed. 'That's it.'

'Still, how d'you come up here?'

'Well, I was out of cash as well as goodwill so I came up here to see an old friend who's a teacher. She told me what you were up to and said it was just up my street.' She looked round. 'You've a lot on your plate here.'

'So I have.' He'd no idea what to do with her. It was like being in the same room as a puppy the size of a leopard.

'I can help you,' she said.

'We're working on an absolute shoestring.'

'Doesn't this Trust thing allow for housekeeping expenses, a place this size?'

'Well, there is an allowance . . .'

'Right then. I'll do that for you. And I can help out with some English and Drama.'

He gave in. Here was a decision made for him. There were a hundred more important decisions he'd have to make. He leaned forward and offered her a cigarette. She picked it up with delicate fingers and held it for a while as he fiddled with his lighter. He lit the cigarette; she inhaled and spoke as the smoke drifted from her mouth. 'So. I don't cost much and you save me from the living death of the classroom.'

'There is an allowance,' he repeated.

'Good,' she said. 'Now, would there be somewhere to stay, here?'

'There are a whole lot of rooms on the next three floors. The place rambles around over two original houses. The rooms on the first floor'll be for Settlement things. I'll have the rooms above them. There are two rooms above that.' Doubt crept back into his voice. 'I thought a housekeeper . . .'

'Done!' She leaned over and shook the hand which had no cigarette. 'The room then, and how much did you say?'

Archie had had friendships and occasional functional intimacies with women in his travelling life but he'd never hit it off seriously with just one woman. In his life, the most glamorous people had been the men: actors like Jack Tarrant and Robert Donat, managers like Tyrone Guthrie. The women to him had always seemed like lesser players. Even Flora Robson who'd had this thing with Guthrie and was said to be a great actress, was unbearably plain and demure out of role. It was the men, still with the fragments of make-up, their lashes still black with kohl, who were the peacocks. This added to the power in the roles such men played; for Archie it made them overwhelmingly fascinating.

Archie even found *himself* glamorous when he looked into a cracked dressing-room mirror and surveyed his own browned skin, his own kohled eyes. This was so, even if he were playing some boring manservant or agricultural worker who came on in the Third Act. His fellow students, when he funked Edinburgh, had clubbed together and bought him a box of stage make-up. The very best quality. He still had it. He still loved an excuse to use it.

Archie had never really been able to work out this man-woman thing. Perhaps it was because women, especially actresses, wore make-up *all* the time, that they lacked the glamour of the men who only put on their mask for the drama. He liked women well enough for conversation and the occasional 'pillow fight' but, for him, they were never as attractive as the men were, at that moment when they were ready to tread the boards.

'Mr Todhunter?' The woman in front of him dragged him back from his reverie. 'Is that it then?'

He smiled slightly. 'That's it. You can go and get your luggage.'

Her curls bounced as she shook her head. 'No need. It's all outside your kitchen door.'

So this was the way that Cora Miles came to the Settlement. She'd been by his side since those early days. She'd done everything, from moving and sorting boxes, dragging furniture, teaching classes, building sets, sewing costumes, making dinners and finally, warming his bed at night.

In his most frustrated moments Archie was irritated by her assurance, her possessiveness and, it had to be faced, her highly studied vulgarity. He was too shrewd to pursue his frustration, though, for he knew he couldn't have done all this without Cora Miles, although it was he who received the accolades and the growing fame for this trailblazing project.

And in *Coal and Blood*, in her role as Maggie Olliphant, Archie knew she would do him proud. He needed her now as he'd never needed her before. Of course he didn't say any of this to her as they sat quietly smoking their cigarettes in the growing dark. It was not his way.

Chapter Eleven

Notes

We're familiar enough with the play now. We've had more meetings in the big room to read it through in sections. That girl Greta Pallister has her words off already. Archie Todhunter stops and starts the action, coaching and cajoling us like a benevolent sergeant-major. He makes me read Arthur's lines from one end of the room to the other, to Greta Pallister, whose voice in return sounds like a chirruping bird spiralling in the space between us.

'Project your voice! Project, don't bellow!' Todhunter says. 'These are intimacies you must share with strangers.'

As he makes us read the lines again and again, I battle to become Arthur, desolate at the impossibility of trying to communicate from this muddy trench to a place back home. Arthur's voice begins to tremble as he covers up the foulness of his situation with his hopes for tomorrow, when the war will be won and he will return and he and his sweetheart will live happily ever after, he at the pit and she in the little house they will share. You can almost smell the roses round the door.

In the end I, Gabriel not Arthur, revolt. 'This is rubbish,' I say. 'How could he say that? Happiness? Safety? Look what happened – poverty, the dole, crippled soldiers begging in the street. Look outside this very door.'

'Rubbish?' says Todhunter evenly. He's leaning back, with his bottom hooked on to the table they use for the books on library days. 'Rubbish, you say, Gabriel?'

'Well,' I slow down a bit. 'It's all very nice to hear, but it's not the truth, is it?'

'We know that now, laddie,' says Todhunter, 'but they didn't know it then did they? They hoped they'd win the war and "Return to a land fit for heroes," as Mr McVay said once.'

Tegger shuffles his feet; I can feel his eyes on me, then on Todhunter as we take each other on.

'Just what I mean,' I say. I'm wary of the man. He's like a fisherman playing us all with his line. 'It's false, making our characters say things we know are a lie.'

Todhunter draws on his cigarette through his fancy holder. 'Irony, my boy! You're talking about the irony of the situation. You'll not be alone in your perceptions.'

'Irony?' I *do* know the word.

'Irony's not confined to Shakespeare, nor the lives of the long dead. It infuses our lives today. That flare of anger which you just described. *A land fit for heroes*. That's the irony. That sense of hypocrisy, of wasted lives. That's what the play's about, is it not? Lives wasted by bad management underground or by cod generals in the trenches. Don't we want people to recognise this? To join it to their own experiences? To reflect on what happens when they put their fate in the hands of incompetents? Colliery managers, generals, princes and kings.' His voice has lost its usual jocular tone. 'All who see unique human beings as fodder for their cannons or their grinding mills.'

Cora, lounging in a corner, waves her cigarette in Archie's direction 'Go lightly, Archie. These are young creatures. Tender birds.'

'It's their lives. Their country,' says Todhunter gruffly.

My brain hums with his words, buzzing like a hive of bees. 'Sounds like treason to me,' I say. 'Scoring off against generals and kings.'

'Now you're getting it,' he says. 'Now, can we please carry on with this rehearsal? Then I'll give you my notes, after which the redoubtable Fraulein Vonn needs this space at six for her stage-design meeting.'

The room empties just on six o'clock, apart from Tegger and me and Mr Conroy, the joiner. At one minute past six the redoubtable Fraulein Vonn comes in with a big black folder in her hands, which she places carefully on the long table. She shakes hands with each of us. Her handshake is firm, her glance as direct as any man's. 'Mr MacNamara?'

'Ah'm called Tegger, er, miss . . . er.'

'That is a strange name,' she says.

'It's for Edgar, Miss. But Ah'm always known as Tegger. You can call me Tegger.'

'And you can call me Rosel.' She smiles at him with her small white teeth. She might not be young and is no beauty but there's something about her. Tegger's eyes go glassy. He's smitten all right.

'And this is my mate Gabriel Marchant, Rosel. You can call him Gabriel,' he smirks.

She shakes my hand. 'I know Mr Marchant from the art class.' She has been civil to me lately, although she leaves me strictly to get on with my own stuff.

'And from the pit heap. She walks by the pit heap, Tegger,' I say, watching her closely. Her grasp is really strong. I look directly into her eyes which are the colour of the grey-blue glass in the side window of the old chapel. 'I'm called Gabriel, like he says.'

'What is it there, at this tip, that you search for with such care?' Her voice is soft, careful, coming from somewhere deep in her throat. I wonder what it must be like to think in one language and speak in another. I can smell her perfume. Lemony. Sweet and light. I imagine some neat German flower. Tight. Symmetrical.

'The petrified forest,' I say. 'The fossils of fish and birds. Insects. That's what I look for.'

'I see.' She pulls her hand from mine with difficulty and turns to Jake McVay, and then to Mr Conroy. 'We know each other, do we not?' she says. 'I see you at the meetings.'

'Aye, so you do. Mr Conroy, you can call me.' The old man is having none of this first-name rubbish.

She nods to us all, avoiding my glance again. Then she spreads her papers out on the table. 'This is Mr Todhunter's rough sketch.' She smoothes out a crumpled piece of paper. On top of it she places another crisp sheet. 'I have sketched the stage in this way. Like so.'

It's Todhunter's scene sketched in much greater detail. The three settings are drawn in deftly: the army trench, the coroner's court, the podium with its cluster of women. She has added figures of the actors in role, depicted us in simple, direct strokes. Nathan, masterfully authoritative as the coroner. Jake McVay, squat and scant-haired as the corporal. Archie, sharp-suited as the pit manager. Me, in uniform with an improbable halo of curls. Greta Pallister, with her crown of plaits, narrow and earnest among more shadowy women. Behind it all is the massive circle of the colliery wheel, the huddle of dark colliery buildings. Above it all, washed in bright colour, is a blood-red sunrise.

Tegger whistles.

'That's good,' says Mr Conroy. 'Clever, like.'

'So how are we supposed to get that on the stage in the church hall?' I say. 'It's very elaborate.'

She looks at me sharply. 'Ha! So you think I am proud, Gabriel, that I show off?'

'I never said that. I'm just wondering how that might be a stage set, like. It'll be hard to get it right.'

She shrugs. That movement is so foreign, so unlike any movement my Aunt Susanah or Greta Pallister would make. Her narrow shoulders move with an elegance that whispers of grand parties and fine rooms. Don't ask how I know this. I just do.

'I do not know whether it will work,' she says. 'I am an artist, not a stage designer. I draw from Mr Todhunter's sketch and from watching the rehearsals. It is for you to make a stage from it.'

Mr Conroy's peering at the paper. 'Need to break it down into parts,' he says. 'It's not impossible.'

Tegger frowns at him, then counts the 'parts' off on his fingers. 'One, painted backdrop of the sky with colliery wheel where the women stand. Could we build one? Two, coroner's court. Furniture. Three. Trench dugout. Wooden framework, papier-mâché? We made models at school like that, didn't we, Gabe? What about some kind of big gun looming over it all?'

'Not enough room,' I say. 'Remember the stage in the chapel. That's the space.'

'The greatest problem is that we need to see one part only at a time,' said Rosel Vonn, frowning. 'I know you have thought of a turntable. But we must make the audience look at that part only, when the action is there.'

I'm peering myself now, as interested as any of them, forgetting about Rosel Vonn and the way she fled from me at the tip and has been ignoring me in the art class. 'Light,' I say finally. 'Lanterns.'

'How's that, marra?' says Tegger.

'Well, when the coroner speaks he turns up this elaborate lamp on his desk so you see him and all around him. When we need to watch the lads in the trench, they can have lanterns, like Tilley lamps. Same with the women. There could be a kind of street lamp beside them which goes on when they talk.'

'Yes,' says Rosel Vonn. 'This is good.'

I squeeze my eyes half-shut, staring at the drawing, imagining the dark stage where the light leads the action. 'And you don't really need a colliery wheel, or a gun, do you? What you need are models, like shadow puppets, see? A kind of outline model of a pit wheel which you shine a light through, so the black shadow shows up against that sunrise. And a machine gun. You could do the same with a machine gun for the trench scenes. A silhouette.'

In the silence that follows I'm embarrassed at my enthusiasm. Then Tegger whistles. 'Why Gabe, man, yer clever devil.'

'Could work,' said Mr Conroy slowly. 'Idea's simple enough.'

'Is a good idea,' said Rosel Vonn. 'Have you seen such a thing Gabriel, on the stage before?'

I shake my head. 'I've never seen a play before, never mind a stage.' I imagine Rosel Vonn on the staircase of great theatres in Berlin: all chandeliers and sweeping dresses.

* * *

I suppose you might say that this is how Rosel Vonn and I have come to something of a truce. We work on the set together, our proximity mediated by the energetic enthusiasm of Tegger and the measured pipe-smoking wisdom of Mr Conroy.

It's still more or less the same in the art class. Here I get used to drawing and eventually painting without much comment or guidance from her. I've been preoccupied with Rembrandt lately. I try to make some kind of sense of his way with light, to come to grips with his sheer sorcery in bringing white exterior light into his interiors. In the class I make crude attempts at mimicking him, which go uncommented upon. What with all that and two nights' play rehearsal a week I seem to spend little time in my father's house. That, of course, is to my liking.

Greta Pallister stayed for every minute of every rehearsal, even those which did not involve her. She sat in a corner, sometimes reading a book, sometimes doing her homework, or writing in a small notebook which she always carried with her.

Greta knew she was clever. She was the only member of her family to take up a place at the Grammar School.

Her eldest brother Robert, who'd emigrated to Canada, sent money earmarked for Greta's schooling. The second eldest, Joss, had moved to London where, after a false start as a dishwasher in an hotel in the Strand, he had found a steady job as a servant to an elderly man who enjoyed being read to. In that job, all found, there was money to send back home to help out.

Contributions from these two brothers kept their parents on their feet and Greta at Grammar School. It also freed their father Dev to get on with his jobs as Union man and Councillor without excessive worry.

At the Grammar School, Greta's slightly dusty appearance and pitmatic talk came to be overlooked as, test by test, examination by examination, she won all the prizes. In the end she not only learned her Geography and History, her French and her Maths, she also learned to round up her vowels and put on her *ings* and *aitches*. Greta was an adaptive organism in the body politic of Brack's Hill.

All this, added to her success in Archie's plays, did her no harm at all at school, where her teachers started to talk of scholarships to Oxford and Cambridge.

Such verbal sophistication, of course, was not called for in the case of this new play *Coal and Blood*. Tegger's laughing and mockery made sure that Greta dropped her new middle-class voice and reverted to the talk of her early childhood. She kept her clarity but she had to flatten her vowels and drop her *ings* and *aitches* to sound authentic.

However, Archie, with more than a little help from Tegger MacNamara, had written a play which had rhythms of its own. The speeches of the soldiers, the women, the miners and the lawyers followed each other like spoken anthems. Greta did not miss the glance which passed between Tegger and Archie when she compared the rhythms to those of Chaucer's *Canterbury Tales*. They could think what they liked.

She wondered what her mother, who rather wallowed in her daughter's ability to *talk posh*, would think when she saw the performance. She'll have a fit, thought Greta. A proper dicky fit. Mrs Pallister saw herself as a bit above her penurious neighbours. And here was her daughter, back talking pitmatic! Wasn't her husband Dev a big man in the Union, which seemed even more important now there was no work? And he was a Councillor as well. Hadn't her sons taken their chances, made their way in the world, and hadn't the whole family benefited? Didn't they have an end house with a bay window?

In Greta's rather myopic eyes the ever-silent Gabriel Marchant was as beautiful as Apollo. She copied some school notes into the notebook which she always carried with her. *Apollo's beauty had as its essence strength, reserve and emotions in full control.*

She somehow squeezed some time to join the Saturday painting group to see more of him. She witnessed his battle with light and colour in the context of the dark of the pit; she watched him poring over the prints of Turner and Rembrandt. She copied more of her notes. *He is the god of light and of inspiration which itself is the soul's light.*

Gabriel moves like a panther and, though he says very little, when he does speak his voice is deep and distinct: it makes profound music. As he reads his lines (it's taken him ages to get them off by heart), his voice penetrates the very corners of the long church hall. He doesn't need to raise it and project like the others. It has timbre.

Greta looked up the *timbre* in her little dictionary to see she'd got it right.

Except in the process of the actual rehearsal, Gabriel would not meet her gaze. No matter how long she hung around it was never long enough.

Greta was not surprised at his rejection. The young men of her acquaintance, even cousins, found her looks unentrancing, her lack of flirtatious skills confusing, her bookishness next door to repellent. She didn't know how to tease and flirt, and if you got off on the wrong foot with her she'd bore you with some facts about the discovery of Australia or the significance of the Magna Carta. On top of that she was clumsy. She had large hands which didn't work too well and tended to knock over things like glasses and cups.

Gabriel said so little it was hard sometimes to tell who he really was *And thereby*, wrote Greta in her diary, *hangs the problem. That German woman fills his eye. She's always head to head with him. There are sparks between them. They say she's a proper artist. Half the time he looks like he hates her. But other times they are over at his board scribbling away as if they are joined at the hip. Siamese twins. There was a picture of some of those in the* News Chronicle. *Weird.*

If Gabriel was the new Apollo in Greta's life, Archie Todhunter was the Zeus. She drank in every word he said, noting the most outstanding of them in her diary. She thought Archie clever, even learned; funny, full of life and a fount of wisdom and anecdote. She compared him very favourably with the male teachers at school whom she was supposed to admire.

Putrid, fossilised timeservers! She wrote this in her diary with a flourish. *If they're not gibbering with shell shock they're inventing stories of saving the Empire. And they pinch your arm to make a point and pat your bottom when no one is looking.*

But even they were livelier than the mistresses. These venerable women retreated to their lair – the female common room – and only emerged to deliver their lessons in parrot voices or give you a hundred lines for saying *pass* instead of *parse*.

Thank God for textbooks, wrote Greta. *There at least is some light, some scholarship.*

After she joined the Settlement she noted: *Hurray for Archie Todhunter! At least he has some fire and believes in what he's saying and thinks he can change the future. He might be wrong but this is still a good thing.*

Greta was wary of Cora Miles. The woman was kind enough. She would take Greta into a corner to show her how your body can reflect the words that are coming out of your mouth. Or how the way you use your body can give meaning without even speaking. More. How your body can *add* to the meaning, help the audience to know what the play's really about. This had been invaluable in *Loves Labours Lost* when Greta despaired of her clumsy body. She was certain that her clumsiness would bleach out the delicacy of Shakespeare's poetry and make it poor fare for the audience. Cora helped her to avoid that, and Greta began to understand that on stage she could be another person, even a not-ugly other person.

But kind as Cora always was, Greta felt that somewhere underneath the kindness, the firm touch, there lay a distinct mockery. Occasionally, when other people were present she would call Greta 'Archie's acolyte'. This would make Greta blush and the others would laugh, not always kindly.

Archie himself was reassuringly bland with Greta. He spoke to her evenly, without the talking-down of the others, or the mocking kindness of Cora. If she made an intelligent remark in his company she would be rewarded with his close attention and a further request for her opinion. The others might exchange glances. Even roll their eyes.

'What's that you're writing?' It was Tegger MacNamara, peering over her shoulder.

She jumped, putting her hand right across the page. 'Nothing. Just some notes. A notebook.'

'Nowt wrong with writing, kidder. I'm a bit like that meself, nowadays.' He looked up and past her, then set off across the room. 'Hey, Gabe! You off, marra? Hold on.'

She watched the two boys go off, heads together, one dark

and one fair. Then she put her books in her satchel and fetched her coat. She would follow them as far as Inkerman Street. At a safe distance, of course.

But she missed them. It seemed they had some business with Rosel Vonn. Something about scenery.

Chapter Twelve

A Manmade Place

Rosel Vonn had settled in quite well in this house which was part-home, part-meeting place, part-office. Todhunter and Cora were kind enough to her, but not curious about her. Apart from the lunchtime meal, which Cora made for them all at twelve noon each day, they left Rosel to her own devices. She made her own breakfast and supper in the office-kitchen, she worked with her artists, painted her own paintings, helped with the scenery and drew in her own sketchbook. She was drawing freely now for the first time in years.

Rosel watched with admiration Archie's management of the place where so much happened. After ten o'clock in the morning, every day except Sunday, the Settlement buzzed with activities: daytime classes in cobbling, watchmaking, French and embroidery, daily visitors to read the newspapers from cover to cover, in the evenings weekly discussions of news and current affairs led by Todhunter, the poetry circle led by Cora, some Economic History with Mr Jonty Clelland, the twice-weekly library, the cornet lessons given by Mr Poppel from the Grammar

School, and now Fine-Art classes and play rehearsals. All these activities seemed to give the building an intense inner light. Despite being very shabby and only half-painted, it outshone the rest of the houses in the drab row. It probably outshone every house in the town.

The activities often went on into the night. This meant Archie and Cora kept theatrical hours, not rising till nine or nine-thirty some mornings.

Rosel, an early riser herself, got into the habit of going out for a walk before they were out of bed. On one of these mornings she cut herself a slice of bread, put that in one pocket, her drawing pad in another, and let herself out of the back door. She walked the length of the High Street past two yawning young men who were opening up shop and sweeping pavements. A ginger-haired man with a high forehead was unloading a wagon of beef and heaving them into the Co-op butcher's shop.

These men peered at this smartly dressed woman with interest. This was no skivvy going to scrub for someone on High Row, no shop-girl going to stand behind a counter all day. It was true that the women who worked in the shops on the High Street were well scrubbed and respectable. They even wore a flash of colour now and then. But this woman had the look of something more than that. She wore a striking red scarf round her neck; another gauzy scarf with silver stars on as a bandeau, instead of a hat. She was no chicken but she was slender and shapely like the mannequins you saw in the Co-op window. But why was she out so early? The way she was dawdling, there was no work to go to. You could bet on that.

Many of the shops which Rosel passed were boarded up. Those which were open were making a brave show, even if the colour of some of the items on display was bleaching down, showing signs of age. The stock was not moving, not moving at all.

She cut through a narrow alley behind the High Street on to a row of low houses with small square windows. These were much lower than the other houses she had passed, perhaps just one storey. Smoke surged from the chimneys to weld itself to the general pall of smoke above the town. Each house in the row differed from its neighbour in fine degrees of visible poverty.

She walked on, making her way round the silent colliery buildings out towards the pit heap and the patch of woodland beyond. Up there, above the low hills which lapped towards the horizon, the sky looked brighter. Her lungs ached for good clean air.

Looking across towards the pit heap she saw the now-familiar figure of Gabriel Merchant. Feeling her gaze he raised his head and saw her. He stared for a minute then put up his hand and started to scramble towards her. 'Hey!' he called. 'Miss . . . er, Roscl.'

She waited. He came level with her and put out his hand, palm flat. 'This is what I look for,' he said. 'Up here on the heap.' It was a piece of slate lined with the delicate tracery of an oak leaf. 'From the petrified forest,' he said. 'Fathoms deep.'

She touched the veins of the leaf with a finger. 'A miracle,' she said. 'All those thousands of years.'

He pushed his hand forward, against hers. 'Here, you can have it,' he said.

She shook her head. 'No. It is your collection.'

'Have it,' he said. 'I have hundreds.'

She took it from him. It was warm from his hand. After

thousands of years in the cold earth, now, today, it was warm. 'Thank you. I shall treasure it.'

He looked at her sharply, to check for mockery.

'Really,' she said. 'It is a treasure.'

He glanced along the pathway she had come. 'So, are you off somewhere, like?'

'I thought I'd make my way towards that woodland,' she said. 'It looks brighter there. Fresh air.'

'You can see Roman stones over there. Not as old as this fossil, but quite old.'

'How do you know they are Roman?'

'Everybody knows. They have Roman markings.'

She hesitated.

'I'll show you.' He set off, quickly moving into his swinging stride. She followed, skipping now and then to keep up with him. They walked in silence. Once in the wood he headed down a narrow pathway through blackthorn bushes, some gorse and a stand of beech trees. Their feet slapped on wet grass. Then they crunched down to a clearing with a kind of gravel beach. Here the river swirled round into a wide basin formed by a cliff of sandstone, before moving on to wend its way seaward. The sun pierced the cloud for a second and lit the edge of the water where it escaped the shadow of a cliff.

Gabriel used his broad forearm to sweep leaves and twigs from a sandstone ledge. 'You sit here a minute. I need to look round. I think they were somewhere near the edge. It's a while since I saw them.'

She sat down and watched as he made his way along the edge of the river, pulling away at brambles and low branches. Suddenly hungry, she took out her paper-wrapped bread and butter and started to eat. She'd just finished and was brushing crumbs from her dress when she heard him shout. She followed his voice and, careful of her shoes and the encroaching water, she edged her way round the corner.

He'd pulled away a thicket of bramble. 'Look,' he said. The surface of the stone had some kind of indented design with letters underneath.

'What does it say?' She traced the lines with her finger.

He shook his head. 'It's a gravestone or an altar, I should think. There's a number there, look. IX. That's nine, isn't it?'

She looked round. Brack's Hill lay to their right, rolling countryside on the left. 'Where does this come from? Is it a Roman place?'

He shrugged. 'It's a place. A manmade place. See there. Five stones flat in a row. Must be a landing spot or something. Upstream though there was a camp, a military camp. There are stones from that camp in some of the farmhouses round here. They shipped them down on the river, so mebbe this one rolled overboard.'

She looked up across the turbulent basin of water, to the cliff on the other side, then back to Gabriel's face. 'This is a magical place,' she said.

He nodded. 'It's that all right,' he said. 'My father showed me it once when I was very little. I used to come here with Tegger before we started work. Used to play soldier games. Huns and British.' He blushed. 'I'd almost forgotten about that,' he said. 'Who you are. You coming here . . .'

'Can we sit down?' she said. She led the way back to her stone seat. He sat further along, his booted feet dangling over the water. She waited until he was settled. 'Do you live with your family?' she said.

He shook his head. 'I live on me own. Me father's dead. Mother too.'

She flushed, remembering the men in the class: what they had said about Gabriel's father. 'Goodness,' she said. 'I am sorry.'

He stared at the swirling water, away from her. The silence went on too long. She reached into her pocket. 'Do you mind if I draw?' she said.

He looked up, frowning.

'That's why I come out to walk away from the town, Gabriel. To breathe clear air. To draw. And this is such a beautiful place.'

'Suit yourself,' he said.

With a speed which surprised herself she executed two drawings: one of his drooping figure staring into the water, one of the whole scene, with the rearing cliff and the circle of trees, the stones at an awkward angle.

In the end he hauled himself to his feet and came to stand beside her. 'What's it you're doing?'

She turned her book towards him. He looked from it towards the river, then handed it back. 'You're very good,' he said. 'A fine artist. I see that in the class.'

'So are you,' she said.

'You never say so,' he said. 'You never say anything to me in the class.'

'But you know it very well,' she said. 'You don't need me to tell you.'

He stared at her. 'Mebbe I do.'

She jumped down. 'I will have to be back to the Settlement. I promised Cora I would get some fresh bread for Mr Todhunter's breakfast toast.'

* * *

She shoves her sketchbook in her hand then and sets off, walking very quickly away from me, away from this place. I watch her swinging stride until she's out of sight and then sit down where she was sitting and breathe in the last of her lemony scent. I look and look at this scene again, through her eyes. She has made it strange, this place where I played Huns and British with Tegger, where I used to tramp with my father when he was still a reasonable man.

I wish now I had my own sketchbook here. Perhaps I should draw this scene myself. Perhaps that will make her begin to talk to me about my painting and what I'm really trying to do.

Chapter Thirteen

The German

Cora was waiting with the toasting fork for Archie's bread and a letter for Rosel. 'It has a German postmark.'

Rosel peered at the writing. 'My father,' she said.

'Archie says he was an artist too. Famous.'

'I would not say this. There was a set of drawings from the war. Archie has the book.'

'I should take a look at it.'

'It might make you very sad. It does not glorify those things. For this it is not admired in Germany now. They have burned many copies of it in the last few years, according to my brother. It seems it is decadent to show the true face of war.'

Cora nodded. 'I can see it's a threat. Like Archie's play. They want glory and sacrifice, not the true face of pain.'

Rosel looked sharply at Cora. 'This is true.' She made her way to the stairs.

'You must be proud of your father,' said Cora.

'Proud?' Rosel turned. 'I had not thought of it like that. At present, I am worried. He is a very outspoken man and has no care for his safety.'

'I hope he's all right.' Then Cora waved the loaf at Rosel. 'Now I'd better see the old boy up there gets his toast. Got to make sure for all our sakes that he gets out of bed the right side. Nice hot toast usually does the trick.'

The letter, in her father's flowing hand, was full of terrible things which were happening to him, but even so he showed an unusual interest in her life in Brack's Hill. *Why do you live in such a far place? London I know has its attractions even these days. Your work with artists there seemed appropriate. But, Liebling, to bury yourself so far away . . .* He was suddenly there, fussing over her in her small room. She could almost smell his cigar and the pomade he wore on his hair. To keep him with her, she wrote back by return.

Settlement House
Queen Street
Brack's Hill

1 June 1936

My Dearest Papa,

You ask of the people with whom I find myself. They are kind enough, these folk of Brack's Hill, but you have to dig deep to get under their hard, sometimes blank looks. If they are curious, it is in a sidelong way. There is a kind of courtesy, a discretion about this, which I like. Their humour is equally oblique. Often I have to get Cora or Archie, with whom I live, to explain. Sometimes I miss it altogether. I only know it has been a joke when the people around me splutter into laughter, half of it at my ignorance of their allusions. Even after my years in England I find it so different from the German way which is more direct, perhaps more intellectual and distinctly more cruel. You write to me in some embarrassment about the current jokes against the Jews and how you are jeered at for not laughing.

But this issue of prejudice is not one-sided. Twice when I have walked into a place – once a house, another time a shop – someone has spat on the floor. Three times I have heard 'Hun' hissed behind me in the High Street and turned round to blank stares. I have had one letter which called me a 'fucking prostitute' and informed me the only good German was a dead one. I went to Archie – Mr Todhunter – with this and he took it from me and rolled it into a spill which he put in the fire and used to light his pipe. 'Leave them to it, Miss Vonn. Don't absorb the poison.' He is a cool person. Did I tell you they call me Miss Vonn? I hope this does not disturb you. I thought it a good idea, as they can't seem to say our second name.

I asked Archie Todhunter if he had fought in the war and he said that, for good or ill, he was in China with his mother at the time and only came back to start his medical studies in 1918.

'Your mother was in China?' I said.

'Aye. She was a missionary.' His face was carved from stone. It was hard to know what to say. I worship form and the intoxication of creation but you know that I recognise no God. 'She must have been a good woman,' I said to him.

'I suppose so. I barely knew her apart from those few

years in China. Though there she was such an icon of virtue and sacrifice she seemed to have nothing to do with me. Other English people there were kind to me.' He sounds brisk, as though this does not matter.

'You didn't help her in her work?'

'God was long lost to me.' He smiled a cool smile. 'I set up childish play-acting with the few English that were there. And some Chinese taught me how to gamble.'

I like this man although he is hard to know.

But in general here in this town I have met a certain tolerance. I feel comfortable with them. You used to say that the English and the Germans had so much in common: a steadiness in the face of difficulty; an ability to organise others; a natural patriotism and an appreciation of good leadership; a sense of responsibility to their worldwide empires. I feel that this is so.

So, I am well, and this is an interesting time in my life. But I worry about you, dear Papa. Perhaps you would be safer here? Write, write, keep writing so that I know you are well.

Your devoted Rosel.

She sealed the envelope, her mind still dwelling on her father. In the years of his youth, this not uncommon view of a special relationship between the Germans and the English was intensified in people like her father by a sense of kinship. Was not the King of England cousin to the Kaiser? As a young man her father had been to parties and soirées with young Englishmen and he'd skied with them in Switzerland and the Italian Alps. In 1899 he was engaged briefly to an Englishwoman whose family had a house in London and a sprawling estate in Leicestershire.

His cousin, Rosel's Uncle Berti, studied architecture and design in London as well as Paris, even though London was not so fashionable then for such studies. This unfashionability suited her uncle, as he liked to be different. Sausage-and-mash and eels, for which he'd acquired a taste in his Limehouse lodgings, were regularly on order in his Berlin house.

Then there was her father's housekeeper's cousin, a woman from Düsseldorf, who'd been a maid attending the English royal children. She'd had to leave the Palace to come back to Germany at the beginning of the Great War. According to Rosel's father there had been tears all round, even from the Queen. The Düsseldorf woman had been quite at home in the Palace as German was commonly spoken there and the Royal children were at ease with it.

As with all patriotic Germans, Rosel's father and brother fought in that war, as did her uncle's son Humbert. After his first sojourn as a stretcher-bearer in the trenches, which provided the inspiration for his famous paintings and book of drawings, Rosel's father had seen no action. He got himself involved with the development of vehicle design for bad terrain and made some modifications to tank design. Her Uncle Berti had been assigned as a kind of errand boy to a general who avoided the Front like the plague, so he was quite safe.

Berti saw the Great War as an unfortunate, wasteful but basically honourable fight between equals. The final Treaty he believed to be disgustingly *dis*honourable. However, Anglophile that he was, he blamed it on the rapacious vengeance of the French who had, after all, suffered defeat, albeit temporary, at the hands of the Germans.

In the years after the war her father had welcomed the crude directness of the National Socialists. He supported their resolve to end the reparation payments; he welcomed their frontal attack on the downward spiral of the German nation. But these days things had changed. Now he was increasingly worried about the campaign against Jewish people. He'd had to stand by while his friends had been attacked and robbed of their livelihood and their homes: he'd had to dismiss his Jewish servants, some of whom had been with him for decades. He could not even consult his Jewish doctor who was a long-term expert on the vagaries of his wayward colon. He wrote to Rosel, *Things are not as they should be, Liebling. They make tyrants of us despite our inclinations*.

Rosel put down her father's letter. At least, she thought, here in Brack's Hill I've not been confronted with such hard decisions of conscience. But sometimes I feel uneasy at escaping from it all. Sometimes, working with Archie and Cora, with the painters and the set builders, I don't think of Father or of Germany for days, even weeks on end. My greatest problem is not to get too excited about the talent of these people. Especially that remarkable boy who feels his way into his art by some kind of instinct. He does not say much. But he did give me a fossil of an oak leaf and showed me that magical place. Perhaps that was saying something.

She took the fossil from her coat pocket and held it up to the mirror. Such a very ancient thing. Her gaze lifted to her own reflection. 'And you, Rosel Von Steinigen you are a very old thing too. You must be careful. Very careful.' Her breath steamed the mirror as she whispered the words to herself. '*Vorsichtig!* Be careful.'

Chapter Fourteen

Shoes

'It's an idea.' Archie stroked his non-existent beard.

'The artists, they will have a purpose. Something to aim for.' Rosel had proposed that some of the artists should draw, perhaps even paint, the players in their roles. 'They need some disciplined work on figures. Some of them draw people as though they are sticks of Plasticine. There is no sense of bone, muscle. The clothes, of course, they are a problem. At the Slade we drew the classical statues. Forms in the round.'

'Naked figures?' said Cora. She whistled. 'Now that could be embarrassing.'

Rosel shook her head. 'We were all women artists in the room. And we drew from statuary, not from models. Only the men were allowed to draw from life.' She sniffed. 'Ridiculous.'

'So did you never draw from life?' persisted Cora.

'Of course I did,' Rosel told her. 'It is impossible otherwise to learn. I made private arrangements.'

'What – you drew men?'

'Cora!' said Archie. 'Leave it alone.' But he was smiling slightly.

Rosel threw up her hands. 'They were no more than limbs . . . the arms, the legs, branches of trees. We are artists, not whores.'

Cora whistled again. 'With one or two curious lumps and bumps, I'll warrant,' she said.

'Cora!' Archie's mild reproof had as much impact as a feather on a rhinoceros.

'Well!' she said. 'In the buff. Art's as good an excuse as any.'

'We'd have problems if you wanted to strip off any of my miners, Rosel,' Archie coughed. 'They're a prudish lot above the ground. It would be round Brack's Hill like fire that we're running a brothel here. We'd lose our funding in a day.'

'Yes,' said Cora. 'They stretch a point with Archie and me even if they disapprove. They go along with the pretence. Hypocrisy is an unkind word for it.'

Rosel shook her head. 'It would be very good if they did take off their clothes. If any of the more talented ones manage to go on with their art, attend a proper art school, they will have to draw from life however prudish they may be. They will have to learn about muscles and bone, the beating heart within.' She sighed. 'But for now I thought we would draw them in the parts they have in the play, wearing their costumes. That child – Greta, is it? – in her apron, the miners in their pit gear, you as the pit manager, and the coroner, in your waistcoat suits and . . .' She paused.

'Gabriel in his muddy army uniform,' put in Cora, her painted mouth in a wide smile. 'Now that boy would be beautiful in anything, don't you think, Rosel? Root and branch. Just like a tree.'

Rosel ignored her. 'We could mount an exhibit for the days of the performance. Perhaps use the images for playbills, the programme. Is there a printer's where we could make some plates?'

'Whoah! Whoah!' said Archie. 'This may be too much. It's only a play, after all.'

Cora scowled at Archie. 'So what're you up, to Archie Todhunter? The play's important, you know it. It's not some end-of-the-pier farce for child miners. It's more than that.'

Archie shrugged. 'I don't want it getting attention for the wrong reason. The play's the thing. These are *your* own works, my dear. Works in the field of art, not drama.'

There was a silence as all three of them contemplated Archie's jealousy of Rosel's burgeoning achievements as though it were a small animal on the floor between them. Finally Rosel said slowly, 'Perhaps, Archie, my miners drawing pictures will have something to say for themselves. Something unique. Some message that will come purely from them. Not through the medium of *your* words and *your* contrived scenes. You do not like this, I think?'

Archie laughed suddenly. 'You've caught me there, Rosel. Fair and square with the wee green gremlin tugging at my heels. Yes, yes. Of course. Paint your pictures, print your posters. We can listen to their message as well as know the play.'

The feeling of rigour and purpose in the Saturday painting group is so strong that I tell no one about my obsessive copying at home, segment by segment, of the Rembrandt paintings in the book given to me by my Aunt Susanah.

I do this in secret because both Rosel Vonn and Todhunter frown on it. For her, copying is a taboo activity, 'That slavish,

slavish habit', she calls it. Todhunter, who, although genius at the drama, I know already to be less of a painter than me – well, he goes on about being 'true to yourself' and how you can 'invent your own way of seeing', your own way of painting. So copying Rembrandt has become my secret vice.

But how else am I supposed to tackle this problem of light as it inhabits flesh, clothes, sky, the very stone walls of this grey town, the very depths of the pit? It's frustrating. The more I pursue the delicacy, the luminosity, the more fugitive these qualities of light seem. At least in this *slavish* process of copying I can explore, however crudely, inch by inch, the way that assiduous master captured light like a butterfly hunter catches his fluttering prey. In this I know I'm training my eye, not necessarily learning how to paint. In this I'm no *slave*, whatever Rosel Vonn might say.

Archie was in his element working intensively on the monologues and dialogues, putting individuals through their paces under hard pressure, in the style of the great actor-managers. He listened when people strained with the dialogue, made changes and adjustments as he went. He kept Tegger by his side, notebook in hand, for the young man always knew just where Archie had gone wrong. 'Nah, he wouldn't say it like that. He'd say . . .' Archie encouraged him to alter the text, pasting and cutting the scripts until some pages were sheer patchwork. Archie talked to Tegger about the balance in a line, a phrase, in a speech, which could be achieved even when that speech stayed true to the way Brack's Hill people spoke.

It was Tegger who suggested using songs of the Great War as part of the chorus. When they tried this, Nathan objected. 'Yer makin' gam, aren't yer? Makes a joke of the whole shebang.

Songs! This is about the death of miners, man!'

'I don't know about that,' said Archie carefully. 'It adds a measure of counterpoint to the whole action.'

'Counterpoint be b—' Jake McVay stopped himself. Women present.

Greta leaned forward. 'I think it gives a kind of . . . rest . . . from the other serious parts,' she said. 'I like it. Some of the Shakespeare plays have dances and concerts in the middle, you know.'

I watch and listen to all this, not, if I'm honest, caring one way or the other. Of course, I'd always support Tegger in this or any other deal. The way he brings Todhunter's grandiloquent ideas into the genuine way of thinking and talking of this place – well, he's a wonder. It's no less telling that way. In fact, it's more powerful.

At this moment I'm more concerned about a large hole in my left boot and whether I'll get home with it on. I had put newspaper in for a sole but that got wet on the way here and now has disintegrated completely.

The rehearsal has finished. 'Comin' down to the workshop to help build the soldiers' trench?' Tegger calls across. I shake my head and hurry out, moving too fast to be waylaid by Greta Pallister. Once outside my feet squelch on the wet pavements and I have to limp to stop my boot dropping off altogether.

I let myself into the house and stir up the fire. Then, as I try to ease off the boot it falls to pieces in my hand. It's hopeless. The boots have been mended twenty times. The edges are totally broken down. They're unmendable, even with the careful craft of the lads from the cobbler's workshop.

It's such a basic humiliation, having no shoes. It stops

children from going to school, adults from going out to look for work. You can't even go for a walk to pass the time.

'Twelve and six for a new pair! Where will that come from?' I ask the question of the empty room and no answer's forthcoming.

I am stuck in the house for days on end. The weather has turned into an unseasonal whirligig of sleet, snow, hail and rain which has set in for a week. No shoes for me means no rehearsal, no painting class. I'm not glad of this. I'd go to both in my stockinged feet but would die at the attention this would bring me. Even Tegger can't 'tice me out, though he's tried.

I'm finishing off the Rembrandt *Night Watch*. It's a bit of a rough and tumble of an effort but I think I've caught one or two of the figures right. I put it beside my copy of *The Old Woman Reading* and in front of that disastrous copy of *Susanah and the Elders* where I got the flesh all wrong.

Yesterday I got out two boards, wooden off-cuts from the workshop. (These, at Rosel's suggestion, I have already primed with a mixture of Flake White and Raw Umber two weeks ago at the class.) I pull away my grandmother's sewing machine from under the window and drag the kitchen table into its place. Here the largest board which I prop up on my grandmother's flat irons will catch what light there is even on the darkest day.

Then, on the table beside it I put the cigar box of paints – some curled up and half-used. These have been supplied by the teacher who talks to me now but not directly about my painting. Rosel said the tubes were old ones from her dead uncle – no use to him, she says. And very high quality.

Now, loading my brush with thinned-down Umber I draw in the scene which has been hammering in my head. Shadowy figures of men slumped in the foreground. The roofline of the seam, the straining props. I am working round the space, back-centre, where the woman must go. The white space.

Even by the window the dark in the kitchen reminds me of the lit gloom of the pit bottom and I recall the weary heart with which you set out into the dark for yet another shift. I hear a sigh behind me and whirl round, sure that my father is there. But of course the room is empty. The fire rustles again and a cinder slips down towards the hearth. I close my eyes tight, then open them and start to paint.

In the middle of the afternoon I'm just straightening my back and stretching upwards to rest my muscles when there's a knock on the door. When I open it my visitor is shaking down his umbrella. 'Mr Todhunter!' I say.

'Hello, Gabriell,' he says, looking past me.

I stand staring at him, my eyes blinking in the stronger outside light.

'Is it feasible that ye might ask me inside, laddie?' says Todhunter, shifting from foot to foot, umbrella in one hand, a bulky-looking sack in the other.

'Yes, yes, come in.' I lead the way through the scullery and back into the kitchen. I hurry to pick up the new painting and lean it to face the wall in the corner. 'It's a bit of a mess . . . just me,' I say.

Archie stares at the opened paints on the table, now otherwise bare. 'Wouldn't say so,' he says. 'Seems very neat. Nice fire.' He places the closed umbrella in the corner beside it, then nods at my drawings, pinned up on every wall. 'Nice decoration, too.' He looks at a study of the defunct winding gear at White Leas Pit, then walks across to peer at each of the drawings in turn. He examines my Rembrandt copies one by one. I resent his cheek. As well as this I'm conscious of my bare feet and equally conscious of the wrecked boots on the hearth. I can't put them on, or my feet will fall right through them.

Archie comes back to the table, lifts up the bulky sack and tips its contents out on to the surface. Shoes tumble out, exhaling the beeswax smell of new polish. There are eight shoes, tied together in four pairs by their laces. He stands them side by side in a line.

'What's this?' I say.

'Shoes,' drawls Archie. 'I'd have thought even you'd recognise shoes, Gabriel, artist that you are.'

The sarky bugger.

'Funny,' I say. 'Very funny. Musta been taking lessons from Tegger MacNamara.' I know Tegger's behind all this.

'I want you to choose a pair that fit. For yourself.'

'I need no shoes.'

'Tegger MacNamara says—'

'Bugger Tegger MacNamara. He should mind his own business.'

'He just wants you there at the Settlement, to help with the sets. He worries that you haven't been painting. There are those portraits need doing.'

'I am painting.'

'So I see.' He puts a finger on one of the boards, still wet, leaning against the press. 'Rembrandt, is it?'

'Aye, the *Night Watch*. Apprentice piece. No matter how many times I try, I canna get the light right. And the figures . . .' I blurt out the confidence and wish I hadn't.

'Old Rembrandt had a bit more time to practise, and more light to practise in than you. He was older than you when—'

'Aye, I know.' I have to say something. 'I know you don't think it's any good to copy.'

'You're right, I don't. It's false and, as you've found out, it can be very disheartening.' It's a flat statement. Unequivocal.

'But that's how an electrician, a cabinet-maker learns,' I argue. 'Copying the master. Seeing how he does it then doing it in his own way.'

'It used to happen with painters too, of course. Whole studios of apprentices copying the master.'

'Well, if it's good enough for them it's good enough for me.'

He stares at me and I stare at him. Neither of us will give in.

Then he breathes hard down his nose and retreats. 'Well. Leave that for another day. About these shoes . . .'

'I told you, I don't need no shoes.'

'Look, Gabriel,' he says, his voice very hard. 'Those paints on the table, they're half-used, aren't they? They come from Rosel's uncle, is that not so?'

'Aye.' I'm annoyed that he knows.

'And you don't object to using them?'

'No.'

'Then think of these shoes as paint.' He stands up. 'You need paint to paint. You need shoes to get you down to the Settlement to work on your paintings. Choose a pair that fits well and bring the rest down to the Settlement in the bag.' He's already at the door. 'Get down there. They need you, you need them.'

The rain has stopped at last but the afternoon has closed in even further now. I shut the door and turn up the gaslight. There are two pairs of shoes which fit perfectly: my choice is a pair of black brogues with hand-stitched tops and barely worn soles. I weigh them, one in each hand. Who wore them last? A man now ensconced in a cemetery these days, or some virtuous individual who has sacrificed one of his best pairs of shoes for the poor in the North?

I put them on, tie the laces tight and walk up and down my grandmother's rug. They're good and strongly made and will mend for ever in the cobbler's workshop at the Settlement. They'll see me through a decade if need be.

When I make my way back to the Settlement the members make no comment. I leave the bag of shoes in the empty office, just by a big sack of clothes with a Herefordshire label on them. No one looks at my feet. Tegger, when challenged, swears blind he'd only said something when Archie tackled him hard about my absences. 'He was like a man off when you kept not coming. I thought telling him about the shoes would shut him up, Gabe, honest I did.' I satisfy myself with giving him a good punch on the shoulder and squat down beside him to slop papier-mâché on to the soldiers' dugout.

It's really good to be out and about again, but the whole thing niggles me. These shoes hang on to the end of my legs like alien objects. I've sunk very low to have to accept charity like this. When I get some money I'll buy my own shoes and will take pleasure in handing these shoes on to some other beggar.

Still, it's good to be here in the workroom at my own easel, pinning on some new bark-surfaced paper that Rosel has got from somewhere. She comes up and watches me square it off. 'You're to paint Greta Pallister for the exhibition, Gabriel, did you know this?' she announces. 'As Dorothy, with her apron and her shawl. This will be good, will it not? Greta is very happy about it.'

Greta? Well then. That'll be an experience, won't it?

Chapter Fifteen

Gossip

'The council are all for it. An honour, the Deputy Chairman claims.'

Dev Pallister and Archie Todhunter were sharing a packet of prime Virginia tobacco which had been included, though Archie didn't disclose this, in a charitable parcel from the city of Chichester to the people of Brack's Hill.

Archie surveyed the bowl of his pipe, pleased that for this occasion he'd forsaken his beloved cigarettes. The tobacco was glowing nicely. 'So what's your view on it, Mr Pallister? Cora tells me there's talk of a royal visit, from Edward, Prince of Wales. Is it true? What do you make of it all?

Dev paused for a moment to collect his thoughts. 'Well,' he said slowly, 'I suppose it shows we aren't forgotten. As far as the national scene goes, like.'

'Mmm.' Archie veiled his throat in the prickly balm of the Virginia.

'The newspapers'll be here. The newsreels. See the state of things.'

'Ye-es.'

'I don't know that it'll make a ha'porth of difference in real terms.'

'They say these things bring cheer to the people.'

'Aye. Thc women like him right enough. My wife was real excited. Prince Charming was mentioned,' he said blackly. 'Worse than film stars. Pantomime stuff.'

Archie pointed towards the window with his pipe, to the wider world of Brack's Hill. 'Good for morale, according to *The Tlmes*. The regions are grateful to the Prince.'

'Oh well,' snorted Dev. 'If *The Times* says so, it must be true.'

'Now, now, Mr Pallister,' said Archie calmly. '*The Times* is the thermometer of the ruling classes. Even we *Manchester Guardian* readers have to take note, whether we like it or not.'

They sat in silent for several long minutes, savouring the fine tobacco.

Then, 'What I keep getting back to, though,' said Dev, 'is the zoo thing.'

'Zoo?'

'A royal visit like this might cheer a lot of people up – I'll credit that. I really do, Mr Todhunter. But for all the world it's like we're a bloody – excuse me – a bloody zoo. The world gawps at us with their newpapers and newsreels. A pathetic backdrop to this Prince Charming, with our clogs and our blackened faces.'

'I don't see you in clogs, Mr Pallister. And your face shines like a rosy apple.'

Dev shrugged.

'Well, do you think others – say those folks he went to see down in Wales – think in that way? In the way you see it?'

'Mebbe others have more sense. Pragmatic – is that the word?

Take everything as it is, on the surface. Don't think deeper than that. Mebbe that's a good thing. Seeing the surface, going by the day.'

'But won't the Settlement make it different from one of the other kind of visits? And what about the things you put on for the men at the Club? There's more to see here than clogs and blackened faces.'

Dev shrugged again. 'Mebbe they don't want to see hope. Doesn't fit their picture. A more elaborate kind of zoo, mebbe. That's all. A zoo with a stage and dressing up.'

'But it *is* different,' said Archie, leaning forward now. 'The play! Your Greta and the others showing their paces. Making their point about just how they've been let down. And the crafts, the paintings – some of them are remarkable by any standards. People look at the product of the hand and eye like this in places all over the country, rich or poor. In pleasure, not in pity! This stuff is not just on show here because the people who make it are poor and starving. The people here show their talent. They show their deep humanity. It is they who have something to offer – insight, pleasure, what you will.'

'Mmm.'

'Mr Pallister, you don't know who'll catch sight of this, who will recognise the grace in the people of this town. Think of your daughter Greta, acting her heart out . . .'

Dev put down his pipe. 'I don't know that they'd actually see the play, like. When His Royal Highness was doing a similar tour in Wales, they say he averaged ten minutes a stop, with thousands of people at each stop. He'd not have time to see a single scene of your play.'

Archie sighed. 'Well, I had thought . . .'

'Ten minutes, that's what I heard.'

'Well, then,' said Archie, 'we'd better make our ten minutes count, then.'

Later that night, after an affectionate if rather unfulfilled wrestle in bed, Archie talked to Cora about the likelihood of a visit from the prince. 'It seems your gossip is correct.'

She sat up, clutching the eiderdown to her generous bosom. 'Oh! HRH – here?'

'HRH? Friend of yours, I suppose?'

She smacked him on the shoulder. 'Sarcasm doesn't become you, Archie Todhunter,' she said. 'Of course I don't know him, but . . .'

'But what?'

'The last company but one I was in, where we did that season in the West End – Mary Charteris who was married to the manager, she still writes to me. You've seen the letters.'

He groaned. 'That scrawl! Not worth reading. God save me from stage gossip. Tittle tattle.'

'Well, her cousin sings in New York in a small way, operetta and stuff.'

'Cora!' He pulled the sheet over his head.

She pulled the sheet away. 'They say HRH – that's what they call him – goes about with this American. Very smart piece of goods . . .'

'Cora, will you . . .'

'You know what I mean. They're always together, apparently – at social events. She's always on his arm. With him on cruises, hostess at his parties.'

'Nonsense. The Americans, how would they know this?'

'It's in the American papers, that's how. Photos and all.'

Her warm, slightly ripe smell suddenly made him want to

choke. He shook his head. 'It can't be so. It would be news here. Just low American gossip. We would know it here. The *Manchester Guardian* . . .' He was all at once very tired. He slid down the bed. 'Mr Dev Pallister wasn't too happy about the visit. Said it would be like the zoo.'

'That old sobersides. Everyone'll love it – you watch. They'll give anything for a smile from the handsome Prince. You just watch. It'll really cheer them up. Not much cheer here after all.'

Archie turned, heaving the eiderdown away from her. He spoke over his shoulder. 'I expect you not to say anything about that American gossip, will you, or nobody will be cheered.'

'Gossip – me? I've been on the wrong end of that too many times myself, to spread it around. I'll be as silent as the grave. You watch me.'

'Is it much further?' Rosel leans against a tree. She lifts first one foot and gives it a shake, then the other. The wet from the grass has stained the fine tan leather, changing it to black in some places. 'My shoes are ruined.'

My 'new' shoes are also wet with the combination of last night's rain and this morning's dew which has lashed the long grass almost to the ground. 'No more than five minutes, honestly.' I hold out my hand. She takes it.

We've made our way through the trees and just passed the sandstone cliff where the river deepens and turns. The shoreline widens and we're crunching pebbles underfoot. We skirt another bend and ahead of us, framed by the trees, rises the fine tracery of the Priory walls and the church spires and bridges of Priorton. In the distance is the winding gear of Priorton's two pits.

'It's all very beautiful,' said Rosel. 'If you take away the mining wheels, it is like fine towns on the Rhine.'

'Without the pits.' We clamber down on to the Priorton road. I drop her hand. 'It might be prettier, but what's any town without its prime work?'

I can feel the heat of the sun now on my back. Our shoes squelch on the drying road.

Rosel glanced towards the boy. His face was so clean that it looked burnished. He wore a white scarf round his full throat and his cap was jammed as usual on top of his overlong curls. There was legitimacy in her looking. For more than a week now she'd been making preparatory sketches of him, for her painting of him in his role of Arthur, the trapped soldier.

'Now up here!' I take the lead as we leave the road again and set off up a steep path. We have to skirt round some farm buildings. 'Keep low!' I say. 'The last time I came by here the farmer threw stones at me, sent a dog after me – a big black and white sheepdog. Took me for a poacher. There's a lot of poaching these days. Who can blame a man for wanting a rabbit for the pot?'

I have never talked so much; I am almost babbling.

How did we get here? Well, she's mentioned more than once how silent I am. I've had to sit in the workroom for her to draw me, sometimes for more than an hour. So we've had to talk about something. Her comments made me more silent than ever, of course.

Then she started to ask me more about the Roman camp I'd told her about, that first morning when I showed her the stone altar. I found myself telling her, then, about the remnants of chambers and the stones scattered on the surface. Then somehow we were arranging to visit it early the next morning, today, when no one would be about. It seemed essential to keep it a secret, though I can't think why.

I stop. The stones in the grass beneath my feet now are butted together in a neat row. 'The road's coming to the surface here.'

She stops and scuffs some soil off the stone beneath her foot.

'They say the camp stretched as far as you can see.'

We cast our eye over the spread of farmland, the scatter of farms and hamlets, the ever-present winding gear of pits. 'As far as the eye can see? How would they know?' she says.

I kick the stone beneath my feet. 'This is one of the great Roman Roads. I forget its name.'

'Is it very famous? Then you must know it.'

'Watling Street – Dere Street. I've heard both said. It goes right down to Yorkshire.'

'I see. But would the camp really extend for miles?'

'They've done excavations. Before the war.'

She shrugs: that elegant movement. 'Gabriel, I don't see . . .'

I pull her over into the little clapboard hut in the corner of the field and close the door behind us. Inside there are signs of excavations, though not recent. Someone has dug here, laid bare a long wall built of dressed stone. Dusty duckboards lead safely over the muddy pit. Two discarded trowels stick out of the wall at odd angles. It makes me think of the soldiers' trench in the play.

'I see.' Her fingers trail along the top of the wall. 'Would this be where they lived and slept?'

My turn to shrug. 'I don't know. Storeroom? Guardroom? It was certainly a room.' I jump down on to the mud, pick up a trowel and start to dig.

'Digging, Gabriel? It is like the mine, is it not, or the soldiers' trench?'

I dig swiftly. 'I never did the digging in the mine. They call them hewers. I never did that. I pulled and pushed tubs, full and empty. There *is* something here.' I start to dig round it. 'Ah!' I palm the thing up to her: a round piece of metal with a blackened pin attached. 'Here.'

'It's a brooch,' she says, peering at it.

I jump up to stand beside her and take a look. My finger touches her palm as I turn it over. 'Another part of the Petrified Forest. The Romans left before the Dark Ages, so this must be pretty old.'

She offers it to me. 'It is an amazing thing,' she says. 'Wonderful.'

I close her fingers round it and hold her whole hand tight in mine. 'It's yours,' I say. 'That's why I brought you here.'

Her hand comes up over mine. 'Thank you, Gabriel. You are kind,' she says. Her lips touch my lips, and the brooch in our joined hands is trapped between us. I push myself towards her and she backs away until she is stopped by the rough lapboards of the shed. She turns her head. I raise my free hand and put it on her long neck, turning her face back towards me with my thumb. In her eyes I see the image of my own face. In my mind's eye I see the dream-woman, that day in the goaf, crosshatched with this pale face before me. Now there are tears in her eyes and I want to jump the hurdles of time and space between us and press myself ever closer to her, into her, until we are one being. She stands still for a second then she starts to struggle. The door to the shed rattles and a dog starts to bark.

I step back, put a finger to her lips, then lead her to a gap in the boards. 'Here!' The door behind us is being pushed open.'Run!' I say. We don't stop until we reach the narrow path which goes back up through the woods to Brack's Hill. I wait for her, leaning on a tree trunk, gasping.

She plants herself before me and holds up the Roman brooch. 'So this is for me?'

I look her in the eye. 'That's what I said.' The whitened early sun turns her putty-coloured hair to gold.

She reaches up now and kisses me on the lips. She tastes of blackberries and mint. My head is swimming. All parts of me are perking up. Even my toes in the new shoes curl up. I grab her hard and kiss her back, my tongue forcing its way against her teeth. Now her hands are on me and her fingers are through my hair and she pulls back to murmur in her own language.

'What d'you say? What d'you say?' My lips are thick against hers. I am mumbling almost into her mouth.

'I say you are a fine boy. A very fine boy.'

With the effort of Titans I pull myself away. 'Boy? *Boy?* Is that what you think?'

Her hands drop to her sides and the temperature drops several degrees. 'This is what you are,' she says. 'You are only a boy.'

I walk away from her then. I am ahead of her all the way home and she doesn't run to catch me up. My heart is like a stone in my chest. My face feels taut as a sail against the air. At the edge of Brack's Hill we part without another word and go our separate ways.

Chapter Sixteen

Images

Archie Todhunter has fixed it up for me to draw Greta Pallister by her own fireside. 'Authentic, fitting,' he said. 'The iron oven, the clothes on the overhead rail. Fitting.'

It's very difficult. I thought she would be pleased; the girl's been following me around for weeks with those sharp eyes of hers. But she's awkward about the whole thing. 'Not so stiff,' I order her. 'Stand like you've just turned away from the oven.'

Mrs Pallister watches us from her sentinel place by the window. 'That one has never *just turned away from the oven*. Never even worn an apron, our Greta,' she sniffs. 'Never had to. She's a scholar.'

'It's just for the play, Mam,' says Greta, wriggling her shoulders. She rolls her eyes at me. 'It's only a play.'

To be honest I can see what Mrs Pallister means. Here's Greta, destined for better things, wearing her mother's old long dark skirt and blouse and a sacking apron covered by one in lighter blue cotton. On her feet are clogs which she's borrowed from her neighbour. Her fine hair is drawn into a long plait which snakes down her back and on her head is a knitted red beret with a pom-pom. This is not the image of a scholar.

As I draw her I note the fine bones of her face, and her long elegant fingers. This is an interesting paradox. Was there ever a pit-lass who looked like this, with fine long hands. Yes, as a matter of fact. Very probably. The Grammar School girl today was likely the pit lass of her grandmother's day. Intelligence is no bar in the pit. Look at Tegger. Look at me.

'Can I sit down a bit? My legs ache.'

'No,' says her mother from the window. 'Stand yourself still. How can the lad draw you if you're fidgeting round?'

'All right then. Sit down a bit.' I lift the sketch from the makeshift table easel and put it beside the others: two quick full-length close-up sketches of her head, her hands, the attitude of her figure; her bare, blue-veined feet in their old-fashioned clogs. Greta and her mother come to pore over the drawings on the table.

'You've got her to the very life!' Her mother's workworn hand touches the surface of the paper, running a coarse finger-nail down her daughter's profile. In that touch is unspoken pride and love. For a second in Mrs Pallister's face I can see the young woman she was, and the young woman her mother was before her. I look at Greta who – her spectacles back on her nose – is peering at these strange projections of herself on paper. 'You're as good as she says you are.' She nods her head.

'She?'

'Rosel Vonn. I wasn't going to let you do this but she told me I'd regret it if I didn't. That you were a proper artist.'

Mrs Pallister takes one full-length sketch across to the window to get a better look. I can see that she doesn't want to part with it. 'You can have that one if you want,' I offer. 'Afterwards.'

She looks across at me hard. 'I thought these were for this exhibition thing.'

I shake my head. 'No. These are my preliminary sketches – the first tries. The decent paints are down the Settlement. These sketches'll set it up and Greta'll pose down there for a proper painting.' I take the picture from her. Turn it over and write *For Mrs Pallister, drawn by Gabriel Marchant* in my best handwriting. 'I'll need it to set the big one away, but I'll give it back to you.'

She looks at me. 'Will you? I wish I had a proper picture of our Robert or our Joss. All I have are those dead things.' She nods at the photographs of her sons which have pride of place on the mantelpiece. They *are* dead things – stiff photographer studio portraits, the same as a thousand others. 'I miss them,' she says suddenly. 'And soon I'll miss our Greta here.'

Greta puts an arm around her. 'You won't miss me, Mam. I'll stay with you always.'

Mrs Pallister shakes off her hand and sniffs. 'Oh no you won't, lady. They're away out of this dead and alive hole, and I'll get you away too if I die in the attempt.' She looks me full in the eyes and I know exactly what she's on about. 'Aye. I'll have this one off you, son, if that's all right. An' I'll find a nice frame for it, or get a nice frame for it in Priorton. So, wherever this one is, she'll be living and breathing on my wall.'

It took three long Saturday mornings in the Settlement for me to get Greta's portrait anything like. Rosel has completed a painting of Nathan but is not happy with it and will not show it. 'Why not?' I say. 'This isn't perfect but I let you see this.'

She shrugs. 'Nathan was unhappy to sit. He is like these people here – he has a peculiar reserve. When he saw the finished article he said I must not show it to anyone. So I mustn't.'

'Well, that's a waste of work!' I say. 'You should tell him—'

She put up a hand to stop me saying anything further. 'A man owns his own image, Gabriel. If we take that away from him, he has nothing.'

'So what will you do with it?'

'I put it away in storage. Otherwise, I believe he would have destroyed it himself.'

It seems that this thing we are doing has power. In a strange way I am comforted by this.

Rosel has urged me to hurry with Greta's portrait as there are others to do. So much for art as a long journey! Rembrandt took months over his paintings. Years. Now she is nagging me like a real schoolteacher.

Since our visit to the Roman camp she and I have been polite, more wary with each other. I'm conscious that she has the painting of me to do. Maybe she won't do that after the fiasco with Nathan. That'll be an ordeal, being painted by her. But whatever happens I won't destroy it. I would never do that.

I seem to have been with Greta Pallister all day. This morning I took her mother the sketch which I had marked for her and a few more. Afterwards Greta and I walked across to the Settlement together. After these sittings I feel easier with her now. How can you feel awkward with someone you have drawn fifteen or twenty times? She talks away about some teacher telling her something about *Ovid*, and I half listen. I wouldn't say I am as easy with her as I am with Tegger, but you'd have to go a long way for that.

Although I've been looking at her on the surface, I feel now I've seen somewhere inside her. I *know* her and wherever we go in the future I'll always *recognise* her. I know now she still watches out for me, even lies in wait for me, but this no longer makes me uneasy. She's young, just a kid, but quite a nice person.

I suppose I am beginning to understand her. She watches for me in the way I watch for Rosel Vonn. Ever since that day at the Roman camp, I have to admit I do watch out for her. Sometimes I lie in wait for her: by the tip, at the end of Queen Street where the Settlement is. I wait and watch.

'He's waiting for you again.' Cora came to stand behind Rosel, peering past her through the window.

Rosel stirred. 'Who? Who waits?'

Cora laughed. 'That one who you watch. Standing by the lamp there. Young Gabriel of the golden halo.'

Rosel backed away from the window into the room and sat down at the small table to rescue the letter she was writing to her father. She was worried about him. Now his friends – so-called – were ostracising him because he had championed Goldstein the dentist, and had actually warned him of a police visit. Now he'd written letters to the government. Rosel had tried suggesting in one of her letters to him that he should come here to England, or go to America. He'd dismissed that swiftly. *This is my country. I will not abondon it. If the people of goodwill run away, who then would watch the fire? And I need to keep the watch for Boris. He is in their hands even more than I am. He stayed here last weekend, we drank French wine. It was like the old days. But he too is unsure about things.*

'I've seen the boy looking at you in rehearsals.' Cora had settled down to stitch the hem of the apron which young Greta was to wear in the play.

Rosel's mind came back from the grand apartment in Berlin. 'Who?'

'Gabriel. Standing on the corner.'

'This is not true, Cora. You imagine.'

Cora held up the apron and peered at her neat row of stitches.

'That portrait of young Greta, it is very fine. I think he works on one of you soon, as Maggie Olliphant,' said Rosel. 'That will be a very fine picture.'

Cora would not be put off. 'Greta watches for him, and he watches for you,' she said.

Rosel shook her head. 'He has done a very fine portrait of the girl,' she repeated. 'In the style of Rembrandt, I fear, rather than Gabriel Marchant. The light licking round. The treatment of the clothes. Pure Rembrandt.'

Cora broke the thread with her teeth and rolled the end in a knot before beginning to sew again. 'Is there something wrong with that? Isn't Rembrandt what they call an Old Master? The lad could do worse.'

'Gabriel must have his own style.' Rosel shook her head. 'Or the old ones will possess him and he will not go forward. It is of great concern to me.'

Cora jabbed her needle into the fabric. 'So you're concerned about him, the angel-boy?'

There was a rustle as Archie put down his newspaper with a vengeful swish. 'For goodness' sake, Cora, will you leave Rosel in peace, with your jabbering! Of course she's concerned for the boy! He's a person of talent. He is her student. And of course he's interested in *her* – she's his teacher. As for your sneaking insinuations, use your eyes, woman. You have a Penny Dreadful mind. The lad's young enough to be Rosel's son. Is that not so, my dear?'

Rosel looked up from her letter. 'What was it, Archie?'

'I was just saying to nosy Cora here that young Gabriel Marchant is of an age to be your son.'

Rosel put her head down over her letter so her face was hidden. 'This is so. But I have no son, then or now.'

Archie raised his paper again, to read of the Italian leader Mussolini rejecting an offer of British land in Somaliland in return for keeping his hands off Ethiopia. 'I told you he'd never do that,' he announced.

'Who?' said Cora.

'Mussolini.'

'So you did.' Cora turned back to Rosel. 'Did you hear about the Prince, Rosel?'

'Prince?'

'The Prince of Wales – Edward comes to Brack's Hill in November and the rumour is he'll come to see the play.'

'Of course she knows. Everybody's talking about it. Even so it isn't certain,' grunted Archie from behind his paper.

'Well, I think he'll come and I think we'll meet him, that seems sure,' said Cora firmly.

Rosel looked at the empty sheet in front of her. That would be something to write to her father. 'Why does he come here?' she said, interest in her voice at last.

Archie folded up his paper and put it on the table by his chair. 'He comes to show pity for the poor and dispossessed of this town. To draw the world's attention to it. To demonstrate his sympathy and that of his father the King. To reassure us that he is on our side. He has done this in many parts of England – and the Empire, in fact. It's called *the common touch*. You have to have it if you're going to be King.'

'They say he's very handsome,' said Cora. 'I've seen him on the newsreels.'

'He's very short,' said Rosel.

'What?' said Archie.

She glanced across at him. 'My father says this.'

'Your father has met him?' said Cora, eyes wide. 'Actually met the Prince? Where? How?'

'Before the war. Austria. Switzerland. Somewhere like that. Skiing. My father is older, but . . .'

'And he said he was short?'

'Barely up to Papa's shoulder.'

'But he would be tall, your father, like you?' Archie was interested in spite of himself.

'Yes. My father is more than two metres,' she nodded.

'But the Prince is handsome. You can tell it on the newsreels,' persisted Cora.

'Perhaps they put only very short people beside him,' said Archie. 'They do it in films.'

'Archie! You're such a misery!' said Cora.

Archie turned his shoulder to address himself more exclusively to Rosel. 'You will have to speak with him when he comes, you know.'

'I do not see this,' she objected. 'There are many people for him to speak with in Brack's Hill. It is not my town.'

'Ah. But he will speak to you in German. He's fluent in that language, I hear.'

'I know this,' said Rosel. 'So are they all, in that family. My father tells me this.'

'Perhaps he won't want to speak German,' said Cora, snapping off her last thread and folding up the apron. 'Not in Brack's Hill.'

Cora – in her role as the stalwart leader of the women – is my next portrait. I do sketches of her in the sitting room of the Settlement before I embark on the painting. Cora is very hard to do. I screw up pages and pages of preliminary tries. From his seat in the corner, Archie looks on with amusement. I wish he would not stay in here while I do this.

Cora is more concerned. 'What is it?' she says. 'Am I that hard to draw!'

'To be honest, yes, you are.'

'So, why's that, then?'

'I look at you one minute and you seem this kind of a person. The next, you seem another . . . You've got me tearing my hair out.'

'Don't do that. Those curls are far too pretty to tear out.'

'Cora!' warned Archie from his chair. 'Will you stop flirting, woman? He's young enough to be your—'

'Whoo, Archie,' she says cheerfully. 'Can't I have a little flirt? Miss Rosel Vonn can flirt away with all and sundry, so why not me?'

Despite my red face I pursue my problem. 'Can't you just *be* Maggie Olliphant for me? Not Cora Miles dressed up as her. Or Lady Macbeth. Or Titania. I want you to *be* her.' I am quite desperate. I can't believe it, but I have to turn away and blink the tears from my eyes.

She looks at me and is suddenly not frivolous at all. She

closes her eyes then opens them. Her face is clouded with grief. Her shoulders hunch forward. The hands holding her shawl clench into knuckles. Then she peers towards me with pain-blanked eyes.

'That's more like it,' I say, flicking over another page of my drawing pad. 'That's much more like it.'

Chapter Seventeen

The Woman

The morning after I've finished Cora's portrait I have a bit of a lie-in. I have been thinking and dreaming in paint for days. I smell of turpentine and linseed oil like a baker smells of yeast. I make myself a mug of tea and drink it slowly. Nothing to eat in the house and two days to dole day. I'll have something when I get to the Settlement. Cora always has bread there, maybe some offcuts of ham from the butcher's. She expects it to be eaten. There's no feeling of charity about this although that's what it is.

I tried one day to thank her for her thoughtfulness but she waved my thanks away. 'It's there for everyone,' she said briefly. 'Was it Napoleon who said an army marches on its stomach? Well, to my mind all who come through these doors are Archie's shock troops.'

Cora's finished portrait is not half bad, though I say it myself.

It's too long a time since I've seen Tegger. There was the business of the shoes, then there was this thing – or this *no*thing – with Rosel Vonn. And all the painting. Tegger hasn't been around. Archie Todhunter has asked me twice where he is. Seems Tegger has some stuff for him – some pages of text. What's he up to? And now I'm missing Tegger myself, like you'd miss the wind in your hair.

So I set off to rout the devil out. I've only been to the van encampment behind the High Street once. The habit of avoiding it predates Tegger's residence there. Tegger always calls at the house for me, doesn't want me there among that flotsam and jetsam. I know this, even though he hasn't said so.

It's already ten o'clock when I get there. The thin drizzle sits in the air like a veil and the vans are a drab sight, pulled into a higgledy-piggledy half-circle. Almost buried in long grass, they're a decrepit collection of wooden and metal wheeled contrivances, some solid-topped, some with canvas drawn across to keep out the weather. One man has dug over a patch ten feet square beside his van and set potatoes in it. At the centre of the arc are the still-smoking embers of what has been a big fire. Last night there must have been quite a blaze.

On the steps of one van sits an old man wearing a lumpy woollen scarf over his collarless shirt. He is sucking hard on a cigarette. His face is crevassed with the sucking pathways of a thousand cigarettes. I ask about Tegger. He has to stop coughing before he can try to answer. Then his eyes bulge as he coughs again and he waves his hand towards a low narrow van painted dark blue. I rattle its battered wooden door and shout, 'Tegger!' I rattle it again. 'Tegger! Come on, man!'

A bear-like groan seeps through the wood and I push the creaking door open. I leave it wide open so that the smell of barely digested beer and cigarette smoke can force its way out. The space inside the van is the size of our back pantry. A narrow bunk. A metal stove of some kind. A cupboard. A chair with clothes thrown over it and boots standing unlaced beneath it. I pull back a curtain on a crude string to let in light through an equally crude window.

The heap on the narrow truckle bed groans again.

'Tegger!'

I pull back the quilt to expose his curled-up shape. He puts his arm up to shield his eyes from the light. 'Tegger! What is it, man? Get yourself up, will you?' I push at his elbow to expose his grinning face, his sleep-sticky eyes. 'What's on here?' I say. 'What's on here, man?'

One blue eye opens wider. 'Go away, Gabe. Get away, will you!'

'All right then.' I turn and put my hand on the knotted rope that does for a doorknob.

His voice comes from behind me. 'No, wait on, man! Sit yourself down out there and I'll join you in a minute.'

When he comes to sit beside me on the caravan steps five minutes later he has his clothes on, but that's the only difference between him and the dormant creature I saw minutes ago. His hair is still greasily awry, his feet are bare, his eyes still squinting at the light. He stretches his dirty feet before him. 'Sorry, marra,' he yawns.

'What's all this?' I say. 'Living here like a stoat.'

'You know why. They won't let me live at home. The dole . . .'

'I know that, but look at the state of you!'

He offers me a cigarette from a battered packet of five Craven-A. I shake my head. 'What's happening here when I wasn't looking, Teg?'

He draws hard on the cigarette and coughs briefly. 'Last Saturday I went to Sedgefield Races with a lad from here at the vans.'

'Races?'

'He'd heard of a brahma[1] horse running there – *Ambrosia the Second*. What a runner!'

'You went to Sedgefield? How?'

'We walked.'

'What for? Why d'you go?'

'I told you. To put some money on this horse.'

'But you haven't got any money.'

'Passed the hat round on the site. Remember the miracle of the loaves and the fishes? Everybody pitched in. We promised them a share.'

'And you lost?'

'Nah. *Ambrosia the Second* romped home. I told you he was a runner. We won. Ten pound.'

'So you shared that out?'

'Nah. Not those winnings.'

'You spent it then? On . . .?'

'Well, yes. In a manner of speaking. We spent them on another horse. *Old Rascal*. He'd heard that was a *brahma* too. It won. Twenty to one.'

'It won?'

'Aye. Two hundred and ten pounds.' He licks his lips as though the words are honey.

'What then?'

'We brought the money back here to the vans and shared it out, fair and square. Not a man on this site wasn't over the moon. Ten pounds apiece for just pennies outlay.'

'So what d'you do with the money?'

[1]Very fine specimen (colloquial).

'Three of the lads went off to the station. Bought tickets to London. One said he was off to America but I have me doubts.'

'What about you. The rest?'

'Well, we put money in the kitty for beer and saved the rest to take home, like. To the family.'

'And you did that?'

There was a long silence.

Then, 'Some did,' he said. 'Me and Tommy . . .'

'Tommy?'

'That lad that knew about *Ambrosia*.'

'What about him?'

'He knew this horse called *Old Licorice*, running on Wednesday. We were going to double our winnings, see? For our families.'

'So, what happened!'

'Well, *Old Licorice* was away like a bat out of hell, so we thought we were in for it.'

'But . . .'

'The silly bugger jumped a shadow where there was no fence.'

'So you lost your money?'

'Not all of it. I had two pounds left.'

'So . . .'

'So we brought it back, pooled it and went for a drink.'

I am weary for him. 'Yeh daft lad,' I say. 'Nothing for your mam, the little 'uns.'

'Ah know that, marra.' He throws his cigarette into the dirt and screws it down with his bare heel.

I stand up. 'Right,' I say. 'Get yer boots on.'

'Why should I do that? I've nowhere to go.'

'Yer can't go anywhere smelling like a stoat. First to my house and we'll get the tin bath out. Then breakfast. Only tea, but that's something. After that we'll go down the Settlement and get some grub. Todhunter's been asking for you for three days. Says you promised to show him something.'

'Some rubbish I've written,' he says. 'About the vans. There's this magazine he wants us to send it to.'

'Get that. Bring it.'

'I don't know where it is. I think we used those sheets to write the bets on, Tommy and me.'

'Well, you can get yourself down our house and write it again, at my table. Come on!'

At the house I make Tegger jump into a tin bath of tepid water from the fireside boiler. It takes the best part of an hour to get the smell of the alehouse and the dirt of the racecourse off him. Then I set him down at my kitchen table with torn-out pages from one of my old schoolbooks.

'I won't remember,' he warns.

'Write,' I say.

As I look at him clutching the pencil in his big hand I feel a sense of fit as close as a key turning in an oiled lock. He rescued me when my father died. And now I've rescued him. Like changing positions in a dance.

So that's how I started calling for Tegger at the vans and bringing him home with me every morning. He wouldn't come if I didn't call for him. It's true there's the risk that someone will lay him in with the dole for coming here, but I can't leave him there with the dirt and the damp. And Tommy the horse man.

And that's how I've managed to become embroiled with a woman called Marguerite Molloy who occasionally serves at The Lord Raglan and who's generous to a fault. If she likes you.

Days after rescuing Tegger I'd been painting all afternoon in the Settlement House, trying to get to grips with the next portrait: Archie Todhunter in his role as the owners' man. He's there in the big workroom when I arrive. The finished portraits have been hung here to make room to work in the painting shed. He peers first at Greta's portrait and the just-about finished picture of Cora in her role as Maggie Olliphant. The room smells of linseed. The surface paint, still soft and malleable, gleams like skin in the light of the overhead bulbs. I see now there's more work to do on both portraits. The light on Greta's face is not quite right. And Cora needs some aquamarine on the edges of her apron where the light catches it. We're out of aquamarine, the dearest of the colours, but Rosel Vonn says she has some on order. She's had a word with Archie.

'You've been putting a lot of time in here,' says Archie. 'These are not bad.'

'Nothing else to do, have I? It'll take weeks to dry, the paint's so thick.' I say this just for something to say. I am never really easy with Archie Todhunter.

Archie takes his glasses from his top pocket and looks at Greta's portrait even more closely. 'This one's very believable, to the life,' he says. 'Stares at you out of history, out of time.'

The light falls on Greta from the left; it bleeds over her, turning her drab shawl to ochre, her heavy plait to pure gold. The thread of light on each hair was a bit of a challenge. I borrowed a specially fine brush from Rosel Vonn to tackle that. The light catches the generous pink curve of Greta's underlip, turns the earnest gleam in her eye into gold. But her cheek . . . her cheek. I have been clumsy there. It's not right. I'll have to do some more work on that.

'A very creditable piece of work.'

'It's not perfect. Needs more work on the cheeks.'

'Rosel Vonn says you can work on something too long,' he says.

'She didn't say that to me.' It was Rosel who talked about the problem of light on full flesh, made me realise the cheeks need work. 'Anyway,' I turn away from the portraits on the wall, 'I'm here to make a start on your picture, now I've got you.'

He's a very hard man to get hold of. We had to sit a clear ten minutes looking at his diary for him to find space for these sessions.

'Ah yes!' says Todhunter, barely concealing a smile. 'Me as the pit manager – where do you want me?'

'I thought I'd do some sketches of you in your office. Like the pit office, see?'

I work away at sketches of him at his desk: with his pipe, without his pipe; with his fountain pen in his hand, without his fountain pen; standing up, sitting down. Then I sketch him in front of his desk, leaning back on it, hands in his pockets. The picture of confidence in his role as pit manager. He chuckles when I ask him to put his trilby hat on and push it back slightly on his head. 'Doing a bit of characterisation, I see, Gabriel!'

I shrug and pin another sheet to my board. 'It's gotta be right, Mr Todhunter.' I'm not happy about that smug smile of his. He thinks we're all children to be led with silken threads. I can't believe I'm the only one to see through him.

'So what . . .'

'Can you sit still, Mr Todhunter? I need to concentrate.' He knows I mean for him to keep quiet. He raises his eyebrows and does as he's told.

As I sketch, my mind goes back to Rosel Vonn. She's getting hold of all this paint for me. She'll give curt advice, now and then when I'm painting; she still worries too much about

Rembrandt. Sometimes I've waited for her, casual like, so we can happen to walk along together, But she never appears. Perhaps she's dodging down back streets to avoid me. So really we're back where we started, with some kind of armed truce, I suppose. I feel like a little lad, stamping his foot and saying, 'It's not fair! It's not fair! Look at me! Look at me!'

All the time I'm thinking, the drawings roll off my pad. Dozens of them.

'D'you think I could move?' Todhunter wriggles his trunk. 'Stiff as a board, old boy, with my knees braced like this.'

'That's all right, Mr Todhunter,' I say. 'I'm done here now.'

'Thank goodness for that.' He shakes one leg and then the other, then comes round to see my efforts. 'I must say, it's been like turning on a tap, getting you started on this art business.'

'I was away with drawing before I got to the Settlement,' I say through gritted teeth. 'My auntie can draw and my grandmother was great with the colours and textures.' I put the drawings one on top of another, roll them and tie them with black tape. 'You've Wednesday afternoon clear in your diary, is that right? I'll have the thing blocked in then and will start to paint. In the workroom, that'll be.'

I can tell I've caught Archie out. I know that his fingers are itching to touch the drawings, to turn them over, to hold them up to the light. They're good. We both know that.

'No need to take them away, Gabriel. I can keep them here.'

I almost give in. He has great authority.

I shake my head. 'I'll need them back at the house. Pin them up. Take a look at them through the day.' I would swear he's blushing. I've caught him out. Archie Todhunter vain? Never!

'Fine, fine,' he says brusquely. 'Wednesday afternoon it is. Now then. Is it three o'clock already? I've the Reverend Coston

Wells of Durham University coming to see me at three-fifteen. He admires your work. Proposes sending some of his students here to—'

'The zoo.'

'No, nothing like that. Something about seeing what we do here and setting up a new—'

'Zoo.' I have to say it again.

'Have you been talking to Dev Pallister?' He manages a laugh. 'You're too thin-skinned, Gabriel. You'll get nowhere with that attitude, my boy. Your talent brings advantages to others in this place, less talented but equally worthwhile. But the greatest advantage has to be with you. To capitalise on it, you must learn to tolerate these visitors. Get your work known.'

I button my jacket over my precious drawings. This watchful, managing side of Archie Todhunter harasses me. He can be too much in charge. Sometimes it's as if I'm a pet dog or something: wheeled out every time he wants someone to be entertained by a few tricks. 'All I want to do is paint, Mr Todhunter, nothing else,' I say. Then I sweep out like some prima donna. I'm only seven steps down the road when I regret my sharp tone with him. All *he* wants is for my own good: the good of all who come through the doors of the Settlement. I say this over and over to myself like a spell. It's just that his sharp little eyes, his plain admiration, do get under my skin. I can't think what to do about it.

Halfway down the road I realise I meant to go and have a word with Tegger in the workshop but in my eagerness to escape from Archie Todhunter I've come away without doing that. From the street I look up at the windows on the upper floors of the Settlement, for any sign of Rosel Vonn. Of course there is none.

I've made a proper fool of myself there all right. She's barely started on her picture of me. Fat chance that that will ever get done; now she can't even bear the sight of me.

All this is tumbling through my head when I turn into the yard to my house and see this strange woman sitting on the brick boiler in the corner of the yard. Beside her is a small enamel pan of fresh eggs. These appear once a week with no message. I know that they're from Steve, my father's old marra down the allotments. The eggs come in very handy in these hungry days but I can't get the will to go down the allotment to thank him. I think I'm afraid I'll find my father there. Or something of him.

I pick up the eggs and survey my visitor.

The woman has bright hazel eyes and her skin is a deep golden brown: a change after the chalk-pale faces which are so familiar round here. Her great cloud of soft black hair is topped with a bright green beret with a feather fixed with what looks like a gold brooch. The feather trembles as she nods and jumps down off the wall, 'Look at me, why don't you? Who're you?' she says. She's nearly as tall as I am.

'Who're *you*?'

'I asked first.'

'My name is Gabriel Marchant. This here is my house. That's my wall you were sitting on.'

'I'm looking for Tegger MacNamara. They said at the vans that he lived here now.'

I glance round suspiciously. 'He doesn't live here.'

'They said he did.' She laughs. 'Don't worry. I'm no official or anything.'

'He visits here,' I say. 'Most days.'

'Is he in?'

'How would I know? He just calls now and then. Here at the house.'

She stares at me, then her gaze sweeps down to my shiny brogues and back up to my face. Various parts of me prickle to attention. I turn away from her demanding gaze and put my hand on the door sneck. I speak to her over my shoulder. 'You didn't tell me your name,' I say, leading the way into the house.

'Marguerite. Marguerite Molloy.' She follows close behind.

We're in the kitchen, too close for comfort.

'Sit down,' I say. Then I squat by the fire and poke at it till flames start to lick up the chimney.

She sits down, very tall on a kitchen chair.

'You don't sound as if you come from round here,' I say.

She smiles. A chip in one tooth on the left side is the only flaw in a perfect smile. Her lips are the colour of mulberries.

'You mean I don't *look* like I come from round here. Where do you think I come from?'

Anything I say will be wrong and she will laugh. 'How would I know?' I say.

'I come from South Shields.'

That's only on the coast. I feel she must have come much further.

'My mother came from Brack's Hill but lived there on the coast for a lot of years.'

'And your father?' Now I'll be in trouble.

'He came from Mauritius. He was a seaman.'

I have no idea where Mauritius may be. 'Did they come here with you?'

She shakes her head. 'He died in an accident at sea.'

'He drowned?'

She shakes her head again and the fine fibres of her hair

catch the light of the fire. 'Not so lucky. He was a cook. The galley caught fire.' Her body moves with a faint shudder.

'Is that why you're here?'

'This is my mother's home-town. She was born here. I brought her here to . . . well, she died here.'

'I'm sorry.'

She shrugs. 'Look, are you going to sit down too, or will these questions go on for ever?'

I'm staring at her, drinking in the sight of her: the golden gleam of the flat planes of her cheeks, the way her night-black hair springs from her high brow. Half of me wants to touch that face, the other half wants to paint it. My fingers itch for my brushes.

She's no spy, I know that now. 'What do you really want with him, with Tegger?'

'Well, I work at The Lord Raglan and he's there from time to time. He's been missing for a few days. He came in a few days ago and treated the bar, then he vanished. I thought sommat might have happened to him.'

'So he . . . are you . . . courting?' What a daft word that is.

'We're friends.' Her voice growls with annoyance. 'Apart from that, you mind your own business.'

Now there's a clatter in the yard and the subject of our speculations bowls into the room. His face lights up when he sees the girl. 'Why, Marguerite Molloy! What brings you here?'

'Well, for one I thought you might be dead, as you were dead drunk when last I saw you, being carried out of the Raglan toes up. You looked like you'd heard the Last Trump.' Her tone is severe.

He laughs easily. 'Just a bit under the weather from the filthy brew you draw in your blessed pub. And other pubs further afield. You could fire cannons with that stuff. Charge of the Light Brigade, all right.' He looks at us, one to the other. 'Now why are you two sitting there like two jars of jam? Let's get the kettle on and have a nice cup of tea.'

I'm aware of the sheaf of drawings stuck in my coat like a corset. I mumble something, then make for the stairs. In my room, I take out my drawings and lay them carefully on the bed. Their laughter floats up the stairs and invades the narrow room like smoke. I'm reminded yet again of how easy Tegger is with women. His mother, his sisters, his various licit and illicit women friends: these are the ordinary taken-for-granted sentinels in his life. For me, in the main, women are intimidating strangers who may not be approached directly. They are the magical sirens of the deep seams.

When I get back downstairs I find another invasion of my privacy. She's peering closely, one by one, at my pictures which still line the walls. Worse, she is singing their praises.

'Yeah,' says Tegger enthusiastically. 'He's all right. Yeh'll have ter get him to paint your picture, flower.'

I'm annoyed now, mostly because he's expressing the very thing I was thinking only minutes ago. I charge back upstairs and drag my jacket back on. I pick up the drawing of Greta Pallister. When I get back down I manage to act much more calmly. 'I've got a message to do,' I say.

'Yer off then, Gabe?' says Tegger, not urging me to stay. The girl is surveying me with sharp-eyed amusement.

'Yeah, I'm off,' I say through gritted teeth. The door clicks behind me and I can breathe more easily. I make my way across the ten streets to the Pallister house on the corner, with its bay window and its demure nets. Mrs Pallister is pleased to see me and delighted with the worked-up sketch which was her final choice. 'I've sorted this frame,' she says, pulling an ornate frame from the back of the press. 'A horrible picture of my grandmother, it was. I've given the frame a nice clean.' She proceeds to put my drawing into the frame, settling it behind the old Victorian mount, then clipping the whole thing together. Then she hangs it on the wall where the other painting had hung and makes a great play of resettling it, making sure it is plumb-line straight. 'Sets it off, doesn't it? Our Greta to the life. Here, get a proper look.'

I stare at my work, somehow given new legitimacy by its heavy Victorian frame. It seems as if someone else drew it. It looks real. It is outside me. It exists. It is art. Is it art? I blush at these overblown thoughts and turn back to Mrs Pallister, who's staring at me, beady-eyed. She's regarding me as though I'm some particularly delectable pudding which she is about to consume.

I become aware that she's actually speaking. 'What do you think?' she's saying. 'Could you do that?'

I frown. 'What?'

'A picture of my Dev, Greta's dad. He's a big man in the town and . . .'

I'm already shaking my head, unwilling to be consumed in one gulp. 'No question of that, Mrs Pallister. Sorry. I'm just learning, really. I'm going to do a special one for a friend of mine.' (Already I feel committed to painting Marguerite Molloy.) 'And I've all these to do for the Settlement. Too many really. Ready for the Prince's visit.'

Her round face lights up. 'November, Dev says. He'll be on the receiving line, of course. He'll shake the Prince by the hand. Did you see him on the newsreel? Handsome as any film star, he is. Better. So concerned for everybody. Me, I read every single line about him in the newspaper.'

I wrest my gaze from her just to stop her going on. I look round. 'Is Greta about?'

She stops in mid-flow, disappointed at my lack of interest in the Prince. 'She's upstairs doing homework or something. Orders not to disturb her. She can be a madam sometimes.'

I can see why. The mother can be very disturbing in her own way.

She goes to the door. 'Greta!'

Greta comes very quickly. She must have heard the commotion and been waiting for her cue. She has a red knitted cardigan on top of her uniform skirt and an ink mark on her cheek. Her plait is down her back and her glasses are firmly on her nose.

'He's brought the picture of you,' says Mrs Pallister. 'Look. Doesn't the frame set it off?'

'I thought you might like it,' I say hurriedly. 'You weren't a bad model.'

Greta takes off her glasses to take a closer look, her finger on the glass. 'A strange thing, looking at a picture of yourself,' she says. 'Not like photos.' She has her nose two inches from the glass. 'It's you and not you. Photos can only be you.'

I'm backing towards the door. The desire to escape this house is overwhelming.

'Stay for a cup of tea, son,' says Mrs Pallister. 'I've got Co-op cakes.'

'No – no. I—'

'We haven't time,' says Greta. She lifts her red beret from the hook behind the door. 'We have to go to the Settlement. Special meeting of the cast. Five o'clock, wasn't it, Gabriel?'

'But your father will be in!' said Mrs Pallister. 'The tea!'

'Half an hour! I'll be back in half an hour.' Greta throws the words behind her like a ball to an eager dog. 'An hour, mebbe.'

We're the other side of the door before I can blurt the words out. 'What meeting? I just came away from there. Archie never said anything about—'

'Did we need to escape from her or not?'

I thought it was me needed to escape. Not *we*. Here was Greta Pallister telling lies at my behest.

'We can easy walk across to the Settlement,' suggests Greta, her tone reassuring. 'That'll make it nearly the truth.'

We walk along awkwardly side by side, a foot apart. Around us a regular drift of people make their way towards the High Street. The town buzzes on a Saturday night, even in these thin times. People gather to reminisce, to joke, even sing. They talk of their gardens, their rabbits, of the horse that nearly won, of the lad that's really coming on in the foot-racing, the new trumpet-player in the Club band. They do this even if they can only afford half a pint of beer in a whole evening. They do it even if they only stand outside the pub to talk. Talk costs nothing and has great value. These gatherings are mostly men with a sprinkling of the most forward women. Perhaps the more respectable women have their own equally momentous gatherings, pondering their own and the world's affairs over cups of tea. I don't really know about that.

This thing about the women is a mere impression, a guess. My experience of such home-life is the skeleton of a memory. For a second I wish it was my father who was striding down to The Saddler's Arms or The King's Head, and my mother who was staying home with her bosom buddies sorting the world.

I really am on my own on this planet.

Chapter Eighteen

The Promise

When Greta and I get there, the Settlement rooms are open and empty. Like church doors, the doors of the Settlement are never locked. Archie Todhunter likes members to go in freely and work on their projects. In the early days there was a problem, Greta tells me. 'Some folks took it for just a club where you could go and have a bit of crack and a free read of the papers, a cup of tea. A break from the house, like. Mr Todhunter made it clear they could only come in if they were registered for courses – proper members, you know.'

'Seems a bit, well . . . mean, like,' I say.

'Yeah. I always thought that. Just coming in here would be a break for some folks, from the four walls of their houses,' she says. 'We get a break, don't we? We need to come and do the plays, and the painting. Sometimes I think Archie's built a world of his own here. Outside the world of the dole and no money, hunger marches and it being so miserable with no work.' She adds this as we come into the big workroom. She goes to stand before her own portrait. She takes off her glasses to peer at it closely. Then she puts them back on and stands at a distance to take in the whole thing, scowling slightly as she concentrates.

I turn on more lights. The girl's close scrutiny of the painting makes me uncomfortable. It's as though she's staring at me and I'm naked. I want her approval. I really want her to like it, to like me. How can I want the approval of this child, this schoolgirl? I'm defensive. 'It's not finished. The cheeks are not quite . . . It's not dry yet. The colours will change. Darken. Eventually.'

She puts one hand palm outward, towards it. 'It's a dark picture but there's so much light in there. The light comes from inside the girl. *From* her,' she mutters. 'It's like she really has a whole past, a whole future. Look at her. Did her mother love her? Did her father beat her? Did she play whips and tops in the spring and skipping in the autumn?'

I stand behind her and try to see what she is seeing, this 'her', this other person. For me the whole thing had been a task, a challenge: the blocking in of the bulk of the girl's body, the drawing forward of the points of light, the depth of colour in the shadows which reflects my observation in the pit of the dense colour in the medium ground.

She turns towards me. The light from the overhead bulb glints on her glasses, making ellipses of light. 'Don't you see?' she says.

'Don't I see what?'

'This amazing thing that's happened. Mr Todhunter – and Tegger now – wrote about all these people. The one you play. The one Cora plays. The one I play. We clothe them with his words. And here you are. You've painted them. Made them real. A kind of magic, that.'

I reach out to grasp her shoulders and clasp her to me in a hug which is sheer pleasure in her delight, her perception. It's an awkward embrace. 'Glad you like it.' My hands drop to my sides. I walk across and sit down at one of the tables, putting safe distance between us. She stands very still for a moment, staring at me then comes to sit opposite.

'Gabriel?'

'Yes?'

'Did I do you a favour sitting for that portrait so you could do your masterpiece?'

'It's no masterpiece.' She has me on my back foot. 'But yes. It was a favour if you think it was.'

'Well, will you do *me* a favour? In return, like?'

She's the cunning one. I'll need to be careful. 'All depends on what you call a favour.'

'It's a very big thing.'

'All depends. Don't matter how big it is.'

Her narrow chest heaves. She takes off her glasses. 'You'll know that I'm, well, very *clever*. You'll have heard that.' A statement rather than a question.

'Pretty obvious, that.'

'Well, they're all talking about college. Even Cambridge. I'll probably get there.'

She is so certain of herself. And I can hardly think of tomorrow.

She takes off her red beret and her glasses and places them on the table. 'It's very *delicate*, like.'

'Get on with it. Stop messing about.'

She puts her hands flat on the table and looks at them. I look at them too. They are fine, well shaped, the nails perfect ovals. So perfect. I recall how difficult they were to draw. 'Well,' she says, 'there's this college thing. Then I'll probably go on to some really decent job. Teaching in a big school. Maybe even a college. Maybe I'll join the Civil Service. My dad says they'll run the country.'

'What're you doing? Showing off how clever you are? I told you – I already know.'

'No. No. There's no virtue in being able to mug things up. Godgiven, my Gran would say. Nothing to do with me.'

'So?'

'There's one thing . . .'

'Spit it out!'

'Well, whenever I look into the future all I see is this dry life. All books and no passion. Like some of my teachers. This clever spinster who's in a wonderful job, lives in a big house and keeps two cats.'

'Sounds all right to me. Better than round here washing with a poss-stick on Mondays with four kids at your skirts.'

She leans forward and puts one perfect hand on my arm. 'But don't you see? In that picture there, the girl Dorothy has a real life. A future with someone else. If it's not Arthur, it'll be some other man.'

I'm getting hot under the collar now.

'Me, I'll be a dried-up spinster, like some of those old trouts up at the Grammar School. And I don't want to be like that.'

I am even hotter under the collar now. First Marguerite Molloy and then this. 'So what's it you're saying?'

'I'm saying that – just as a favour, a great big favour – I want you to do *it* with me. That thing that men and women do. So I don't go on to be a dried-up old spinster. So I know what it's like when it's not out of books. I've read it up, you can be sure of that.'

'Bloody hell!'

She laughs. 'Yeah. It does sound weird when you say it out loud, like. You're blushing. Even I'm blushing and I'm the brazzent[1] one.'

'Brazzent fond!' I nod vigorously.

'Well?'

I stare across at the portrait and back at her.

She grins. 'If you'll do it I'll mention you in my memoirs when I'm a famous undried-up old dame.'

I still can't think of what to say.

She glares at me now. 'Don't tell me you don't know what to do!'

'Dinnet be daft. Of course I do.'

It's all hearsay, of course. I've had these urges that I've had to deal with myself. Practice runs, you might call them. It's all in working order. And that tongue-kissing. But I've never done *it* with a woman. Never.

'Go on!' There's a thread of desperation in her voice now. 'Just think of what you're saving the world from. Me as a miserable, frizzled-up old trout raging at the world in vengeance at my virgin state.'

'All right, all right, I'll do it!' Anything to stop her going on and on like this. 'But . . .'

'I've thought it out. You'll need to find out how we can do it so I don't have a baby. This is not one of those traps, you know. I know you can do it without getting caught but I'm not sure how.'

'Oh! So there *is* something you don't know.'

'Don't you be sarcastic!' she says fiercely. 'This is serious.'

[1]Cheeky.

'What I was going to say was that we shouldn't do it till after the play's been on.'

'Oh, I thought . . .' Her bottom lip comes out and now she looks very young.

'Look, Greta, it'd be impossible. Too much going on. All these rehearsals. The paintings. The sets. This fuss about the Prince.' I had to put it off somehow.

'After then?'

'Yes.'

'Promise?'

'Yes.'

'Say it!'

Girl-games. 'I promise. I promise. After the Prince's visit.'

She stands up and jams her beret on her head, threads her glasses on to her ears. 'That's that, then!' she says brightly. 'I'd better be off. I told Mam half an hour and I've got some homework to do.'

'I . . . yes, half an hour,' I say lamely. I watch the door as it clicks behind her. She's got me outranked, outflanked and quite defeated. And what's more she has me all worked up and I'll have to go somewhere to calm myself down before I can get on with anything, anything at all. Couldn't paint a bucket in this state.

My house feels deserted when I re-enter, although there is a faint, cinnamon smell of woman in the air. No sign of Tegger or the girl. Disappointed as well as relieved, I take my pictures, one by one, down from the wall. As I place each one on the table I examine it carefully. It's just as well that they're down from public view. Those which are not mere apprentice-pieces are rough, half-conceived things. My copies of the precious

Rembrandt *Supper at Emmaus*, and *Night Watch* from Aunt Susanah's book look as though they've been painted with pokers. The portraits I'm working on are not great art, maybe not art at all, but they are a world better than these daubs.

'So you make out you're a good drawer then?'

I spin round. Marguerite Molloy is looking at me through the open stair rails. She is as neat and finished as she was earlier, but her soft cloud of hair is free now from its cheeky feathered cap. My gaze searches behind her, in the dark reaches of the staircase. Tegger looms into sight, bustles her down the stairs. 'Gabriel, mate. Yer back!'

'I do live here, like.' I bring the pictures into a neat pile, pick them up and make for the door of the front room. 'Your friend says she's just going,' I say over my shoulder. Then I slam the middle door behind me.

Two voices, man then woman, trickle to me through the closed panel for a moment. Then there is complete silence. I stack the pictures carefully in my grandmother's big press, then go back through the kitchen.

Tegger is sitting there, alone, smoking a cigarette, as calm as you like. 'What cheor[1], marra,' he says.

'You cheeky bugger!' I answer. Well, what would *you* say?

'Sorry about that, Gabe. Her just turning up like that.'

'Her?'

'She's the bar woman at the Raglan. Helps old Flaherty out, like. She's off there now. Starts at six. Finishes when they close.'

'And you . . .?'

[1]Traditional Northern greeting. Goes back to *What cheer?* Used in Shakespeare.

'I was just there at closing time a few nights. She's a nice woman. Likes a laugh.'

'So I see.'

'She was dead interested in your pictures.'

'None of her business.' I fill the kettle and press it so hard on the fire hob that the coal grinds and moves.

'She says she's seen pictures at a big gallery in Newcastle that's worse than those.'

'She can't have. They're bad pictures. Just apprentice-pieces, my private affair.' I am curious though. 'Which gallery was that?' I've never been to a proper gallery.

'Just a big gallery. She didn't say.'

I could not resist it. 'Were you in my bedroom?'

'Nah.' He surveyed the glowing tip of his cigarette. 'The other one.'

I wondered about that gallery with its rows and rows of pictures, proper paintings. Then I thought about those two, her and him, upstairs on my father's bed. These days it just has a flock mattress on the bare springs. When Tegger was last in there he was with me, attending to my dead father. To his dead body.

I wanted to ask just what it was they did together – apart from the broad mechanics, which any dog knows. And I desperately wanted to know how you stopped the worst happening. The very worst. That unwanted baby which could anchor a man as sure as any sea anchor. There are seven men in this street alone, anchored in such a way, with mouths to feed and no wage. That will not be my story. Nor will it be Greta Pallister's.

'She wants you to paint her.' Tegger lit another cigarette. 'Marguerite.'

It's a great relief to laugh at such a stupid idea.

'She has money,' he says. 'She will pay.' He looks me in the eye. 'You'll enjoy it. Be sure you will.'

To be paid to paint that woman. Now that *is* a thought.

Chapter Nineteen

Energy

Two weeks later I'm on my own in the painting shed finishing the first stage of Archie Todhunter's portrait when the door opens and Rosel Vonn comes in. In my painting, Archie's standing by his desk. His blue fountain pen, his black-bowled pipe and his amber cigarette-holder are in their stand on its polished surface. The black cigarette-holder with a smoking cigarette is in his hand. I have imagined the pit manager to be something like Todhunter at his least creative: overbearing, overconfident, meticulous; fussy about small things.

But now Rosel is in the room and I have to stop while she looks at the paintings one by one. I've brought them back from the big room to be finished. They all need some more work on them and I am short of bone black and aquamarine.

Rosel is focused, but quite natural. You'd not think she'd neglected me these weeks at all. Now suddenly she's acting the teacher, carefully appraising my work. I know I shouldn't be moved, excited by her; she is my mentor, after all. I should expect her careful appraisal.

But she moves me. She excites me.

Then she laughs and I nearly jump out of my skin.

'What? What is it? What's wrong? Are they so funny?'

'You work with such *brio*, Gabriel, such *élan*!'

'*Brio? Élan?* What're you talking about?'

'Such energy! Such speed! Such style! You've gobbled up Rembrandt and Turner. You've ploughed your way through all my new brushes, new paints . . .'

I wait.

'And you make something good, something very brave.'

'You're saying these are just big, clarty daubs, aren't you?'

'Clarty? What is this?'

'Muddy, sticky. The opposite of *élan*!'

She laughs up into my face and it is like light. 'No, Gabriel. It is as though with your energy you have shaken all the rules in a bag and pulled out any one which suits you. But you make them work. For you.' She takes a step back and the bare swinging bulb gleams on strands of her putty-coloured hair. 'Perhaps you are right. Perhaps it is little bit *clarty*. Still, there is character here. Delicacy.'

I stand behind her now and try to look at my work with a stranger's eye.

'What do *you* like about them,' she asks, 'these paintings of yours?'

'They were all very good subjects, Cora, Archie and Greta,' I begin. 'Patient. Waiting for me to do what I really can't. Or couldn't. As I drew and painted it's like they tried to show me the daylight and dark places, not just in the people they were playing, but in themselves. Their real selves. It seems like two things are happening.' I'm frowning with the effort to think. 'No, many things.'

She nods, willing me on with my thoughts.

'All the time I'm painting, having, like you say gobbled up Turner and Rembrandt, I'm thinking about the pit. How the dark works with the light. I'm thinking about my grandmother who knew the magic of colour and pattern in ordinary things. I'm thinking about my Aunt Susanah who painted kingfishers. How nothing comes from nothing . . .' My voice fades on the dusty workshed air. It's the longest speech about painting I've ever made in my life.

'These paintings are good, Gabriel. Be sure of that,' she says slowly. She nods, her face turned slightly away. I will her to look at me but she resists. I want her to take me to her. I want to engulf her. I want to stroke her hair and put my lips to her mouth. To her cheek. I want to be part of her. To be in her and to have her in me. She knows. This is why she won't look.

She moves hurriedly to the door, then turns and looks somewhere near my left ear. 'Oh, Gabriel. I have a terrible thing to ask of you. For your portrait – will you get someone to cut that mane of hair of yours? Mr Todhunter tells me that in the trenches they do not allow such abundance. *Short back and sides*, he says.'

I laugh now, my inner tension melting away. 'So you're not frightened I'll bring down the walls of the Temple?'

She frowns. 'The Temple? Ah, yes. Samson. I see.' She smiles. 'Even close-headed, Gabriel, you will stay strong. A Roundhead perhaps, not a Cavalier. You see? Don't I know my English history?'

The door closes behind her and I set about my work again with – what was it? *Brio*.

* * *

It's Marguerite who cuts my hair in the end.

She's in and out of my house regularly now, to see Tegger. I've given up worrying about what my neighbours will think of this regular visitor trotting down the back street and letting herself into the house like she lives here.

I listen to their laughter, up there in my father's bedroom, and I wonder when there was ever laughter in that place. You would probably have to go back to the time of my grandmother and her husband. And he was killed in the South African wars. It was a grim place when my father slept there, to be sure.

One morning I come in with some milk to find Tegger sitting meekly on one of my kitchen chairs, shouting and yelping as Marguerite cuts his wiry locks with some very small scissors. She is making a very good hand of it, her brown fingers fluttering round his head like butterflies.

I watch for a second then ask, 'So would you cut my hair?'

'So would you draw my picture?' She's quick, I'll say that.

I shake my head. 'It doesn't work like that,' I say.

She pouts. Tegger yelps as she snicks one of his ears. 'Hey, man! You got me pouring with blood here!' He pulls his shirtcuff down over over his hand to mop his ear. Blood seeps on to its greyish surface.

'Well,' she says, 'if I do cut your hair, will you at least think of painting my picture?'

'I was thinking about it anyway.'

She smiles brilliantly at me then ducks her head to concentrate on Tegger's hair, trimming it to not more than an inch all over. Finally, 'There you are, you baby. What do you think of that?'

He tucks away his bloody sleeve and examines himself in the over-mantel mirror. 'Not bad for an amateur, like.' She flicks him with a handy tea towel. 'Bad boy,' she says. She turns to me. 'Next for shaving?' she says.

I sit down in the chair and watch as my yellow curls mix with Tegger's black hair on the stone floor. I wriggle in the chair, then settle. It's quite relaxing, having Marguerite move around me, snipping away. There is a lot of hair and it takes her quite a long time with her tiny scissors. 'There!' She pats my shoulder just as she patted Tegger's. 'See what you think.'

I peer in the mirror and for a second my father looks out at me. I blink and chase away the resemblance. The girl has certainly done a good job: cut it close all over so my pelt is as smooth as rabbit fur.

Tegger has the brush and is sweeping the stone flags and pushing the hair into the fire with the hearth shovel. He tips the shovel on the back of the fire and for a second the air is full of the sharp tang of burning hair.

'Tell you what,' says Tegger. 'I've to go down the Settlement. I'm gunna read this thing to Archie.' Tegger is the only one, apart from Cora and Rosel Vann, who calls Archie Todhunter by his first name. I don't know how that came about. Perhaps it's a writer's privilege. Anyway, it seems Archie sent Tegger's story about the men in the vans to a magazine and now it's to be published. And now Tegger's written this play about the Hunger March. Believe it or not, it's supposed to be funny. Not much to laugh about there, you'd think.

There's certainly nothing to laugh at round here, is there? We have no work, no money, hardly enough food to keep body and soul together and the undertaker's having his best year yet. But somehow you have to build a way to live like this and still be human. Now, our way is the Settlement. Others use their garden, or their pigeon-breeding, or dog racing. Seems to me now that if you do things to obsession you can stop the pain of having to live like this, in this half-human way. Like this you can declare your membership of the human race.

Anyway. The legend is, Tegger's new play'll be the next one after *Coal and Blood*. If it works out.

'I tell you what,' Tegger says now. 'Why don't we all go down and Marguerite can look at them paintings you've already done? They're canny grand, Marguerite. Canny grand. Just wait till you see them.'

In the street she walks between us, linking our arms as we march along. We draw quite a lot of glances. I'm not sure whether this is because of our saucy promenade or because Tegger and me are shorn like sheep and look like a pair of bookends.

At the Settlement Tegger vanishes into the office to see Archie and I lead the way to the dingy workroom and turn on the lights. The paintings have been brought out from the shed to finish their drying in the warmer atmosphere. Marguerite stands in the centre of the room and whistles. *A whistling woman and a crowing hen brings the devil out of his den.* Where have I heard that? My grandmother? I can't remember.

'Hey, Gabriel' she says. 'These are really good.' She walks along the line, stopping in front of each one. 'I tell you what,' she says. 'If I cut your hair for the rest of your life, will you do just one for me? Of me?'

I keep my face blank, although my fingers are already itching to do it. Cadmium red, Yellow Ochre, Veridian Green, Aquamarine . . . It's important, though, that I don't let her know this. I want to do it so much. I cough. 'If I did one, then it'd not be for you. You'd not own it. It would be mine. I need to keep the paintings together.' This thought has suddenly come into my head. I didn't know I thought this, but I do. Maybe I should be anxious to sell them. I'm wearing charity shoes and I haven't got the price of a new jacket or my next meal.

'Oh dear,' she says, 'I did think . . .'

I shake my head. 'It's not possible. I need to keep them together.'

But she's so crestfallen I have to make an offer. 'There'll be drawings,' I say. 'Mebbe you can have one of those. I did that for her.' I nod towards Greta's picture.

'Right!' She's happy again. She pulls closer to Greta's image. 'Is she your sweetheart then? Wonderful-looking kid.'

'Well, in the play she is. That's what these are, portraits of the characters in the play. And she's no beauty. She's really just a schoolkid.'

She laughs. 'See that look in her eye? She's no school-child.'

I sit down at the table. It's lined up with books now, for the Wednesday afternoon library. The library tickets sit in a long box, like a little coffin. The tickets are all filled in, in Archie's immaculate script. Marguerite comes to sit down opposite me. 'Tegger was saying to me that you'd never seen proper paintings, hanging up in a gallery, like. On a wall.'

'Tegger should keep his mouth shut.'

'Looking at these paintings, that's hard to believe. They look like proper paintings.'

'That's what they are.'

'There's this gallery at Newcastle.'

'I know. Tegger told me. I couldn't fathom how you ended up there.'

'Well, it was a rainy day and . . . Don't worry about why.'

'Is it very big, this gallery?'

'Yeah. Really big. Enormous. We could go and see it, on the train. There's this really big station at Newcastle. You should see it.'

I'm tempted. 'Will Tegger come?'

'No reason why not. Anyway, d'you think he'd let us leave him behind? We could take some of your pictures and—'

The door clashes and Rosel comes towards us, her head tilted in enquiry. 'Good morning, can I . . .? Gabriel, your hair! I did not recognise you. You look . . .'

The table wobbles as I get to my feet.

'Older?' says Marguerite cheerfully. 'I thought so too. Made quite a man of him, didn't I?'

'She cut it,' I say. 'This is Marguerite.'

She gets up to her feet and shakes Rosel vigorously by the hand. 'Doesn't look quite the same without his golden locks, does he, our Gabriel?'

Rosel frowns. 'You are his sister?'

A peal of laughter. 'No. I'm nobody's sister. More a friend, you might say. It was a bargain. Exchange of skills. He's gunna paint my picture.'

'Is he?' The words hang on the air.

I'm all hands and feet. I want to go into all kinds of explanations; that Marguerite is really Tegger's friend; that she has this wonderful face; this wonderful apricot glow on her skin; that my fingers itch to paint her. But of course I can't.

Rosel nods. 'I am sure that will be a great task for Gabriel.' Icicles hang from her words. She moves closer to me, putting Marguerite out of her eye-line. 'The hair is good, Gabriel. Will you have time today to come down to the painting shed? Nathan and Tegger now have the dugout constructed. You will know this, of course. I need some preliminary sketches of you there. Archie tells me Mr Pallister has an old army uniform which will fit you. I did not believe this at first but it seems he has become very fat as he grew older. But first you must collect it, this uniform.'

I glance along at Marguerite who is still sitting at the book table. Her fine black eyebrows are raised and there is a shadow of a smile on her lips. I'm like a ball being patted gently between them. I look back at Rosel. 'So, then, what time?'

'Perhaps one o'clock this afternoon? While there is still natural light from the skylight?'

'Right. Right.' I clear my throat to stop myself choking. 'Marguerite? Let's get on. I need to go to the Pallisters', to get that uniform.'

Marguerite stands up, comes to full attention and gives a remarkably authentic military salute. 'Yes, sir, Captain. Anything you say, *mon capitaine*!'

I bustle her out of the room. 'There's no need for that,' I burst out as we tumble into the street outside.

'No need for what?'

'That saluting business.'

'Hey, Gabriel. Where's your sense of humour? It's just a bit of fun. What an old glum-sides you are.'

We walk along the street passing a woman who's pushing a cart with three bawling children in it. She glances at us with dull eyes.

'I have to go to the Pallisters',' I say. I don't want her to tag along there. What would Mrs Pallister make of her?

'And I've to get home. This is my way. Don't worry your head.'

'Home?'

'Two rooms at the Raglan. I have an outside staircase. That's something.'

'Is your mother with you there?'

The laughter drains out of her. I can feel the loss. 'I told you,' she said. 'I brought her home . . . to spend her last days here.'

I remember this. 'I'm sorry. I shouldn't have . . .'

'So she's not here at the Raglan. She might be hovering somewhere above it but if she is, she'll have very raggedy wings. So, you can come there and visit, any time you like. Like I say, I have an outside staircase.'

'Like I say,' I say, 'I've gotta go to the Pallisters'.'

She shrugs. 'Suit yourself. But you will come, Gabriel. Oops! Nearly past my corner. See you!' She gives another military salute and clicks away on her bobbin heels, the feather in her hat trembling as she walks.

I don't know whether she makes me mad or amused. I do know that I'm looking forward to that train ride to Newcastle. The only problem is, I don't know how on earth I'll find the fare. I'm in debt to the corner shop for my daily bread, I've no spare money. None at all. Not even the fare to Newcastle.

Chapter Twenty

A Triptych

When I get to the Pallister house Greta is at school, Dev is out on council business and Mrs P. is ironing at the kitchen table, which is padded with blankets and covered with a singed sheet. A large clothes horse squares on to the fire and Mrs Pallister has one flat iron on the hotplate and one on the table. There are piles of clothes ironed and unironed on every surface, and the air smells of singed wool and vaporised bleach. My grandmother's house smelled like this on ironing day.

Mrs Pallister laughs when she sees me. 'Why, Gabriel Marchant! I'd' a passed you in the street. You look a good ten years older.'

'Why, thank you for that.'

'No, no. Still a bonny face. But where are those curls?'

'At the back of our fire, seeing as you ask. They made a good blaze. I've come for Mr Pallister's uniform.'

'Yes. Mr Todhunter came and talked to Dev about it. It's all laid out in the front room. Our Dev says you'd better try it all on to see if it suits.' She bustles me through the middle door which she bangs shut behind me. I can hear the clink of crockery. The dreaded cup of tea. I'll not get out of here very fast.

The uniform is immaculate except for a couple of neatly mended holes in the left leg. The buttons shine out of their bed of folded khaki; the trousers have knife-edged creases, the boots gleam like new tar. On the table are three medals.

I strip off and step into the uniform. It fits perfectly. Against the back wall is a black japanned press whose three mirrors are cobwebbed with wear and damp. In their milky surfaces, for a second I see a stranger: someone who fought through many hard battles and came back unscathed. How hard it is to connect the heavily built, round-jowled Dev Pallister with that young man. I mimic Marguerite Molloy's salute in the mirror. Then I drop my fraudulent hand and shake my head at my presumption.

The door clicks and in bustles Mrs Pallister. Her eyes bulge. 'My life! It's a ghost here. You could be Dev standing there. He was always a good-looking man. Even coming home covered in mud with lice in his seams. Always. So many lost friends.' Her voice trembles and I am helpless. 'My own two brothers . . .'

'But Mr Pallister came home,' I say urgently, to relieve myself of some responsibility for her pain.

She sniffs. 'Aye. That's true.' She puts her hand over the medals. 'What about these? He said you should wear these.'

'I can't do that, Mrs Pallister. It'd be such a fraud.'

She frowns. 'But according to Dev, Mr Todhunter says the painting was of a lad who's fought in the war. A brave lad. You can wear it for that brave lad, and for all the other brave lads. You can wear it for the brave lad Dev himself was, not much older than you were then. And for all the lads that didn't get back.'

Words like this have been said over and over so many times that it's a wonder they have any meaning left after twenty years of hard use. But here I am nearly crying myself now. Such a gowk. 'It'll be an honour, Mrs Pallister.'

'Now you can go off and get your picture done. It suits.'

I look down at myself, more immaculate in these borrowed plumes than I've ever been before in my life. 'I cannot walk through the streets like this,' I tell her. 'I'll get arrested for false pretences.'

She stares at me, then laughs uncertainly. 'Well, mebbe not.' She ducks down behind the horsehair sofa. 'There's his kitbag. But all my good pressing'll have come to naught.'

'I'll roll it up carefully and shake it out as soon as I get back to the Settlement. Archie Todhunter'll keep an eye on it in between times.'

She nods and leaves me to it. When I go through to the kitchen she has tea and Co-op cakes on the little table under the window. I eat my cake standing up, pleading great urgency, that the 'painter woman' is waiting for me at this very minute.

'You go, son!' Her glance is dreamy; the image of young Dev just returned from the war printed for a little while on her retina.

I reach the end of the yard and she calls, 'Gabriel, son.'

I turn. 'Yes?'

'I'll tell our Greta you called.'

'Aye.' Now, what's she after? 'Aye. All right.' Then I swing down the back street, borrowing a soldier's heel-down hard-won gait.

When Rosel sees me in the uniform she shakes her head. 'But it is the trenches, Gabriel. Arthur is down there in all the mud. Is that not so?'

I look down at the immaculately pressed uniform, the white puttees. I imagine how long it took Mrs Pallister to get it this way. 'We can't mucky this,' I say. 'Mrs Pallister'll be mortified.' I shut my eyes tight. My head is tumbling with notions and images. 'What about, say, an image of Arthur as an immaculate soldier and then him in the trenches and mebbe as a miner before the war. Like, shadows behind.'

'That's three paintings, Gabriel!'

'It's the message of the play, isn't it? A land fit for heroes – a fight worth fighting? I'll wear my old pit hoggers[1] for the trenches, and my old pit jacket. And you can make it look like khaki under the mud . . .'

'Stop! Stop!' She holds her brow and shakes her head. Then she walks around to stand close to me and I get hot under the collar and in other places too. 'So one in full uniform. One in the trenches. One in the pit. A triptych. I will have to work very quickly. It is illustration rather than art, but . . .'

'A what?'

'A triptych. A painting in three parts. Sometimes joined, sometimes not.'

'Triptych! Well, I keep learning these new words from you, Miss Teacher.' I'm grinning like a fool now, pleased to get my own way and pleased that for once she'll have to pay me full attention while she paints me. At the very least I'll watch and learn.

I had thought these sessions with her drawing me would be personal, close. But I'm wrong. As the days go by she's very focused on this task of the triptych. All about the place she pins

[1]Work shorts which miners wear underground.

drawings she's already made, of colliery wheels and Durham skies. She brings in a wonderful sketchbook – her father's, I think – which has pages and pages of scenes from the trenches. It's only when you look closer that you can see it's German trenches, not British ones which are pictured there. I don't mention this. It seems too rude somehow.

She tells me exactly how to kneel, how to handle the shovel, how to hold the gun. She looks and looks at me but it's not personal. I might be a tree in the forest, or one of her marble statues. Still, I relish these times. I feel I know her better by her very actions, by the very furrow on her brow as she does a tricky bit of shading. At least after this we can never be strangers.

I'm in a bit of a muddle these days. I look at Rosel and I think of Marguerite Molloy. When I see Marguerite messing on with Tegger I think about Rosel and I even think about Greta Pallister and imagine myself with each of them in turn being close to them like Tegger is with Marguerite. Some kind of tryptych, that.

Then, from time to time I remember the promise that Greta squeezed out of me and wonder how I'm going to do *it* with her after all this is over. What's more, I've got to find out how to do *it* without Dire Consequences. There must be someone round here who can tell me. Show me.

Apart from Sundays, when things are a bit quieter, the weeks now for both me and Tegger are very full. I've little time to be angry at my father or bemoan the empty house. Tegger only manages to get away to the races with the horse lads once in a while. He's preoccupied with Archie Todhunter now, and their new play. Then there are long rehearsals for *Coal and Blood* on Wednesdays and Fridays. The problem is, Todhunter is getting more and more dissatisfied with everyone's performance, just when us actors are becoming more confident that what we're doing is right. It's making us unsettled.

Todhunter insists on going, line by line, breath by breath, through everyone's part, making the rest of us sit and listen when all we want is some time out for a smoke or a gossip. Tegger's usually there by Todhunter's side, changing words and phrases, still tightening the whole thing up so it almost pings in the air.

Todhunter's concentration and passion make it impossible to complain out loud but there are mutterings behind his back. Nathan has said more than once that it is worse than the bloody pit. Greta frowned at him once when he said this, telling him that Mr Todhunter was only trying to get it right for all of our sakes. 'We'll all look like fools on the day, if it's not right. Think of the Prince!'

Nathan turned away so she doesn't quite catch him saying, 'Bugger the Prince.'

'What d'you say, Mr Smith?'

'Nothing. I said nothing.'

My scenes with Greta are not so uncomfortable now. Becoming more natural, I suppose. I wish I could be as objective about this as Rosel is about painting me. But I'm not as pure as that. Each time I find myself looking forward a little bit more to laying my lips on Greta's soft mouth. It makes me tingle.

Archie is still raging on about continuity. He has it written down and reads it to us:

a) The connection (through the girl-and-boy-romance) between the trenches and the women seems to be working.

b) The connection between the trenches and the goings-on in the coroner's court is working. The description of the miners in jeopardy and the soldiers' dilemma has strict parallels.

c) However, the connection between the coroner's court and the chorus of women – led by Cora – is lacking.

Cora comes in for some stick from him regarding this, even though it's not her fault.

Tegger pipes up. 'I know what to do,' he says. 'Baffer Bray.'

'What?' says Archie, scowling at him. 'Who?'

'Baffer Bray. He's this funny old gadgie. A bit . . . well, a shilling short. He must be seventy-five. Always with the women, he is. Chatting, gossiping, like he's one of them. Should've been a woman, so they say down at the Raglan.'

'Well?' Archie glowers at him through a veil of cigarette smoke. 'What's your point?'

'He could be like that herald in Shakespeare. You know, bringing news back to the village. Every time a new thing happens in the court he can run to the women and tell them.'

'Sounds a bit of a clart to me,' Nathan's voice bells out from the back.

'Not a bad idea,' says Archie. 'Write it!'

'What?' says Tegger, blinking.

'Take the blasted play away and write in this herald of yours. What shall we call the old man?'

'Baffer Bray!' calls Nathan.

'Canna do that,' says Tegger. 'Not right. Taking from life.'

'Call him Granda Pew,' says Greta.

'Where d'that come from?'

'Search me,' says Greta.

Tegger turns to Todhunter. 'When d'you want we should do this then?'

Todhunter shrugs. 'Bring it here tomorrow night at seven and you and I'll go through it. If it works we can rehearse it on Friday. It will touch everyone, so we'll need a full rehearsal.'

'New material – at this stage,' groaned Cora. 'Oh Archie, really!' Only Cora could object to Archie's face and she's quite willing to do it.

'Let me do my job, Cora, will you!' I've never heard Todhunter speak to her like this and she goes red. 'You mind your own business and I'll mind mine.'

Because Tegger knows he'll be working that night and all the next day and the next night with Archie, he'll miss seeing Marguerite at the Raglan. 'Gan on, Gabe. Will you get down there and say why I can't come myself?'

I go there early evening but even so the public-house is already busy with men drinking single pints very slowly. There are the rhythmic clicks and calls from the two domino tables, the bustle of a darts game and the quieter hum of groups of men playing cards, with piles of spent matches taking the place of money. I join the few stragglers who sit up at the bar.

Marguerite is serving at the other end of the bar, her hair an iridescent purplish black in the light of the gas mantel. She's pulling pints and laughing, showing the cracked tooth which is her only imperfection. I feel tender now about this flaw, which makes her somehow accessible, less like a goddess. She laughs and talks with one old man as she serves him. It must take patience to humour people like that. Perhaps that's what she does with me when she praises my paintings and promises me a visit to the gallery at Newcastle.

There's no denying, though, that her face lights up when she sees me. 'Gabriel! You're a sight for sore eyes.' Her gaze slips across my shoulder. 'No Tegger? Lost your twin?' As she speaks she pulls a pint of draught and puts it before me.

'That's why I'm here. Tegger's down the Settlement doing some work for Mr Todhunter. Shouldn't think he'll get out tonight, or tomorrow night.'

She grins, unfazed. 'Well then, honey, I'll have to make do with you, won't I?' She pushes the glass towards me. 'Here.'

I shake my head. 'Can't buy that, Marguerite. I'm saving for new paints. Nowt to spare.' In fact, like a lot of the men in here I've nowt to spare for food, if truth were told. The new paints are a dream. But I wouldn't admit this to her.

'Nah. Take it. Mr Flaherty over there includes two pints a night in my pay. Tegger gets them, so why not you, that's here in his place?' She pushes it even further towards me. It's almost touching my chest.

My father was never one for the public-house and as a consequence I've never really bothered, except for the odd pint or two with Tegger when we were both in work. Tegger, though, he loves the pub. The gossip, the practical jokes, the storytelling are all meat and drink to him. Some of it – like Marguerite – he keeps to himself. Other bits resurface in these stories he's writing, with Archie's encouragement. It was at the Raglan that he heard the story about the two brothers and the deputy's kist[1]; that's the story that he's making into a new play, with Archie's help.

I sit back on my stool, take a sip of the smoky-tasting beer and watch Marguerite at her work. She's as neat as an egg: deft, smiling and efficient. A glow settles on her wherever she is in

[1]Deputy's toolbox: his managerial station.

the room. In this sea of pasty underfed faces she is exotic, a flame of warmth in a cold place. No wonder old Flaherty gives her a bonus of two pints a night. She probably brings a hundred pints of business in, some nights. Even in these hard times.

Around ten o'clock a surge of song bubbles up from a gang of Irish ironworkers in the corner. The ironworks has been closed for two years now so their beer money must, I imagine, come from more diverse sources. The Irish are very resourceful.

Marguerite drifts in my direction.

'How long before you close?' I say.

She glances up at the mahogany wall clock behind me. 'Two hours, I'd say.'

I tuck my pint behind a card advertising Players Cigarettes. 'Will you watch this?' I say. 'I'll be back soon.'

I hare through the streets and am back on my corner stool in eighteen minutes. I put my drawing pad and my pencils down on the stained bar. Taking a sip of my beer I square the room with my eye. The elaborate gaslights illuminate the bulky bodies, leaving the corners in smoky darkness. My pencil touches the paper. I draw Marguerite about her work: leaning over the bar, her head tilted, listening to some confidence from a very old man on the other side. I draw her narrow figure weaving its way through the tables, hands aloft clutching five empty beer mugs cleared off a vacated table. Then I move on to the men who are playing, talking, singing. The cameos grow under my hand and I become engrossed.

Someone whispers in the ear of Flaherty. With the edge of my eye I see him wending his way towards me. My sketching rate slows. Marguerite hovers behind the bar, watchful.

He's at my shoulder. 'Now, marra,' he says quite kindly, for he is a jovial man. 'What's it yer up to here?'

I put down my pencil. 'I'm drawing.' I keep my tone neutral. 'I like to draw, I do so every day. Everything and anything.'

He sits on the empty stool beside me. 'Gissa look then,' he says comfortably. His fat hand with its sausage-like fingers flaps towards me.

I hold out the book and turn the pages myself. He peers first at the sketches then out at the room. 'Bliddy hell, man,' he says. 'Yeh've got Joss Allenby to the life. And old Marshall Kidd. Yeh've got a good hand all right.' His eyes, sunk a little by the high pouch of his cheeks, bore into me. 'Tell yeh what, son. We need a new sign outside. That one's falling to bits. Musta been there fifty year. Mebbe . . .'

I interrupt him. 'I don't do that sort of thing. Mr Flaherty. Sorry.' I can feel Marguerite's tension from behind the bar. Perhaps the fellow's not that jovial. 'I just draw and paint pictures.'

Clearly, he's not pleased. I flick through the book and carefully tear out the page which shows the scene by the dartboard with Flaherty himself looking on, pipe in hand. 'Mebbe you'd like this one for yourself? Stick it up behind the bar. Put a frame on it, mebbe?'

He holds it up to the light. 'Yeah. Yeah. I'll have that.' He nods at Marguerite. 'Hey Lass, give yer friend a whisky. I'm on that bit o'paper for posterity. Immortal. Nice frame and it'll sit behind the bar a treat.'

They're all watching me now, which I don't like. So I close my book, put my pencils in my top pocket and slip away. I pass Marguerite who's clearing the table of the Irishmen who are leaving too. One of the older men pinches her cheek as he leaves. Her eyes meet mine, full of patient endurance.

* * *

Later, perhaps eleven-thirty, a loud knock rattles the back door, the sneck clicks and in comes Marguerite Molloy, her green coat caught at the waist with a big black belt, her hair tied down gypsy-wise with a red silk scarf.

I stand up from the table where yet again, I've been poring over Aunt Susanah's book of Rembrandt plates.

'Marguerite!' I say.

'Gabriel!' In her voice is a drawling echo of my own.

'What?' I try not to think of the neighbours.

She sits down easily in the hard-backed chair opposite mine. 'You asked what time did I finish. Well, I'm finished. Just five minutes ago. So-o. Maybe it's for me to say "What?" '

I'm hot under the collar again. I sit down to face her. 'I just wanted to ask you about something. There was no need to come here.' I glance round the room uneasily. The desire to escape from my own house does strike me, even in this tense moment, as ridiculous.

'Oh.' One slender hand comes up to her forehead. 'What a disappointment.'

'It's just . . .' I am conscious of feeling my way towards something. 'I don't know . . .'

'Oh! *What* a disappointment.'

Why did I ask her, in the pub, about the time she finished? I didn't think it out. The words just came. I licked my lips. 'I wanted to talk to you, like.'

'What about?'

'Well, there were two things.'

'What two things?'

'One, I wanted to fix up that Newcastle gallery. Visiting it. Does it have a name, this gallery?'

'The Laing. The Laing Art Gallery. That's what it's called.

We'll go any time you want. Mr Flaherty permitting, like.' She sits back in the chair. The collar of her coat slips down and her slender brown throat gleams like honey in the firelight. 'And the other thing. What was that?'

Instead of answering her, I jump up, go into the front room and come back with a sheaf of papers. I put the big Rembrandt book on my mother's sewing machine under the window and spread the papers and sheets of cardboard across the table. One half of me can't believe I'm showing these things to someone who, to all intents and purposes, is a stranger. They're sketches and half-botched paintings representing that time underground when I saw the woman. They are fumbling, clumsy things. Clumsiest of all is my depiction of the woman who is somewhere between Christmas card pictures of the Virgin Mary and the faded print of Rembrandt's *Danae* in Aunt Susanah's book.

Marguerite peers closer. 'What on earth are these?'

I begin to talk to her about my vision underground. How I saw the woman in the goaf. How I may or may not have gone to sleep. I can hardly believe my own ears: I've never explained this properly, not even to Tegger. 'It's just like the whole of the earth is a woman. And that time, somehow I saw her. This is something I really want to paint, more than anything else. And I want to do it right.'

She looks up at me, very direct now, not a trace of mockery in her bright eyes. 'Now, there's a story. But what's all this to do with me, I'd like to know?'

I take a very deep breath. 'I want you to be the woman. To . . . er . . . pose for the woman.'

'Mmm. Well. I should'a known you didn't want me for my bright blue eyes.' Her bright blue eyes pierce through me now and the heat under my collar has spread across my skin, all over my face, right to my hairline.

I shuffle the papers together. 'Don't bother, don't bother. Stupid idea anyway.'

She puts a hand on my arm, stops my manic gathering of paper. 'Woah, tiger! I didn't say it was a bad idea, did I? I never said I wouldn't do it, did I?'

I stand very still with her hand over mine, not daring to move. Now the heat has spread to every single part of my body and is having the worst effect. At last she releases me and with a swift movement unbuckles her coat and throws it across the back of the chair. 'How do you want me?' she says. 'Standing up? Sitting down? Lying down?'

Sweat is pouring out of me. 'What?' I say hoarsely.

Then she laughs a wicked, wicked laugh. 'Gabriel Marchant! You little tinker!'

I close my eyes and wish to vanish into the rug, into the very heart of my granny's sunflower. I close them even tighter, wishing that when I open them she will be gone. Bugger. A tear. There are tears in my eyes, trickling through my squeezed lids on to my cheeks.

'Gabriel, Gabriel!' Her voice now is all tenderness. 'Come on, honey. I'm only having you on. Only teasing. You should know that.'

I open my swimming eyes and look into hers.

'Oh, baby,' she says, blinking. 'You'll have me blubbing next.' She moves away from me and sits on my father's chair by the fire. She leans forward, her hands slack in her lap. 'Now then, pet. We'll stop the teasing. What is it you really want?'

I sniff and knuckle my eyes to clear them. If I'm honest, what I really want is to take her and kiss her. I want to pull her with me on to the rug beside the fire and do that thing I know how to do in theory but have never put into practice with any woman.

'What I really want,' I say, sniffing, 'is to make some drawings of you. I want to place you at the centre of this painting. I want you to give some life, some energy to this drawing of the earth woman. Then I will paint you. I want this to be my best painting, I want it to be the beginning of me really as a painter.' I'm embarrassed by the pretensions of the words coming out of my mouth but this is what I want to say.

And I know for sure that my world has changed now that I've actually said it.

Chapter Twenty-One

Mother-of-pearl

After the clash between Archie and Cora at the rehearsal, Rosel noticed that Cora did not bounce around the Settlement any more. She stopped wearing her theatrical make-up in the day and her curly hair was often grimy, unwashed. The house stopped ringing with the broadcast banter between her and Archie. Doors were slammed. Grumbling voices penetrated even these stone walls.

One morning Cora brought a letter up to Rosel's room. She hovered when she had handed it over. 'That will be a letter from your father,' she said. 'German postmark.'

Rosel glanced down at the letter, then up at Cora's strained face. She opened the door a little wider. 'Will you come in a moment?' she said. 'I have some lemonade here. I made it myself.'

Cora followed her in and sat on the bed. She glanced round. 'You have it very neat in here,' she said.

'Ah,' said Rosel. 'This is because all my mess of things are in the painting shed.' Rosel's rooms were always neat. As a girl of fourteen she'd revolted against the Bohemian squalor of her father and her mother's apartments and decided to be neat. It suited her.

She handed Cora a glass of lemonade. 'So what is this, Cora? Is there something wrong? You seem so different. *Down in the mouth*. This wonderful phrase.'

Cora stared at her with hard eyes. 'I *am* "so different".' She hesitated. 'There has been a difficulty. Something difficult turned up.'

'Difficulty? What is this difficulty?'

'I was pregnant.'

'A baby? Oh dear. You *were*—'

'No baby. Not now. I went to a woman.' Her voice was steely, neutral. 'She knew what to do.'

'And Archie? What does he . . .'

'Archie doesn't know,' she said heavily. 'No one knows except the woman who did it. And now you. It's not worth knowing. It doesn't matter now.'

Rosel grasped Cora's hand in hers. 'And you? How do you feel?'

'It's left me low, certainly. I'm too old for any of this.' Cora hesitated. 'It happened once before – twenty years ago. I was fine afterwards. Fine. It was a relief.'

'You should have told Archie. He—'

'Is too busy with all these people, with this play, with talking to the great and the good. Debating the Depression and his practical strategies to anyone who'll listen. Me? I'm just a carpet to be walked on. A nuisance. A fusspot. I criticise his play to make him feel small.'

'He says these things to you? He shouldn't. They are cruel words.'

'Perhaps he shouldn't. But I'm the only one in the world he can wail at, or demean. He is here for the public good. With everyone else he . . .' There were tears falling unchecked from her eyes, and dripping by her mouth. She licked her cheek and snuffled.

Rosel leaned across to pick up a neatly folded handkerchief from her dresser and blotted Cora's eyes for her as if she were a child. 'Now then, Cora. Don't cry. You have been ill. You *are* ill. You need to rest.' She pressed lightly on Cora's shoulder and the older woman collapsed back on to the bed and turned her head into the white pillow, where she cried her last tears into its downy surface. Rosel pulled the eiderdown up around her and patted her shoulder. 'You stay there, my friend. You must rest.'

Then Rosel went in search of Archie. She ran him to earth in the big room where the Wednesday library was in progress. He had perched himself on the edge of the smaller table and was talking to Mrs Stewart who was doing sterling duty stamping books. Mrs Stewart adored Archie.

He stood up to greet her. 'Ah, Rosel. How are we today?'

'We are very well,' she said shortly. 'Archie. I need to speak with you.'

'Fire ahead! What can I do for you? The stage set is beginning to shape up. And the portraits by you and young Mr Marchant are going great guns. I only wish I could say the same for the play. There is so much still to iron out. They think learning the lines is sufficient.'

Drat the man. He was in love with the sound of his own voice. She broke into his wordy flow. 'I wish to speak to you in private, Archie.'

He raised his eyebrows. 'Oh. Better go into my office, then.' He looked down at the adoring Mrs Stewart. 'We'll talk about the new book order another time. Perhaps I'll catch you at the end of this session?'

He swept off without waiting for an answer and led the way to his office. He settled behind his desk, chose his amber holder and lit a cigarette. He drew on it, closed his eyes and opened them and spoke to her. 'So, Rosel. What is it?'

She was conscious of the theatricality of his actions. That he was demonstrating his resentment at her sharp tone.

'It is about Cora, Archie.'

He wrinkled his nose. 'What about Cora?'

'She is upstairs at this minute on my bed. She is in great distress. She weeps.'

He put his cigarette into a convenient ashtray. 'I can't think why she's up there. What on earth is the matter with her?'

'You must go to her. Comfort her.'

He shrugged. 'She's a moody soul, our Cora,' he said comfortably. 'Artistic temperament, you know. Feelings first, brain comes after.'

'She is very, very distracted. I cannot calm her down.'

'She'll calm down soon. Been working up to something for a week or so now. Sulking, shouting, unreasonable. In front of the cast the other night, you know! It's not on, and I let her know it. How can this project be run with—'

Rosel crashed her hand on the table. 'You . . . you obtuse man! Is it only the mirror you see everywhere?'

He stood up. 'There's no need to be offensive, Fraulein. I think—'

'I'm going out to the hut now to do some work. I will not be back for two hours. You *must* go up and see her. Go and see her, Archie.' She slammed the door on the way out.

* * *

Cora was still bundled up on Rosel's bed when Archie entered the room. She hauled herself up, rising like a seal from a sea of eiderdown. 'Rosel, I'm sorry . . . Oh. It's you.'

He stood at the end of the bed, his hands loosely at his sides. 'Well now, old girl, what's this?'

She rolled back into the bedclothes. He could not see her face. Her voice when it came out was muffled. 'Go away.'

The bed creaked as he sat on the end of it. 'Of course I won't. You'll have to talk to me.'

Cora continued to hide. 'What did she say, Rosel? What did she tell you?'

He sighed. 'All she said was that you were very upset and I must talk to you. She's very bossy, that young woman. It's because she's German, I suppose.'

Cora emerged from the eiderdown. Her hair was half up and half down, her eyes were red with crying, her face was creased. 'Do you really want to know why I feel like this?'

There was a pause. 'Yes, of course.'

'No, you don't.'

'Cora, what kind of game are you playing?'

'It's not a game. Something very bad has happened. It has happened to you and it has happened to me.'

He threw up his hand. 'Happened? What are you talking about? How can anything have happened that I haven't seen? We live in the same house, for God's sake. We share a bed.'

'You never notice anything.'

'I have noticed lately that you're in training to play Kate in *The Shrew*. Everything is wrong. The slightest criticism and you berate me, despite the fact that we are behind with everything when there's so much to do.'

She brought her legs round so that she was sitting on

the edge of the bed. Then she put her hands up to pin her hair back into place. There was a forced grace in her movement: a theatricality. 'It is about you, Archie. It is always about you.'

He went to stand beside the window, peering out into the afternoon gloom. 'Not me, Cora,' he said patiently, reasonably. 'It's about the Settlement. If this place doesn't survive we will have let down these people. This town. You, me, everyone. This place is the only thing that matters.'

She sighed. 'In one way you're right . . .'

'That's the ticket,' he interrupted her. He looked down at his watch, a present from his father on his majority, imported to China from Switzerland, then posted, carefully wrapped, to Scotland. 'Look, it's nearly four o'clock. Your literature class will be waiting. Very successful, that class is. Several people have told me how lively it is. How you encourage everyone. What is it you're reading now?'

'Mark Twain. *Tom Sawyer*.'

'Ah yes. Accessible stuff. That'll cheer them up. It'll cheer you up.'

She began to remake Rosel's bed, pulling and patting it to make sure that no wrinkle or dent showed her recent presence there.

Archie paused by the door. 'Oh, and Cora?'

She looked at him blankly.

'How about a bit of warpaint, old duck? You don't look the same without it.'

The door slammed before she had a chance to answer.

She leaned against Rosel's neat dressing-table. 'Bugger, bugger,' she said. 'And bugger again.'

* * *

I have to wait in the painting shed for Rosel longer than I thought. I'm all togged up in my pit shorts and jacket: on my feet are my father's scarred and patched pit boots with the metal bands and segs on the soles. The last time they were worn they were on his dead feet. It was quite a decision to use them. She comes through the door behind me as I stand before her nearly completed portrait of me in the character of Arthur in uniform. It's lightly done, with washes of ochre and yellow for the khaki cloth and a splash of red on the cap badge and the medals. The face which is surely me but is not me, the eyes straight and steady under the close helmet of golden hair. There is fear and tension in the set of the shoulders, the way the hands clasp the cap in front of him. Somehow the sparing use of paint on the canvas allows a tremulous, uncertain light to sing through.

'Do you like it?' Rosel is very direct behind me.

'Yes. Yes.' I struggle to say something sensible. 'It's very light. To get that much effect without using so much . . .'

'Paint?'

I look across at my efforts which now seem like heavy daubs, a consequence of me trying to work up depth of shadow, the state of light that I am striving for. My painting, to be honest, has more in common with Rembrandt than Rosel Vonn. Perhaps Rembrandt would not agree. 'Makes mine look like right daubs.'

She was slow in denial, but quite definite. 'It is not the case, Gabriel. You find your own way. You use the old painters as your tutors and it is their image you strive for, not your own. One day you will find your own way. These paintings are wonderful, but you are on a journey, my dear, and this is not your destination. But you are on your way.'

Then she is all busy, pulling on her smock and dragging

across the easel on which sits a canvas which has already been primed. She whisks away a cloth to reveal that she's already blocked in the picture of 'Arthur' kneeling down in the seam. His hair is long and tangled, not his military crop.

'You started without me. And with hair.'

'Your hair was there when I drew them first, Gabriel.' She opens her black folder and shuffles through drawing after drawing. They all show me. Down at the pit heap. By the river. In the rehearsal room. 'Now, will you brace yourself to push the edge of that table as though it were a tub full of coal. Your arms like so . . .' The touch of her hand, cool and dry, makes me shiver. 'Fine. Now if you will just stay there.'

She works on for twenty minutes then throws down her brush. I stand upright and ease my shoulders, wriggling them this way and that.

She perches on a stool and lights a cigarette. 'Is this how you'd be, Gabriel, down below – wearing your jacket and your shirt?'

'No. Too hot. You have to strip down to the buff. Just my pit hoggers and my scarf to mop up the sweat.'

'Pit hoggers?'

'Short trousers.'

She breathes out. 'Well then, could you take off your things? Be like you really are? No shirt. Only the scarf. And the pit hoggers.'

I obey. She arranges my arms, the tilt of my head and we are in silence – thirty or forty minutes until my straining muscles can stand it no longer. I ease myself upright and wriggle my shoulders.

'Gabriel!' she says.

'You can't paint me if I fall over, now can you?'

She stands back from her easel. 'Would you like to see?' she says. 'To see the picture?'

I don't know whether I want to do this, but I go to stand behind her and look over her shoulders. The head is just about complete. She has caught the closed, intent, intense effort. She has somehow enlarged the muscles of my shoulders, making them bulge. She has caught this more in lines than dense painting. The power in the painting is simply in the line of the brush. You can see it is a brushmark. There is no attempt to disguise this. Though I regret having to admit it, the portrait is somehow the better for its lack of paint. 'You are very good,' I say.

Her narrow shoulders move in a shrug. 'I do not think so.' She leans forward and looks more closely at my painted head as it presses the metal surface of the tub.

In front of me, the nape of her neck gleams like mother-of-pearl under her thick, bobbed hair. There is no thought in the action as I lean down and kiss it. She smells of lemon and musk, linseed oil and turpentine. She tastes of delight. My hands go to her shoulders and turn her round. She reaches up and puts her lips on mine. All these movements happen in the blink of an eye. Then her slender, paint-stained hand comes up to cup the back of my head. Her body fits itself to mine and we kiss properly. Oh, how we meet each other in this touching of lips. She twists somehow and seems even closer. Her lips move against mine. Her tongue flickers and my mouth opens and a sense of her, who she is, the sheer *womanness* of her threads through me like a wire. It reaches my toes and inside my father's boots.

Now I'm pressing her to me. I can feel her small breasts, her long legs. I am all heat. I want to be further into her. My body is showing me the way. I want her.

Suddenly she breaks away and it's as though the world has broken in half, making me cold as the worst winter. She looks at me, then puts the back of her hand against her mouth. 'Do you want this?'

'I want you.' My voice is reduced to a growl. 'Oh yes.'

She comes near again and puts her hands on my shoulders. 'We can have this, but only this. No past. No future.'

'But Rosel . . .'

Her finger is on my lips. 'No past. No future. Just this.'

'Well . . .'

'Or nothing.'

I pull her closer. 'This, then,' I say. 'I will have this. Bloody hell. I do want this.'

Chapter Twenty-Two

The Woman in the Goaf

Rosel crept up the narrow staircase past Archie and Cora's silent room. Even in the aftermath of making love to the boy Gabriel, concern for Cora flittered through Rosel's mind like a persistent moth. She must go to Cora. Talk to her. There was truly a desolate woman.

But once in her room she stripped off, crept along the corridor to the bathroom basin with its single cold tap and soaped herself and dried herself all over. She combed cold water through her hair, scraping it back off her forehead and tying it with a dark green ribbon. Only then did she look in the cracked mirror. For a second the younger Rosel looked out. The Rosel who'd laughed her way through life with her friends in London and in Paris. The girl who'd painted into the night and had gone to visit much better painters to appreciate their fine skills.

That Rosel had been a quiet girl, a keen friend, a devoted lover to the two men whose lives, for brief spaces of time, she had shared. With these two men she had shared her youth. To these two men – who had lives of their own – she gave the non-returnable gift of her young years. At each parting she sought the relief of cutting herself, but somehow once she had recovered from the cuts she got on with her life.

Now tonight it had been her turn to share in someone's youth, someone who was as young to her as she had been to Philippe and Viktor.

She made her way back to her bedroom and sat on her bed, knees drawn up under her chin. She could see herself in the dressing-table mirror. She could see this woman who had made fumbling, ultimately exquisite love to a boy half her age, a boy who had never done this before. For whom she was the first. Suddenly the face in the mirror looked all of its thirty-eight years. Yes, the forehead was fine and smooth, the chin taut. But lines round the mouth suddenly looked deep and the tender skin under the eyes was loose and faintly creased. What had she done? How had she come to make this mistake? She'd gone to the boy upset and concerned about Cora and somehow her defences had been down. While she painted him, the tension in his shoulders, the earnestness in his eyes had made him more than an object to be observed and painted. His cropped hair made him seem, for a moment, older, more like a man and therefore desirable and accessible.

She looked hard in the mirror to see if this woman knew what she had done, had any shame in it. No. She saw a woman whose skin was glowing with the residue of desire, whose eyes were sparkling with satisfaction and mischief. She groaned. 'Rosel, what have you done?'

But still she did not regret this thing. She stretched her feet down the bed and as she did so, she noticed the letter underneath the intricate shelf of the dressing table. Her father's letter! She'd forgotten all about it amidst Cora's drama and the rush down to the shed to paint Gabriel.

She padded across to take the letter down, tear it open and carry it back to the bedside lamp to read it.

It was not from her father. It was from her brother.

Meine liebe Schwester,

I write to you in some despair in consequence of recent events. You will know that our father has angered the authorities with his vigorous protestations regarding the proscribing of his friends Herr Doktor Goldstein and Herr Bellig. He insists on consulting them and paying them, but he does not do it discreetly or quietly as some are supposed to do. He shouts it abroad. He makes his objections. Now the consequence. Two days ago he was arrested and imprisoned. He was in a cell, stripped and humiliated for two nights. Yesterday I went for him and brought him back to the apartment. It caused me great embarrassment, but I alleviated this by not wearing my uniform. He was shouting and incoherent. It seems they did not actually abuse him physically but he was very frightened. He is now at the apartment being cared for by old Frau Schmidt. I stayed with him one night and he talked about you. Perhaps you should come, I do not know. I am not certain whether or how my position in the army is compromised. I do know that he is not safe, outspoken as he is.

Do you think he would be safer in England? That may be so, although having a sister and father in England would probably compromise my own position further. I am not sure how much I care about this, if I am honest with you. Things are very difficult here. The virtuous way is turned up on its head. I cannot understand the arrest and the frightening of a harmless old man, nor the proscribing of equally harmless old doctors. You know how I have criticised the moneylenders and financiers who held the country to ransom in its hardest times. You know I have gloried in the reinstatement of Germany, in the rebuilding of her pride. Only now am I wondering whether the price is too much. Too much altogether.

There are men here who feel something should be done. But what possibly could be done without, well, great risk. So much is at risk. Even this letter to you is risky. It may be the last time I may write to you in these terms, except via a messenger.

Our father has an old friend who lives in London – Sir Peter Hamilton Souness. He worked once at the Foreign and Commonwealth Office. Perhaps he could arrange for our father to come to England? Will you go to visit him, to tell him of all this? An invitation from him. Perhaps . . .

Greetings from your loving brother,
Boris.

Tegger is intrigued by my idea of painting the women in the goaf. He questions me closely about it but I don't say much because I don't know what to say. I can only paint it.

'I was there when he saw it,' he asserts to Marguerite. 'I think it was a dream, me. But he said not.'

Last night I made love with Rosel Vonn. I think the whole of my life will be marked with this date. Anno Domini. AD. Anno Rosel. AR. I learned more about being alive and living in those hours in that rackety shed than I had ever known in the previous nineteen. I understood about power and communion, about the two into one. I understood the weakness, the draining afterwards, followed by the almost instant hunger to experience it again. We did do it once more, just before we had to go. It was impossible to resist.

I came home then, and after reflecting just a bit on what it was to be a man, I had the best sleep I've had in this house since my grandmother was alive.

The arrival this morning of both Tegger and Marguerite on my doorstep made me blink. Then I remembered the arrangement I had made with Marguerite. Weekday mornings only, as the rest of the day right up to eleven at night really belonged to Mr Flaherty.

'Where y'gunna do it?' says Tegger, looking round the crowded kitchen. 'In here?'

I laugh. A bit uneasily, I admit. 'You sound like I'm gunna do a murder, marra.'

He frowns. 'Isn't there some primitive tribe somewhere who think that if you make their picture you take their souls? Watch out for Marguerite's soul, marra.' He's no fool, is Tegger.

I am looking round the room seeing the orderly clutter through their eyes. 'You make me sound like a bloody vampire, Tegger.' He's right. This is no good. I can't paint her in here. There's too much of my father around.

'Hey, you. Language,' Tegger says idly. 'Lady present.'

I open the middle door. 'Right. Sorry, Marguerite,' I say absently. The front room is in darkness. The curtains have been shut since my father died. My grandmother's heavy parlour furniture sucks what light there's left out of the room. Yes, this will do. 'Hey, give us a hand.' I throw the words over my shoulder and start to push the heavy table to the wall. They help me pile the chairs on top of it. The space becomes a tangle of chair legs and leather-bound boxes.

There's one upholstered chair. I pull it this way and that in the room until it occupies the darkest space. 'Right. That's it.'

Tegger is red with all the effort. 'What a bloody jungle. Sorry, Marguerite.'

The girl is staring narrowly at me. 'What has happened, Gabriel? Something's happened to you.'

'What're you talking about?' I say. But my cheeks burn.

'You're different. You're more . . .' She pulls me round and stares at me. Her pale eyes bore into me. Reflected there I can see myself, sweating and plunging, making the double person with Rosel Vonn. Then she nods. 'You're more certain.'

I drag myself away and heave the press into the corner. Then I cover the looking-glass with my father's old black coat. There is still dust in it, after all this time. It smells of the pit.

Tegger claps his hands. 'I get it. The seam! You're making the seam. Well, kind of.' His voice trails off.

'Where do you want me?' says Marguerite, still staring intently. She goes to stand beside the chair. 'Here?'

Her instinct is fine.

'Yes. Yes. But . . .' But how can I tell her that the earth woman was not wearing a neat jacket with frogged buttons on it, nor was she wearing lisle stockings and shoes with brass buckles. She was, in fact, more or less naked.

She reads my mind and takes off her little hat and the jacket with the brass buttons. She bends down to unbuckle her shoes and looks up at me. 'How was she, this woman in the goaf? Was she naked?'

'Hey Marguerite,' says Tegger. 'Steady on.'

'Well, I'm right, aren't I, Gabe?' She stretches up to unbutton her blouse at the back. 'She'd have no clothes on.'

I look at her steadily. 'Yes.' I say. 'That's right. But there was something over her shoulder. Something with red. Like a flower.'

She continues with her unbuttoning.

'Hey Gabe, yeh canna do this.' Tegger is grim now. He means it.

She folds her blouse neatly and lays it across one of the inverted chair legs. Then she slips out of her skirt. 'It's a picture. Tegger,' she says crossly. 'I've seen them in the gallery. It's art – nothing else. Isn't that right, Gabe?'

'Yeah. Yeah.' I rummage in the kitchen cupboard for my father's old pit lamp and light it. When I return to the front room she is naked except for a cross-cut slip which reaches just above the knee. 'Is this all right?' she says, her eyes still burning into me. Tegger is huffing and puffing beside me.

I place the pit lamp on the edge of the table. Already in my mind the table is a shelf in the seam, a natural consequence of the shot-firer's blast. I look at Marguerite and I know it's not really *all right*. Then she picks up the hem of her petticoat and pulls it over her head, and her full breasts settle slightly lower than they were before. She is larger than Rosel, more generously curved. But she is beautiful.

She drapes the silk petticoat over her shoulder. 'Like this?' she says.

I nod.

Now she reaches up to take down her hair which must be very tightly wound, because once down it falls around her like a rippling black ocean.

I root about in my grandmother's press and emerge with a tangle of red knitting wool. I pin it to the draped petticoat.

'Marguerite!' Tegger sounds desperate now, very young.

'Oh Tegger!' says Marguerite. 'Go and make yourself some tea, will you? Gabriel and me have work to do here. It's work, that's all. Get it into your head.'

This can only happen because Marguerite is so businesslike. I think for a second or two I've been in severe danger of getting punched on the nose by Tegger. As it is he blunders past me and we can hear him clashing the pots in the kitchen. He's not pleased.

'Now,' she says, standing in exactly the right spot. 'Do you want me here?'

It's hard to explain just what happened that morning and all the mornings this week. Bit by bit my father's dark parlour becomes the pit: the area behind Marguerite darkens and condenses itself into the goaf. The struggling beam of the pit lamp touches on the female form before me. The darker shadows in Marguerite's undulating figure and her cloud of black hair seem to join the darkness of the goaf so that she becomes insubstantial. Sometimes she is there; sometimes she is not. Her eyes become passive receptacles of light, only existing because the rays of the lamp call forth some response.

For two days I achieve almost nothing. I am looking and thinking, feeling my way back to that time in the goaf. A line. A marker for distance but that's all. I am thinking about the woman before me; about Rosel who has made me know a woman's body . . .

Rosel has vanished. According to Cora, who is a bit of a sourpuss these days, she's gone down to London. In one way this is a relief, as I didn't know how I would look her in the eye again after that night. In another way it's bad because I long for us to be together in just that way. But she wouldn't permit it: she made that very clear. 'Only this time.' She said it as we parted that night. 'Only this time, Gabriel!'

But without that time how could I now be looking at the body of Marguerite Molloy with such dispassion? I would not be able to conceive in my heart, my brain and my busy fingers what the woman in the goaf really means. But now I know.

She is my grandmother who could pluck beauty from dross; she is my mother who barely mothered me; she is Rosel Vonn turning over and under me, unlocking delights in my soul; she is Marguerite Molloy shrugging herself out of her blouse, knowing me with her eyes; she is the pit, the earth herself opening to receive the miner's tribute then spitting him out again touched by magic even if through his life she breaks him down entirely.

It is not till the third day that I start to work swiftly, blocking the body in, using my miner's sight-memory to raise up the image of the seam with the rainbow gleam on the out-jutting coal in the foreground and the eternal density of dark behind the woman.

Tegger still keeps sentinel, making us cups of tea, banking up the fire for Marguerite to warm herself when the standing still makes her too cold. He goes out now to cadge coal and pick up a sporting paper, lays out his own notebook on the kitchen table, scribbles and crosses out, scribbles and crosses out.

None of this is easy. The way the light works on Marguerite's beautiful brown skin has to be studied. I have scraped off and started again twice. But it is coming.

I will not let them see the picture until the sixth day. Even then I am unwilling, but Tegger has been very patient and wants his reward. So at dinnertime on Saturday I drag the canvas through to the kitchen and pull off the flimsy green cloth I've been using as a cover and turn the canvas towards the light from the kitchen window.

'Oh.' Marguerite sounds a bit disappointed.

'Why,' says Tegger, growling. 'There's nothing there. It's all black.'

'Look!' I say.

They move about the canvas, standing further back.

Marguerite narrows her eyes. 'I see her! I see it!' she says, smiling. 'There is the red wool. Like a pinpoint of light. Or a poppy from Armistice Day.'

'Why, you bugger!' says Tegger. 'One way it's all black. The other it's all there. The woman. The seam. The goaf. Aye. Yeh've got something here, marra.'

'It's not finished,' I say. 'Some of it is not right yet.'

'But you don't need me no more, do you?' says Marguerite Molloy, who seems to know everything.

'No.' I shake my head. 'You've been just right, Marguerite. Thank you for that.'

'So that's the picture for you,' she says. 'Now what about a picture for me? For my own?'

'No,' protests Tegger. 'No more. Let's go down the Raglan. I can't remember the last time I had a pint. All this art makes me very thirsty.'

I let them go then and drag the easel back into the front room. The mocked-up seam is in there, and I need only half-close my eyes and the woman is still there. So much to do to the painting yet but, for the moment, I am satisfied.

Later, I sit at the table with my drawing pad and, from memory, make three sketches of Marguerite. In one she is pinning up her hair. In another she has one hand on her face, in that characteristic way of hers. In the other she is perched on a chair leaning forward, listening, it seems, with her whole body.

I make a roll of these, tie it with string and set out for The Lord Raglan.

Chapter Twenty-Three

Drying

Rosel has not been around for some time. Again I feel two ways about this. One part of me is glad, as I feel too close to her now to be near her casually. I think she feels that, too. The other part of me is dying to see her again, even if it is just to see, not to touch.

But there is plenty to take my mind off her. The goaf woman picture. And the rehearsals are really coming on now. Tegger's alterations have now embedded themselves into the text and drummed themselves into our heads. The words are as natural to us now as breathing. It seems like we've moved on to some other plateau in the play. Archie Todhunter is now focusing on refinements of movement and demeanour; he is adjusting the pace of the whole thing, sometimes speeding it up, sometimes slowing it down.

I've never seen a man conducting an orchestra, although I hear music on the wireless and read pieces in the paper about Sir Henry Wood, but this is how I imagine it happens. A flick of the wrist, a hoisting of the eyebrow and the whole tone changes.

In painting all these clamours and changes, tightenings and adjustments happen within yourself, during that crackling flicker from the eye to the hand. It's an interior, individual thing. With the play it must all be communicated and acted upon.

I have to admit many of my reservations about Archie Todhunter have just about faded away. He *is* obsessed. He *is* self-absorbed. He can be cruel. But I know now he can also be very kind, even insightful in an oblique way. Think about my shoes. And on top of this he has these magical qualities which are tightening this play like a bowstring so that when it takes flight, its message will hit its mark.

This afternoon we run the play right through. Archie has some mate of his here, from his theatre days. I think he wants to show us off a bit. It sharpens us up, puts an edge on us, to perform before the eyes of this stranger. Even Archie, normally so solid, so confident, is all a-flutter.

It goes well. The moves are right, the timing is perfect. My main scene with Greta – halfway through the action – goes particularly well. Her lips part a little as we kiss and cling together. I can feel her body – small, firm as a young branch – against mine. Her look of faint surprise and involuntary joy add to the impact. Yes, all goes well until near the end, when Baffer Bray as Grandpa Pew puffs on to say that the tribunal looks like it's turning our way and that in France the Somme offensive has started.

Cora looks at him. Now's the time for her to embark on her big speech as Maggie Olliphant, in which she sums up the similarity of the situations in the village here, and out in the trenches. Tegger has done some good work on this scene, bringing life and energy into what had been rather a wooden lump of summary from Archie's pen.

Cora sets away, frowns at Baffer Bray, then stops. She starts again, frowning. We can see the lines fading away from her. Mrs Gomersal, the prompt, has found the place and does her prompting in a hoarse whisper. The thing is, the text has been altered by Tegger, pasted over and she gets it mixed up.

Archie's face is white with anger. 'Go back, all of you,' he growls. 'Back to the herald.'

So Baffer does his bit again. This time Cora makes her speech perfectly, stretching it out and slowing it down in just the way we have discussed in recent days.

The play comes to its poignant end where, finally, the names of the dead are intoned on one side by Nathan as the coroner, and on the other by Jake McVay as the corporal in the trench. The final voice is mine, as Arthur writes his last letter to his sweetheart about his hopes for the future.

The visitor out front claps his hands. 'Well done,' he says. 'Well done, everyone. It is a fine play.'

He and Archie begin to talk under their breath, excluding all of us with the intimacy of their conversation. They leave the dusty room, still talking as they go. Archie offers not one glance in Cora's direction.

'Who is he?' asks Greta as we cluster round Cora, who pours tea for us from a large tin teapot.

'Corinthian Small,' says Cora. 'Actor-manager, leading light of The Corinthian Players. They're playing the Newcastle Theatre Royal next week. Chances are that he might put on one of Archie's plays. Perhaps even this one. Archie reckons Small's a coming man. Pity. I spoiled his pudding.' Her voice grates dully, bereft of the actress's normally round tones.

'No!' protests Greta earnestly. 'It can happen to anyone . . .'

Her voice trails off as Cora clashes down the teapot and storms out. 'What have I said?'

Now it's Greta who's upset. Tears glitter in her short-sighted eyes. I jam my cap on my head. 'You off now?' I say. 'I'll walk you, if yer like.'

Cora was sitting behind the desk in Archie's office when he came in to retrieve his heavy coat and his trilby from the coat-stand.

'Where are you off to, then?' she said, standing his pencils up in order of size, like soldiers in a line. 'Off with your friend, are you?'

He shrugged his way into his coat. 'Sarcasm doesn't become you, Cora.'

'It was just a simple question.'

'If it is so important, I'm going to The Three Tuns in Durham to have dinner with Corinthian and the Dean and a few other fellows involved in the Project. Corinthian is very interested.'

She kept her eyes on the pencils. 'You'll enjoy that then, away among your own kind.'

'Cora, what is it? You've been a proper sourpuss for days now. Not your usual self.'

'So you noticed?'

'And then this embarrassment today.'

'Of course you think I did that on purpose. I was mortified. I've never dried on stage. *Never*.'

He tugged down his shirtcuffs and pulled on his pigskin gloves. 'No, no, Cora. Don't worry. We've all dried in our time. And your recovery was the mark of a true professional – Corinthian said so himself. A true professional. Said you'd be an ornament to any troupe.'

'Thank you, Corinthian,' she said with a jabbing nod of her head.

'So?' he said.

'So what?'

'So what *is* the matter with you?'

She stared at him and wondered whether she should tell him the truth of just how she'd made the decision to deny him his immortality; to prevent his having any part in her decision to get rid of the baby.

He glanced at his watch. 'So, Cora?' he said.

She toppled the pencils down on to the desk and forced a laugh. 'Just put it down to women's troubles, Archie. The bane of my life, that.'

Archie relaxed. He became what he saw as his really kind self. 'You have no idea, Cora, how many times I thank God that I'm not a woman. You have my every sympathy in these matters.' So saying, he swung out and the door clashed behind him.

She put out her tongue at the closed door. 'Thank you for that, Archie. That's all I need. Your sympathy.'

Something of the drama that occurred behind us in the big room has affected Greta and me. We're over-conscious of each other as we walk briskly through the bitter damp of the late afternoon. Our hands bump twice mid-swing and the third time I grasp hers so our arms swing together. Her hand is smaller than I thought and soft in mine.

She starts to talk about Cora and her troubles, speaking faster than usual. We reach her gate too quickly and she uses our joined hands to pull me round so I'm facing her. 'Have you thought about what I asked, Gabriel? The favour?'

I'll say one thing for her. She's forthright.

'I've been too busy. These portraits, the play . . . anyway, I said not till November, after the Prince has been.'

'But you have to find out. Have you?'

I've found out a lot of things since we last talked, Greta. The words stay in my head, unspoken. 'No,' I say humbly. 'Not quite.'

'Well, don't forget,' she says, very seriously. Then she reaches up and gives me a good, hard, smacking kiss on the mouth. For a second we are Arthur and Dorothy. Then I watch her go swinging down her yard and catch her mother's face at the kitchen window. Pauline Pallister won't have missed this little episode at all. It's a wonder she wasn't out with her fire iron to give me a good clattering.

She's very protective over Greta.

Chapter Twenty-Four

London

'My dear Rosel! It must be such a relief to be actually *doing* something up there.' Vanessa Bell leaned over to pour tea for Rosel. 'We've done what we can here. Parcels for Spain. Money. We had this fundraising exhibition in Pimlico, did you hear? And we boast to everyone how one of our number is working up there among those unfortunate miners.'

Rosel looked round at the comfortable room with its painted cupboards and its hand-printed curtains, and back at Vanessa's beautiful, slightly worn face.

'There is need for this, Vanessa. Also your efforts with Duncan and the others. Without such efforts so much less would be done.' Rosel had not planned to have tea with Vanessa. She had bumped into her in Bond Street and Vanessa had insisted on calling a taxi and bringing her home to tea.

Rosel had never been intimate with Vanessa or any of the other members of the Artists International group. Still, she'd spent time with them raising funds, going to meetings and agonising over the state of the poor and oppressed. In the end it had been quite a relief to get on the train North and actually do something real.

'It must be too terrible up there, my dear. How can you bear it? I suppose it is far too depressing for you to get any work of your own done?' The other woman seemed genuinely concerned.

'It is very hard, yes. But, no, I am painting again for the first time in years. There are some very fine people there. People of talent. Of course, there is the poverty, so much illness.'

Vanessa nodded gravely. 'You are so brave, dear. How you can work in a place like that . . . well! The mere vagaries of family life perpetually stop me working.' She laughed briefly. 'Although my sister would have it that if I wanted to be an artist I should have resisted the desire to procreate. As she has.' She frowned. 'You, Rosel. Do you have children?'

Rosel laughed and stood up. 'I am afraid not. And now it is rather late.' She looked at the fine clock on the mantelpiece. 'I think I will be late. I have an appointment with Sir Peter Hamilton Souness . . .'

Vanessa raised her brows. 'Peter? He's a dear. You wouldn't believe it, he looks such a stuffy old thing, but he gave us a very generous donation for our Spain fund.' She stood up and shook Rosel heartily by the hand. 'So good of you to report back on your Durham adventure. The others will be fascinated to hear.'

Rosel was outside on the pavement before she realised that she had, in fact, told Vanessa nothing at all significant about her 'Durham adventure'.

Despite this little diversion Rosel was glad to be back in London again. What a relief it was to see the brighter, fuller faces, the more distinctive colours, the newer clothes in the streets and the shops. How restful to be among people unmarked by the stigmata of poverty and consequent starvation.

In her months in Brack's Hill, Rosel's understanding of the specifics of poverty had become more refined. She was beginning to distinguish between those who were out of work and active – albeit dressed in battered clothes and ten-times-mended shoes – and others. Somehow such people, like Gabriel and Tegger MacNamara, seemed to draw luck to them: they manufactured the materials for their own salvation and remained optimistic.

Different from these were the unemployed and inactive people who occasionally flushed on to the street to stand on corners, lean on walls, to pass the long stretches of time before returning to a cold, desolate house. Then there were those very still people who sat in doorways or lurked down alleyways as though there was absolutely nowhere to go. Such stillness had the feeling of the cemetery about it.

Rosel knew very well that London had its own poor and its own hungry. She knew the Depression bit at the heels of people even in this ancient, crowded and wealthy city. But perhaps the pickings from this affluent place were greater. Perhaps the poor were hidden in closed neighbourhoods. In the main, the places where Rosel strode in her quest for her father were peopled by the city dwellers, sober-suited, that you would find in any cosmopolitan city. This she was used to, in Berlin. So in London she felt at home.

On her first day she'd endured a cautious, even uncomfortable interview with a young Secretary at the German Embassy. He'd asked her sharply about her residence in England and her plans for returning home. When she told him about her artistic enterprises in the North he softened a little.

'The much-vaunted greatness of Britain is somewhat invisible these days. It would not be tolerated in our country, such poverty.

It is conquered now, despite the vengeance of our neighbours.' He smiled slightly. 'We have policies, programmes, which will deal with such problems for ever. We are systematic, unlike the British who bumble along with their *ad hoc* do-gooding.'

She let that sink in, then took a breath and asked him about the possibility of her father coming to visit her. He raised his eyebrows.

'He has been ill. I thought he might come here to convalesce.'

'Here?' A high-pitched laugh leapt from the narrow mouth like an escaping rabbit. 'In London with all these fogs? This rain?'

'No,' she said. 'I'll take him to the North.' She took to outright lies. 'The air is clean and clear there. Not like these London fogs.'

To build up her courage for the next visit on her list, Rosel went to a little millinery shop in the West End and spent too much money on an elegant brown hat with a feather. She popped into Marshall & Snelgrove and bought new lingerie and a simple black dress. In Bond Street she came across a small boutique where she purchased a dark green coat with silk frogged fastenings. This was when Vanessa had come upon her and spirited her away for tea.

Later it was with a strand of guilt that Rosel sank into the luxurious bath in her comfortable hotel, and ate the substantial luncheon which was put before her by an attentive waiter. Still, the guilt did not quite mar her pleasure in her new silk stockings and underclothes, in the smooth surface of her fine wool coat. It was a long time since she'd thought the way she looked mattered.

Her appointment with Sir Peter Hamilton Souness was at three-thirty. At three twenty-nine precisely she rang the bell by his name at Frobisher Mansions, a high Edwardian block not far from her hotel in Bedford Square. There were four bells and four names. Would Sir Peter come pounding down the stairs?

The door opened and a long, very young face stared at her. 'Ye-es?' he said.

'I have an appointment with Sir Peter Hamilton Souness,' she said, her chin up. 'My name is Rosel Von Steinigen.'

The door opened wider, revealing the body which went with the face. It belonged to a young man of perhaps nineteen. He wore the dark jacket of a servant and an incongruous green striped tie with his soft-collared shirt. He nodded at her. 'Yes, Miss. Sir Peter is expecting you.' The words were chanted like a learned script. He opened the door wider and she stepped in. 'We're on the top floor, Miss. But fortuitously there is a lift.'

Fortuitously! The accent was high-pitched, nasal. Gabriel came into Rosel's mind. His voice came from somewhere deep, near his immaculate second-hand brogue shoes. This boy was somewhere near Gabriel's age. Rosel couldn't imagine Gabriel fetching and carrying for a gentleman. Even young Tegger would not do this menial stuff.

The lift was small, its door ornately designed as a parade of cast-iron pelicans. She noted the fine workmanship. The boy stood by her side. His eyes slid round to appraise her. 'I see you like green, Miss.' His tone was cocky. Not so subservient after all.

'Yes, I do.'

'Me too. Green's my favourite colour.'

The lift whirred to a halt and he pulled upon the door. 'Here we are, Miss.' He opened a heavy mahogany door. Then he altered his demeanour and spoke out of the side of his mouth.

'I'd watch him this afternoon, Miss. Got up in a paddy and has got worse as the day's gone on.'

They were in a square hall furnished with a fine Turkish carpet, with a single table holding a silver tray placed precisely at its centre. The boy knocked, then opened the door on his right. 'Miss Rosel Von . . . Von . . .'

'Steinigen,' she supplied, moving forward into a room which, to compensate for the dingy afternoon light, was illuminated by two large standard lamps which stood each beside its own winged armchair. Peter Hamilton Souness raised himself from one of these, moved towards her and took her hand. He was taller than she was, grey-haired and slight. He had an scar on his left cheek.

'Miss Von Steinigen. How good of you to call. Brownson!' He looked away from her towards the boy. 'Tea, I think.'

'Yes, sir,' said the boy called Brownson. 'Thank you, sir.'

Sir Peter drew Rosel into the circle of light cast by the taller lamp. 'Ah, Fraulein. I see in you traits of both your mother and your father.' He paused. 'Your mother was a great beauty.'

She laughed. 'In that I do not favour her.'

'Won't you sit down?'

She sat in the circle of one lamp and he settled down opposite her, the smaller lamp throwing light on to the unblemished side of his face, showing his delicate profile.

'Perhaps not, Miss Von Steinigen. Perhaps you inherit more of your father's elegant demeanour. Handsome rather than . . .'

'Sir Peter, I don't think . . .'

He put up a hand. 'You're right, my dear. It is rude of me to be so personal. We have just met, after all.' He settled back in his chair and his face dropped into shadow.

'My father has told me that you and he were good friends in your youth.'

'So we were. We skied together, swam together, fenced together.' His narrow hand touched his scarred cheek lightly. 'We also danced together and gambled together, in the summer before old King Edward breathed his last. They were such happy times. All was right with the world in those days.'

'He always spoke of those days with great nostalgia, great affection.'

'He was fine company. And a fine artist.' Sir Peter stood up. 'Anticipating your visit, I looked out some old papers and I found this.' He went to the desk and returned with a drawing mounted on card. It was unframed. The man depicted was clearly Sir Peter himself, but he was younger, fuller-faced; his cheek was not scarred. The hair curled more fully and fell over his face a little. He was smiling a peculiarly sweet smile.

'You must have been very young, Sir Peter. It is a good likeness.'

He nodded. 'We thought of nothing but travelling about and sport and larks in those days. In retrospect it seems we were filling the cup which we knew would be spilt.' His voice fell away and he stared at the painting as though seeing it for the first time. 'Of course, your father did not just sport and play. He drew and painted. Made us feel like lazy oiks.'

'It is his life,' she ventured. 'Drawing and painting.'

'Life!' He surveyed her from under beetling brows. She had the sense that he was put out by her interruption of his idyll. 'Yes. Yes. He did some fine paintings during the war, you know.'

She didn't like to say that yes, she did know. This was her father they were speaking about, after all. 'Saw him in 1923 and he gave me that book.' He nodded at the familiar tome on the table, the twin of the one in Archie Todhunter's office. 'Their trenches. Ours. What's the difference? Such wonderful drawings. A terrible war between old comrades.'

His monologue was interrupted by a rattle at the door. Brownson, now dressed in a white jacket and white gloves, entered, pushing a small trolley on which sat a silver teapot, two china cups and saucers and a plate of plain ginger biscuits.

'Ginger biscuits?' said Sir Peter. 'Can't we run to cakes, Brownson?'

'Sorry, Sir Peter. I would if I could. I could always nip out to Longton's for a few cakes, but—'

Sir Peter put up a hand. 'Cease! Cease! Ginger biscuits will do.' He looked at Rosel. 'Will ginger do, Miss Von Steinigen?'

She nodded. 'I like ginger biscuits. I do like them.' Oh dear. Too emphatic in her anxiety for the boy.

'That is a relief. Leave the teapot, Brownson. Miss Von Steinigen will pour.'

She sat forward on the seat to attend to the teapot as Brownson backed off and shut the door behind him. They could hear him whistling in the hall. Sir Peter raised his brows. 'I had hoped I would make something of that boy but now I am in doubt. Can't abide serving women about the place, but these boys take some bringing on.'

Rosel laughed and handed him his cup. 'I think he is an exceptional young man. Such cheer. He seems very keen.'

'You think so? I am relieved to hear it.' He sat back again in his chair and sipped delicately at his tea. He looked at her over the rim of his cup. 'Now then, my dear. How do you find yourself here in England?'

Having put her at her ease he now proved to be a good listener. His intent gaze and his occasional query prompted

Rosel to tell him all about living with her uncle in Sunderland, of her studies in London, her attempts to make a living from painting and her work at the Settlement.

'Now that must be a thankless task for you,' he murmured. 'There is so much to do about this poverty and no will to tackle it head on here in England. As always we wait for it to fade away. Your own Government has it all in hand, I hear.'

She stared at him for a moment, and could not deny what he said. It had been the message of the man at the Embassy too. Some might claim they were right. Roads were being built, guns were being made. There was a new prosperity in the land. 'It is my father, Sir Peter. I came to talk with you about him.'

'Perhaps you would be kind enough to call me Peter. How is he these days?'

'Well . . . He is physically well.'

'And does he still paint?'

She shook her head. 'I can't think so. He's in some kind of trouble. He was arrested.'

He frowned. 'Arrested? Old Max? Now that *is* a surprise. What has he done – robbed a bank? Acquired a work of art by nefarious means?'

'He was arrested,' she said, 'because he spoke out. About his friend Herr Doktor Goldstein whose house was taken.'

'And what had this man done? Had *he* robbed a bank?'

'No,' she said impatiently. 'It is the prohibition on the Jews. Many of my father's friends have been affected by this.'

Sir Peter frowned. 'I read of new arrangements . . .'

'Well, my father was in prison for two nights. They humiliated him and he is not even a Jew. Goodness knows what happens to the Jews.'

Peter took a sip of his tea and his glance strayed from her to the window. 'So what do you wish me to do?'

'I wondered if, somehow, he could come here. He would be safer here.'

'Would he come? He's a great patriot. He would not leave Germany, surely?'

'It is not the same. The country is not the same.'

'No? We have good reports of it. We hear that the future is being forged.'

'We?'

'No matter. So you want your father here?'

'It's the only thing I can think of. To keep him safe.'

As she nibbled at a ginger biscuit she noted his teeth which were too large and slightly yellowing to be anything but his own. He looked at her from under those beetling brows.

'I shall see what I can do, my dear. A word in a few ears works wonders, don't you know? I will give you my telephone number here in London. Telephone me one week from now and perhaps there'll be something to tell. Now then, your father's address in Berlin . . .?'

Chapter Twenty-Five

The Honourable Thing

'Can you do something for us, kidder?'

I look up into Nathan Smith's lined face. I'm drinking a welcome cup of tea in the Settlement kitchen as I've run out of everything, even tea at home. Tegger has just gone in to see Mr Todhunter. The news is, another story he has written is to be in one of these magazines he's always talking about.

'Aye. What is it, Mr Smith?'

He sits down opposite me and looks at me earnestly. 'D'you know that the German woman . . .'

'You mean Rosel Vonn?'

'Aye, her. Well, she painted this picture of us, you know like the ones you did of Todhunter and Greta Pallister.'

'Yes. But she says you had second thoughts about it.'

'Aye. Seemed like such vanity, like, sitting there. And when I saw myself, why . . .'

'You were embarrassed?'

'Aye. Seemed like so much showing off?'

'So you didn't want it shown.'

'No. I told her so an' all, and I think she's put out. Not too pleased.' He sits there staring into space a second.

'Well, Mr Smith, I'd'a thought that was your right, if you didn't want it seen.'

'Aye, but the trouble is, now I've seen the others round the place and see it's all about the play, not about the folks in the pictures. And I'm a bit, well . . . I thought it wasn't right on her.' He's still looking away from me, out of the narrow window.

'So . . .?'

'I went looking for her to say mebbe we *should* put it up with the others, but she's nowhere around. Cora Miles says she's gone to London and she doesn't know when she'll get back. So I wondered if you could get it for me and I could have another look, and mebbe we could hang it alongside the others.'

'Well, I don't know . . .'

'Look, I'm gunna have to tell the woman I'm sorry, isn't that enough? If she sees it up when she gets back, that'll be half the battle.'

In the painting shed are the racks Tegger has built from old floorboards, so we can leave work there. Nathan's portrait is tucked in Rosel's space alongside a big battered folder with her name on it. I haul it out and put it on an empty easel underneath the skylight. It is really good. It is lightly painted in her style but he is there to the life. She's done something very clever. Nathan sits there, the respectable coroner to the tip of his polished boots. But also it is still, ineffably, Nathan the big miner who has spent half his life scratting for coal underground and yet still retained his dignity and humanity. 'It's good,' I say. 'Very good.'

'Aye, I thowt you'd say that,' he says. 'Now can we get it in the room beside the others?'

It'll be nice for her to see it hanging on the wall when she gets back. But maybe she won't bother to come back. Maybe London is a softer option than up here. Who could blame her?

I would. I want her here. I'm refreshed by tea and stirred by thinking of her and suddenly I want to go back home and get on with my painting of the woman in the goaf. There are still things about it that are not right, not right at all. I turned the bundle of red wool into an actual poppy and that was a big mistake. It'll have to come off.

Rosel arrived home to what seemed like an empty Settlement House and a letter which looked as though it had been dipped in seawater.

Liebchen,
I understand Boris has recounted to you my rather difficult news. To explicate: it was not just the fact of the arrest. In that dark place they made me strip off my clothes. I was so much reminded of that first time as a boy when I came to England to school. They made me strip as well, then, to my bare skin. In the cell here, at least they shouted at me in my own language. What language! What words! They talked about betrayal. I told them of my work in the war and my medals. I shouted to them that there was no greater patriot than I. That was when they struck me, with their fists and the butt of an old rifle. And they laughed and joked as they did it. Lachelt! It was so much worse than the laughter of those foreign boys in that English school. Two nights of this and I was sure there would be worse to come. I slept in snatches and I dreamed of you and Boris and the time you visited Berlin. Do you remember? On

the second night in prison I thought I saw your mother, ghostlike, before the bars. She was wearing that long, red scarf. Do you remember it?

Then the next morning they came into the cell and I looked at the wall, not wanting to look towards them. They threw my clothes on the floor and leaned on the wall and laughed and nudged each other as I dressed myself. This was hard, with the injuries to my right hand. It passed through my mind that at least at one's execution one was allowed the dignity of trousers.

Then the officer came in, clicked his heels and called me Meinherr and told me he knew quite well my book of war sketches and that his father had fought in France.

It seemed that there was to be no execution. Boris was there and I think I babbled and moaned to him I know not what. He was not in his uniform but is still as beautiful as ever. He is worried now, with some justification, about his own position.

The apartment was open when I returned. For a day I thought things were back to normal, except for the injury to my right hand which meant I could not execute my daily drawings. Then the next day when I went to the Institute the doorkeeper barred my way and told me that no man of my name worked in that august institution and that I should launch myself back into the gutter where belonged all traitorous scum.

So I am safe for the moment. I thought you might wish to know this even though our paths have diverged in recent years and your uncle, my much-mourned brother, became your father in my place.
Your affectionate Papa.

* * *

Rosel stood in the passageway between Archie's office and the stairs and read the letter twice. She closed her eyes and leaned against the wall, clutching it to her. It was strange that at this stage in her life she was being called on to take care of her father; that having escaped his suffocating care as a child it was now her turn to care for him, to feel protective love towards him, instead of the wary regard she had cultivated all her adult life to keep him at a distance.

When she was a girl his obsession, his rapt attention to every detail of herself and her life had been oppressive. Now though, she felt affection, appreciation, even love for him. A victim himself, he no longer held any threat for her. Somewhere inside her she relished the change.

So she was glad that she'd done what she could. Sir Peter seemed confident that things could be taken in hand despite being rather vague about the options. But now this letter meant there *was* only one option. Her father had to get out. She would have to take care of him. She looked along the narrow hall cluttered with books and boxes, stage props and dumb-bells. He could not stay here. She would have to make enquiries about renting a house. There were empty houses enough in this half-derelict town. The rent would be cheap.

On the second landing she bumped into Cora, who was reeling from the bathroom to the bedroom she shared with Archie. She was as white as a ghost. Rosel shoved the letter into her pocket and took the other woman's arm. 'Cora, you're ill.'

Cora smiled wanly. 'Yes. Not quite tickety-boo. Bleeding again. Bit of reaction, perhaps. I thought it would be all right, like last time.'

Rosel helped her into the bedroom and on to the bed. 'I should get a doctor.'

Cora shook her head. 'I need to rest, and then I will be all right. It only took a couple of days last time. It will take longer now as I'm such an ancient wretch. Rehearsal Wednesday night. So long as I am well by then.'

'I thought that it was over?'

Cora smiled wearily. 'That's what I told you. But there's this bleeding.'

Rosel tucked her into the bed and leaned across and plumped up her pillows. 'You should really tell Archie.'

Rosel felt rather than saw Cora's vehement rejection of her idea. 'Not his business, darling. Not his business.' She took a breath. 'So how was dear old London? Nice to get away from the dark satanic mills into the bright lights, eh?' She managed a chuckle. 'And did you get your business done, darling? Paramour, was it? A good-looking woman like you is wasted among these poor dejected folk.'

'Even if, like you, I am a bit of an *ancient wretch*?' Rosel laughed. 'No, it wasn't a paramour, you bad thing. And as far as I can see, the people here might be poor but they're not dejected. At least not those who come to the Settlement.' She thought of Gabriel and wanted to see him, talk to him. She'd go, first thing in the morning. Not for . . . *that*. Definitely not that. They had agreed. But she wanted to talk to him about her father and her brother. With Cora in this state and Archie so distracted there was no one else to tell. She would go tomorrow, after the morning class.

That night she sat in Archie's study and turned over the leaves of her father's war book. She looked into the faces of the men and boys there; she appraised the sensitivity and the specialist skills of her father, the artist. She looked at the crumpled bodies, the strained faces, the weary eyes. The images scattered by explosion: bodies dismembered, without centre. The sense of civilisation in breakdown. The Kaiser, now in exile, had a copy of this volume, and was said to be very fond of it. He had attended the ceremony in person to pin the medal on her father's chest, in recognition of his artistic valour.

Some of the faces shown were so young, embittered but lacking in guile. Surely there was some honour, even in these slimy sodden trenches. But there was no honour in the way her father and his old friends were being treated. None at all. Were there still men of honour in Germany? There must be. Her brother Boris was surely not the only one. So what would they do now? And if they did it, would they themselves be shot? Or worse. Her father was in danger but surely so, too, was Boris. How could they tolerate this?

She sighed, closed the book and put it back in its canvas case. She would see Archie. Perhaps Gabriel could have the book. It would go alongside his Rembrandt book and be another authority for his reference. So he would know that, in her country, there were still men of honour. Her father and her brother were among these. One could only pray it would not lead to their downfall.

Chapter Twenty-Six

The Gallery

You might think it strange that at my age I've never been as far as the twenty-five miles I'm travelling this morning. I've been in a train all right; to Priorton, the nearest big town, and to Durham for miners' meetings when I still had faith in the Union.

As well as that, Tegger and me once went on the train to spend a day at the coast. That day we walked up and down in caps and mufflers, heads bent against the cutting wind. I liked the roaring sea which continually made and remade itself. I picked up two stones, smashed them and opened them up to ammonites more ancient maybe than my father's fossils. I have them now in the same box as the fossils. Tegger wrote this ragged rhyming poem about our time that day by the sea with the coal sludge tippling from the coal staithes into the seething foam.

But Newcastle is a different thing altogether. This is a city, a big black sprawling place spiked with shipping. The long streets and the warehouses cling to the shores of this great greasy river which moves and ultimately flows out into the very sea that me and Tegger walked by three years ago.

The train puffs its way over the high bridge and the line of high buildings is laid out before you like it's this great canvas. Even the smoke and grime cannot disguise the grandeur and grace of the buildings rising up behind the massive warehouses on the quayside.

Parts of the quayside are ominously shadowy and quiet. There is little work; the unemployment affects dockers and shipbuilders the same as us coalminers.

Once out of the station, which is some kind of big cathedral, the city surges around you. Marguerite Molloy knows her way around and leads us up this great busy street like it was her own front yard. She takes us into the Old Lion Café where we're served meat, potatoes and carrots by a woman in a crisp white apron. I have to admit we wolf it down. It's a good while since I've had a meal off a plate like this. My life does not involve meals on a whole plate. It might for some of the lads, whose wives weave wonders, but not for me there in the house on my own.

Marguerite pays for the meal like she paid for the train. We can't object, as there's no money in our pockets. She's wearing a pale grey coat with cloth buttons and a grey cloche hat piped in red. She draws glances wherever she goes, from men and women both.

It was Marguerite who suggested I bring some drawings along with me, to show the people at the gallery. I told her they'd not be interested in some lad off the street. She called me an old sobersides and bought this music case from the pawnshop, insisting I fill it with sketches. I did so to humour her but I know I'm right. They won't be interested.

Still, it's a day out and the company is all right. Tegger's on good form, spinning like a top across the wide pavements, peering into shop windows, swinging round stone columns like a street kid round a lamp-post. Now and then he grabs Marguerite's hand and she suffers it for a few minutes then wriggles away.

All this liveliness fizzles out of us a bit when we stop before the double doors of the Laing Art Gallery and look at them with some awe, taken aback by their height and dignity. An old woman with severe hair and a black coat comes up the steps behind us and glares at us until we give way. The doors don't worry *her*. She opens them as though these great doors were the doors to her own house.

One door is just swinging back when Tegger catches hold of it. 'Come on, marra,' he says. 'You and me's been in scarier places.'

The big hallway inside smells of wax polish and mild chemicals, and looks like the main hall in the Grammar School. A woman at a table behind a kind of glass partition looks up. Her glance falters down past our threadbare coats to our shoes and back up again. Maybe she doesn't see lads in their dusty Sunday best each day. Maybe it's just the shine on my black brogue shoes.

'Yes?'

'We've come to see the pictures.' My voice echoes in the high room and trembles in the dust.

'We brought some pictures,' Tegger rushes in. 'My mate here is a painter.' He grabs the music case and pushes it towards her on her table.

She takes off her glasses and peers at me. 'A painter, is he?'

'I told you,' he said. 'Look at them pictures. You'll have seen nowt like them.'

'It's not up to me,' she sniffs. 'I don't know whether the assistant curator is at the gallery today.'

'I bet you say that to all the artists,' grins Marguerite. 'You should look at them. I've seen some of your pictures here. These are as good as some of those. I'm telling you.'

The woman's mild eyes sweep up to Marguerite's smart hat and drop to the bobbin heels of her shoes. '*You* tell *me*, do you?' She sniffs again.

I reach out for the case. 'No need to bother,' I say.

But the woman's hand comes down on mine, preventing me from taking it away again. It is a surprisingly smooth hand: small, white and well-kept. The nails are polished. The fingers are plump, like little white rolls of dough. I look back up at the woman's mild, lumpy face in surprise.

'Leave it,' she says. 'I'll ask someone to take a look at them.'

'We have to get off for the three-forty train. We can't leave it,' says Tegger firmly.

'Go and look at the exhibits!' She is equally firm. 'Come back in an hour.'

We wander off, not quite knowing where or even how to look. Gradually I begin to take it all in. The walls are heavy with great dark canvases, pictures of men of importance with the accoutrements of their high trades around them. Shipmen and judges, aldermen and patrician women. In some the paint has dried and is chipped with age, and the characters of the people protrayed are masked rather than revealed by the painting. I think of the lightness, the sheer transparency of the way Rosel paints and the jewel-like depths of Rembrandt even in book prints I know I've seen even better than these pictures here.

Then I come across smaller pieces with more recognisable

contexts. Moorland landscapes where the painters have captured the peculiar qualities of the light. I think of a painting in my Rembrandt book, of a landscape in a thunderstorm. I turn a corner and come across a seascape where the turbulence of the sea is perfectly captured by the still magic of colour. There is a seascape by Turner which tops them all. It is just sea and sky, but is sheer light. The breath is knocked out of me. I am winded by it.

'Gabe! Gabe! Come on, marra!' Tegger is tugging my sleeve. 'It's after three! Yer standing there in a daze.'

The woman at the table is smiling slightly. 'Did you enjoy the exhibits?'

I nod. 'It's a great eye-opener,' I say. 'I liked the Turner.'

She nods. 'He is not so fashionable these days, but that is a great painting. His handling of light . . .'

My turn to nod. 'It's magic.'

'Well, Mr . . .'

'Marchant.'

'Mr Marchant. The assistant curator has looked at your drawings and has told me to inform you that we have a summer exhibition for amateur painters, and that he would welcome a submission by you.'

'He's not an amateur,' says Tegger, jutting out his chin.

'Well,' I say. 'Mebbe aspiring rather than amateur.' I'm properly humbled by what I've seen.

'He did say this was promising work.' She hesitates. 'These two drawings . . .' She has them under the case rather than on it. One is a sketch of Marguerite bending to unbuckle her shoe, her long arm a graceful arc down the side of the page. The other is an old one of my father asleep in his chair, his head to one side, his mouth slightly open. One arm hangs over the side of the chair, the other, calloused and workworn, is curled in his lap.

The woman looks me in the eye. 'I have a friend who works in a small commercial gallery in the town. Do you mind if I show her these?'

I shake my head dumbly.

'Man!' says Tegger.

'If you give me your address, I will write to you with what she says.'

I scribble it down. It's probably the last I'll see of these drawings. But it has to be something if somebody – especially somebody who works in an art gallery – thinks they're worth showing to someone else.

There was no answer when Rosel knocked at the door of the low house. She knocked four times then, very tentatively, reached for the sneck and clicked the door open. She found herself in a narrow scullery with a shelf containing a row of empty jars and an enamel bowl on a stool beneath a single tap. Dishes were stacked on another shelf and a single gas ring stood on the table under the window.

An archway led into a square kitchen with the customary black range. The fire was dead ash, but when she touched it, the iron range still held residual warmth. The room seemed chaotic at first, with piles of papers and books scattered around and half-done drawings pinned up on the wall. It dawned on her that there was some order in the piles, some sequence in the drawings. The kitchen table was set up with rows of paints, two wooden bread boards for palettes and jam jars containing, she presumed, turps and oil. On the sewing machine under the window lay a hefty volume of Rembrandt prints, which was open at *The Ascension of Christ* with the foreground figures almost entirely in the dark and the background figure of Christ illuminated from above. She turned the pages to another painting Gabriel had marked, of *Bathsheba*, the woman opulently, luxuriantly naked, a note clasped in her powerful hand.

Rosel turned her head this way and that to listen to the house. It was quiet; there was no noise from the street. Then she opened the door to the front room. It was in complete darkness. She had to squeeze past upturned furniture to turn up the gas lamp to illuminate the curtained room. Here indeed was chaos. Chairs and tables were pushed back against the wall, heaped higgledy-piggledy on top of each other. She turned to survey the room and blinked hard. In the middle of it, on a clumsy joiner-made easel, was a very large painting. She peered at it, then dragged it round to face the light from the kitchen door. Now she could make it out. A dark foreground with a barely lit figure of a man – intent, rigid with fear or wonder. In the deep middle ground was the figure of a naked woman, more slender than Bathsheba but borrowing her glowing flesh tones. She had some kind of drape over her shoulder with a flower pinned to it. Her gaze was not Bathsheba's modest sideways glance; this woman looked directly, powerfully out at the crouching man and past him, out of the picture at whoever else might dare to look.

The way the woman was lit was strange. At one angle she was entirely in the dark. At another angle she was in the light. Unlike Rembrandt's Christ with light streaming from above, this woman drew light from somewhere inside herself. Behind her, surrounding her, framing her, was the densest of black; a blackness enhanced by graining of purple and red, green and aquamarine.

Rosel took a breath. What had the boy been up to? This was

in a different class from his naively gifted paintings of Greta and Cora. Derivative as it was, this painting had something unique, something of himself in it. Obviously he was keeping it secret. She frowned. Why had he not spoken to her about it? Perhaps he'd taken too much to heart what she and Archie had said about copying. How many hours had this taken? He must have burned the midnight oil. Is that not what the English said?

She heard the click of the kitchen door and froze. Then she sighed. She'd been caught snooping and would have to pay the consequences.

'Gabriel?' she called.

'Gabriel?' came the echo.

She went through the middle door to face, not Gabriel but another woman, tall, a little stout, not much older than herself.

'Gabriel?' repeated the other woman, fine dark brows arching. 'Is he here?'

Rosel smiled. 'I was looking for him myself,' she shrugged, and put her hand out to shake the other woman's. 'I am Rosel Vonn, Gabriel's art teacher. Or friend, perhaps. I teach him to paint.'

The woman shook her hand warmly. 'So you're responsible for all this?' She nodded at the walls. 'More like a studio than a kitchen, isn't it?' There was an attractive lilt to her voice.

'And you're . . .?'

'I am his auntie, Susanah Clelland. It is a while since I saw Gabriel and I wondered how he was doing. Seems like he's doing all right.' She moved to the window and peered at the Rembrandt book. 'Ah. He made some use of it, then.'

'You gave him this book?'

Susanah smiled happily. 'Well, there's no college for him round here, so I thought the book might help.'

'He is certainly inspired,' said Rosel.

Susanah peered at the sketches on the wall. 'Goodness, what progress he's made. Look at those figures. You must be pleased with your pupil. You are obviously a fine teacher.'

Rosel shrugged. 'He teaches himself. He finds his own way.' She hesitated. 'There is a big piece in the front room . . .' She led the way. 'Nothing to do with me. I believe it was something of a secret.'

On seeing it, Susanah let out a long, unladylike whistle. 'Well, what's he saying here? Look at that woman.'

'It's a very ambitious piece of work. The first time I have seen it.'

'So what do you think of it? Do you think it is good?'

'Yes.' She went into the kitchen and turned the leaves of the Rembrandt book. 'It is full of references. Look – see those dark figures in this painting? And see how he's used Bathsheba as a reference for the woman figure?'

Susanah frowned. 'Yes. Yes. But this woman is entirely herself. Lit from within, see? See the way the black hair spangles up with the wall behind? Yes! It's in the pit, and this man here, scared nearly witless, is a miner. She's kind of . . . a dark goddess.'

'I see this,' murmured Rosel. 'Before I was only seeing the references, but now . . .'

'Have you had an eyeful, then?' The voice that came from behind them was hard, jeering. 'Poking in where nobody invited you?'

Chapter Twenty-Seven

Caught

They whirl round like a pair of thieves caught in the act. My Aunt Susanah is the first to break the silence. 'Well, Gabriel, we didn't hear you coming.'

'That seems likely, seeing as you're poking around.'

'We were just . . .' says Rosel. Here in my house, among my things she takes on the aspect of a stranger: a woman nearer my aunt than me.

'Poking your nose in other people's affairs.' I push my way past them to turn down the gaslight. The front room and the painting sink into darkness. The women back into the kitchen. I follow them and throw shut the room door firmly behind me.

My Aunt Susanah is the least embarrassed. And to be honest it's really difficult to stay on your dignity with someone who was witness to your naked childhood. She sits down in my father's chair and says, 'Well, Gabriel, no cup of tea for your old auntie or your teacher?'

You never know when she has her tongue in her cheek, that one.

I'm still fuming as I fill the kettle, and put out my father's best cups and saucers. When I parted from Marguerite and Tegger at the railway station, I wanted no talk. I only wanted to think. To see with my inner eye the magical light on that canvas of Turner's. All light, no surface, no outlines. Only light, only dark. What I wanted most this evening was to sit and close my eyes and think of the Turner. And to imagine those pictures and those frames and those people walking by in the gallery, sharing with me the visions of the painter. What must it be like, for people to see your work at its best like that, and to understand what you're trying to say without a word said? Brack's Hill now seems to me a small place, away from everything that means something. This makes me sad and I want to pursue the sadness on my own.

The two women are talking round and through me: about art and painting and Germany and the problems of German rearmament: about Berlin and the way things are the same there as here, only in some ways so very different. Rosel tells Susanah about her father and some problems he has, living there. And my brain is still hanging on to Turner's wonderful swirl of light.

I put cups and saucers into their hands and now it's like they are *both* my aunties, even though Rosel is more slender, more youthful. 'I'll leave you two to it,' I say. 'I've gotta do something.' I grab my cap and scarf and race out. At first it is just to escape but I find myself making my way up through the town towards the pit heap and the reservoir. I walk the paths of my childhood, scramble the heap and pick up a fossil of what looks like half the body and the wings of a firefly. No head. After a while my breathing returns to normal and my vision of Turner's sky stops thumping away on the core of my brain.

I get to thinking that it was Rosel there, in my house, when I had this brainstorm. Rosel there, talking to my Aunt Susanah. My body quickens as it remembers making love with her in the workshed and I wonder what tricks my brain has played on myself in seeing her as my auntie's mirror. This is *Rosel*. My friend. For a moment my lover.

When I get back to the house the door is open as usual but the house is empty. I've no idea how long I've been out. My father's old wall clock tells me two and a half hours. So I set out again. Rosel will be back at the Settlement. I have to talk to her about the Turner and that great building in Newcastle stuffed full of pictures and frames like a Rajah's palace.

As I go into the Settlement there is a kerfuffle in the small vestibule and my heart sinks. Jake McVay and Greta. I've missed the rehearsal.

Greta is beside me, her eyes glittering fiercely behind her glasses. 'Where were you? Tegger had to read your lines and do you know what? He really kissed me! I had to kiss Tegger! I slapped his face. Archie was mad.' The sides of that full mouth are pulled down. 'Archie was shouting at everyone. Ready to cut his throat as far as I could see.'

'Sorry, sorry. I forgot.'

'*Forgot?* Well!' She pouts, looking older now than her sixteen years. 'Better things to do, have we?'

I catch up with Archie in the office. 'Look Archie, I'm so sorry . . .'

He flicks a hand at me. 'Don't worry, dear boy. You didn't let me down – you just let down young Greta and Nathan. All the people who've been your friends and comrades all these months. We started half an hour late and not one of them turned in a performance worth a bucket of fish.'

'Look. I've been to Newcastle today, and this just slipped my mind . . .'

'Slipped your mind, did it? Well, it didn't slip Tegger's mind. Here on the dot was young Tegger. And he, I believe, accompanied you on your afternoon odyssey?'

The sarcasm of the man.

'Well, mebbe Tegger should be Arthur. Mebbe he's a better type, being on time and all that. He might as well. Seeing as he wrote all the words, like.' I pause. Archie likes to keep up the fiction that the play is his alone. 'All the words that count.'

My betrayal hangs in the air. Archie busies himself with inserting a new cigarette in his holder and lighting it with the butt of the old one. He grips the holder with his teeth and speaks through it. 'Get out,' he says. 'Get out of my office.'

Only Cora is left in the hallway. With a turban round her head and that white face she looks twenty years older. Seems like she's making a good fist of the role of Maggie. Lives it outside the play. 'I'm looking for Rosel,' I say. 'Is she here?'

She frowns at me as though she doesn't know me from Adam. 'Rosel? Oh, Gabriel! Where were you tonight? Archie was spitting coals. Big trouble. You mustn't cross him, you know. It doesn't pay.'

'I got . . . I got delayed.'

She takes off her character-shawl and folds it carefully into a square. 'Well now. You should remember that to Archie Todhunter, what preoccupies *him* is the centre of the universe.'

'Seems like.'

She takes off her turban and her abundant toffee-coloured hair falls about her shoulders. This should make her look younger, but it doesn't. 'But you got here,' she says, 'in the end?'

'I am looking for Rosel,' I say again.

'Oh.' She stares at me very hard. Her eyes spread very wide as though we are deep in water and she can't quite make me out. Then she glances back at the empty corridor. 'She's upstairs in her eyrie,' she says. 'Keep going till you can't stop. Yellow door.'

She is my conspirator. I belt up the stairs three at a time but hesitate outside the yellow door. Push my hand through what's left of my hair; straighten up my necktie. Then I knock on the door. A strangled voice invites me in and I am inside.

Rosel is tying a green silk dressing gown with a yellow tasselled tie. The room smells spicy and over-warm. The tall single lamp softly illuminates the side of her face.

'Gabriel!' she says. 'I thought you were Cora.'

'She sent me here. I was looking for you.'

She picks up a brush to smooth her already smooth hair. 'Archie was raging about you at the rehearsal.'

Back at my house she looked as old as my Aunt Susanah. Now she looks as young as Greta Pallister. 'I know. Everyone has said so, and you can see it on his face.'

'Why did you run away?' She sits down on the bed.

'You were there, poking about my things. With my aunt.'

'I apologise. I apologised then. It was wrong. It was . . . a moment.' She looks up at me. 'I see Nathan's portrait is beside the others. How did that get there?'

'He talked to me. Seems he changed his mind. It looks well there, doesn't it?'

'I am pleased that you think so,' she says, staring at me with those light eyes of hers.

I sit down on a chair beside the door and stretch out my legs in front of me. My brogue shoes – highly polished for the trip to Newcastle – shine in the lamplight.

'Your auntie seems very nice,' she says.

'She's all right. I only see her now and then, but yes, she's all right. She's very intelligent. Her husband's a teacher. She gave me . . .'

'. . . the Rembrandt book. So she says.'

'You had no business, being there in my house, poking about my things,' I burst out.

She throws the hairbrush at the mirror. There is a loud crash but the mirror refuses to break. 'Gabriel Marchant! You are as bad as Archie Todhunter. You live in your own little world. You need something to worry about.' She picks up a letter from the bedside table and throws that at me. It floats to my feet. I open it up. *Liebchen*. I can't understand a word. 'What's this?' I drop it back on the floor.

She comes across and kneels down to pick it up. I can see the shadow of her small breasts in the neck of the gown and one part of my mind registers that she is naked underneath.

She smooths out the paper on the sparse carpet and, haltingly, begins to translate it. As the story of her father's persecution falls from her lips I begin to understand her despair at my truculence, my self-absorption. I've read of nasty things happening in Germany. I've heard the old men in the Raglan turn it over then turn it back to their own experience on the Somme. I've mouthed Arthur's words in the play, about a land fit for heroes and injustice to the survivors of that terrible war. Maybe the Germans too needed a land fit for heroes and look what was happening to them.

But this story is about an old man being beaten in his own

country for acts of simple humanity. And here is his daughter doing her bit for people here, not looking to her home country.

'My brother Boris also wrote. He, who had great faith in the New Germany, is faltering. He is in the army, doing well, but all this makes him doubt. I think there are plots, plans to get rid of the cause of all this problem. This will certainly put him in danger.'

'I can see that.' How poor words are in this situation.

'I was in London to try to get help for my father. He needs papers to get out. Money. A welcome in a strange land.'

'Did you manage to get some help?' I say. Very humble now.

'I don't know. Gabriel, I don't know.' There are tears in her eyes.

Now I am kneeling beside her, take her near-naked body in my arms. I comfort her as a mother comforts her child. I think this must be how they do it, although I have no memory of it myself. I stroke her and murmur half-words. I push her hair from her face and smooth it down.

Then she takes hold of my hand and presses it beside her throat where it swells into her shoulder. This makes me groan and before I know what I am doing I am carrying her to the bed and there we make love for what seems an eternity of time.

Afterwards she tells me stories of her father and her mother: very unusual types to say the least. She talks about her childhood with her brother, of the wild times with her mother and the choking, over-attendant care of her father, who seems to have tried to put her into her mother's place, to make a lover of her.

Then she's raining kisses on me again and we make love for a second time, more slowly. Then we sleep awhile. My arm is stiff underneath her when I wake, so I ease it out and she wakes too. Now at last I start to tell her of the gallery and my delight in seeing those great paintings as real objects. I babble on about the sheer driving power of the paint, the eternal quality of the light. 'Made me think. Seems stupid to think I can paint at all, seeing that. Here am I, painting the dark. However can it compete with the light?'

'Always the dark and the light, Gabriel.' She puts a finger on my lips. 'You can paint. I saw your painting. In your house.'

'Did you?' I know she did. Wasn't that why I was so angry, feeling exposed like that?

'It is a very powerful piece of work. Such depth.'

I am silenced.

'You've learned so much, Gabriel. Taught yourself. Tell me about the painting.'

Now I'm telling her about the woman in the goaf and there are no secrets between us. She talks to me about the way I've referred to the Rembrandt pictures in my painting. I know about this, but I listen, wait for the criticism.

'But somehow that painting is purely your own. No one else could have painted it – none of those painters you have seen today.'

With that I have to be content.

Suddenly we're hearing voices, sharp and unpleasant in the room below us. I sit up, dragging her and half the bedclothes with me. 'What's that?'

'It's Cora and Archie. They quarrel a great deal these days.' She paused. 'Cora's not well,' she whispers.

'I thought she looked under the weather, like.'

'More than a bit.' She hesitates.

'What?'

'Nothing.' Then she pushes me. 'You should go home. Archie will be furious if he knows you're here.'

'Cora knows I'm here.'

'She won't have told him. She knows how to keep secrets.'

'These rehearsals get later and later. Don't they know you've got school to go to?' Mrs Pallister put a jam sandwich, neatly cut into triangles, beside Greta's cocoa.

Greta closed her eyes, savouring the smell of chocolate. 'It's full performance rehearsals now. Takes some time, with Archie's notes afterwards. I've got to get it right.'

'How many weeks are there left? Three? It'll have to be right for the Prince of Wales.'

'You don't think he'll have time to see the whole play, do you?' Dev Pallister's voice came from behind his newspaper. 'There is the visit to the Club, and the allotment project. He'll have no time to sit through a play.'

'But that's what we're doing it for. For the Prince's visit.'

The newspaper crackled as Dev crumpled it in his lap. 'I'd'a thought you were doing it for yourselves, for that swaggerer Archie Todhunter, even for the poor folks in this town. Not for some Prince who dips his toe in the working class and gets his footman to polish it off.'

'You've changed your tune,' said his wife.

'Only within these four walls,' he said. 'Do you know what was being said in the meeting today? That another war was the only thing to wipe out this misery. They'll need coal then. And steel. Uniforms. Manufacturing.' He sighed. 'And d'you know, I found myself agreeing? After that last lot! And losing our Ernie and Alan? But let Mosley and his gang get a hold here and still we lose all that we fought for. They're saying we've go to fight again. Got to.'

'Why can't the countries come to an agreement?' said Greta.

'Talk instead of fighting? Seems stupid to me, war. Rosel Vonn – her brother and father were soldiers last time. Her cousin died, like Uncle Ernie and Uncle Alan.'

Dev shook his head. 'There are them who say let the Germans get on with their own affairs and we'll get on with ours. But ugly things are happening in Germany and it'll spread like the Black Death right across Europe if we don't watch out. Even self-interest says we should rearm. I'm sure of it now. They'll leave us behind, else.'

'My teacher says if we rearm as well there's bound to be another war.' Greta wiped a crumb from her lip. 'She says it's inevitable. A drawn sword must strike.'

He laughed. 'Ha! The easy comforts of pacifism!'

His wife collected the dishes. 'Seems like the last one never really ended,' she said, shaking her head. 'Not twenty years gone and here we are again.'

'Now there speaks a wise woman,' said Dev, drawing up his newspaper like a fire curtain before him.

'So you're right, Dev. It *is* a bit trivial to worry whether or not the Prince will watch the play.'

Dev grunted agreement from behind his rustling newspaper.

Greta stood up, grabbing the battered book by her plate.

'*Wuthering Heights*!' said Pauline Pallister. 'Reading it again? How can you stand that Heathcliff. He's a cruel one.'

'He has passion, that's all,' said Greta. 'And lots of it.'

'Well, passion or no passion, don't you read too long. The light in that bedroom's not what it should be. Your eyes are bad enough already, my lady. And there's school tomorrow.'

Chapter Twenty-Eight

The Bogie

Later in the week, Rosel catches me after the Thursday long rehearsal. She's keen for me to take the painting of *The Woman in the Goaf* down to the Settlement, but I'm not so sure about that. For one thing, I don't think it is finished.

'Work on it down in the shed. The light's better there than in your house. Your front room is good for atmosphere, but for painting, no.'

'I don't need the light. I need the dark.'

'Don't talk nonsense. All painters need light. The point about that painting is the light with which you've imbued the figure of the woman, set off against the goaf.'

'You're wrong. The point about the painting is the quality of the dark. The goaf. The black behind the black.'

She stares at me for a moment. 'Well . . . yes. That is true. Look, it's your decision, but I think the real reason you don't want it there is because you're frightened.'

'Me – frightened?'

'Frightened, perhaps, of something people might say. It

always makes one afraid – I know this. A stranger's eyes on your canvas is like his eyes on your naked flesh.'

'My portraits are already there. People see them.'

'Ah, my dear.' She shrugs. 'They're portrait exercises. Illustrations, merely. Very good. Admirable. Skilled. But how much of yourself is in them? But in that one . . . you are there. You have invested much.'

I know I'll give in to her but I delay it. It's easy to give in to her. I've been closer to her than to any other human being, but between us it seems again that we have to maintain our distance now. I take my cue from her. I change tack. 'So what has happened about your father?' At least I can exploit this intimacy: the intimacy of a confidence between friends.

She shakes her head. 'I telephoned the man in London and he says, he is making enquiries. That is all.'

'He was a toff, that one, wasn't he? The one you visited.'

She frowns. 'A toff?'

'A posh lad. A lord or something? *Sir* something or other?'

'Is that a toff?'

'Didn't he live in a grand house?'

'Well, no. Yes. It was rather grand rooms in a grand house.'

'Like I say. How old was he, this toff?'

'What does that matter?'

'As old as my Aunt Susanah? As old as you?'

She frowns. 'This is ridiculous. About as old as Archie, if you wish to know.'

I don't think she likes this talk of age. 'Oh well, that's all right then.'

Her face hardens to a mask. 'No, it's not. You have no right to question me.'

'Oh,' I say softly, 'I have a right.' I put my hand on the top of her arm and rub the ball of my thumb over her shoulder-bone.

She slaps me so hard that I reel. 'I have told you.'

I stand upright and rub my injured cheekbone. 'Rosel. There's no need . . .'

She moves swiftly to the door of the echoing rehearsal room and looks at me over her shoulder. 'You have no right, Gabriel. No right at all. You are a child. I have no more in common with you than your Aunt Susanah. Like her I am fond of you, but more than that – no. Never, never again. It is ridiculous. It was ridiculous. We make ourselves look foolish, doing that. No more.'

I find that to make up for my gaffe with Rosel I have to give in about the picture. But now there's the problem of getting the canvas down to the Settlement. It's too big to manhandle, even if that were possible and it isn't, because the paint is still wet. It takes weeks for this stuff to dry.

Tegger has the solution. 'We'll have to get your dad's bogie[1] off the allotment.' I don't let Tegger see how my heart jolts at his suggestion. I haven't been there since we cut down my father's dead body and carried him home. It occurs to me that we didn't think of the bogie then to carry him back home. I'm glad we didn't think of it. I'm glad I carried him home in my arms.

I thought the allotment would be derelict and overgrown, but it looks much as it did. The chickens still cluck away in and out of their cree[2], and the soil has just had its winter turnover.

[1] Small homemade chariot made of a box on pram-wheels.
[2] hut.

My father's friend Steve is backing out of the cree. In his hand he is clutching his cap: five eggs nestle in it.

'Why Gabe, son, how's it going?' he says, smiling slightly. 'I'd given up thought of seeing you down here again.'

I look round. 'I thought it'd be overgrown, like.'

Steve shakes his head. 'Saw the allotment committee. Said I'd tek it on. Called on you with eggs now and then, but you were never in. Left a note.'

'I found the eggs. And the note.' I feel guilty for making no response to his kind gestures. 'I should have come.'

'Canny eggs,' Tegger butted in. 'We enjoyed them, those eggs.'

'We wanted me dad's bogie,' I say. 'We need it for a job we're doing.'

'All in there, in the big cree. Yours by rights. Tek it back any time, Gabe. Garden, too.'

'Nah. I couldn't.'

'In the cree, take a look.'

The bogie is in the cree, upended. It's a kind of long box, home-made, set on wheels. A kind of coffin on wheels. Maybe that was why it was unthinkable that we'd take my dad home in it, that night. I close my eyes and there is his body, swinging on the tree.

Tegger pulls the bogie out into the daylight. 'This'll do fine. Could mebbe do with it down the Settlement anyway. Always hauling things down there, one way or another.'

We take our leave of Steve. 'Always remember, son, it's here when you want it.'

'I won't want it.'

At the house we find the canvas barely fits on to the bogie. Tegger knocks up a kind of frame so we can stand it upright. I protect it with an old tablecloth from the wooden press, then a blanket off the spare bed, where Tegger and Marguerite do their courting when they're in the house. Tegger insists on wedging it in with the easel. 'It'll stop it moving about. And you'll need it down there in the shed.'

'I'll need an easel here. I like working vertical now. An' I like working on my own.'

'I'll make you another one. It's just a few planks and screws. Nae worries.'

We draw a few interested glances in the street, but a couple of lads dragging God knows what through the rainy streets on a bogie is not a new sight in Brack's Hill. Potatoes, coals scrounged off the heaps, furniture, livestock, sickly relatives: homemade bogies have been used here for such tasks for many years. And before that it was probably medieval barrows and Roman sledges. But never before, I think, has a bogie carried a still-wet painting of a near-naked woman. So it's just as we are trundling it down the narrow side-street that I start to wonder for the first time what the people of Brack's Hill will make of the woman. There'll be a few raised eyebrows.

Todhunter's brows certainly climb towards his silvery-grey thatch when we unveil the picture in the big room. He caught us in the alleyway and smiled a little at our bogie. Seems like he's recovered from his paddy last week about my absence from the rehearsal. He doesn't hold a grudge, I'll say that for him.

He watches inside the long room as we put up the easel and carefully place the painting on it. I hold my breath and listen for some kind of judgement from him. I'm much more worried now than when I'm delivering my lines as Arthur. This is funny as, though Archie knows everything about drama, he's a less than competent painter. But he's studied pictures in those books of his, and talks knowledgeably about what one should or shouldn't do as a painter.

He walks up to it and away from it, as Rosel and Susanah, Tegger and Marguerite have done. He goes and opens the door to the hallway to dredge more light into the room. Like others he's disturbed by the darkness in the painting.

'Extraordinary,' he says. Then he turns it so it's even more in the light. 'Extraordinary. The effect of that drape and that . . . is it a flower? Decadent, somehow.'

'Extraordinary. What does that mean? You don't like it.'

'I do. I do. It's very . . . *very* well done. Compelling. Such depth. Incredible, the progress you've made, young man.' He does the dance again. Near and far. Near and far. 'So what inspired this masterpiece?'

I don't tell him of the dream. I describe it to him as an idea. Of the woman as the earth and all that.

'I see. And,' he coughs, 'it can only have been painted from life.'

'Yes.'

'I haven't seen this person in the painting, here, at the Settlement?' He has a question in his voice.

'You would have, if you'd ever been to The Lord Raglan. She works there,' says Tegger. 'Her name's Marguerite Molloy.'

'I see. She has the looks of a . . . of a colonial.'

'She's my friend,' says Tegger. 'And she comes from South Shields.'

'I see.' Todhunter pulls the painting back into the corner so that it's alongside the portraits which now line the walls, but still slightly in the shadow.

'It could go up on the wall, I suppose,' says Tegger. 'It'd need a bracket, like. You'd not believe how heavy it is.'

Archie shakes his head. 'It can't be in the exhibition, of course.'

'What!' I say. 'Why?'

'Well, it wouldn't go with the others. They are all to do with the play. It would be out of place.'

'It *is* to do with the play,' argues Tegger. 'What's the play about except miners and their lives in peace and war? When you look at this, this one's all about a miner and his life, and what goes on inside him as well as outside him. And see the red? That's the poppy. The Flanders poppy.' I've never said that to him. In fact, I've never worked it out myself till now.

Archie lights another cigarette. 'That's all very well, but then there's the problem of the woman. If it had been an ordinary underground scene, perhaps. But the woman . . .'

'That's what it's about,' I say. 'The woman.'

Archie stares at me then back at the picture. He draws a lungful of tobacco through his amber holder. 'People . . .' he sighs.

'What he's saying,' says Tegger, 'is that he can't have a picture of a naked woman on these walls. In this town.'

'What? We've just been to the best art gallery in the North and there's plenty of naked and half-naked women there. Statues too.'

'Ah,' says Todhunter. 'But that's—'

'Proper art? Not a pitman's daubs?' I spit the words. 'Howay Tegger, get that bloody bogie and we'll have this away home.'

'You must show it, Archie.' Rosel's voice comes from behind us. 'How could you not show it?'

She's standing in the doorway to the house. Cora, looking haggard as she has recently, is at her elbow.

'There'll be difficulties, Rosel. You don't know about this

place. There's a reserve. They're not used to this sort of thing. I depend on the goodwill of the local people. A section of my money comes from the council. They'll have it that I've led young Gabriel here astray.'

He seems to have forgotten that the town knows he's here in this same building living tally with his fancy-woman.

Cora takes a closer look at the picture. 'I can see what you mean, Archie. That scarf on a naked body. What will Mrs Pallister and Mrs Stewart think?' She looks at me, her white, tired face smiling slightly. 'You're like a mushroom, Gabriel, growing to full strength in the night. It's very good.'

I look at them all and beyond them to the picture where the woman in the goaf glows at me from her dark nest. 'It's my work, honestly done, saying something I want to say.' The words come out of my mouth very slowly. The thought is dawning in my head as I speak. 'If that can't be shown, then neither can the others that I painted. Greta, Cora, yourself, Mr Todhunter.'

'Oh dear,' said Cora. 'My moment of eternal glory vanishing before my eyes.'

'Cora, shut up!' The words are like a whiplash. Todhunter is very still now, a rock carved against the dusty air of the room. 'You can't say that, Gabriel. Those paintings don't belong to you. They belong to the Settlement.'

'What?' The word explodes from me.

'The paints, the materials came from here. You'd never have painted them without the inspiration you found here. Without Fraulein Vonn's instruction.'

'And that makes them yours?' I am speaking through grinding teeth. 'It means they all belong to you?'

Archie opens his mouth to answer, but Rosel interrupts him. 'This can't be so, Archie. An artist owns his own work. He's no slave, nor Russian serf. Do you know in Russia before the Revolution the Tsar owned artists as well as actors and ballet dancers? We must be beyond that, Archie.'

'Don't interfere with something which is none of your business, Fraulein.'

She goes to stand in front of him and looks him in the eye. 'It's so much my business, that if you rob that boy of his paintings, I will take mine away. I will take an axe to the stage set which I have designed. And I will be off these premises within the hour.'

Todhunter stares at her.

'Archie!' says Cora.

He coughs, then blows his nose, making a great bit of business about it. 'Very well. Of course the paintings do belong to the boy. A slip of the tongue. I wasn't thinking . . .' Now he looks at me and when he speaks, his tone is more conciliatory. 'Don't you see, Gabriel? The painting will get such attention, will cause such a scandal, that the whole point of the play, the whole message that I . . . that young Tegger here and I have worked so hard to plant at the centre of the play – all that will be lost as people discuss, or rage around your painting.'

There's logic in this, and the room is silent. Then Rosel speaks up again. 'But the painting has its own message, Archie. Why should the world be deprived of that? And if there *is* controversy, has not art always caused controversy? Are not artists fleeing my own country even now because their paintings are being called decadent and they cannot practise their art because they live in fear? My own father's books with his drawings have been burned.'

'Look,' I say finally. 'I don't want to spoil the play, far from it. But this is still the best thing I've done and it means a lot to me, just like the play means a lot to you. It's something I've been dreaming about for a long time without even knowing it. And somehow, though it's not perfect, there it is. Outside my head.'

Todhunter puts his hand up and pulls it down his face, dragging his flesh with it, distorting his large features. It seems like he's wiping years of tiredness out of himself. 'It is good. I acknowledge that, Gabriel.' He glances at Rosel. 'And I'm no ogre, whatever you might think. Perhaps I should get Dev Pallister down here to take a look at it, alongside the other pictures? He's close to what the people here think. He's a sound man.'

'Aye,' says Tegger.

'What if he says it'll cause too much of a ruckus?' I still can't let it go.

Cora breaks the silence. 'What say that we still have the painting, perhaps in Archie's office or in the room upstairs? So anybody who likes Gabriel's paintings could be shown it.'

'No!' says Rosel sharply. 'That is like . . . like . . .'

'. . . dirty pictures,' says Tegger.

It seems insoluble. One part of me is sympathetic with Todhunter's concerns. Another is not. 'I tell you what,' I say. 'Why don't we wait to hear what Mr Pallister has to say? There really is no way I would spoil the painting exhibition or the play. Let's just see. If he says no, I'll take it home. There's others that might be interested.'

So the tension fades a bit and we leave it at that. The painting stays in the corner. The bogie is tucked into the painting shed and we get on with tonight's rehearsal which focuses on the women. The spotlight's off me, thank goodness. I sit in the corner watching Todhunter put Cora through her paces like she was young Greta. He's a perfectionist that one, and no mistake. Greta and me play draughts in the corner and she beats me twelve games to three. Todhunter calls her up and she whispers in my ear that next time she'll bring her chessboard and thrash me. Her breath tickles my ear.

Later on, when we play the kissing scene, I remember that tickle and clutch her harder and put my hand on her face as I kiss her, a move which goes unreproved by Todhunter, despite the fact that it's not in his movement plan. He's not usually keen on us using our initiative, so this is something new.

Chapter Twenty-Nine

A Popular Girl

Tegger has brought me some wooden offcuts from a cabinet-maker's where he's been working. At least the furniture factory has kept going, although the cabinetmakers are on short time. People out of work do not buy furniture.

Tegger's been leading some scrap away for them with another fellow and his van. It's tally work, like, done at night so no spies can get him into trouble. Seems Marguerite knew this foreman from there. Regular friend of hers, he says.

Tegger and Marguerite are not round here as much together. More him on his own. When I ask him about it he just shrugs his shoulders and lights another cigarette. Then one night he loosens up a bit and tells me, 'Looks like I'm getting in the way of her work.'

'They don't like you hanging round at the Raglan?'

He looks at me strangely then and shakes his shoulders in that way he has. 'Sommat like that,' he says. Seems she got him this tally job at the cabinetmakers as some kind of compensation for him losing her constant company.

They were funny together, those two. Not inseparable, not really like a girlfriend and boyfriend. Marguerite is a very kind person. Look at her treating us to the Newcastle trip. Look at her getting Tegger this tally job. Her heart's in the right place.

So I'm the beneficiary. There are some lovely bits of pitch pine and elm here. All kinds of shapes. Well seasoned. They're raw wood, so there's nothing to scrape off. I pick three big rectangles and set about sanding and sizing them. Even as I do this I have two images pricking at my brain like swords. One is the heap where I pick my fossils, the way it was the other night. Black against the white sky. I have some more ideas about light since I saw the Turner. The learning-by-copying gremlin still grabs at me.

Rosel would disapprove – but then she had her college and her teachers, didn't she? She had her father in his studio, her uncle in his. Maybe when she was little, she copied; her hand was guided by one of greater authority. I have no greater hand to guide me apart from those Old Masters speaking to me from their canvases. Maybe one day I won't be looking for techniques, but now I am. There's so much ground to make up.

The other painting in my mind has something to do with the effort of pushing tubs up an incline. I have knowledge of that in my sinews which I'd like to set out for others to see. This one will be about the depths of the tunnel. All the time when I am visualising it, the petrified fireflies and lizards are staining my mind. Maybe they'll find their place in that picture.

I'm in the middle of priming the boards when my Aunt Susanah drops by. She's taken to doing that lately. She examines my work. 'Lots of scope here, Gabriel. Seven boards ready primed. A year's work, is it?' She glances around the room. 'More like a workshop than anybody's home, this room.'

'It's the way I like it. Only meself to please.'

'Yes. I can't think any woman'd tolerate it.'

She sits down in my father's chair. 'So, love, what fetches with you?'

'As you see, I'm fine.'

'I feel guilty, you being on your own across here and no family to support you. I was saying to Jonty.'

She takes off her gloves and I am impelled to make her a cup of tea. She talks about her husband whom she has left at the Settlement to teach his Politics class. 'The Settlement has certainly brought you on, Gabriel. That Archie Todhunter is a remarkable man. The difference he's making to so many lives. It puts us to shame.'

Working with Todhunter day to day, with the play and the paintings, you don't think of him like that. You think of him as obsessed and pernickety, rather domineering and a bit of a know-all. You take for granted, I suppose, that it's his sheer drive that underpins our lives, the fact that without him those hundreds of people would not have their classes or their library books, their plays or their painting. Without him – and Rosel – I'd still be scribbling sketches, cursing in my father's shadow. Without him I'd not have painted *The Woman in the Goaf* which I count as my real painting, as the beginning of something.

She reads my mind. 'That painting – it was very good. Individual. Dramatic.'

'Glad you think so,' I mutter.

'And the woman, Rosel, isn't it? She is your teacher?'

'Aye.'

'And your friend as well?'

I wish she'd lay off. 'Aye,' I repeat.

'She must be thirty-six, seven.'

'What's that to do with anything?'

'Nothing. You're right.' She drinks off her tea and stands up to go. She pulls on her gloves. 'It's none of my business. It's just, after what happened with your father, if you ever want any, well, help, I'm here. And there's Jonty. There might be something . . .'

'There's nothing. But thank you.' I hate how grudging that sounds. 'Thank you,' I say, more heartily this time. 'I appreciate the thought.'

'You know where we are.'

It's only when she goes that I think of a question I'd have liked to ask her. Or Jonty. The one about how not to get pregnant. For no reason at all Greta has been on my mind recently. I notice her more in rehearsals and I notice her noticing me.

Rosel is still there in the centre, like. And still in my mind. Many, many times in bed do I go over what we did together, frame by frame, like they do in a film. No one will ever be the same for me. Not like her. But she's taking one step back these days. She's genial enough, but there's a glass wall round her. To be honest it's a bit of a relief. I have this feeling that if it had gone on, somehow the painting would have been a problem. Maybe it would have stopped. I don't know why I think this.

I think, too, she's worried about her father. He's been in trouble for sticking up for his Jewish friends. Not many of them around here, mind you. Jews. There is a doctor on Back Row. And there's a new factory set up near Priorton. It was in the paper. They've built new white houses for some of the key workers, and the place is nicknamed Jerusalem. There's some shouts about Jews in the papers. Blackshirts, fighting Jewish types in London. But not much round here. No one moves in here. They're all moving out to get work elsewhere.

No. I couldn't ask Rosel that particular question for Greta. It's funny, that. When you've seen someone virtually naked, you'd think you could ask them anything. We did nothing to stop anything when we were together. Risky when you think about it, but that was the last thing on my mind.

And I can't ask Tegger 'cause that'd make me look like a twerp. Maybe Marguerite? She's open and knows a lot of things that would surprise you. She's a woman. She might know. But I've been trying to think of a situation where I could ask the question, but that defeats me.

Maybe I'll go down the Raglan tonight. I have the price of a half. Tegger's gone absent without leave with some dog-racing friends. He won't surface for a while.

Dev Pallister was having a problem finding Archie Todhunter. The library was in full swing but he wasn't there. There was an argument going on in the little classroom. He recognised the teacher, the pacifist from Priorton called Jonty Clelland. He was going at it hammer and tongs with Nathan Smith. Something about Russia.

Todhunter wasn't in the dusty workroom or his office, so Dev mounted the stairs and knocked on the living-room door. On the instruction to come in he pushed open the door. Cora Miles was sitting curled into a chair clutching a large cup of something. Dev glanced round the room. 'Is Mr Todhunter around? I had a message from him.'

She shook her head. 'He has a meeting in Durham but should be back,' she glanced at the mantel clock, 'about quarter to. Off the three-thirty bus from Durham.'

'Oh,' he said.

She unwound her long legs and stood up. 'You could wait

here. I'm sure he wouldn't want to miss you.'

He smelt the not unfamiliar waft of whisky as she wove her way past him. 'I have to go. There are chores to do.'

The door clicked to behind her. A fine-looking woman, Cora Miles. Good shoulders, but more than a little haggard these days. Letting herself go. He hated to see that in a woman. His Pauline was a homely person but she was as trim now as the day they were married. Good ankles and a fine bust – that's what had attracted him when he first met her at the chapel dance they held for the lads on leave from the war. 1915 it was. He'd been more than a bit downhearted at the thought of going back to France, but Pauline with her quick ways had cheered him up. Not a bad reason for getting married. They got on well, him and Pauline. No fireworks. But that suited. He was so busy. Her too, with the lads, then Greta to see to and everything.

He didn't have time to pursue that thought because Archie Todhunter came in then, rubbing his hands against the cold, delighted to see him. Seemed he wanted help with a problem. 'I want you to look at a painting.'

'Why?'

'It was done by young Gabriel Marchant.'

'Now that's not a bad lad. Turns up with our Greta sometimes.'

'Well, he's painted a very good picture, but . . . I want to show you something.' He led the way down to the big workroom, clicked on the overhead lights and walked with Dev along the row of paintings. Dev nodded his approval of each of these, standing before Greta's in special appreciation. He lingered a while too before Cora's portrait. 'Our Greta says Cora Miles takes a right good part in the play. I saw her upstairs here. Thought she was looking a bit tired and poorly. Has she been ill?'

'Ill?' Archie frowned. 'No. Cora's as strong as an ox. A bit on the stubborn side lately, but that's mood, not substance. Now then!' In the corner was a crude easel and a painting covered lightly in a green cloth. He whipped off the cover and carefully adjusted the painting.

Dev's mouth dropped slightly at the sight of the picture.

'Yes!' said Archie. 'It's good, isn't it? Fresh. Powerful. But you can see the problem, can't you?'

'Once you make it out, you can see the pit seam. It's clearly there. Well shown, in fact – any miner would recognise it, but as for the scarf and the figure. Is that a poppy? The problem . . .' said Dev.

'The youngster wants it displayed on the day of the performance, along with the others. Insists on it, in fact.'

'Insists?'

'This is the problem. The subject-matter. The naked woman. He speaks very well of its symbolism. What it means and so on. The red wool on the shoulder for the Flanders poppy. All very well, I say. But would the good folk of Brack's Hill understand?'

'Good folk, you say?' said Mr Pallister, brows raised. 'You think those "good folk" might think it was a dirty picture?' His tone was very careful.

'Let's say, in questionable taste. They would be wrong, but it gives me a dilemma.'

'Is that why you're showing it to me?'

'I respect your judgement, Mr Pallister. You know the people of Brack's Hill. Would they see the art in it? Or would they be offended? Therefore offended by the whole exhibition, and the play, and the Settlement for that matter. I'm reluctant to censor anything which is a true artistic expression. But there are sensibilities.'

'I can see that.'

Archie Todhunter started to defend the painting. 'It is very tastefully done, of course. And the boy is an innocent. Earnestly defending his muse, as it were.'

'I can see this.' Dev coughed. 'The model – is she a person from the town?'

'I believe so, although we've never seen her here. She's friendly with young Gabriel and his friend Tegger. She works at The Lord Raglan.'

'It's a good picture. He's got the pit. And many of our "good folk" would get this message you're talking about. Yet this young woman, who lives hereabouts . . .'

'Yes?'

Dev walked up and down the line of pictures again. 'You'll know that the men have a very big objection to women in the pit? Like sailors – see it as bad luck. Many of them would view this as wild fancy, at the very least.'

'But this is not a woman in that sense. She's an idea.'

'She looks like a real woman to me.' Pallister paused. 'Showing this picture could do two things, Mr Todhunter. It could get you a great deal of publicity. Draw attention to your play, and the work here at the Settlement. That could be very good.'

'Or the opposite,' said Archie. 'It could swamp it, perhaps even destroy it. It depends on the *kind* of attention it would get.'

'Could you not display it separately, in another space?'

'Where? In my office? What would that say about me then? We thought about that but Tegger MacNamara talked about dirty pictures, and I'm inclined to agree with him. It's not just a concept, then, is it?'

'I tell you what, Mr Todhunter. I'll talk to the lad, see if there's some give there. Then whatever the decision is, it'll be part mine. So the pall of prudishness did not sit completely on your shoulders.'

Archie shook him by the hand, very satisfied and harbouring a degree of admiration for Dev Pallister's tact.

As he swung out of the Settlement and down the road Dev blew air from his lungs in quick relief. The fact was that Gabriel Marchant's young model was quite well-known to him. Quite well-known to a few prominent citizens of Brack's Hill. It was true that she did work at The Lord Raglan. It was also true that she occasionally showed great kindness to these citizens – for a modest payment, of course.

Perhaps for this reason the painting would be more than embarrassing if it were displayed here. It could be downright dangerous.

Since receiving the first letter from her brother Boris, Rosel Vonn had drawn and painted very little. She'd not even completed the final touches to Gabriel's triptych. She attended the painting classes, sharpened pencils, laid out paints. She responded to requests for advice and praised good efforts. But she no longer sat beside a painter and painted with him. She no longer set up her own easel to lead by example.

Gabriel had a new easel – a new version of the scrapwood contraption which held the big painting. That big painting was still under wraps in the big room, until the great decision was made. Nathan Smith and the others had lifted the veil and taken a look. There were smirks and embarrassed half-laughs about the subject-matter.

Rosel watched with interest as Gabriel set about his current work on a primed-up rectangle of timber. It was a study of the pit heap where she had first seen him, the one with the glittering pool beside it. At some points the penetrating grey light of the sky swirled into the white light of the pool and the two became indistinguishable. From a distance it might be a study of Switzerland or the English Lake District. It was only when you got nearer that you realised that the mountainous heap consisted of an intricate jigsaw of jagged stones. All these were marked with the insignia of petrification. There were leaves and lizards, tree barks and sea creatures. Each stone was a different shade of black or grey, thickly layered in paint. The insignia were scratched into the paint with a knife, which gave them a faintly shocking crude quality. They were like those chalk drawings children drew on pavements. As the days went on, and Gabriel laid on more and more paint, all of the slag became covered with gouged-out reflections of the flora and fauna which grew unchecked in crevasses and around the pool below.

Now here, thought Rosel, Gabriel was at last beginning to show his own hand. Only he could have painted this one. At least on the surface it owed little to the artists he admired.

Rosel did not voice her opinion to him. In the main she was keeping her distance. The open sensuality and directness of his painting *The Woman of the Goaf* had disturbed her. She found herself thinking of the girl who had modelled for him. Under her calm exterior, she still worried about the closeness of herself and this boy. He was far, far too young. She must keep her distance. There was security, and dignity in that.

In any case she was preoccupied these days with thoughts of her father. She turned over the pages of his war book in her room. She'd taken Archie's copy for Gabriel that day she'd met his Aunt Susanah. She'd taken it as an excuse to see him, and brought it back when Gabriel ran away. The faces of the men there leaped and surged across the pad, often disembodied from the swirly mud of the trenches. She thought of her father at the Front, with his pencil in his hand, peering at them in that short-sighted way of his. When he drew and painted them he was not much older than these young soldiers themselves.

He was younger than Rosel herself was now. Through his eye you saw each soldier as an individual; a young man writing home; a bewhiskered captain standing by a staff car; a boy curled up as though asleep, blood seeping from his footless leg; a game of cards in a dugout; two men peering over the edge of a trench into No-man's-land. Each one was an individual. These were no ciphers, no pegs on a board, no toy soldiers marching off to war.

You could see why the new militarists had had the book banned from the university library, had even recommended that copies be burned. Perhaps it *was* decadent to show the sheer vulnerability of the human frame and expose the ridiculous inhumanity of warfare; a retreat into the easy delights of hubris. But such images would not encourage a young man to throw himself into unquestioning defence of his Fatherland. No wonder they wanted to burn the book.

She received another letter by an English messenger from Boris, saying that their father had settled back into his apartment and had been undisturbed since the last onslaught. The police had taken some of his books – including the original war notebook – and had not returned them. Some of the drawings were removed from a gallery which regularly sold them and had vanished without a trace.

* * *

So, dear sister, although he is physically safe he is, with some cause, full of melancholy. So many of his friends have emigrated; some have been arrested. I had not realised so many of his friends were Jewish. One did not think like this, did one? Among some of my fellow officers my attitude is seen as wilful blindness. But there is one fellow, who I shall not name, who has other ideas. His father was one of the Kaiser's generals and he has ideas of honour other than these tin-pot bullies who're rising like scum to the top. He thinks something should be done about it and I am not far behind him. I will join him in his endeavours. But first I am concerned to get our father away. He is very vulnerable here. He is still writing letters of objection to the wrong people. He is still voicing his protest to anyone who listens. But these days, those who listen to you are Janus-faced. There are few whom you can really trust. You have to be careful.

Beside such considerations Rosel's own anxiety about her obsession with a man young enough to be her son was, she knew, essentially trivial. After the first defence of his work to Archie she could not stir herself into genuine concern about whether or not Gabriel's painting *The Woman in the Goaf* should be displayed at the Settlement.

So as the days went on she ignored the young man's soulful, sometimes angry looks and avoided being on her own with him. It was the only way. She could only see his angry looks through smoky glass. She had other things to worry about.

Chapter Thirty

Money

For all the attention I'm getting off Rosel Vonn these days, you'd think we were strangers. You'd never believe that a little while ago, for a spark in time, we were as close as a man or a woman can be. I wish it were otherwise but there are new things to think of.

I had a letter this morning from a strange address in Newcastle. The signature, as far as I can make out, is Edwin or Edward Crump. Tucked into the letter is a postal order for ten guineas.

Dear Mr Marchant,
Your sketches were passed to me by Sybil McNeil from the gallery. I should tell you that they were displayed in my gallery a mere five days before they were bought by a Northumberland gentleman, who expressed interest in further work by you. I also had a visitor here from the Shipley Gallery, Gateshead, who evinced an interest. Alas, when he returned to purchase, the paper birds had flown.

So, dear sir, should you have further examples of your work, they will certainly find space in my gallery. Next time you find yourself in these parts I trust you will call, as I am certainly keen to make your acquaintance.
With respect,
Yours truly,
E. Crump.

To say I was stunned at this would be an understatement. I'd almost forgotten those pictures I left in Newcastle; forgotten the snobby woman at the gallery. My mind was more on the paintings I had seen, and the sheer wonder of the gallery itself. Now it seems this same woman has done me a favour.

Just at present I'm almost entirely on my own day by day. Rosel's not talking so there is no point in going to her. Tegger has gone on one of his trips with the dog-man. I think he and Marguerite have fallen out and he's in a huff.

When it came in the post I did this daft thing. I held this postal order, a flimsy thing, up in the air and whirled round and round the kitchen. 'Here, Dad, here! Look at this! Money for drawing.' But my voice rang as though the house was a hollow cave and there was no one to receive it. 'Beats slaving in the dark!' I shouted the words. I felt foolish then, so I stuffed the postal order in my pocket, put on my cap and went out of the empty house.

So this is how I find myself walking through the swing door of the Raglan at dinnertime, peering through the fug and the crowd to catch sight of Marguerite Molloy. And here she is, flashing smiles and pints in good order.

I squeeze to the corner of the bar and wait for her attention to get to me. She gives me a quick grin. 'I needed to see you. Be with you in a sec, Gabe.' She works through her orders and leaves me till last. Now here she is. 'That's those seen to. Pint, Gabe?'

'It'll have to be one of your tally pints, 'cos I've got no money.' I can be the beggar here, as I know tomorrow, once I've been to the Post Office I can treat her royally.

She's already drawing the pint. 'Where's that rascal Tegger? I only told him he didn't own me and off he goes with a pet lip on him like a gorilla.'

'He's gone to ground with the dog-man. He does this sometimes. He'll be back soon.'

The foam from the beer slops over her slender fingers as she places it before me. Then she folds her arms, leans on the bar and looks up in my eyes and says, 'So how have you been, Gabe?'

'Well . . .' I take a large mouthful of that bitter velvet. 'Very well, in fact.' Like a magician producing a rabbit, I produce the postal order. She peers at it rather short-sightedly and frowns. 'What's this?' she says. 'Money, is it?'

I tell her about the letter from the gallery man. She squeals with laughter and claps her hands. The noise in the bar dips for a second and a dozen or so men stop talking and look across at Marguerite. And me.

She turns her back on them and the hum restarts. 'What a thing, Gabe! What a thing. And you do have more sketches, don't you?'

'Oh yes. Plenty of sketches. Boxes of 'em.'

'Well. Now it's beginning. Something is really beginning.'

'Hey, Marguerite! Get some beer in, will yer?' She's called away and has to pull six more pints before she gets back.

'So when are we going there again?'

'We? When are *we* going?'

'Look, sweetheart, if you think you're going there without me you've got another think coming.'

I laugh at this. This girl always puts a smile on my face. 'Well this time it'll be my treat – when I've been to the Post Office, like, to cash this postal order.'

When I finally get out of the Raglan, leaving Marguerite with her last customers of the afternoon, the world is spinning around me as a consequence of my delight at my good luck and three pints of the Raglan's strong ale. I had drunk both of Marguerite's free pints, bless her, and then the landlord stood me another. He's pleased as Punch with his picture, which now hangs behind the bar in a neat mahogany frame. I really do need some fresh air to clear my head.

As I turn into the High Street I bump into a lad wearing a Grammar School blazer and cap. He apologises to me despite the fact that I'm the one at fault. My feet turn in the direction of the school; as it's home-time, the blazered and capped legions are soon spilling round me like a river in flood.

Greta is just making her way through the ornate iron gates. Her satchel is slung over one shoulder, her school hat is awry, her glasses have slipped down her nose and her head is bent over a book which she reads as she walks. I want to hug her where she stands. Instead I clap her on the shoulder. 'Hey! Bookworm!'

She drops her book and scrambles to rescue it from the wet pavement. 'Gabriel! What kind of trick is that?' She pushes her glasses back up her nose. 'You shouldn't go scaring people out of their skin.'

'Never, never!' I shake my head. 'Never would I scare you out of your skin.'

Her pert nose wrinkles. 'You've been drinking.'

'Not much. Not much.' I shake my head very carefully. It is still spinning.

She grins a bit at that. 'Here. Walk me home, will you? Everyone's looking.'

It's easy walking along with her. We know each other now, and are calm together. After a few minutes' walking, she looks up at me. 'What is it?' she says. 'Something's happened, hasn't it?'

'Yes, Yes. So it has.' I stop and take out my postal order. 'Look. Look at this.'

She adjusts her spectacles again and looks at it. 'Ten guineas. Where's this from?'

'Seller in Newcastle paying for my sketches. My drawings.'

She sets up a whoop at this, reaches up and kisses my cheek. 'Hey, Gabriel. Isn't that wonderful?'

I grab her and kiss her full on the mouth and for a second every part of my body is alive to her. I can feel the cut of her glasses on my cheek, the rectangular shape of the book she holds in her hand. She struggles away.

'Sorry,' I say.

'No,' she says. 'It's nice to celebrate. You're pleased, that's all.' She starts to walk. 'Come home with me and have a cup of tea. My mam'll have shop cakes. We'll tell her about the drawings. Dad, too. They'll be pleased. Dad was on about that painting of yours. The naked woman. I wasn't supposed to be listening.'

Dev Pallister's in the house when we get there and he asks me about the painting.

'Ah took a look at that picture of yours, lad.'

'Aye.' I watch his face. He runs the council. Manipulates his comrades and his constituents. How do they ever know what he's thinking? I don't.

'A bit rich, I'd say.'

'It's what I want to paint.'

'I'd have thought a lad like you . . .'

'What?'

'Well, there's things to do in this town. Clever lads like you should get involved. The council. The state of the place. You could make changes. But painting . . .'

'It's what I can do. Those other things are not for me.'

He stares hard at me. 'Aye, the painting. Well, to tell the truth I can't see what the fuss is about. Archie Todhunter seems to think that we're out of the egg here at Brack's Hill. Never seen a naked woman afore.'

'And we're not?' I force him to meet my gaze. 'Out of the egg?'

'Are we buggery,' he says.

'An' the picture in the exhibition won't cause a riot?'

He frowns a bit at this. Something's on his mind. Then he shrugs his massive shoulders. 'A bit of a stir, mebbe. But they need stirring up now and then. These are sluggish half-alive times. Can't see no harm in it myself. But mebbe it needs a bit further thought.' He puts his head round the door and shouts to Greta's mother, 'Two hours – no more.' Then he looks back at me. 'I reckon that picture of you in my army togs does me credit. Reminds me of myself before the scales fell from my eyes. That German lass did a good job on you.'

'She's very good,' I agree. I think again, of those hours of intensity, with me just standing and her just looking and drawing.

Then looking and painting. They were the most intimate times, before I laid a hand on her.

'And she's done a good job *with* you, too – showing you how to paint.'

I want to protest that I could paint before, but don't.

'That picture, the one Archie's so uneasy about.'

'I've called it *The Woman in the Goaf*.'

'Aye. A funny thing. All goaf one way you look at it. Any miner would know it. All woman the other way.'

'You see it like that?'

'I've seen the goaf many a time. But I've never seen no woman.'

'All depends on the way you look.'

'Aye. I see that. Aye. I was thinking . . . mebbe the town *is* ready for your picture.'

Then he is gone and I am left alone in the cluttered parlour, thanking heaven that Dev Pallister is an intelligent man.

Greta bursts into the room. She's still in her school uniform. One of her grey socks has fallen round her ankle; on her cheek is a smudge of navy-blue ink. 'What was all that about?' she says.

'About that picture I did for the exhibition.'

'The one with the woman?'

'You've seen it?'

'Everybody has. Easy enough to lift the cover.'

'Oh. Are you not bothered about the woman?'

'Because she's bare?'

'Aye.'

'You can hardly see her. I had to go to one side and squint my eyes. Then I saw her. At first I thought it was all black and wondered what you were doing, painting a picture all black.'

'Archie Todhunter doesn't want it put up. Says it will shock everyone.'

She laughs.

'But your dad seems to think it's all right.'

'He would. He's not stupid.' She paused. 'Mr Todhunter doesn't really know the people around here, does he? Aside from the Settlement people.'

'How do you make that out?'

'I heard him talking to that vicar pal of his, the one with the dog-collar. He was saying the people here had no culture. One step from the barbarians.'

'Cheeky bugger.'

'I thought so too. Look at everything that happens here. The men who breed pigeons and know lineage as well as any horse-owner. And breed new strands of flower. What about the choral societies and the women's poetry and discussion groups – my dad's political stuff.'

'Makes you feel like punching him.' It does for a second.

Greta throws up her fine head and laughs once more. 'Poor old Todhunter. "*He knoweth not of which he sayeth*".'

'Is that the Bible?'

'No. It's me.'

I make for the door and those strong fingers grasp my forearm. 'Did you find out?' she says.

'Did I find out what?'

'What I asked you to, about stopping . . . you know what. Babies.'

I'm blushing, of course. I've forgotten all this. 'No.'

And then I am standing in the middle of this plush parlour and kissing this schoolgirl with ink on her face. Her soft form is pressed to me and her slender fingers are thrusting their way through my short hair. For a split second I want her more than I have ever wanted Rosel, or even desired Marguerite.

Her mother's voice calls in from the kitchen and I drag myself away. 'I'll find out, Greta. I will.' I throw the words over my shoulder as I flee.

Through the fog of worry about her father, Rosel watched Gabriel's increasing familiarity and intimacy with Greta with some detachment. Not long ago she'd been drawn to him with his intensity and his bud-like sensitivity to life around him. She'd been floored by his undoubted self-taught accomplishment and flattered when she saw that her own approach to painting had influenced him. She was relieved, of course, that he did not imitate her as he did his beloved Rembrandt and Turner. He was making progress, though. These days he looked, he pondered, and transformed what he saw into something peculiarly his own. Modernism had not touched him and perhaps never would. He'd never fit into a trend or school of painting. He would always, stubbornly, plough his own idiosyncratic furrow. That might very well mean that artistic success in worldly terms would pass him by. He would be his own man.

Greta had passed on to her the news of Gabriel's success in selling sketches to the Newcastle dealer. This struck alarm bells in her. It was far too early for him to sell! It could easily fix him in a style and stop him making proper progress. She smiled at the possessive, maternal trend of her thinking. Quite clearly there was no way she could, or would sleep with that boy ever again. It would be little short of incest.

Her father now leaped back into her mind. Those intimate, playful rompings in the big white bed in the Berlin apartment. How she and Boris would run round and round the room to escape their father's insistent tickling. How at last they would all subside on the bed, the last exhausted giggle escaping their mouths. How she would wake in the early morning to find her father stroking her face, her shoulder. How eventually it was a relief to get out of that flat, away to Uncle Berti, who kept his distance and loved her like you would love a dog who gave you occasional pleasure in his company.

She wondered what she would do if she were successful in getting her father over here to England. Could she really take a house for them in Brack's Hill? They were cheap enough. But this place would be too desolate for him, she was sure, after Berlin. No. It would have to be London. She closed her eyes briefly. To be back with him would be a mixed blessing. She would make sure there was no big white bed.

A noise on the staircase told her Cora was on her way up. She came up most days now, sometimes to talk, sometimes just to sit at Rosel's window looking out, preoccupied by her own thoughts. She was definitely in retreat from Archie and her work in the Settlement. Sometimes Archie called for her from downstairs and she shook her head at Rosel and did not go down.

'Any news about your father, Rosel?'

'I've had another letter from Sir Peter saying they're taking steps. Still taking steps.' She paused. 'I've been wondering what I should do with him when he arrives. Perhaps rent a house here in Brack's Hill, or . . .'

'Not here,' said Cora sharply. 'He'd die here. Anyone from any other place would die here. It's so dark. So intense. The end of life. You should go to London. Bright lights – a bit of life.'

'Do you hate Brack's Hill so much?'

'Not at first. It was a bit of an adventure, to be honest. But now, I'd go like a shot. I *will* go like a shot, once the play is over. I'd go this minute if . . .' She glanced around the room.

'You don't want to let Archie down.'

'Not him! Not him!' The words rapped into the air. 'No. It's for the sake of the people who've worked so hard on the play. And because of the Prince coming.'

Rosel wondered at this. When she first came here she'd admired the funny, dry, mutually respectful relationship between Cora and Archie. Now all that had vanished and Archie seemed hardly to notice the change. The baby, of course. It was about the baby. And he had never known about that.

'Where will you go,' said Rosel, 'when you leave?'

'Perhaps to London. It's a while since I've been there. I could do with a bit of excitement. You should take your Pa to London, Rosel. You go there with him. Stay here too long and you'll rot on the stump, believe me.'

Chapter Thirty-One

A Deal

Marguerite and I have decided to go to Newcastle on the bus. It takes longer than the train but it's cheaper. I'm treating Marguerite this time and I want to conserve my money. It'll be nice to buy my own paints instead of having to be grateful to Rosel, who has receded even further into her shell these days. She is kind enough, tender even. But distant.

And me? Well, I'm very confused. I want Rosel like I did before. I need to be near her like I was before, but I don't know how to make the moves. So I, in my turn, am kind and polite and distant with her. What goes round comes round.

And I find that I'm kissing Greta every opportunity that presents itself. We don't go out together but she wants me to kiss her and I do. It feels very nice and she's excited, grateful. It's not like Rosel, but it's easier really.

And now here I am. I've just been sitting thigh to thigh with Marguerite Molloy on this long journey. Tegger's back from his sorties with the dog-man but is a bit grumpy these days. He's cutting with Marguerite now she's finished with him and short with me over the fact that I go to see her at the Raglan. Seems to think her finishing with him is something to do with me. Although I protest strongly, in my heart of hearts I think there might be something in it. Especially after this bus journey where she has laughed into my face, clutched my arm with mirth, allowed her musky perfume to invade the air I breathe. I've had to take some very deep breaths to keep myself from grabbing her and kissing her on the spot.

As the bus wends its way through Chester-le-Street she starts on about the painting. 'I was talking to Dev Pallister about it.'

'You know Dev Pallister?'

'Everybody knows him. Used to come into the Raglan now and then. He thinks the painting is very good. Recognised me straightaway.'

'It's not you,' I rap this back. 'It's *her*.'

'We know that. I explained it very carefully to him. But none of the other people in Brack's Hill will realise that.' She hesitates. 'A lot of them know me. They drop in at the Raglan.'

I'm about to ask her why she's suddenly so bothered about it when the coach swings into the station and we are preoccupied with getting off it and finding out just where we are.

Apparently we have to get a town bus down to the Haymarket where E. Crump has his gallery. It's a shop downstairs, with fine art copies of paintings and statuary. On the walls there are original paintings of the Tyne Bridges, and spookily lit scenes of Northumberland high country. There is one of an old house with a cherubic child laughing out of the window, ringlets falling on either side of her face. One of the paintings is a dark cityscape in which lights sparkle through the pall of smoke settling the city into twilight. I like this one and look for the painter's name.

The woman behind the desk in the shop has a childsize body

with an old woman's face. She knows all about me and my work. She is the friend of the woman in the gallery. It seems she, in fact, is my fairy godmother. She leads us straightaway up the steep stairs to a large room that is half-gallery, half-office. The walls are hung with pictures. There are three long tables with black folders on them. At one end is a large desk, littered with papers. On a small table beside it is a smart black telephone.

Sitting at the desk is a large man with a bulky, square head. His silk tie is slightly loose at his neck and he is jacketless. He stands up and nods at the small woman once. Her voice flutes like a blackbird. 'Here's Mr Gabriel Marchant, Mr Crump. We sold his drawing to Mr Herberts of London and Morpeth. You'll remember – Mr Herberts was very keen. Wanted more.'

He scowls at her as she leaves the office and then stands up and takes his jacket from the back of his chair and pulls it on with urgent, clumsy movements. 'Well . . .' he says, his hands reaching forward.

The man moving towards us is heavily built, turtle shouldered. His jacket has a red silk handkerchief hanging untidily from the breast pocket. He has long cheeks and these dark eyes which are almost all pupil. Hard to read.

He pumps my hand up and down then turns to Marguerite. 'And this is?'

She takes his hand in hers. 'Marguerite Molloy, Mr Crump. I am—'

'My friend – she's my friend,' I jump in.

'I model for Gabriel, too. He draws me,' she says.

'Does he now?' He frowns at her for a second, then says, 'Sit down, sit down, won't you? Have you brought some more work for me? I may have buyers.'

I lift up my battered music case; he grabs it and takes it to an empty table by the window and spreads out twelve drawings of various sizes. Two of them are practice sketches of Marguerite. He pays special attention to these. He holds them up to his face, peers across at her, then back at the paper.

I find myself resenting his eyes on my drawings and on Marguerite. I've seen that same look on butchers' faces as they assess plump herds of cattle at Priorton Mart.

He comes back to his desk, wedges himself into his seat. 'I can give you two guineas apiece for these drawings, Mr Marchant. I'll take the chance on the buyers. My risk.'

That's such a lot of money. Twenty guineas. Twenty-one pounds. There's paint and brushes and even a new jacket in that. There could be a pretty scarf for Rosel, another for Marguerite. A fountain pen, even, for Greta Pallister. That would be nice.

I take a breath and open my mouth, but before I can speak Marguerite jumps in. 'There's another way, though, Mr Crump, isn't there?'

He turns towards her. 'And what way would that be?'

'A percentage. You sell it an' you get twenty per cent of what it goes for. I saw a drawing downstairs in the gallery, not a patch on Gabriel's, for sale for twenty guineas. By that count, you're giving Gabriel twenty per cent and keeping the rest. Should be t'other way round. That's not fair. It can't be right.'

He smiles slightly, but his smile has no warmth. 'Ha! Not born yesterday, Miss Molloy?'

'No. Nor the day before.'

'You're used to doing deals, then, Miss Molloy?'

'You might say that.'

'I can see you are.' He turns to me. 'I see she's not only your friend and model, Mr Marchant, she's your guard-dog.'

I've caught Marguerite's drift. 'We're only after fair pay for fair work, Mr Crump.'

'I see.'

He hauls himself to his feet and goes to the window, leaving a trail of old tobacco scent in the air. He stares into the busy Newcastle street below, humming slightly under his breath. He does this for ages. He must be quite mad, this man. Perhaps he'll tell me to go away and take my scribblings with me and I'll have lost those precious guineas. Marguerite reads my thoughts. She presses my arm with her gloved hand. *Don't weaken, do* not *take the money and run*. I can feel her thoughts.

Crump turns back to face us and comes to stand before me. He holds out a podgy hand. 'Thirty per cent for me, Mr Marchant, and I'll give you twenty guineas on account against any money they make. This is not charity, mind you. My instinct is that you're a fine craftsman. You may be even better than that. I'd like to see more substantial work. Do you paint as well as draw?'

'Painting's what I mostly do.'

'So where are they? I see no paintings here.'

There's nothing wrong with the truth, I decide. 'They're too big. We couldn't bring them on the bus.'

A snort emerges from that fleshy mouth which might almost be a laugh. 'How am I to see these paintings, then? I can't buy them unseen.'

I don't want him to come to see me, to come to my father's house. 'There's an exhibition,' I say slowly. 'An exhibition in November, at the place where I paint. Not just me, others too.'

'The Prince is coming,' puts in Marguerite. 'The Prince of Wales is coming to see a play and look at the paintings.'

'You'll have paintings in this exhibition?' he says to me. 'How many? What are they?'

'A couple of portraits,' I say. 'And . . . and a kind of underground landscape.'

'I'm in that,' says Marguerite, eyeing him narrowly. 'That's the one I modelled for. Brr. It was really cold. Not a stitch on.'

Crump blinks very slightly at this, but keeps his gaze on me. 'I'd like to see this exhibition, Mr Marchant, especially the underground landscape. When is it? And where?' He scribbles the details down, then he asks my address and writes that down. 'Now,' he says, pulling a book towards him. 'Your cheque.'

'I can't have a cheque,' I say hurriedly.

He scowls. 'Why not?'

'Because I haven't any way of getting the money. You can't have a bank account if you've got no money.'

Muttering, he reaches into a bottom drawer, pulls out a battered black box and extracts some notes and some coins. I scoop the cash from the desk and stuff it into my top pocket without counting it. 'Thanks, Mr Crump.'

I'm dying to be away from here now: full of feelings of delight at the deal, mixed up with distrust and dislike for this bearlike man.

He comes round the desk and shakes me by the hand again. Now his tone is warm, his face not so severe. 'Could be we'll be able to help each other a fair bit, Mr Marchant, you never know.' He turns to Marguerite, takes her hand in both of his and looks at me across her shoulder. 'You have a fine watchdog here, my boy. Take her advice and you'll not go wrong.'

Outside on the pavement Marguerite dances around me; she hugs and kisses me, oblivious of the disgusted looks of the passers-by. 'Now, Gabriel, for a slap-up dinner,' she says. 'We deserve that.'

'Why did you tell him about that? About being painted with *not a stitch on*?'

She laughs at me. 'You are silly, Gabe. Innocent as a babe, you are.'

I leave it. 'Very well. Slap-up dinner it is. And then what?' It's really dawning on me now. I've twenty guineas in my pocket. And the promise of more.

She puts an arm through mine. 'And then what? Who knows? Who knows, Gabriel Marchant!'

Chapter Thirty-Two

Nights Away

'There's a chap downstairs for you, Fraulein.' Archie had struggled up the second staircase himself: an unusual event. His heavy smoking was taking its toll on his breathing and he measured his physical efforts carefully. 'I've left him in my office.'

'A chap? What chap?'

'Sir Peter Something. Tall fellow.'

She turned to the round mirror and ran a tortoiseshell comb through her hair. She straightened her collar and dabbed her nose with a powder puff. 'Is there anyone with him?' she said carefully. 'Is he alone?'

'Alone? Oh yes. Entirely. Came in a Daimler car, would you believe? All the way from London,' he ventured.

There was a question in his voice. She realised Archie was impressed. He would never admit it but he tended to flutter a bit when those Durham professors were around. Then there was all this tension, all this fuss about the Prince.

'His name is Sir Peter Hamilton Souness,' she said. 'He has

or had something to do with the Foreign Office, I think.' She put on some lipstick. 'There! That's better.'

Archie led the way. 'The Foreign Office, you say?'

'He was a friend of my father's. He offered to help me. Perhaps get him to England.'

'He'll have news of your father? Cora tells me there's some concern about your father.'

'I hope he might have news for me.' She was impatient, wanted Archie to get out of the way so she could fly past him down the stairs and rain questions on Sir Peter.

Her visitor was sitting in a wooden chair, Homburg hat on knee, hands joined over his silver-topped cane. When she entered he stood up, discarded his hat and cane, removed his right glove and shook her hand, half-bowing over it in the continental manner. 'Miss Von Steinigen! At home I see.'

For a second she was dazzled by his sheer elegance.

He glanced round the cluttered none-too-clean office. 'I thought, perhaps, I was mistaken.'

Archie edged into the room behind Rosel and started to fiddle with things on the desk. Rosel stared at him for a second, then said, 'Perhaps you would like to come to the workroom, Sir Peter? We can talk there.'

'Good, good,' said Archie heartily. 'Show your friend round the Settlement, Fraulein. Show him the work we do. The woodworking class is on, and the library's open. All our work here is voluntary, Sir Peter . . .'

Rosel swept her visitor away, sympathetic with Archie's desire for a convert to the cause, but eager for news of her father. She set up two of the folding chairs in the long room and they sat opposite each other. Then she said urgently, 'Well, Sir Peter? What is it? It can only be bad news that brings you so far.'

He shrugged his smoothly clad shoulders. 'This is where you are wrong, my dear. I was already up here, on my way to the wedding of my niece in Northumberland. I am half a day early so the thought occurred that one might seek you out.'

Her head went down. 'So, my father? You have no news of him?'

'I did not say that, my dear. I've a note from the Embassy. Someone called on your father and he is well, although a little distracted.'

'Distracted?'

'It seems he eats little and does scarcely any painting these days, although he had a lively conversation with our chap on the decline of Futurism. The same fellow took him a letter from me and sent me his return in the diplomatic bag. I have it here.' Sir Peter dipped into an inside pocket and drew out a large envelope. The letter, addressed to him, had been opened.

Rosel scanned her father's close writing: a ramble about things he saw or thought he saw, in the flat and out of the window. Drawings clipped on to the letter showed nightmarish images of the men who invaded his flat, who attacked him in cells. 'Oh!' The paper rattled as she gripped it tight.

Sir Peter's fine fingers were on her sleeve. 'Don't disturb yourself, dear Fraulein. There are things we can do. Things we *will* do. The documentation is all in place now. The papers are ready.'

'But how will he deal with all this? See this garbled rubbish? He's not fit to set out, not by himself. He will be silly and will get arrested.'

'Do not worry, dear lady. I have a journey planned – semi-official visit, don't you know. Bring him back with the baggage myself.' He smiled slightly. 'He's a friend, after all.'

She looked at him. There had been little mention of this friendship at that rather stiff meeting in London. But her father had sent her to this man. He'd known him.

'A friend?'

'We were very close – for a short time – when we were very young men. Before the Great War.'

She blinked. Into her mind came the thought of the young servant; Sir Peter's kindly attitude to one who was obviously not of his class, as though the two of them were playing some kind of game. This man had no problems with friendships across all kinds of barriers.

'You were intimate?' she said abruptly.

He chuckled. 'How very German, my dear. How very direct. We were young, he and I. We thought we knew the world.' He looked round. 'What a dreary place you have wound up in, Fraulein. I do admire missionary works, but to do it in the cold and wet seems to be rather an error. Why not try Africa? My brother is there – some kind of judge, I'm told. Not missioning, of course. But at least in Africa the sun shines and the sky is clear blue.'

'I am not missioning,' she said sharply. 'These are people like us. It is the times which are dark, not the people.'

'No, my dear, the people you help in this town were never people like us,' he said softly. Then he stood up and leaned on his silver-topped cane. 'Perhaps you would like to show me round your haven for the down and the desolate? Mr Todhunter was very keen for me to see it all.'

'He's eager to gain support so his work can continue. That is all.' She flushed, resentful of his patronage of Archie, angry with him for his condescending tone. She wanted to dismiss him, show him his place, but there was something about him that she found appealing. Also, he had her father's safety in his hands and this she couldn't jeopardise.

'Yes,' she said. 'I should show you around.'

She led him through the rooms, and talked defensively about the fine work being done here. He spoke with benign grace to some cobblers and cabinetmakers, asking quite intelligent questions about their crafts. He talked to the people borrowing library books, and placed one manicured finger on the back of a rather soiled copy of *The Mayor of Casterbridge*.

He hesitated beside the growing wall of paintings. 'Interesting but rather immature except . . . this.' He laid a finger on her triptych of Gabriel.

'I painted that.' She looked at the images, now more than a month old. The portraits of Gabriel with his long, then his short hair, showed change in him. It might have been two different people.

'This reminds me, I spoke with your friend Vanessa at an opening. She sends you her cordial greetings and asks me to say that your artist friends wish you well in your work up here. She also told me that you were accomplished yourself. That you had worked with this fellow Henry Moore.'

She laughed. 'It was not so much *worked*. He was kind enough to talk to me about some reliefs I had done. To tell you the truth, he put me off the idea of being a sculptor altogether.'

'Well,' he said heartily. 'Look at this! Perhaps he is right. You are a painter not a sculptor. And these . . .' They had come to Gabriel's little group of paintings. 'These are more the ticket.'

'Ah, they are by one of those down and desolate people whom you mentioned. A very young man. He is a member of my class. This also is his.'

They moved on to the last painting. To *The Woman in the*

Goaf. Rosel slipped off the green cover. Like all the others who had viewed the picture, Sir Peter first drew very close, then retreated. Only when he moved back again did he really see the woman. 'Well, I'm blessed! I see you have taught him well.'

'I have taught him hardly at all. He is talented and highly observant. He uses books a great deal.'

'Ah – an autodidact! Very wearying, I find. Always spouting their learning in their braying voices.'

'Gabriel is not like that. He is quiet. Too quiet, I would say. Many people in this town are quiet. Reserved. Perhaps even taciturn. He is like this.'

'Ah.' His laughter pealed out. 'I sense a protégé, even.'

She flushed.

'Are these paintings for sale? Perhaps I should buy one.'

'No.' She was surprised at how vehemently she did not want him, or anyone, to buy Gabriel's paintings. 'They are for exhibition only. For when the play is performed and the Prince of Wales comes.'

'Well now, how old is this young genius?'

'Nineteen. Perhaps twenty.'

'Ahh. I see.'

She knew how he saw it. Twenty years. The difference between her and Gabriel in one direction, between her and Sir Peter himself in another.

'You don't see,' she said gruffly, stalking ahead, back towards Archie's office.

Archie stood up behind his desk and looked from one to the other. 'Well, Sir Peter,' he said heartily, 'how do you like our little kingdom here?'

'Very commendable,' said Sir Peter, reaching for the hat and gloves which he had left on Archie's desk. 'Very fine work,

Todhunter. Crucial in these difficult times.' He made for the door, then turned back. 'Perhaps I could make a contribution,' he said abruptly. 'A small sum?' He took out an enormous flapping chequebook from an inner pocket of his voluminous tweed coat.

'That's very kind, Sir Peter,' said Archie, his eyes glinting with satisfaction. 'Very kind.'

Peter leaned on the desk to write the cheque, then paused. 'Do you think you could spare Fraulein Von Steinigen this afternoon, Todhunter? It would be a good opportunity to take her to lunch. Useful to find out more about her work here, don't you know?'

'Archie, I . . .' protested Rosel.

Archie beamed. 'What a wonderful idea. And perhaps the Fraulein can tell you of our outreach programme in New Morven. You would be delighted to go, wouldn't you, Rosel?' He turned the beam of his pleasure on her and she could not refuse.

Later, sitting opposite Sir Peter in the rather stuffy dining room of the Royal County Hotel in Durham, Rosel wondered that she had allowed herself to be manipulated by these two older men. The one pressuring her because he could save her father, the other because he knew she would help him for the sake of his beloved Settlement.

Over lunch, however, Sir Peter transformed himself into the most entertaining companion. He told her of his travels in America and Russia, shared with her tales of slight scandal in the British Government and certain rumours about the Prince of Wales. He referred to the changes in Germany but only in passing, as a background to some escapade of a member of the Romanian royal family.

Her reluctant smiles turned into laughter as his anecdotes became more risqué. He stopped mid-sentence. 'You laugh just like your mama, my dear. She had the most surprising, hearty laugh.'

Her laughter died. 'You know where she is now, with all her wild laughter? In an asylum. Boris tells me there are proposals. Ugh!' she shuddered.

Then his hand was on hers. 'Don't be sad, my dear. We may even be able to do something about that.' His tone was soft, reassuring.

'But you said that about my father.'

He stared at her. 'If I say all things are possible, then will you start to smile again?' There was something in his tone which gave her confidence, despite herself. She managed a smile, reluctantly deciding that she liked this man, really liked him.

He took his hand from hers. 'May I ask you a question?'

'Yes, all right,' she said.

'You have no husband?'

She shook her head.

'But you have had lovers?'

She lifted her chin. 'How would you know that?'

'Have you ever seen a bud that has died on a tree without ever being opened? That is like a woman in middle years who has never known fulfilment. Beauty unresolved. I have some such in my acquaintance. You are not one of these poor souls.'

She was made uncomfortable by his comfortable certainty. 'And you, Peter? You were obviously beautiful.' He was still, in fact, a very handsome man. 'Is your beauty unresolved? It is harder to tell in a man.'

He blinked at the turned table, then laughed. 'Well, I was married once. And I have had lovers.'

'And these lovers,' she persisted. 'Were they men, or women?'

That shout of laughter again. 'Ha! No Englishwoman would have asked such an indelicate question.'

'And being an Englishman, you didn't answer it.'

He stared at her. 'If you want honesty, I don't feel there is a great deal of difference between the two, as far as affections are concerned. I become interested in the person. We'll leave it at that, shall we?'

It was her turn to touch his hand. 'Sir Peter, when I first met you I thought you were typically English. Boring. Restricted. But now . . .'

His hand turned against hers and grasped it firmly. 'But now, I am just like any man. Even a young painter of the dark!'

She let her hand lie in his. She felt warm and comfortable with this man. Safe in a way she had never felt with any man in her life. She glanced around the restaurant where the scattering of well-upholstered guests were tucking into substantial repasts. What a world away from Brack's Hill with its soup kitchen and its thin children. She closed her eyes. Just let me enjoy this comfort for a little while, she prayed to anyone who was there. Let me enjoy it without feeling guilty.

'Rosel?' Peter was looking at her intently.

She blinked. 'Sorry. What was it?'

'I wondered whether you would care to stroll up to the cathedral. I believe it is very fine. Or perhaps you need to get back to your beleaguered town?'

'Yes,' she said, 'I would like to stroll to the cathedral. And no, I am not in any hurry to go back there, to be very honest.'

* * *

'Three hundred pounds!' Archie threw the cheque, made out in Sir Peter's sprawling hand, on to the couch beside Cora. 'Feller gave us three hundred pounds just on a walk round the Settlement by the Fraulein. She should give guided tours all the time.'

'I wish you wouldn't call Rosel that, Archie. The Fraulein. Sounds so sarcastic.'

'Three hundred pounds, Cora! What good we can do with that. Re-equip the joiner's shop – those tools are falling to pieces. New books! New *art* books! No doubt Sir Peter would approve of that.' The couch creaked as he sat down beside her. 'Perhaps we could get the main hall painted for the Prince's visit. Bright canary yellow. That'll make His Royal Highness blink.' He laughed wholeheartedly, then coughed and spluttered.

She smiled slightly at him. His joy at his visitor's generosity had stripped him for a moment of his hag-ridden obsession with the place, and made him optimistic again. His usually smooth hair was sticking up all over and his tired eyes were gleaming with pleasure.

'You should buy yourself a little car,' she said suddenly. 'Traipsing around like you do, going to meetings, carrying all that charity stuff. You're getting worn out. With a little car you could do so much more.'

She watched as he considered the suggestion, then rejected it. He hugged her absently, as though she were a cat. 'No, no,' he said. 'I couldn't justify that. I can spread it out to so much more benefit. Yellow paint!' He stood up. 'I'll pull together some volunteers and we'll paint the main hall.' He made for the door and she called him back.

'What is it?' His gaze was preoccupied. In his mind he was already distributing brushes and yellow paint into willing hands.

She held the cheque towards him. 'You need this,' she said. 'You'll have to put it in the bank.' She threw it. He caught it, and vanished. A second later his head came back round the door. 'Cora?'

She looked up from her book. 'Yes?'

'Are you all right?'

'Why?'

'It just seems that you've been a little *hors de combat* lately. Lost your *joie de vivre*.' His tone was hearty. She knew his sudden caring was some kind of a residue from his recent goodwill about the cheque.

I've lost more than my *joie de vivre*, she thought. 'It's nothing,' she said quietly. 'Nothing at all.'

'Good. I'm pleased about that.' His head vanished and Cora knew that she vanished just as completely from his head in that very instant.

Marguerite and me ended up in Newcastle in this little hotel she knew. It was not far from the station and you could hear the trains steaming in and steaming out, rattling on the rails. Sometimes the passing trains made the room shake. I think it was the trains. It could have been something else.

I asked Marguerite how she knew of this hotel and she told me she used to come here once, with a friend from London whom she'd met on a trip down there. Seemed he travelled selling fine goods from India and such places. He sold them to the big department stores in Newcastle. 'A bit artistic, he was. He was the one who first took me to the gallery.' I suppose that this man was the reason why she knew more than the average Brack's Hill person about pictures and things.

The wizened old woman who sat by a table in the hotel

vestibule was not troubled by our lack of luggage and did not blink when we signed ourselves in as *Mr and Mrs Smith*. Above us were *Mr and Mrs Jones*, with *Mr and Mrs Thompson* before that.

We spent the afternoon raging round Newcastle. With its high buildings, broad thoroughfares and teeming side-streets it vibrated with our own need to celebrate. Marguerite dragged me in and out of noisy pubs. We would have one drink then glower at the people there who glowered at us (resenting our jollity, I think) and leave. We went to one cinema where we saw Charlie Chaplin acting in a very heart-rending love story. Then we went and bought me a new tweed jacket and cap. I put them on, leaving my old tattered things to be handled by the delicate assistant. Then we went to another cinema and saw Claude Rains in *The Invisible Man*. We talked for quite a time about how on earth they got the effect of the man being invisible. After that we had high tea in a place where the women wore frilly aprons and pursed looks.

I was just dragging Marguerite through the majestic portals of the Central Station when she stopped.

'What is it?' I said.

'I think we've missed the last train.' She looked into my eyes. Deep. I started to pull her along again. She pulled back.

'We don't know that we have,' I said. 'Missed the last train.'

'Believe me?' she said. 'We'll have to stay overnight and get the first train back.' Again she looked hard into my eyes.

'How can we do that?'

'I know a place.'

So here we are. We've spent the night here at the hotel, pretending to be Mr and Mrs Smith. The trains have woken me up and I have opened the window to let some air into the stuffy, overfilled room. The window gap sucks in air which has salt in it from the tidal river, soot from the city fog. The buildings out there, still looming and dark, are edged with the butter light of the winter dawn and are full of promise of a very fine day.

I turn back to the room. Marguerite is lying, long legs half out of the stifling blanket, one hand under her cheek like a child, her mass of black hair spread on the pillow like moss.

Greta Pallister should be pleased with me. I finally know how to stop yourself from making babies. Marguerite showed me how to do it tenderly and with great laughter. Having a baby is not, she said, a risk she'd ever take. I can't remember how many times we made love. We seemed to be waking and doing it, languorously, again and again. Sometimes I might have just dreamed that we did it. One time I mentioned Tegger and she put a finger on my lips. 'We belong to ourselves, Gabriel. Remember that. Humans imprison each other and they start to shrink.' She gurgled with laughter. 'In more ways than one.'

Rosel is on my mind too. I know now I love her – I am sure of that. But the way she has been with me makes me think. Well, what's the use? Now you might say that's very convenient in the light of what happened last night, but I don't feel that's true.

I would not make comparisons but the wonderful thing here has been the ease and the freedom of what we've done. Here there has been no hole-in-the-corner lurking, no agonising about how old one person is, or the other. Here there has been a whole bed for a whole night. True luxury.

Now in the grey-gold of the morning, Marguerite's eyes snap open and stare into mine. 'What is it, Gabe? Never seen a sleeping woman before?'

'Well, now you ask it, no.'

'But you have done the deed?'

'Yes.'

She swings her legs on to the floor, stands up and stretches like a cat, unashamedly naked. My eyes, my mind, are filled again with the woman in the goaf.

She clips on a small corset and pulls on her stockings. 'Come on, Gabe. The early train. That was what we stayed over for, wasn't it? The early train?'

It was nine-thirty in the morning when Rosel returned from her trip with Sir Peter. He dropped her at the end of the road and speeded north in his Daimler. In the sitting room Cora looked at Rosel over her newspaper. 'What was that about, Rosel? A night out? Thoughtful of you to send a telegram. We would have worried otherwise. So this must be quite a fellow, this Sir Whatsit. Archie was telling me about his generous cheque.'

'Peter Hamilton Souness is his name, Cora. Do you know, I believe he will save my father. I think he may even save my mother.'

'Do you like him?'

Rosel shrugged. 'At first I wasn't sure. I thought he would just be useful. But now I see he has such kindness. And he is entertaining.'

'And, I bet, not bad you-know-where.' Cora's tired eyes sparked with their old humour.

Rosel blushed.

'Don't worry, darling. You're among friends here.' She winked. 'You must like him quite a bit if you ask me.'

Rosel sat down beside Cora, slipped off her shoes and stretched her slender feet in front of her. 'I must like him. I *do* like him very much. How could one sleep, Cora, with someone one does not like?'

Cora put a hand on hers. 'Happens all the time, dear girl. Believe you me.'

Chapter Thirty-Three

Changes

When I get home Tegger is there, sitting in my house, chewing on a heel of *my* bread. I glance at the roaring fire. 'I was running out of coal,' I say.

'S'all right, marra. I've been on White Leas tip. Got a couple of bags.' He's looking just a bit rough around the eyes. Apart from that he doesn't look too bad.

'Where've you been?'

He shrugs. 'Down the dogs a bit. Then there was a paying snooker tournament on. Won eight shillings.'

'Not to be sniffed at!' I'm almost too hearty.

'I came round here last night. Slept in the back bedroom. Took a look at the new painting.' He nods at the board, covered with a soft cloth, which stands by the windows. 'Pit heap, eh? Never looked like that but in your imagination. Makes it look like some place of wonder.'

I'm patient with him because he's Tegger. 'Good. That's what I'm after.'

He chews the last of the bread and looks me in the eye. 'Bin out on the tiles, have you?'

'Nah.' I shake my head. I tell him about the gallery man and the twenty guineas.

He whistles. 'Yer bugger.' He looks at me very directly again. 'Stay with him overnight, did yer?'

'Nah,' I repeat. 'We had a bit of celebration . . .'

He cocks his head. '*We*, you say?'

'. . . Aye. Me and Marguerite.'

'And you stayed over, the pair of you?'

'Aye.' I wait.

'She jacked us in, yer know. An' now she takes up with you.'

I protest. 'She hasn't taken up with me. Like she says – nobody belongs to anybody.'

'Ships that pass in the night? She told me that, too. She certainly does exactly what she wants, that one.'

'Isn't that a good thing? How many people are driven to do what they must? Look, Tegger, we're mates. I don't want this thing . . .'

'It's all right, marra. It'd take more than a woman, wouldn't it? Anyway, she's only . . .' He cocks an eye at me. 'Never mind. Are yeh gunna make us a cuppa tea or what?'

We're both due at the Settlement later today. Me for one of the interminable, near-final rehearsals of the play with the Prince's visit only a week away, and Tegger to continue fine-copying the final version of the play which will be bound in a presentation copy for the Prince. He's spent hours picking it out on Archie's old typewriter and he's getting very quick at it, considering.

Despite his hearty words, between us now there is the faint shadow of Marguerite Molloy. In some ways, the ways of experience, she's brought us closer together. In other ways she's come between us like a dagger drawn.

Despite that, I'm not sorry about what's happened. I see that Marguerite will jack me in just as sure as she's jacked old Tegger in. But that's not the point. If I'm learning anything from Rosel and now from Marguerite it's how not to be tied. How to be free is to know how free you are. For me that's free to go on painting till it becomes who I am; not to be tied to the oppression of my father's life and death, not to be shackled by the helplessness, the hopelessness I see around me every day.

I've not mentioned love out loud to anyone. I don't know that what has happened with Rosel or with Marguerite is *love*. Perhaps that makes me selfish. But maybe you have to love yourself and who you are before you can look outwards and love someone else.

The rehearsal goes very well. We're now using the Church Hall out the back of the Settlement. At least here there's a small stage. However, the way the sound works here is different to the long room at the Settlement, so there have to be some adjustments. Still, everyone is word-perfect. Better than that, once into their togs they seem to *become* their character. In fact, Nathan talks like the coroner even when he's not in his togs.

Today Cora seems to have screwed herself up another notch. I've heard her say the lines a hundred times, but even *I* have tears in my eyes and anger in my heart when I hear her speak them today.

I must say, I'm still relishing the bit where I have to kiss Greta. There's a certain joy in feeling her soft young body yield a little under mine, even if it is only part of the drama. There's this thing I've noticed about Greta. She's a serious girl but when she laughs heartily there's an explosion of giggles, like shooting rain. What a far cry from her serious face, her owl-like glasses. I like it.

Archie, for a change, seems moderately satisfied. After he's pulled us together and given us the usual notes on our performance he puts a hand up to stop us scattering. 'One moment, everyone! I have good news. We've been given a surprise donation from a friend of Fraulein Vonn.' He nods to the back of the hall, where Rosel is standing in the shadows. 'Sir Peter Hamilton Souness.' He goes on then to describe some crazy ideas about painting the long room yellow.

'Yellow?' I say.

'Yes,' he beams. 'Brighten things up a bit.'

'It'll be like working in a bowl of custard,' say I.

A rumble of laughter bubbles up from the assembled people like porridge.

'Ah, Mr Marchant!' Archie permits. 'The artist speaks. What would you have, then?'

His sarcasm. I hate that. 'Something lighter? Cream, maybe.'

'I tell you what, Mr Marchant. You shall come to the Priorton Co-op with me, to give me the benefit of your expertise.'

'That'll teach you to open your gob,' says Tegger, his eyes gleaming. I have to say there's a new note of malice in his voice.

'I'm not going with him,' I say. 'I'm working on the new painting. Lost enough time as it is.'

The crowd of us, all speculating about the Prince's visit, make our way out of the hall. As I move through the double doorway I'm conscious of Rosel hovering there. She has a brief word with Cora as she passes: touches her arm. Then as I pass she calls across to me and I go to her. The crowd parts round us.

Some of them glance at us with curiosity; others ignore us, absorbed in their own business.

Close to her I catch her perfume, that subtle hint of lemon. Her skin is clear. Her fair hair shines in the harsh electric light. She's the cleanest person I know. Her attraction is pristine. She is day to Marguerite's night. I can acknowledge now I'm equally attracted to both of these women. I'm amazed at my heart, which seems to know no loyalty. In recent weeks I've learned that real life is no Sleeping Beauty fairy tale where I kiss a princess and she awakes and we live happily ever after.

'Gabriel?' Rosel's tone is sharp. 'What are you staring at?'

'Just thinking about a fairy tale I know. How are you doing?' We make our way through the double doors together. 'It's a long time since I've seen you properly, like.'

She stops by the steamed-up windows of the Gaunt Valley Café. 'Here. Shall we have some tea?'

The bell clangs as we go through the door. She orders tea and cakes at the till and leads the way to a corner seat. 'Why have I seen nothing of you?' she demands. 'It seems to be you who've vanished.'

I'm uneasy. Not sure of what she's saying. 'You said one time, that one time . . .' I mumble. 'Apart from . . .'

She smiles slightly and there's a world of age and experience in that smile. 'I meant it, Gabriel. I really did. But I missed you at the art group yesterday morning. Where were you?'

'I was in Newcastle,' I say. 'There's this man who has a gallery. He bought some of my sketches.'

Her fair brows rise into her fringe. 'Greta told me this,' she says. 'You are taking steps forward.' She hesitates. 'They will be very excited about you, Gabriel, but don't be too eager to sell your work. You have a long way to go. These works are markers on the way. You will need the reminders of these early stages. You should not sell just now. You are still growing.'

I scowl at her, seeing her for what she is, a creature from another place. She is like one of my fossils. Entirely recognisable but out of another civilisation. 'Easy to see you've never been out of work, or out of money for that matter. See this jacket? I bought it in Newcastle yesterday with some of the money I made. My other one was falling to pieces. It was already worn when my father had it. I left that in the shop, to be put in their rubbish bin. I also have a debt to my corner shop to pay off. He's stopped serving me 'cause I can't pay. And then I need to buy materials if I'm to make any progress.'

She leans across and puts a finger on my lips. 'I'm sorry, Gabriel. I should not have said that.' She hesitates. 'As a matter of fact, I just turned down an offer for your paintings, the ones already in the hall. The man who gave Archie his donation would have bought them all. He really liked *The Woman in the Goaf*. He has taste.'

'Taste? Rich bloke? Is he the London toff, *Sir* Peter something?'

'Toff! That is an ugly word.' A faint blush stains her pale cheek.

'You're right, though. I wouldn't want to sell the paintings anyway. Not just yet. Not the goaf woman ever. The drawings are different – I see that.'

'I suppose so.' She looks very sad.

I put a hand across the table and cover hers. 'Did the feller have news of your father?'

She shakes her head. 'They're looking into it. He was very kind.' Now she looks me very clearly in the eye. 'I like him. I stayed with him, Gabriel, in his hotel.'

My hand moves away from hers as if it were burning hot. 'Why? Why d'you do that?'

She shrugs that wonderful shrug of hers. 'He was kind. He told me stories. He is a sweet man.'

I can't say, tit-for-tat, that *I'd* stayed out last night in the arms of Marguerite Molloy. That would reduce it to some playground Yah! Boo! game. As I am unable to say that, there seems very little to say. In silence we watch the woman lay the cups and the teapot and the cake plate on the table.

We move on now to casual chatter. We talk, inevitably, of the play and the yellow paint, and I know truly, that the other things between us are in the past. That's why she has been so open with me, has told me about her new lover in this blatant manner.

Greta listened with amusement to her father's conversations with her mother about what he should wear when the Prince came. 'They say I have to have a bowler hat to meet him. I've never had a hat. My cap suits me.'

His wife looked at him thoughtfully. 'Yes, I can see that. The other lads'll be wearing caps. You won't want to be different.'

'Not that I have to. Wear a bowler, that is.'

'No, you don't, do you?'

'I'll make my own mind up.'

'You always do.'

The next day, Dev told her he thought now he *would* wear a bowler. 'The chairman's wearing one. Mebbe it's not such a good thing to stand out, like.'

'Anything you say, Dev. You'll have to go to Priorton to get it. The Co-op, probably. Or Doggart's.'

'You go, I've too much to see to here.'

She had to put her foot down. 'I will not do that, Dev Pallister. What if I come back with the wrong size?'

'Try it on yourself. You'll have an idea.'

'I'll be a laughing stock, the joke of the year. No, you're coming, my lad. We'll go tomorrow. And you can come too, Greta. We can get you a nice new pinafore dress. I've got money saved.'

Greta shook her head. 'No need. I'll have my sacking pinny and my clogs 'cause I'll be Dorothy.'

Her mother groaned. 'But what will he think, the Prince? You'll be talking pitmatic. He'll think you're really like that.'

'I hope so. It'll show I'm a good actress.'

'You could still come. Help your Dad choose his bowler hat. First thing tomorrow.'

Greta shook her head again. 'I've got homework. And after school I'm painting the long room in the Settlement. Bright yellow. Two more days to go.'

'I wondered why you looked like you had yellow fever,' said her father, before retiring again behind his newspaper.

I've lost far too much time lately on my painting of the pit heap. There's such a flurry now about the Prince's visit. Even with five of us working, the long room's taking days to paint. Archie won the battle over the colour and I'm right. The room *is* beginning to look like a bowl of custard.

Back home, I've just washed the last of the yellow speckles off the backs of my arms and taken the cloth off the painting when there's a knock on the door.

Marguerite walks through the door without waiting and gives me a peck on the cheek. Her fine nose wrinkles. 'Now then, tiger! You smell of paint.' Then she kisses me on the lips and one part of me delights that this thing is continuing, at least for now. It's not to be put in a funerary box like my intimacy with Rosel. Another part of me is terrified in case Tegger walks in on us. He probably won't, though. After the hall-painting he was off to the printer's seeing about the binding of the copy of the play, I think.

Marguerite inspects the painting. 'Different again,' she says.

'Aye. Different again.'

'Sit down, won't you! You make the room look small.' She pushes me so that I'm sitting in my father's chair. I grab her clumsily to pull her on to my knee but she pulls herself away, takes off her coat and hat, and sits on a hard chair by the paint-laden kitchen table. 'I've come to talk to you about something serious.' She smiles widely. 'Well, that's the main thing I've come about.'

'So what's this something serious?' I find it hard to concentrate. She's wearing a shortish, well-fitting dress in deep purple, which calls up tones in her dark hair. In the popping gaslight her eyes are almost green. 'What's wrong?'

'Nothing wrong, not really.' She hesitates, then speaks in a great rush. 'Your painting of *The Woman in the Goaf* – I don't think you should leave it on show like that, with the others.'

I stiffen at this. 'Why not? It has to stay. I've told Archie Todhunter.'

She nods. 'I know it's your best thing yet, Gabe, I do. But, well,' she hesitates. 'Dev Pallister came to see me at the Raglan.'

'You know Mr Pallister?'

'Yeah. In a casual sort of way – I think I said.'

'Well, what's he have to say?'

'He was saying that lots of local men will be there, on that day. He named some. Some that I know quite well.'

'What's that to do with anything?'

She takes out a cigarette without offering me one and lights it with matches from my mantelpiece. She inhales, then talks to me through the smoke that trails out of her mouth. 'Do you know what I do, Gabriel?'

'You pull pints at the Raglan. You make people feel all right.'

'Well, yes, I do make people feel all right. More than that when the fancy takes me. Only when I want to, remember. And I get presents, Gabriel. Money.' She sits back now in her chair. 'From some of those men who know Dev Pallister. Nice men, mainly.'

The realisation floods in on me and I'm brick red. I wish for my father's chair to swallow me. I curse myself for my ignorance and understand in retrospect Tegger's half-aggressive despair at my simplicity. At last I sniff. 'So. Right, then. What's this to do with *The Woman in the Goaf*?'

'Nothing. I know the woman in the painting is not me, but the problem is that up there on the wall, she *looks* like me. And these men, they'll recognise me.'

My thoughts are racing. 'Then they're seeing the woman as a siren and that's OK. That's part of what I'm trying to say.'

Her finely arched brows lift. 'Siren? That's a new one.'

'So. What's the problem?'

'Gabriel, they'll be angry – furious. They'll feel exposed, embarrassed. Especially before the Prince.'

'So what? I want it to rouse people. It'll have done its work if they get angry, whatever the reason.'

'But their anger'll turn against you . . .'

I shrug.

'And against Archie Todhunter and the Settlement. And these are the men who vote money to keep the Settlement going.

Archie Todhunter acts very independent, but there's ways he has to fit in. Dev Pallister explained this to me. Came back a second time.' She looks at me hard; the boldness is gone from her eyes now. Her gaze is rueful, appealing. 'If I'd realised this, Gabe, I'd not have agreed to pose for you. If I'd realised what would happen to the painting.'

'You weren't to know.' I cough hard to clear the disappointment, the despair from my voice, to make it brisk and business-like. 'Well, that's it then. I can't, and wouldn't, have it on display without your say so and there's an end of it.'

She throws the last of her cigarette in the fire and leans forward. Her breasts move under the purple fabric as she does so. 'No, Gabe, not the end. Look, I've had this idea. You don't want to actually sell the painting just yet, do you?'

'No, not yet.'

'So why don't we lend it to Mr Crump to exhibit in his gallery, to show what you can do? He'll be selling some of your sketches alongside, so he's not losing out.'

'Your friends can see it there. Won't that upset them?'

Her hair trembles and dances as she shakes her head. 'No. No. It's away there out of their world here. Me, I'm rendered anonymous up there. Your woman will be herself in that gallery, not me.'

Somehow I'm relaxing. She's very clever, is Marguerite. 'It's an idea.'

'He's coming, isn't he, Mr Crump, to the performance? We can show him the picture here.'

'Here? In this house?'

'He'll be charmed. He knows artists are eccentric. He'll have been in many a worse artist's garret.'

'You're very wise.'

'Me? From the looks you were giving me half an hour ago I thought you thought I was a demon or something.'

I smile slightly at this. 'You told me once that nobody owns anybody.'

'That's the truth.'

'Do you still help these . . . friends?'

She waits a second before answering. 'I'm not saying I wouldn't, if I wanted to. If someone needed me. But . . .'

'But?'

She comes to kneel beside my father's chair, on my grandmother's sunflower mat. 'But right now my hands are full of you and your paintings and Mr Crump and . . . it's good fun.' Then she kisses me and I am made to learn again how, just for a while, we *can* belong to each other.

Chapter Thirty-Four

Yellow Light

Operating without my advice, Archie Todhunter has had his way over the colour. Our joint efforts have made a great impact on the long room at the Settlement. It's taken five of us two days to put two coats of yellow paint on everything that does not move. The place is blazing with a yellow light that hurts my eyes.

In the end, just Greta Pallister and me are left to do the final touches. The very last task is to put a second coat on the cupboard in the corner.

'This must have been a bit of a comedown for you,' she says.

'How d'you make that out?' I'm squinting at the narrow cupboard door-return. I've been given all those things to do which demand a small brush and any degree of accuracy.

'More used to painting masterpieces.'

'Get on!' I'm unmoved by her sarcasm. She's been good to work with: neat and able to concentrate. I don't have to say much. She's been talking as usual about school and her ambitions, about books she's been reading and how her normally imperturbable father is in a bit of a flap about the Prince's visit.

'It's really funny, this, as he's no time for royalty or what he calls "all them up there". But here he is, getting carried away.'

'He's not on his own. I think people like to put on a good front whoever's gawping at them.'

With only two days to go, the place has been humming with a sense of suppressed anticipation. Archie Todhunter has been very tight-lipped, complaining at how long the painting was taking. He only has tomorrow now to get the pictures rehung and the display tables laid out with the quilting, the joinery, and the samples of shoe-mending.

As well as this, there's the Church Hall, where the play will be performed. Even at this moment he's across there in workman's overalls wielding a brush. I'll say one thing for him. he will get stuck in when needs be.

'So, where's your naked lady?' says Greta. 'Why has Mr Todhunter banished her to the outer darkness?' She has finished her bit. She starts to dip her brush in a bucket of turpentine and rub it with a rag. Her slender fingers are freckled with yellow paint.

'Nah. I took her home. She didn't fit with the rest, see?' I stop talking to concentrate on the last tricky corner. 'Took the attention off the business of the day.'

'Poor thing. I really liked her, even under her veil. Mind you, I did hear my dad say to my mother that she'd cause a bit of havoc in the town. Here, give us that brush if you're finished.' She takes it from me and I sit back, watching her as she makes a very efficient job of the cleaning.

'I didn't withdraw her for that. I withdrew her for reasons of my own,' I say.

I'm still not certain it was the right thing to do; to keep her on display or take her home to allow a few men in Brack's Hill to sleep more comfortably in their beds. I suppose it was really for Marguerite.

Archie Todhunter was very pleased, of course, when I told him of my decision to remove the painting. Said that naturally he didn't believe in any kind of artistic censorship, but there was so much about this 'day with the Prince' that could go wrong. He had to admit to some relief in not having to ride the storm which the picture would inevitably have raised.

Greta wipes her hands with the rag and comes to sit beside me. 'Personal reasons?'

'Yes.'

'It's a shame though.'

'Not really. She'll eventually be hung in a gallery in Newcastle, so more people'll see her than would have here. More people that know about proper painting and art.' I have to cross my fingers at this. There's no saying Mr Crump will agree to Marguerite's plan.

'So, that should do you some good?' Her head is on one side. There is a smut on her nose.

'I hope so.' I've been through all this with Marguerite and it seems right. As she said to Crump that day at the gallery, she knows how to strike a bargain. As *he* said, I could do worse than having her keep an eye out for me. But there's more to Marguerite than just that. There's lessons to learn about how to belong to yourself. Not to look to the past nor the future; just be, and belong to yourself. There's intoxication in it.

'Here, d'you want one?' Greta is nudging me with a crumpled bag of toffees.

'Don't mind if I do.'

'I'm pleased I've got you here. I wanted to talk to you about something.'

'About what?'

'Our bargain. You remember?'

'Greta, I—' I am just about to tell her that at least I've discovered how not to make babies when she puts up her hand like a policeman on traffic duty.

'Stop!' she says. 'I said I wanted to say something. *Me*, not you.'

Very humbly I concentrate on chewing my toffee.

'Now Gabriel, I know we had an agreement for after the performance. That you were going to show me.'

'Greta, I . . .'

That hand again. 'Shush, I said. Now I don't want your feelings hurt, but I have to tell you I've changed my mind.'

'Why's that?' I say, trying to make my voice neutral.

'To be very honest, I didn't know what I was taking on. I didn't know you that well then. It was easy to strike the bargain, when I didn't really know you.'

'Now . . .'

'Now I know you better. We're . . . well, kind of friends. And that – although it might be very useful to me, doing that thing would spoil everything, I can see that. There'd be no future – for you and me, I mean. Our friendship is too important to spoil.' Her eyes are sharp as a hawk behind her spectacles.

'D'you think so?'

'Yes. My mother always says there's a time and a place for everything.' Now she leans across, puts a hand on either side of my face and kisses me. I think it must be the toffees because the kiss is very sweet indeed. Then she jumps up and dashes off and I'm left not knowing whether I'm relieved or disappointed by her decision.

* * *

Rosel Vonn moved to one side to avoid the hurrying girl. She'd seen the two young heads close together and witnessed the fleeting kiss. She stood still for a second until all was quiet in the room and then rattled the door and bustled in, pushing her makeshift trolley that held all the paintings, except *The Woman in the Goaf*, while the hall was being painted.

It's Rosel, making all that noise. I make my way across the room with the turpentine bucket in one hand, cleaned brushes in the other. 'Well!' she says. 'So the hall is transformed into our new gallery?'

'Looks like it. Todhunter insisted on the yellow.'

'It's very cheerful.'

'The paintings'll look like decorations on a birthday cake.'

'But not your *Lady in the Dark*?'

'Not her.'

'Do you really think it will be better this way, Gabriel? You have a right to hang it, you know.' She still sounds angry on my behalf.

'It's better this way – I know it.' I look down so she cannot see what I'm really thinking. 'No one pressured me,' I tell her. 'It will take attention off the portraits. They're more important on the day.'

She puts her hand on the trolley. 'I have the other paintings here. I will lay them in place on the floor. The paint on the walls should be dry enough by tonight for Tegger and Mr Conroy to come and put in the picture hooks. Perhaps you would like to help me lay them out?'

I shake my head. 'Sorry, Rosel, I promised Mr Todhunter I'd

go across and help them finish the Church Hall. He's in a flap because we're all behind.'

'Very well. That is fine, Gabriel. Cora said she would come down to give me some help. She will only be a moment.'

Rosel watched him walk the length of the room and disappear out of the door. Out of the door with Gabriel, she suddenly thought, went the final shreds of her own youth. Now all the two of them would ever be was a fragment, a spark of memory in each other's life. There was a certain comfort in that.

The door clattered and she shook off the sentiment as Cora came through the door looking very grim. 'There's two fellows in long coats in the office and Dev Pallister and a vanload of men at the gate talking about cameras and boxes and ladders. Where *is* Archie? He's impossible. Never anywhere when you want him.'

'Archie?' asked Rosel. 'He's across at the Church Hall, according to Gabriel Marchant.'

'Church Hall?' said Cora wearily, looking around in despair at the bright yellow room. 'D'you think your friend would have made his donation, Rosel, if he realised his generosity would contribute to *this*?'

Rosel fetched a folding chair from a stack in the corner and set it by the window. 'Sit here, Cora. I will go and tell Archie of his visitors.'

Cora was still sitting there when Rosel returned. She was staring at her hands and her eyes were full of tears. Rosel put a hand on her shoulder. 'What is it? What is it, Cora?'

'I don't know.'

'You are bound to feel bad, Cora, after what happened.'

The actress pushed her hand away and sniffed. 'I thought we were here to place pictures, Rosel. Although whether it's worth bothering, I don't know. I don't know anything about painting but my guess is, this colour will drown them out of sight.'

Rosel shook her head. 'You sit there, Cora. I'll spread these paintings out and you can give me your advice. Which beside which? The problem is, balancing out the work coming from the class with the portraits, the ones to do with the play, and the other odd paintings the class has done.'

Cora perked up a bit. 'I see that Gabriel's naughty picture is not to be included.'

'It seems not. I would prefer that it were here. It is a better painting than anything else.' She frowned. 'I fear that pressure was put on him.'

'Yes, I reckon Archie must have leaned hard on him. Drat the man.'

Rosel came to Archie's defence. 'I do not think so. He was reluctant, but it was Gabriel himself who withdrew it.'

'Kind of him, I'm sure.'

'Cora! This is not like you.'

'Shall we get on placing these pictures? We can't give Archie anything else to go frantic about.' Cora's tone was not just weary, but cold. Rosel knew there'd be no more conversation about Cora, or Archie for that matter.

Archie stopped in his tracks when he saw the Daimler.

'Visitors, visitors, the Fraulein said! It's Lord Chase, for goodness' sake, and God knows who else. And Cora playing silly beggars yet again.' He glanced down at his overalls and his hands, still covered with grime from the Church Hall. 'You go and talk to them, Gabriel, while I scrub up.'

'Me?' said Gabriel. 'I'm covered with paint as well as dust.'

'Well, it doesn't . . . it doesn't . . .'

'Matter about me? Thank you very much.'

'I don't mean that. I don't, man,' said Archie as they reached the door.

'I don't like talking to strangers,' said Gabriel flatly.

'Do it. It's good for you. Something you have to learn.' Archie pushed past him and hurried up the stairs to restore himself to the state of a man who could face such visitors on something like equal terms.

I don't want to do this for Archie but I have to admit to a certain curiosity about Lord Chase. He was, after all, my father's and my own employer for a while. It was on his direct order that activists like my father should find no work in the mines and should be condemned to live without work for the rest of their lives.

I thought he would be very tall but when I look him in the eye I look downwards. He's wearing a country cap, rounder and softer than the miners' cap, and a long tweed coat. He stares at me with a blank look which takes me in but doesn't see me. The man beside him is even shorter than he is, and is wearing a military uniform of some kind.

'Mr Todhunter says he'll be here in a minute. He's just gone to change.' His Lordship nods but fails to ask me who I am.

He glances at his companion. 'This Todhunter fellow's done great work among the poor in the district. Old-fashioned sort, a man of principle.'

The other man makes sounds in his throat of agreement, of appreciation.

I might just as well not be there. These men have forgotten me. I want to rage at them, to tell them of my father hanging from a tree, but they strike me dumb with their easy assurance and the way they fill the space around you so you almost suffocate. They ignore me but I can't find a way to get out of the room without backing out like some serving maid.

Now at last Archie Todhunter comes breezing in, scrubbed immaculate, with his filmstar hair just *so*. He's wearing a very dark suit I've never seen and his round spectacles gleam with recent polishing. 'Ah, Lord Chase.' He moves into the room and takes possession of it. He shakes his Lordship heartily by the hand and turns to the other visitor.

His Lordship introduces him. 'This is Colonel Black, who will oversee arrangements for Thursday.'

'Good, good,' says Archie. He turns towards me. 'And you will have met the wonderful Gabriel Marchant here.'

Lord Chase turns to me. 'Mr Marchant?'

'Gabriel is a coming man, your Lordship. A credit to the Settlement. A painter of great talent. A coming man.'

'Is this so?' My hand is grasped now in a wiry, close grip. 'Are you a painter of great talent, Mr Marchant?'

'I wouldn't say that.'

I rescue my hand, only to have it pumped by that of the Colonel who says, 'So you are one of the unemployed?'

Archie interrupts with, 'Gabriel's very much employed these days. Apart from his remarkable painting he's been working very hard rehearsing the play and getting ready for the visit, as have all our Settlement people. We don't define people here by their unemployment, Colonel.'

I delight in the way Archie Todhunter has reproved the pair of them, put them in their place. I gather courage. 'I *was* a miner,' I say. 'In fact, I worked in Lord Chase's pits. My father too, until 1926. Then he was blacklisted.'

Lord Chase's jaw hardens. 'It is all very unfortunate. These are hard times for us all.'

An image of the glossy Daimler rises before my eyes and I open my mouth but Archie Todhunter gets in before me. 'Now, then, your Lordship, Colonel! I will show you round the Settlement, just as I will show the Prince. Then we will go to the Church Hall where the play will be performed.'

'Play?' raps out the Colonel. 'There was no mention of a play.'

'This is the whole point,' says Archie. 'The play *is* the Settlement. It shows the best of what we have to offer here. Talented writers, artists, performers, people of ideas . . .'

'How long is this play?' The military voice raps out.

'Not long, Colonel. Just over the hour.'

Chase and the Colonel exchange glances. 'Impossible,' says the colonel. 'We have a schedule.'

'Just the First Act.' Todhunter goes into bargaining mode. 'These are scenes on the Front in the Great War. I know that His Royal Highness served at the Front. Perhaps he would be interested.'

'And it tells of the state of the mines in the middle of the war,' I butt in. They all look round at me. It's as though a duck has spoken.

'Yes, yes,' says Todhunter, 'and that.'

'The schedule is very tight,' says the Colonel. He glances down at a small notebook in his leather-gloved hand. 'Mr Pallister wants His Royal Highness to meet old soldiers at the

Working Men's Club, and there is a poultry project and this allotment project . . .'

Lord Chase claps his hands together in his peculiar way and we know that this bit of the discussion is over. 'Well, Todhunter? Lead the way. Walk us through it. The Colonel can get out his stopwatch and we shall see if His Royal Highness can fit in some scenes from your play.'

'I'm gunna wear my cap for the visit,' Dev announced at teatime that night. 'Not the bowler.'

'I see,' said his wife grimly. 'That was a waste of money we couldn't afford.'

Greta looked up from *Brave New World* which she had propped against the teapot to make it easier to read. 'You didn't suit the bowler anyway. Made you look like a grocer.'

'You should wear it, now we've got it,' said Pauline.

Dev shook his head. 'Stand out like a pea on a drum. I was talking to these film lads today. Seems the Prince wears a soft cap, so the other toffs do as well. No top hats, even bowlers. Wouldn't do to stand out. Bad taste.' He scooped a spoonful of rice pudding and looked at Greta. 'And you can say goodbye to any thoughts of him seeing that play of yours. According to these film lads he's through in ten minutes, fifteen at the most.'

'Oh dear,' said Greta. 'Mr Todhunter'll be really upset.'

'That one! He was enjoying himself today hobnobbing with Lord Chase and the Colonel. Glowing with it, he was.'

Greta frowned. 'You don't like Mr Todhunter, do you?'

Dev put down his spoon. 'I wouldn't say that. I do and I don't. He means well – you can see that. It's just that Todhunter's an unusual type. Can't place him, somehow. I can place Lord

Chase and his colonel. I can place young Gabriel Marchant. But Todhunter, his heart's in the right place, but he's all things to all men, so who the hell – sorry Pauline – who *is* he really? Does he know himself?'

'That's very clever, Dad,' said Greta approvingly. '*Issues of identity and characterisation*. We've done that at school with the novels of Charlotte Brontë.'

'Thank you very much, Miss Knowall,' said Dev. 'I'm honoured to know that. Now, Pauline, is it out of order to take a second helping of the rice pudding?'

All this cleaning and painting has me whacked. I must be getting soft. I wonder how I ever lasted a shift pushing and hauling tubs up and down inclines in the pit.

Tired as I am, when I get home I'm pleased to see Tegger sprawled in my father's chair reading a sporting paper. He has the fire stacked with filched coal. He grins. 'What cheer, marra! You look paggered.'

'So I am. Where were you, when all this work was being done?'

'I've been down the Wetherill's printers all day. Took the play down for them to bind it. A gift for our Great Visitor. You know!' He nods to a slim volume on the table. I pick it up and flick through it. I look back across to his grinning face. 'But this is . . .'

'Aye. Properly printed. I took my typescript down to get it bound and the old man there asked about it. When I told him who it was for he said it should be properly done. Put his other jobs on hold and set the thing up himself.'

I flick to the title page.

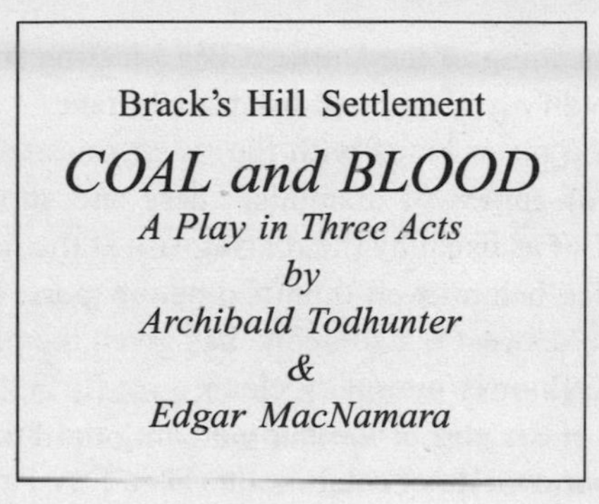
Brack's Hill Settlement

COAL and BLOOD

A Play in Three Acts

by

Archibald Todhunter

&

Edgar MacNamara

'Edgar! Sunday name, eh?'

'Archie Todhunter said I'd gotta put my name on.'

'Only right. It looks very good, Tegger.'

'Doesn't it? The old man printed me twenty copies at a go. Beats typewriting any day. Bound three very fine like that: one each for me and Archie, and one for the Prince, of course. And the rest, more ordinary bound, for the Settlement, for if they do it again.' He's still grinning ear to ear.

I wink at him. 'Proud of you, marra!' And we laugh together like mad things.

He splutters to a stop. 'Now then, what say we go and have a pint to celebrate?'

'Yeah. Yeah.'

'Raglan's no good like,' he says, looking at me closely. 'Not these days.'

I return the look. 'Mebbe not.'

'We'll go to the Club. Build the fire up afore we go, lad. There's plenty o'coal.' He grins. 'Little visit to the coal dump with me sack.'

It's a very long time since I've been to the Club. The last time was on the morning of the Durham Big Meeting in 1932. I had a pint then with my father and his friend Steve.

Tonight the place hums with the usual routines of talk and the playing of games of draughts, chess and shove-ha'penny. The old men sit as usual by the roaring fire at the far end. A few men are buried behind well-thumbed newspapers. It still smells of hops and old sweat but someone has given the place a lick of paint and the floor is unusually clean.

We stand at the end of the bar watching the buzz around us and having our own quiet celebration. Then Dev Pallister comes up behind us and nods at the barman, who silently fills us another pint.

'Strangers here these days, lads?' he says, leaning easily against the bar. 'I thought the Raglan was your usual haunt.'

'Not tonight,' I say, conscious of Tegger who is suddenly tense beside me. 'We fancied a change.'

'Aye. A change is often a good thing.' He looks very directly at me. 'I hear that the big painting of yours won't be in the display.'

'No, it won't. I already have three paintings in that show. I decided there were better places for this one.'

'Did you? Our Greta went on about it not being there. About censorship.'

'Did she?'

'Said it was like censors cutting a piece out of a newspaper. A dangerous thing.'

'She has a way with words, your Greta.'

'She's on her way up and out of this place and that's no bad thing.' Then Dev does something unusual. He puts a hand on my arm. 'You too, lad, if I'm not mistaken. Just one thing though. Be careful not to leave the best of this place behind you.'

Then Dev leaves us with our pints and rejoins the man he was talking to, who doesn't look like any miner. He's wearing a coloured shirt and tie under a tweed jacket with leather patches. Dev Pallister hangs about with all sorts.

But we're here to celebrate. I take a sip of the strong ale and suppress my wincing reaction. Tegger tells me of a sure thing that's racing at York on Saturday and can I lend him the wherewithal to get there on the train? If I can see my way to that, he'll go halves with me with the winnings he'll inevitably make.

'Honest, kidder.'

Dev Pallister took an appreciative sip of his flowing pint and eyed his companion. 'I forgot that you were not much of a drinker yourself, Mr Grossmith.'

'I've said it a hundred times if I've said it once. It's not the drink, Mr Pallister.' Herbert Grossmith patted his creased waistcoat. 'Dicky stomach. I'm a martyr to dyspepsia. Beer is poison. A single glass of port in a week is all I can take. The rest of the time I stick to plain water. Adam's Ale, if you like.'

'I'd have thought that a bit of a disadvantage, myself. There's a lot of information in public bars.'

Grossmith shook his head. 'It causes me no problems, Mr Pallister. No problems at all.' He took a delicate sip of his water. 'So, you were saying? Everything in place for tomorrow?'

'Absolutely everything. The committee has covered all eventualities.'

'Good.' Grossmith's slightly bulging eyes dropped casually to the notebook, which stood guard on his glass of Adam's Ale. 'His Royal Highness will be here at the Club, seeing the war veterans at the Cenotaph, and will look in on the poultry project, the new allotment project and, er, the Settlement.'

'That's right. Colonel Black, who's been doing recces for the Lord Lieutenant, says the arrangements are fine.'

Grossmith scribbled something on the page. 'And the Settlement? What's on offer for the Prince there?'

'Well, there is the play. *Coal and Blood*, but we're still not clear whether the Prince will have time to see that. The actors'll be there in costume and the Prince will receive a copy of the play. And there'll be an exhibition of the other work they do there – painting, woodwork and such.'

'Painting?' Grossmith turned back a page in his notebook. 'I was talking to Nathan Smith. He was saying that one painting, by a lad who's shown great promise, had to be removed. Questionable subject-matter. Offensive.'

'Did he say *offensive*?'

'Not in so many words, but . . .'

'I know nothing about any such painting.' Dev flicked out a hand, rejecting the question as you would swat a fly.

'How do you find Archie Todhunter, Mr Pallister?'

'Fine man. A visionary. Idealist. His heart's in the right place.'

'I've heard him called big-headed, pretentious.'

'You must have been talking to some very ignorant people.'

'Well, I . . .'

Again the dismissive gesture. 'If you want to know about Archie Todhunter, you go and talk to him.'

'I am not the biggest fanatic for amateur theatrics, but you can be sure I will, Mr Pallister.' Grossmith stood up. 'Perhaps I could get you another drink, Councillor?'

Pallister smiled slightly and stood up himself. 'No, thank you, son. I buy my own beer – I make it a rule.'

Grossmith shook hands with him. 'Perhaps I will see you

tomorrow, then. We'll have our photographer there. I hear the newsreels will be there, too. How d'you feel about going to the pictures and seeing yourself on *Pathé News*? Now that *would* be something!'

'To be honest, Mr Grossmith, I don't like it at all.' Dev's gaze strayed over the man's shoulder. 'Oh, there's Hughie Masterton. I need a word with him about the football team. If you'll just excuse me.'

Herbert Grossmith watched his retreating back. Cagey number, Dev Pallister, with a finger in every pie. There was no pinning him down. Never mind. Herbert thought he would have a go at this young painter. Bound to be a bit of resentment there. Worth a stir.

Chapter Thirty-Five

Searching

I am in a bad state. It must have been the strong beer, followed by a very late session in my kitchen poring inch-by-inch over the pit-heap picture. I spent at least half an hour scraping off the part by the edge of the pool, where the single lime tree sticks up at its funny angle. That was the third time I've cleared that square of board and still I can't get it right. Even with four pints of strong ale inside me I could see the problem but not the solution.

My head thumps with a steady rhythm and I try lifting it off the pillow. The thumping doesn't stop. I stagger to my feet and shake my head. Even the violent movement will not get rid of the thumping.

Knocking. Someone's knocking at the door. I have to lift my father's tin clock to the window to peer at it in the grey November light. Eight o'clock.

It must be Tegger. There's some kind of trouble. I leap down the narrow stairs three at a time and scramble to open the door. My bleary eyes make out Rosel Vonn in the dark light of morning. 'Come in, come in! You should've come straight in,' I say. 'The door's not locked. Never locked.'

'I did not wish to surprise you.' Her glance takes me in, head to toe. I am wearing the old shirt of my father's in which I usually sleep. 'Come in. Sit down,' I say and bolt back upstairs.

When I get back down, decently covered, she's there in the kitchen peering at the new picture. I turn up the gas and the room is bathed in pallid light. 'What is it?' I say. 'What's the matter?'

'It's Cora. Archie came to get me half an hour ago. When he went to sleep last night Cora was there beside him. When he woke up she was gone. We've walked the streets around the Settlement and there is no sign of her. He kept saying "Today of all days. Today of all days." At last I fear I lost my temper with him and told him to go to the police. He said he couldn't, because it would cause an uproar. She imitated him. ' "Today of all days, the police will be busy enough." He said that we should find her ourselves, that she would not have gone far. And that when we did find her, there should be no fuss. He is a very obsessive man.' She shudders inside her heavy coat. 'I do not know where to look.'

Already I'm tying a muffler round my neck and reaching for my cap. 'Where have you looked?'

'Everywhere within five streets of the Settlement. Then I came for you and Archie went for Tegger.'

'Why us?'

'Because Archie thinks that you know the town, that you will find her and will keep silent.'

'Right, let's go. Come on!'

We meet Tegger and Archie two streets from the Settlement. Tegger and I divide the town between us and then street by street, back-street by back-street, we set out on our search.

'Why's she run off?' I ask Rosel as we hurry along. 'What's happened?'

'She has been ill lately. So very unhappy.'

'I thought she looked, well . . . ragged. But we're all ragged these days, trying to put on this show. And I don't just mean the play.'

'But Cora is different. She has a real reason to feel this way.'

'What's that then?'

'It is something about which I cannot tell you.'

We're in the alley behind The Lord Raglan. Looking up, I can see the light in Marguerite's curtained window with her shadow moving behind it. It's early for her. Perhaps the excitement of the day has even got to her. She has her invitation to the play.

Rosel's hand is on my arm. 'Come on, Gabriel. Cora is not down here.'

In twenty minutes we're at the edge of the town. We've scoured every street, every doorway, every back alley.

'Not here,' said Rosel sadly. 'Poor Cora. What has she done?'

'The colliery buildings!' I pull her by the hand and start to run. 'She could have holed up there.'

We make our way through the warren of buildings, thankful for the thread of dawn light which is now illuminating our search. We rattle rusty padlocks, peer through dusty windows, call and call. But Cora is not here.

'Not here. Not anywhere,' says Rosel. 'We must tell Archie, perhaps he and Tegger; the police.'

My eye sweeps across the dark buildings, past the pit heap to the empty horizon which is shimmering now with white light as the day really begins its journey. Then my gaze comes back to the heap. 'There's places here. She might have wandered on to the heap.' I walk on quickly.

'Gabriel!' she calls desperately. 'No, not here!'

'Yes,' I say. 'Come on.'

We skirt round the heap, first scanning the heights where the spoil has curled into ridges like a tide of shale and then the places where the persistent whin bushes have started to grow. This is where the children make dens to play. I did this myself. Here are the trenches where the children play Germans-and-English. Here are innocent stretches of slag where treacherous holes open up to steal lives.

We follow the path round and blink now at the pool, which glitters in the morning light as bright as any Swiss lake. I've tried and probably failed to catch all of this in my new painting. My eye automatically seeks the spot with the lime tree: the spot which has given me so much trouble.

And there she is. Not on the edge by the crooked lime tree, but in the water up to her knees and walking, arms out carefully for balance.

'*Cora-a-a!*' screams Rosel, and starts to run. I run beside her, shouting and whistling the crudest playground whistles; anything to take Cora away from her deadly intent. As I run, in my mind's eye I see my father walking steadily, steadily from his allotment, the broken chair in one hand, the strong rope over his shoulder. He too had a tree. '*Cora-a-a!*' My voice is roaring now, enveloping Rosel's birdlike cries.

At last Cora looks up from the water and sees us. She freezes there, arms wide like a crucifix. We slow down, walk gently towards her, breathing hard. 'Cora,' calls Rosel softly. 'Wait there, *Liebchen*, we are coming.'

'Stand still, flower,' I gasp. 'Just stay there and we'll come and get you.' *Flower! My grandmother called me this when I was a child. A term of endearment.*

'Rosel, where've you been?' Cora's mumbling now, through frozen lips. 'I went for a walk. Clear the head.' She's wearing a man's mackintosh over a nightdress.

'Ssh,' says Rosel. 'We come now, Cora,'

We wade out and stand beside her. We each take an arm and half-pull, half-lead Cora out of the icy water. She has nothing on her feet. I take off my scarf and wind it round her head then her neck. Rosel takes off her coat and puts it round her, peels off her warm gloves and fumbles them on to Cora's chilled hands. 'Come on! We must get you back. Quickly. The Settlement.'

Cora puts a gloved hand on her arm. 'Not the Settlement,' she says. 'Not Archie.'

'My house,' I say. 'You can come to my house.'

I hoist her into my arms and thank God for the thousand tubs I've hauled through the years that have given me the strength for this task. Cora's much heavier to carry than my father was and yet I welcome the extra strain on my back, the pull on my muscles. This body is alive. There is the difference.

There are quite a few people about as we make the journey back to my house. We get a few curious looks, but as we're not asking for help, no one interferes with us. At the house my muscles scream with gratitude as I settle Cora into my father's chair. Then I rake out and build up the fire while Rosel starts to rub Cora's hands and feet.

Cora's teeth start to chatter and Rosel stands up. 'Clothes! I need to get her out of these wet things.' She looks round the paint-strewn kitchen despairing. 'Blankets?'

I have the fire blazing now. 'I'll get you the blankets off my bed. And in the front room, there's a press – a big cupboard. In the bottom drawer are clothes off my grandmother. My father never touched the press, so her clothes are all still there.'

When I come back down with the blankets, Rosel's already starting to get Cora out of her clothes. 'Run, Gabriel. Go and tell Archie,' she says over her shoulder. 'He will be very relieved. Tell him she's here, and that she's safe.'

'No Archie,' mumbles Cora. 'Not Archie.'

'Tell him to leave her here and just get on with his day. We will take care of her here.'

When I reach the Settlement, Archie and Tegger are in the office. Archie has his head in his hands; his normally immaculate hair is awry. He looks up at me, then straightens his back and stands up. 'You've found her. How – where?'

'Sit down, Mr Todhunter. We found her in the pit pool. She's a bit wet but she is all right. Rosel's taking care of her in my house. Getting her warmed up.'

'Your house? Go back and bring her here immediately. Your house is no place for Cora!'

'She wouldn't come, Mr Todhunter,' I say steadily, ignoring the man's rudeness.

'Then I'll go and fetch her.'

'She doesn't want to see you.'

There are bright red patches on his cheeks. '*What are you saying?*'

Tegger shuffles his feet and scowls at me. 'Steady, marra.'

'She says to get on with what there is to do. This is the big day. She doesn't want to be in the way.'

His brow clears at this, and he runs his hands through his hair to tidy it a bit. 'Well . . . well. Did she say why she has done this? She knows how inconvenient it must be.'

I can't believe him. 'I just saved her from drowning, Mr Todhunter, I don't think—'

'Gabriel!' warns Tegger.

'Will she be better this afternoon. Will she be here?' He persists.

He's a selfish bastard. 'I'll get back,' I say. 'I have to see to the fire.'

'Gabriel!' His tone is odd – reprimanding and pleading all at once. 'I know it sounds hard, uncaring. But I need to know about her. First I need to know that she is safe. Then I need to know if she'll be here this afternoon to play Maggie Olliphant. If not, well . . .' He coughs. 'It's all for nought, that's all.'

Across Archie Todhunter's head, Tegger throws me a powerful glance.

I rein in my feelings. 'Look, Mr Todhunter, I'll go now and see what I can do. Rosel will come and talk to you later.'

'Just assume she'll be here, Archie,' says Tegger. 'That's all you can do for now.'

I call in for bread and milk and jam at the corner shop, using what is nearly the last shilling from my sales to Mr Crump. When I get back I have to blink. Cora is sitting there in my father's chair dressed from head to foot in my grandmother's clothes – a closed-necked blouse and long skirt, with a thick black knitted shawl round her shoulders.

Rosel is kneeling at her feet making a bit of a job of pulling on my grandmother's homeknitted socks.

I throw the bread and jam on the table. 'Well, Cora. I coulda sworn it was my old grandmother sitting there!'

Cora manages a weak smile. 'Cheeky boy,' she whispers.

'Is that milk?' says Rosel. 'Then perhaps we can make some tea. For the English, tea is medicine. Is that not so?'

Halfway down her second cup of medicine, Cora shouts, 'Ophelia!'

I blink. Rosel puts a hand on Cora's. 'What is it?'

'Who did I think I was? Ophelia? I've played her before, but never for real.'

'I saw *Hamlet* in Berlin. In 1929,' offers Rosel. She's smiling slightly but her eyes are watchful.

'That would be in German, I suppose.'

'Of course.'

'What did you think of Ophelia, Rosel?'

'Well, I . . .'

'Miserable as a drink of watered milk on a cold morning. If ever there was miscasting, it was me in that role, in that play.'

'That's not so,' I say stoutly. 'Greta Pallister reckons you can be anyone you want. That you have a gift.'

Cora's eyes light up at this. 'Does she, now?' The light fades a bit. 'But then, what does she know? She's just a kid.'

'Did you think you were Ophelia, out there at the pool?' asks Rosel.

Cora frowns. 'I can remember putting on Archie's coat and having to get away. I can remember running out of the house. The next thing I know, I am standing up to my bottom in that freezing water and you two are shouting like a pair of hoydens.'

'So you didn't want to?' I have to ask her this. 'Did you want to finish it all?'

'Not when I heard you shout, I didn't.'

'When I was young I cut my wrists, twice,' says Rosel suddenly. 'At the point when I cut them, I wanted to do away with myself. And then, when the blood flowed, that was sufficient.'

'You?' I say.

'Now that's a surprise.' Cora smiles. 'Seems like she's impregnable, Gabriel, doesn't it? But she's not. No one is.'

I try to say something, but Rosel is preoccupied, putting my paints in rainbow order on the table.

Two whole pots of medicine later Cora is looking much brighter.

'Tell Archie I'll be there this afternoon,' says Cora bravely. 'I won't spoil his show.'

Rosel frowns at her. 'Are you sure?'

'I'll be there for this shindig, and I'll be there to be Maggie Olliphant.' Cora's tone is firm, resolved. 'Between you and me, I'm not going back to him. But I'll do that. You tell him I'll be there.'

Herbert Grossmith stood astride his motorbike, pulled it back on to its stand and watched as the elegant woman let herself out of the back-yard gate and closed it with a click.

'That a Triumph, mister?' Two lads of eight or nine were sitting on the next-door wall. Their mother – at least he assumed it was their mother, although she looked quite old – was leaning against her gate, smoking. She had long creases in her cheeks.

'So it is. Called a Silent Scout.' Herbert leaped off the bike with a flourish and hung his goggles over the handlebar.

'Why's it called a Silent Scout?' asked the older lad.

'Because it doesn't make much noise.' Herbert nodded at the gate whence the elegant woman had just emerged. 'Was that Mrs Marchant?'

'That?' The woman sniffed. 'Hasn't been a Mrs Marchant in years.'

'Just a visitor?' Must be. The woman was a bit too smart for this street. Compare her with this one leaning on the gate.

'Plenty of visitors to that house. All sorts. You wouldn't believe it.'

'Is that so?' Herbert made his way down the yard. Experience told him that going in the back way in these streets put you on a much better footing when you tried to talk to the folks inside. Front door was death and the landlord. No good for a newspaper reporter.

The tall good-looking youth who came to the door proved to be the Gabriel Marchant he sought. Apparently neither troubled nor impressed by the fact that this was Herbert Grossmith of the *Priorton Chronicle*, the boy led him through to a kitchen which smelled of linseed oil and turpentine mixed with fire smoke. Paintings and drawings were slung on the walls in no particular order and a half-completed painting was leaning on an easel which stood at right-angles to the window. By the roaring fire sat an old woman in a shawl.

'This is . . .' Gabriel paused.

'I'm his grandmother,' the quavering voice came from the depths of the shawl. The old woman didn't seem to notice the hand Herbert held out to shake hers.

'What can I do for you, Mr Grossmith?'

'Well, son. I'm just making the rounds of people involved in the Prince's visit. Getting some opinions, colourful background – you know the kind of thing. Six pages to fill.' He glanced round the room and sat down, unasked, at the kitchen table. 'This'd make a fine photo – the artist at work. I could get the photographer down.'

'No, you couldn't,' said Gabriel, pulling out the chair opposite him and sitting down. The boy certainly had a very direct look, thought Herbert. Wouldn't like to cross him on a dark night.

Herbert took the small notebook out of his inside pocket. He was surprised he hadn't been offered a cup of tea. He was offered endless cups of tea in these forays into the streets. It wreaked havoc with his poor stomach, but you couldn't turn it down. Not when you wanted people to talk to you. 'Now, then, Gabriel,' he said genially. 'Seems like you're very involved in this business this afternoon, with the Prince.'

'How d'yer make that out, like?'

'Well, I was down there with Nathan Smith this morning. He told me you act in the play and also helped to build the set. Oh, and I saw your paintings, too. One triple thing, very clever.'

'I didn't paint that. It was done by Rosel Vonn. She's the art teacher.'

A penny dropped with Herbert. 'Ah! Was she the lady who was leaving as I arrived? Very attractive lady.'

Here the grandmother had a coughing attack, covering her embarrassment with the edge of her shawl.

'That would be her,' said Gabriel.

'Nathan said she'd had a great deal of influence on all the painters.'

'Aye, she has.'

Herbert glanced round the walls and back at the easel by the window. 'He mentioned a painting that was in the exhibition and had to be withdrawn.'

'Did he now?'

'Bit of a naughty picture, by all accounts.'

The boy stood up and took a big book from the sewing machine which was standing in the corner. With a clattering sweep of his hand he cleared half the table of its paint tubes and brushes.

He opened the book and turned the pages almost too swiftly for Herbert to make them out. 'Look at this one, this, this and this! Is this lewd? Is this offensive? In case you didn't know, Mr Grossmith, this is the work of the great painter Rembrandt.' The boy shut the book with a slap, returned it to its perch, then crouched down on the floor to retrieve his paints.

Herbert watched while Gabriel reassembled his table into what he now saw was a very formal order. The rackety appearance of the room was deceptive. Then he said. 'So your painting was banned?' he persisted.

'He didn't say that.' A squeaky voice came from behind the old lady's shawl.

'I just decided,' said Gabriel wearily, 'that it didn't go with the other pictures, that it would draw attention away from them. Nobody banned it.'

'Can I see it?' Herbert looked round.

'No, you can't.'

'Fair enough.' The journalist scribbled in his book. Then he looked up, pencil poised. 'And what would you say the Settlement has done for you, Gabriel?'

The table was now back in order, and the boy sat down again. 'Well,' he said slowly, 'do you know *The Pilgrim's Progress*?'

'Yes. Yes. Of course.'

'It's like I was plodging about in the Slough of Despond and suddenly I came upon the Settlement, which was the House Beautiful.'

Herbert's pencil was still poised. He frowned. 'But what do *you* yourself feel about your experiences there? About Archie Todhunter and the German woman?'

'Archie Todhunter is a magician who turns base metal, the most ordinary ingredients, into gold. He converts a difficulty to a possibility. People going there have had chances, experiences, that'll live with them all their days.'

Herbert was writing furiously. 'And the German woman?'

'*Miss* Rosel Vonn is the other side of an equally bright coin.' Gabriel frowned, thinking hard. 'She freed in me what I could do and has made me realise how little I know and how much there is to learn. She's given me self-respect and a life challenge at the same time. And I think it's the same for the others.'

'Good stuff!' said Herbert, still scribbling. He glanced round. 'And what do you think you'll do with all this work, when it's done?'

The boy eyed him narrowly. 'What'll you do with that piece when you write it? Show it and sell it? Well that's what I'll do. I'm no fancypants hobbyist doing this for fun, any more than are the cobblers working at the Settlement. I'm a workman. An artisan. I'll sell the fruits of my labour.'

Herbert jotted down some more notes. 'You reckon you'll sell them?'

'I've already sold some, and I have someone waiting for others.'

'Now who would that be?'

The grandmother was taken again with a fit of coughing and the boy went over to help her. When he had patted her on the back and adjusted her shawl, the boy looked up at him. 'I don't think I should talk about that just now, Mr Grossmith, do you?' He went to the door and opened it. 'Now then, we must have finished here. I need to get my grandma on to the bed.'

Outside, the woman and boys were still there. 'Manage all right?' she said. 'Did you meet the lad?'

He pulled on his goggles. 'Yes. The grandmother too.'

'Grandma?' she chortled. 'They're having you on. There hasn't been no Grandma there for twelve, fifteen years.'

Herbert looked at Gabriel Marchant's door, now firmly shut.

Then he shrugged. Whatever had gone on in there he had some good stuff for the paper. He stood hard down on the motorbike pedal, the engine roared and he made his way back down the back street, throwing up the packed earth as he did so.

Behind him the two boys had jumped off the wall and were miming the pedal action and making *bru-u-mming* noises ready to set off on their own motorbike race. The older boy put his hands on his hips. 'Not much noise be buggered,' he said. 'Silent Scout? Not flippin' likely.'

Chapter Thirty-Six

Recovery

When Rosel got back to the Settlement, Archie Todhunter was in the main room surrounded by excited groups of quilters, carpenters and cobblers who were setting up their displays on the long trestle tables. On the wall behind them someone had hung the paintings in Rosel's designated places. The blazing yellow had dimmed a little under this onslaught of colour and texture, and the effect was bright and positive. It worked very well, despite Gabriel Marchant's misgivings.

Rosel reflected that Archie had an instinct for things that worked: like toiling on with the play as though the Prince were really going to see it when Dev Pallister and the others had said there was no question of this. Ten minutes, they'd heard. That was the limit.

Archie hurried towards her. She held up her hand. 'Don't worry, Archie. Cora is well. She is a very resolute lady. She is most definite that she will be here. She is resting at this moment.'

'Good, good,' he said almost absently. 'Cora is a trooper, and this is so whatever kind of brainstorm has assailed her.' He led her to one of the seats along the walls. 'Sit down, Rosel.' He sat down beside her, and took hold of her hand. She had never before felt his touch. His hand was very dry. 'Now dear girl, prepare yourself. Your friend Sir Peter is here.'

She looked round.

'Not here precisely,' he said quickly, 'but here in Brack's Hill. He came an hour ago, took one look at this chaos and insisted on leaving. He has perfect manners, that man.'

'He left?' she said.

'He asked where they could get tea and I directed them to the Gaunt Valley Café.'

She stood up. 'Them?'

'There was someone with him.' Archie paused. 'He introduced me to your father, Rosel. We talked of his war drawings . . . Wait!'

Rosel wrenched her hand away, ran out of the hall and hurried along the pavements into the café which, perhaps because of the royal visit, was unusually crowded with people who weren't from Brack's Hill.

She scanned the crowd. Her eye passed over them twice before she recognised them. Peter's tall frame was almost hidden under the shadow of an overhanging staircase. At the table with him sat a little old couple; the woman's face was almost hidden by the large fur collar of her cape and the wide brim of an old-fashioned hat. Rosel squeezed and pushed her way through the tables to them.

Peter stood up, cracking his head on the underside of the staircase. She felt a flush of affection for him, returning his smile.

Her father, when he stood up, seemed half Peter's size.

'Rosel,' he said. '*Meine Rosel.*' He took her hand and kissed it, then drew her to him and kissed her, first on one cheek then the other. She stood away from him. There were dark rings under his eyes and he looked twenty years older than Peter, who must almost be his contemporary.

Her father turned to the elderly woman who sat beside him. '*Lilah! Hier ist Rosel.*'

Rosel looked down at her mother, who stared back at her blankly from a wrecked face. She bent down to kiss her cheek. 'How are you, my dear mother?' Her mother struggled away from her and looked at Sir Peter. 'The cakes are dreadful here,' she said in German. 'Such dreadful cakes. I wish to go home. At home the cakes are so good.' She looked back at Rosel. 'Who is this woman?' she said.

Peter turned Rosel towards him and kissed her on both cheeks. The familiarity was comforting. 'Sit down, my dear. I fear your mama is somewhat *hors de combat* after the journey from London and the longer journey earlier this week.'

Rosel could hardly speak. 'Peter, how on earth did you do this? Never will I be able to thank you properly.' She sat down, then leaned over and took her father's hand in hers and held on to it.

Peter signalled for the waitress who came scurrying across. 'Another cup, some fresh tea and more of those delightful cakes, if you please.' He turned to Rosel. 'Your brother was enormously helpful. Broke into the asylum and stole your mother from right under their noses, don't you know. Brave young man.'

'Is Boris all right?'

Peter paused a split second too long before he said heartily, 'Of course he is all right. A resourceful man in adverse circumstances. And in your country I find there are many circumstances.'

Max squeezed his daughter's hand. 'You look well, *Liebchen*.'

She gazed at him. 'I am well. And I am painting again. Not very much but more than for a long time.'

'Good, good.' Max von Steinigen looked at his wife who was cutting the cake on her plate to ever-smaller pieces, staring vacantly. 'Your dear mother has been through some bad times, but we will make her well, you and I. Is this not true?'

'Yes, Papa. We'll make her well.' She was desperately thinking of her cramped quarters at the Settlement.

Peter read her mind. When the waitress came back with a laden tray he asked the woman, 'Is there an hotel where one might stay in this unfortunate place?'

'Where *one* might stay?' The waitress looked at him. '*An* 'otel?' Rosel, accustomed to the ironies of Brack's Hill talk, heard the sarcasm which went over the heads of the others. 'Well, there's public-houses that take people in, but mebbe The Grosvenor (she pronounced it Gros-ven-or) at the top of the town's your best bet. They do commercial travellers. I worked there once.'

'Grosvenor!' said Peter genially. 'That sounds very grand.'

The waitress replaced the empty cake plate with a full one. 'Oh no,' she said. 'You couldn't call it grand. You can't miss it though. Up the length of the High Street, under the railway bridge past a row of big posh houses and it's on your left. If you get to the Co-op you've gone too far.'

'The Grosvenor will do for tonight, Rosel,' said Peter. 'Then you must decide what you all want to do.'

'I was thinking I might rent a little house here, for us all,' said Rosel. 'Then I can continue my work and—'

'Here?' He raised his brows. 'Are you quite sure, Rosel? Don't you think perhaps your work here is done?'

The screech of Lilah's knife on her plate, as she decimated another cake, impaled the hum of talk in the café.

Max von Steinigen was looking at his daughter with shining eyes. He spoke almost timidly. 'We need some special help for your Mama, *Liebchen*. Doctors. A hospital for a while. I thought perhaps London?'

Peter coughed. 'I have a pair of small houses in Chelsea, my dear. One of them is empty at the moment. It is quite small, but the second floor has a top light. It has been used more than once as a studio.'

She put both her hands over her face. 'I can't think about this now. My father and mother are just now here and there is the play, the Prince.'

'So Todhunter tells me.' Peter poured out a cup of tea and handed it to her. 'Just relax, my dear girl. Relax, won't you? Nothing is insoluble. We will see. London seems the obvious choice, but we will see!'

Lilah von Steinigen's knife clattered to the ground as she leaned across and grabbed her daughter's hand. 'You must help my son, Fraulein. He is in great danger. They will kill him.'

Rosel put her hand on her mother's. 'Boris?' she said.

Lilah shook her hand hard. 'They will kill him, Fraulein. Such a handsome boy and they will kill him. They think he is naughty. Do you know, Fraulein, I saw them kill people in that place? They killed the naughty ones.' A cunning light came into her eyes. 'Those were the days when you had to be very, very good. You had to be very good, on those days.'

* * *

My Aunt Susanah, who turned up at the house ten minutes after Rosel left, is getting on like a house on fire with Cora. The first thing she did was explode with laughter at the sight of Cora in my grandmother's clothes. 'I thought for a second it was old Mrs Marchant sitting there.'

My aunt is concerned about how Cora finds herself in this state, but soon they are talking in the safer areas of their mutual experience: the Settlement; Cora's acting and all the work Aunt Susanah's husband Jonty has been doing there. 'He's over there now, seeing what he may do to help Mr Todhunter.'

'I should be there too,' says Cora, pushing her shawl to one side.

'Don't let her do that,' I warn my aunt. 'She's had a shock. Nearly drowned this morning, in White Leas pool.' It's only as I say this that I recall a tale once told me by my grandmother about Susanah's own mother drowning in those same waters.

My aunt sees the memory in my eyes and shakes her head slightly. 'Why don't you get off and do something, Gabriel? I'm sure Mr Todhunter can use a fit young man today. I'll stay here with Miss Miles. We'll talk. I'll make her tea. She'll be fine.'

Cora nods her head in agreement. 'And you'll tell Archie that I'll be there by the three o'clock cast call, Gabriel. Do that for me, will you?'

'I'll bring her myself,' promises my aunt. 'Don't trouble yourself, Gabriel. I'll take care of Miss Miles like she was my sister.'

As I tie my scarf round my neck, my eye falls on the painting with the scraped-out place by the pit pool, the place which has been wrong all the time. Now I know what it wants: a figure in the water, holding her arms out like a crucifix. *Cora*. My fingers itch for my brushes, my paints. I want to throw those irritating women out of my house and paint. I can't do this, so I start to paint it in my head as I walk.

I'm nearly on to the High Street before I remember that I've left Cora Miles to get across to the Settlement with only my grandmother's clothes on her back. Oh well. They're two resourceful women. They'll come up with something, I'm sure.

When I call in at The Lord Raglan, the clientele is in its best bib and tucker: white silk scarves rather than mufflers, with here and there a bowler hat. The place is alive with an air of unusual celebration, optimism. I suppose this is what the Prince's visits are about. To cheer people up a bit. To make them feel *visible*.

Marguerite's wearing a pale mauve, shiny frock I've never seen before. It has artificial violets at the shoulder. Her hair's pinned up on her head but there are tiny curls falling on her fine-boned cheeks.

I watch her for a while before she sees me. She talks to one man then to another, making them smile and stand straighter in their battered boots. In a way her presence here's like a Prince's visit every day. *Into these poor lives a little light must fall.*

She grins when she sees me and then brings me my tally pint. 'Now, then. How's my golden-haired genius?'

'Shut up, Marguerite.'

'Everything all right at the Settlement? I've arranged with my boss to get off at four o'clock to come and join in the merriment.'

'There've been dramas already.'

'Dramas? I thought that was later.'

Her green eyes widen as I tell her the tale of my morning. 'Well It's a relief that Cora's all right. D'you think she meant to kill herself?'

I shrug my shoulders. 'I don't know. Rosel says not.'

'Rosel!' Her eyes narrow. 'I think that teacher has a soft spot for you, Gabe.'

'Come on, Marguerite.' I am about to say that Rosel is my teacher but she interrupts me.

'Yeah, I know. She's old enough to be your mother, but you wouldn't believe how many times I've been proposed evil things by men old enough to be my father.' Just then she's called across to the other end of the bar and I stand there a while, watching, talking and laughing with the customers.

As I sip my way down to the bottom of the glass I consider the miracle of Marguerite. I'd thought loving somebody was wanting them to belong to you alone. I do know this is not on the cards with me and Marguerite. But still what I feel for her is something akin to love.

I come out of the Raglan to the sharp cut of the November wind and a driving drizzle. I push my hands deep into my jacket pockets, dip my nose into my muffler and head off for the Settlement at a run. As I turn the corner into Cheapside, I get tangled up with a tall man in a fur-collared coat who smells of cologne. He holds me away from him, smiling slightly with his large teeth. Now I'm in the middle of a crowd of well-dressed strangers. One of them addresses me. 'Gabriel! You are in a great hurry,' says Rosel Vonn.

I pull myself away from the man.

'Peter,' says Rosel. 'This is the young man I told you about. The one whose painting you wished to buy.' The man called Peter shakes me heartily by the hand and Rosel introduces me to her father and her mother, whose hand drops listlessly from mine. I am all bones and elbows in this company, in a rage with Rosel that I can't explain.

'Dreadful weather, what?' says the tall man.

'We're just taking my parents to an hotel,' says Rosel. 'They have just arrived.'

Now I notice the Daimler that's purring on the road beside the pavement. At the wheel is a lad no older than I am. He winks at me and I watch as the man called Peter ushers the two old people into the back. Then he turns to me and shakes me by the hand again. 'Good to meet Fraulein von Steinigen's protégé. You have great talent, young man.' And he vanishes into the car's plush interior, sitting in the front seat next to the driver.

I turn to Rosel. 'So the posh fellow got your father out of Germany for you.' Stating the obvious seems the safest thing.

She puts both her hands in mine. 'And my mother,' she says. 'They got her out of an asylum. Can you believe that? The Government have plans to kill people in the asylums.' She shudders. 'Can you believe that?'

'And your brother?'

She frowns. 'Boris is still in Germany. My mother babbles that they will kill him too.'

'But at least she's here. And your father.' I forget about my wet jacket and hold her close. A woman walking by clicks her tongue. 'That's something.'

'Yes, of course it is. But my brother – I must also do something about him.' Her hands loosen from mine. 'You must be going to the Settlement?'

I nod.

'Will you tell Archie that I will be there for the cast call at three? And could he mark chairs for Sir Peter and my parents as they will attend for the performance?'

'Right.' I clunk the door shut after her and watch the Daimler as it purrs away along Cheapside on to the High Street. One thing's sure. That car carries Rosel Vonn back to her world and her life: a life that's nothing to do with Brack's Hill.

The rain is thinning and the white light behind the clouds hints at the sun. I set off for the Settlement, arms swinging and heels down as though I really am young Arthur setting off for war in 1915.

Chapter Thirty-Seven

Bearing Witness

Dev Pallister, designated one of three council marshals, had a busy time after leaving the house, and an excited Pauline, that morning.

He and his two colleagues had walked the length of the town on the Prince's route. All was in order. Of course, there were depressing sights here and there but that, after all, was what His Royal Highness was here to see.

They talked to the men in the *Pathé News* van and the BBC motor car. They were parked outside the Club, ready for the first sighting. They all agreed it was a pity about this cold drizzle. The poor newsmen had had quite a wetting. But the sun was coming out now and things looked better for the afternoon.

They went to the police station to talk to the inspector there, and then checked out the allotments. The allotment men were already there, clustered into the new goods-exchange hut, smoking like fury.

They called on Archie Todhunter at the Settlement. He was marching around looking a bit white about the gills, also smoking like fury. Even so, everything looked remarkably well organised. The display was particularly impressive. Dev lingered with some pride before Gabriel Marchant's fine portrait of his daughter and stopped again at the sight of the lad himself portrayed in Dev's own uniform, decked out with his medals.

Then they went to Archie's little office, had a glass of single malt and toasted the Prince. Archie Todhunter showed them the leather-bound edition of the play, which young Greta would present to the Prince.

He talked about the timing of the performance. 'Of course we're expecting to put on the play for His Royal Highness. We need to get the message over to him, and the gathered dignitaries. We'll start at approximately four-thirty. I imagine he'll be just about at the end of his tour by then?'

Dev shook his head. 'I think I indicated to you that it wouldn't be on the schedule, Mr Todhunter. It is impossible. The Prince will be moving through. Moving through and moving on.'

'He's a busy man,' put in one of the other councillors. 'A very busy man.'

'In that case,' said Archie flatly, 'I can't for the life of me think why we've been doing all this work all these months.'

'He'll see the exhibition. He'll get a copy of the play,' said Dev.

'It's not the same. The live performance, that's the best of what happens here. The people at their finest.' Archie was grim. 'He'll be seeing them at their most desolate, won't he? Shouldn't he also see these good people at their best? There's balance in this.'

There was no answering this. The trio drank off the last of their whisky and began to move out of the room. Dev Pallister turned impulsively and shook Archie by the hand. 'By rights

His Royal Highness *should* see the play, Mr Todhunter, I am quite aware of that. But I can't think that he will. I'm sorry, I really am.'

By three o'clock there was a full turnout in the Church Hall for the last cast call. Even Baffer Bray got the time right. Cora came hobbling in on Susanah Clelland's arm at three minutes to three. Archie blinked when he saw her, dressed in old woman's clothing. 'Changed your costume for Maggie Olliphant, Cora? I thought you already had that backstage.'

Cora hugged the shawl around her. 'I found these. They're much more suitable. It'll freshen up the part. I just need to find poor Maggie's boots.' They looked down at her dirty bare feet.

'What have you been up to, Cora? On today of all days, walking through the town with no shoes on.'

She had Archie's full attention at last. 'I was at Gabriel Marchant's house, and his auntie here.' She nodded at Susanah. 'She very kindly ran to the corner to get Mr Soulsby's taxi. So I didn't walk barefoot all the way.'

Archie shook his head. 'You're making my mind spin, Cora. I will not ask you to explain further.' He turned away. 'At least you're back and I thank heavens for that.'

She put a hand on his arm. 'I'm back for this show, Archie, that's all. Not back to the Settlement or to you. Afterwards I'm going to Priorton with Mrs Clelland. Seems she has a spare room. Then, who knows? Somewhere.'

Archie frowned at her, then shook her hand off his arm. 'We'll talk about it later, Cora. Later.' Then he strode off, making for Rosel Vonn, who had just come through the doors.

Susanah Clelland touched her shoulder. 'Don't worry, Cora. He has things on his mind, poor chap. Are you really sure you want to do this? – come back with me?'

Cora sniffed. 'Course I do. I don't know what it is about the cold water I nearly drowned myself in, Mrs Clelland, but it doesn't half give you a clear head.'

Archie Todhunter gets to Rosel before I do, so I hang around while they talk, impervious to the old boy's sour looks. Rosel's hair is shining and she's wearing a smart black dress I've never seen before. At the neck, just near the collarbone, is pinned the Roman brooch I gave her. I want to say something about it to her but Archie is in the way.

He's close to her, speaks in her ear. 'I need a favour from you, Rosel. Perhaps your friend Sir Peter could help.'

'What is it, Archie?' She's flushed from running I think, but she looks so bright, so full of life, I want to touch her. But something is happening to her, taking her right away from me. I can tell.

'Anything, Archie,' she says.

'I wonder, is your friend on terms with him? His Royal Highness? Does he know him?'

'Perhaps.' She sounds more foreign than before, somehow. She'll have been talking to her mother and father in their own language. 'Some things he says . . .'

'What about you?'

'I do not know the Prince.' She hesitates, frowning. 'I think my father, he has known the Prince. Once a very, very long time ago. Before the war.'

'Right!' Archie beams. 'Perhaps he will talk with him? And you, too – in German. Anything to take his attention away from the fact that this is just another routine Royal visit.'

She shrugs. 'Why? What will this do?'

He draws nearer to her. 'Rosel, I want you to persuade him to stay to watch the play. Dev and the councillors say no, it's impossible. Out of the question. But it will be his final stop here at Brack's Hill. He *must* see the play. Why else have these people – young Gabriel here, and his friend Tegger, Cora and Greta and the rest – worked so hard? Have they worked so hard for so long to have their endeavour valued no more than a bit of quilting or a cobbled shoe?'

'Mr Todhunter!' A voice calls him from across the room and Rosel and I almost fall into each other's arms in laughter.

'Poor Archie!' says Rosel.

'I've never seen a man so frustrated,' I say.

'Or so very determined,' she adds. 'This is his great quality.'

'So what will you do?' I ask. 'If the councillors say it's impossible, it must be impossible.'

She frowns. 'Archie's right, you know. He's how do you say it? Pigheaded. But he is right. What better way of showing the truth about the people in Brack's Hill than the play?'

'So . . .?'

'So I will do it. Or try. See if my father will recall their meeting, see what Sir Peter can do. Perhaps, perhaps . . .'

'Gabe!' Tegger is bellowing from the other end of the hall. 'Come and get thy clothes on or thee'll never fight a war.'

So I have to leave Rosel, with so much unsaid.

Tegger has taken on the role of chief harasser and director and is bustling everybody into their togs backstage, checking the set, checking the prompter's copy, checking that the pianist has her music.

Tegger for one thinks it's certainly going to happen. The Prince *will* see the play.

I'm busy pulling on Dev Pallister's army boots when Tegger

comes to sit beside me. 'Still on with Marguerite, marra?'

'Is anybody ever *on* with Marguerite?' I say.

'You gotta point there. You realised finally, did you?'

I bend down to tie the long bootlaces: round the back then round to the front to tie in a double bow. 'What about us, Tegger? Am I off your friends' list, then?'

He knocks me on the shoulder and I only just save myself from falling off the stool. 'Dinnet be daft, man. Like I say, it'd take more than a woman to come between us.'

Greta comes bowling across the room, looking the complete pit lass in her canvas apron and clogs. 'Hey, you two! You're to come across to the Settlement. The Prince is nearly there and you've gotta be beside the portraits, to talk to him.'

'Who says?'

'Archie.'

Greta takes me by the hand and leads me through the house door into the long front room of the Settlement. There's this flurry of activity at the other end of the room as His Royal Highness comes in and makes his way down the room. He has a very decorated soldier by his side and a man behind him whose long tweed coat and bowler hat match his own. He flashes his smile everywhere, paying close attention to the quilters and the cobblers. He looks people directly in the eye and listens attentively to Archie who is murmuring in his ear.

I can hear his clear, slightly high voice. 'The paintings are done by people here, you say? Amazing!'

He reaches Greta, who curtseys deeply to him. He is quite a short man. Just about reaches my shoulder. 'A fine portrait of you, my dear,' he says to Greta.

'It's not me, sir.' Her grammar-school voice flutes on the air in contrast with her ragamuffin appearance. 'It is me in the role of Dorothy, who's an historical character from 1915 and is important in the play.'

'A jolly good likeness even so.'

She points to me. 'Gabriel painted it.'

He moves to me, and, not being able to curtsey, I duck my head forward as I've seen the other men do.

'This is Gabriel Marchant, sir,' says Greta, not fazed at all by the Prince. 'He has painted three of these portraits and, as you see, is the subject of this tryptych in his role of Arthur in the play. That was painted by Fraulein Vonn who is the painting teacher here. In the play Arthur's both a soldier and a miner as many Durham men were.' Greta's doing Archie proud.

The Prince casts an eye back at Archie Todhunter. 'And the German teacher painted this young man in his magnificent uniform?'

Greta leans sideways to keep his gaze on her. 'That's my father's uniform, sir,' she says. 'From the Great War.'

One elegant brow is raised. He glances back to the man in the long tweed coat behind him. 'Curiouser and curiouser, Robbie!' he says. Like in some private joke. I decide his face is far too brown for real life. And his cheeks are pink. Rouge. For God's sake, he must be wearing make-up! For the *Pathé News*, very likely.

Archie leads him on. 'This is Fraulein Rosel von Steinigen, our art tutor,' he says. 'Fraulein von Steinigen has exhibited her work alongside that of Vanessa Bell and Duncan Grant. She has also collaborated with Mr Henry Moore, the sculptor. We're lucky to have her here in Brack's Hill.'

Now Rosel, elegant in her black dress, is curtseying deeply beside me. The two of them speak together in rapid German and I've no idea at all what they are talking about. Now she has made him laugh and he shakes her hand again.

He turns to speak to the man behind him again. 'Amazing coincidence, Robbie. Fraulein von Steinigen is the daughter of a chap I learned to ski with, before the war.' He addresses Rosel once more.

'Sir! In English!' his companion says urgently. He looks very uncomfortable. 'We must move on.'

The Prince kisses Rosel on the hand with a flourish. 'And your father, Fraulein?' he says, in English this time.

'We have just got him away from Germany. He was in difficulties there, sir. He will be present in the hall where they will perform the play for you.'

The Prince frowns. 'This play. No one mentioned it before, did they, Robbie?'

The soldier beside him is muttering under his breath.

Archie coughs. 'We have been rehearsing it for months, sir. It's about the war. I understand you were a serving officer, sir.'

'So I was, Mr Todhunter. So I was.' The Prince turns to his companion, shutting everyone out of his eyeline. 'Where do we go next, Robbie?'

'The train, sir. Home.'

'In that case, perhaps we should see something of this play. It might do us all some good, don't you think so, Fraulein?'

The soldier beside the Prince starts to object. 'Sir, you can't,' but the Prince cuts him short, repeating, 'Don't you think so, Fraulein?'

Rosel nods so vigorously her head nearly drops off. Archie Todhunter whispers in my ear, 'You get straight back across there, Gabriel. Tell Tegger to get everyone in their places.'

Across the road, Tegger sets everyone in their starting place and reminds Maggie, as if she needed it, that hers is the first speech. 'But where's Archie?' She demands. 'He has to get over here yet.'

Archie comes in on cue, fastening his braces and buttoning his coat up for his role of the pit manager. 'Listen, everyone,' his voice barks out. 'She did it! The Fraulein did it! She has persuaded the Prince to watch the play.'

Everyone cheers him to the roof and Tegger has a bit of a job to settle us down again. Everyone in their places. Defying Tegger's cross looks I climb out of my trench and peep through the side of the curtains. There are five empty rows at the front. In the sixth are Rosel's posh friend and her parents. Behind them the seats are filled by town dignitaries with chains, soldiers in uniform, men in caps, women in their best hats. The senior councillors are there with their wives. I can see Dev Pallister and his wife, Mr Conroy the joiner and his wife, alongside teachers from the Grammar School. Jonty Clelland and my Aunt Susanah are sitting halfway back. Squashed on the seat beside my aunt is the reporter fellow, Herbert Grossmith: the one with leather patches on his elbows. The doctors and the clergymen take a row to themselves. Marguerite, wearing a purple hat with a veil, sits beside a man. I focus more closely on him and realise it's Mr Crump, the man from the gallery. They look very cosy.

So. All these people are here for a sight of the dashing Prince. It might be secondary in their heads but the most important thing they're here to do, whether they know it or not, is to see the first performance of Archie Todhunter's – and Tegger's – play, *Coal and Blood.*

A kind of humming quiet settles on the hall as the Prince, with Rosel on his left and his fretful friend 'Robbie' on his right, comes through the double doors, followed by a gaggle of people who are part of the tour party. Behind them strides the much-decorated soldier who's obviously in charge, then the insignificant figure of Lord Chase, and two senior policemen who stay by the door. They all, apart from the Prince, look very glum. Perhaps they thought they would be getting away from Brack's Hill soon and here they are, having to watch a poxy play.

Rosel introduces the Prince to her friend Peter and the old man who is her father. There is all this standing and bowing and shaking of hands. Then the Prince leads them all to sit with him in the centre of the front row. Now the whole following group of people, whether they want to or not, have to sit on the rows behind them. More uniformed policemen stand at the end of the front row where the Prince sits. Is this to protect him from us? What do they think we'll do to him?

I return to my starting position and find my hand grasped very tightly in Greta Pallister's slender fingers. 'Good luck to us all, Gabriel!' she whispers.

Archie stands behind the centre curtain perfectly still for a second, then he puts his shoulders back and steps through them.

The room melts into total silence. His voice, slightly muffled by the curtain, comes back to us. 'Your Royal Highness, my lords, ladies and gentlemen. In these hard days, our suffering is greater because we feel the cruel wheel of our lives grinds away unseen by anyone. Yet the presence of His Royal Highness here in Brack's Hill reassures us that our sufferings are visible. But I ask you, ladies and gentlemen, is it just about suffering? In Brack's Hill, especially at the Settlement, we have people of spirit and courage, culture and dignity. It is by their endeavour in the Arts and in the Crafts that they express their relationship with, and significance to, the whole of our society.'

Archie's voice rolls on. Tegger's harsh whisper spits from the wings. '*Get on with it, will yer?*'

'The play we have written, called *Coal and Blood*, shows that it has always been so. It is our privilege today that you, sir, and the wider community will bear witness for the people of Brack's Hill.'

He steps back. Closes the curtain tight, and takes his position. The pianist plays her few mournful chords and as the curtains open Cora swallows a small smile, becomes Maggie Olliphant, and begins her first, powerful speech.

Epilogue

22 November 1963

I stumble through my eulogy to Archie Todhunter, conscious that my speech is not a patch on the oratory of the clergyman, a plainly dressed Presbyterian who'd been friends with Archie in his retirement years in this seaside town.

The minister talked of the heritage of Scottish mission and faith into which Archie was born, how he had lost that faith and sublimated it into the fine lay missionary work in the dark areas of England during the Depression. How, after the war, his work was gradually superseded by the changed society for which he had fought. And how, after all his labours, he had found rest here by the sea.

I'm pleased now that in my eulogy I decided to talk about Brack's Hill. Otherwise the people who pack this tall seaside church might have gone off with the wrong idea about us as anonymous creatures of the Depression. Perhaps Archie Todhunter knew this, and this was why he wrote that if anyone was to say something for him today, it should be me.

I relish the nods and the ripples of agreement that sweep the room as I say what I have to say about him, and about our experience of him in those years. I scan the long aisle of the church for the familiar faces.

First and foremost, of course, is Greta in the front row with her Kaftan and her sheepskin coat, her spectacles slipping as always down her nose. She's still Greta Pallister as she never took my name although we've been well and truly married for years.

And I can see Tegger right at the back, bulkier than ever with his grey-white beard. Thank goodness he made it. We timed the funeral for four o'clock so he could make the long journey down from the North.

Tegger's the only one of us who kept the faith, who stayed up there in Brack's Hill. He doesn't live in a van now, but in one of the houses by the Grosvenor Hotel with his third wife and two elderly greyhounds. Doing all right, is Tegger. His first broadcast, just after the war, was a performance of *Coal and Blood* on the wireless, with him named as writer. He wrote to me that Archie insisted on this. They did it with Yorkshire actors, so the accent was Yorkshire not Durham, but it worked very well. This year he's had three plays on the BBC and a book of short stories praised to the heights in the quality press. These stories give me shades of our almost forgotten younger selves and bring tears to my eyes when I re-read them.

Archie should have asked Tegger to do the eulogy. He's the *word* man, after all. He wrote a fine extended obituary for the *Guardian* in appreciation of Archie's life-work. It was he, though, who telephoned me out of the blue to tell me Archie'd asked for me to do the eulogy. He reckoned Archie had asked for me because he thought it was time I started using words as well as images. 'Always a silent witness, you are, Gabe. "Such a silent boy, Tegger," Archie said to me. "Get him to say something, for God's sake".'

I had a twinge of guilt then. In the end, I left Brack's Hill and barely looked back. First there was art college courtesy of a mysterious scholarship that I finally discovered came from Rosel Vonn's friend, Sir Peter; then the war and surviving the North African campaign. Then Italy. Like Rosel's father I, too, have a book of my images of war. After that I was submerged beneath the bouncing tide of work and exhibitions and a modest degree of success. Exhibitions, a cosy post as Head of Department in a Lancashire college.

What with all this I'd kind of lost touch with Archie when he retired after the war. I know that Tegger spent a great deal of time down here with him in those last months. In this way, too, Tegger kept the faith.

I finish my eulogy with the reference to President John Kennedy and today's tragic event, then nod at Greta. She stands up, turns round and in her clear academic voice reads Maggie Olliphant's fine speech from *Coal and Blood*.

When she ends, there is a slight pause. Then a patter of applause emanating from Tegger at the back crackles through the church and suddenly everyone is clapping and smiling. They nod at each other. Some of them even shake hands with each other. Strange for a funeral, you might think. The plain Presbyterian clergyman looks quite bewildered.

We're shepherded to the church hall next door for an alcohol-free wake. There are tables and chairs and a long buffet with vol-au-vents and quiches. The room is painted bright yellow and on the walls is artwork, some representational, some pastiches of Picasso and Braque. There are even collages, which are very fashionable now. Those of us who were at Brack's Hill recognise Archie's hand everywhere here.

Holding a cup of tea, and standing with my back to the wall, I watch Greta and Tegger working the room like professionals.

A voice sounds in my ears. 'She is such a *person* now, little Greta, is she not? Remarkable, all, those books and articles of hers. A fine academic.' The accent is much thicker than before but the voice is recognisable.

I turn round and we almost bump faces. 'Rosel!'

The body I hold to me is slender to the point of brittleness; the cheek I kiss is still soft but very lined. The fair hair is white now, longer and swept up on to her head. Her smile is wide with delight. 'Rosel. Rosel.' I say it over and over again like a daft thing.

She stands back to look at me. 'That was a very good eulogy, Gabriel. Archie was an exceptional person. He touched so many lives. So how are you, Gabriel?'

'How are *you*? They said you were in Berlin.'

The morning after the play, Rosel called on me at my house. She heaped praise on the pit-heap painting, now graced by the vestigial cruciform figure of Cora by the tree. Then we walked out of the town and along by that same pit pool. She told me how her time at Brack's Hill would always be significant for her. Always. But now she had to go to London to settle her parents there. 'Peter says he will take care of them. Then I must go to Germany and seek out Boris. He is at even greater risk than my father, I feel this.'

'This Sir Peter Whatsit,' I said. 'Is he . . .? Are you . . .?' I couldn't bring myself to say the words.

Rosel shrugged her infinitely foreign shrug. 'As I say, I must go now to help Boris. My father understands this, Peter understands this.'

I wrote to her, via Peter, seven times before and during the war. Then I gave up. I thought she must have married him or something.

It was Tegger who wrote to me in Italy during the last stages of the war to tell me otherwise. It seemed she'd returned to Germany and got mixed up with her brother. In 1943 he, and three fellow officers, were executed for plotting against Hitler. Rosel stayed and was part of a group that carried on his fight. It was in the English papers after the war. She was mentioned in the post-war articles about the plot, as living in Berlin. She wasn't painting. She was helping displaced persons.

I suppose I could have contacted her then, but I didn't. It was all too late.

'Yes,' she says now, 'these days I live in Berlin. In my father's old apartment, in fact. Is that not strange?'

'I read about your brother. And your brave work during the war.' We are talking like strangers which is what, ultimately, we must be now.

'Poor Boris. I always hope he did the right thing, but I am never sure.'

This is the person who changed my life. 'So, you'd be in Berlin during the Blockade?' The words are so ordinary, so polite.

'Yes.' She shivers. 'It was not good.'

'Rosel!' I put my arms round her and hold her close. Then I stand clear and take her arm. 'Come on. Sit down here at this table, and I'll grab you a cup of tea.' I need to get away from her. To put the past in its place.

While I stand in the long tea queue, I watch as Greta and

Tegger join Rosel at the table. Then a dark-haired girl sits down with them, followed by an old woman with pinkish hair.

As soon as I get back to the table, the hum in the room is silenced and the lights are suddenly turned down low. A screen is set up at the front of the room and at the back of the room, film reels start to whirr.

In the dark I sit on the chair between Rosel and Greta. There in front of us, flickering on the screen in black and white, is the outside of the Settlement in 1936. There are crowds of people held back by a couple of policemen. Everyone is wearing caps and hats. And there is the Prince of Wales, as glamorous as any film star. He has his friend at his side, the one who was so worried about his speaking in German to Rosel. The soundtrack is quacking away but I can't hear it.

And then we are standing there, shockingly smooth-faced. So very young. I hardly know myself. The Prince is shaking us by the hand and looking us in the eye. I remember newsreel of Hitler doing the same to his young scouts. I remember the rouge on the Prince's cheek.

Now, here is Archie talking to the camera about his ideals, about the Settlement and the work he was trying to do in Brack's Hill; about honesty and dignity and justice. And here is Cora as Maggie, doing her *Coal and Blood* speech, very comfortable before the whirring cameras.

Cora, incidentally, continued to be comfortable with the cameras. She never stopped working after that day. Corinthian Small, her new agent, got her into films, radio, television even. She played English character parts, of course: with a good deal of comedy. Such a long way from standing like a crucifix up to your thighs in pit-water. No joke, that. That painting last changed hands for twenty-five thousand pounds. We borrowed it back for my Retrospective in 1960. Sir Peter Whatsit came to that exhibition and that's where he let slip about my scholarship.

The lights go up now in the hall and it is filled with a gale of sustained applause. The old woman at our table stands up and bows, a mischievous grin on her face. 'Cora!' I lean towards her and she gives me a very theatrical kiss on both cheeks.

'You said all the right things about Archie in there, young Gabriel,' she tells me, her voice still beautiful.

'I meant every one of them.'

'Good,' she says. 'You also said he was ambiguous. That was right, too.'

Tegger is prodding my shoulder. 'Aren't you gunna say hello to Pearl?' he asks. He nods at the young woman beside him. She's in her mid-twenties, perhaps. Her hair is short and sharply cut; she has black lines round her wide green eyes.

I stare at her and then I know. 'Marguerite . . .'

'My mother,' she says.

I look round the room. 'Where is she?'

'She's in America, living on the West Coast with husband number four, my second stepfather. She wrote me about this Archie Todhunter thing and told me to get in touch with Mr MacNamara here,' the girl says. Her American drawl adds to her glamour.

'Pearl's a singer,' said Tegger. 'In cabaret.'

'Your mother was a free spirit,' I tell her.

'Do you think I don't know that?' She pauses. 'She got me to go to your Retrospective in 1960. I saw the painting you did of her. *The Woman in the Goaf*. Spooky.'

I just don't know what to say to this. I feel like crying. I am missing Marguerite and Archie. And Rosel. This is ridiculous.

'Our children are in America,' says Greta, suddenly putting

her hand on mine. 'Yale. Both of them. International Law! Can you believe that? How small this world has become.'

'*Your* children?' Rosel leans forward and round me to look at Greta.

The tears dry behind my eyes. My hand tightens on Greta's. 'Oh yes, Rosel. Greta here was twenty-six when I finally got her to say yes. Very hard to pin down, is our Greta.' I've been thinking a lot about the younger Greta in the last few days while I've been mulling over Archie's eulogy. She finally let me read her diaries from those early years, which were a revelation, I can tell you.

'Well!' Tegger leans back in his chair and grins broadly. 'Look at this constellation of talent! If Archie were here he'd be bullying us into making a musical film about the Berlin Blockade, American Imperialism and its impact on the common man. What d'ya think?'

The whole of my life, one way or another, is personified around this table and was just expressed on that flickering screen. I think, all in all, I have been a very lucky man.

The Jagged Window

Wendy Robertson

Edward Maichin's eloquent sermons and blond good looks have ensured his popularity amongst his congregation in the small Welsh mining community where he and his family live. But at home, the dark side of Edward's character runs riot, and since his errant father ran away to America, his mother and younger siblings have been powerless to prevent Edward's cruelty which dominates their lives.

Only his younger sister Theo, a gifted writer haunted by her stillborn twin, is brave enough to defy Edward's hypocrisy. But her promising career as a journalist is cut short when the suspicious death of their grandmother's maid – rumoured to be bearing Edward's child – forces the Maichins to flee the valley for the pits of North-East England.

There, on the wild moors of Durham, Theo takes up the position of companion to an old lady who lives with her shambling bear of a son. Theo realises that she has found a family even more vulnerable and fractured than her own. But will the price of healing this family – and hers – be more than she is prepared to pay?

Praise for Wendy Robertson:

'A cross between the yarn-spinning style of Catherine Cookson and the powerful literary talent of Pat Barker' *Sunderland Echo*

'This wonderful historical saga has to be on your reading list' *Woman's Realm*

'A blend of accessibility and total sincerity' Pat Barker

'Wendy Robertson's characters are wonderful . . . quirky and interesting people, utterly believable . . . A triumph' *Northern Echo*

0 7472 5978 X

headline

Now you can buy any of these other bestselling books from your bookshop or *direct from the publisher*.

FREE P&P AND UK DELIVERY
(Overseas and Ireland £3.50 per book)

My Sister's Child	Lyn Andrews	£5.99
Liverpool Lies	Anne Baker	£5.99
The Whispering Years	Harry Bowling	£5.99
Ragamuffin Angel	Rita Bradshaw	£5.99
The Stationmaster's Daughter	Maggie Craig	£5.99
Our Kid	Billy Hopkins	£6.99
Dream a Little Dream	Joan Jonker	£5.99
For Love and Glory	Janet MacLeod Trotter	£5.99
In for a Penny	Lynda Page	£5.99
Goodnight Amy	Victor Pemberton	£5.99
My Dark-Eyed Girl	Wendy Robertson	£5.99
For the Love of a Soldier	June Tate	£5.99
Sorrows and Smiles	Dee Williams	£5.99

TO ORDER SIMPLY CALL THIS NUMBER

01235 400 414

or e-mail orders@bookpoint.co.uk

Prices and availability subject to change without notice.